YELLOW BLUE TIBIA

Also by Adam Roberts from Gollancz:

Salt

Stone

On

The Snow

Polystom

Gradisil

Land of the Headless

Swiftly

YELLOW BLUE TIBIA

ADAM ROBERTS

GOLLANCZ
LONDON

The right of Adam Roberts to be identified as the author
of this work has been asserted by him in accordance with the
Copyright, Designs and Patents Act 1988.

First published in Great Britain in 2009 by
Gollancz
An imprint of the Orion Publishing Group
Orion House, 5 Upper St Martin's Lane,
London WC2H 9EA
An Hachette Livre UK Company

A CIP catalogue record for this book
is available from the British Library

ISBN 978 0 575 08356 1 (Cased)
ISBN 978 0 575 08357 8 (Trade Paperback)

3 5 7 9 10 8 6 4 2

Typeset by Input Data Services Ltd,
Bridgwater, Somerset

Printed and bound in the UK
by CPI Mackays, Chatham, Kent

The Orion Publishing Group's policy is to use papers that
are natural, renewable and recyclable products and made
from wood grown in sustainable forests. The logging and
manufacturing processes are expected to conform to
the environmental regulations of the country of origin.

www.orionbooks.co.uk

'You are right. I understood this myself when I read your novel *The Time Machine*. All Human conceptions are on the scale of our planet. They are based on the pretension that the technical potential, though it will develop, will never exceed the terrestrial limit. If we succeed in establishing inter-planetary communications, all our philosophies, moral and social views, will have to be revised. In this case the technical potential, become limitless, will impose the end of the role of violence as a means and method of progress.'

Vladimir Ilych Lenin, in conversation with H. G. Wells

PART ONE

'We have internal enemies. We have external enemies. This, comrades, must not be forgotten for a single moment.'

Stalin in 1928

'The war will soon be over. We shall recover in fifteen or twenty years. Then we'll have another go at it.'

Stalin in 1945

CHAPTER 1

1

At dawn we boarded a special train. The track had recently been
repaired. We all commented on the extraordinary and heroic efficiency with which war damage was being repaired all the way
across the city. Sergei declared that the sunrise resembled a frozen
explosion: clouds strewn about the sky like shreds of raw meat, and
a vivid orange-yellow billowing-up of colour behind the eastern
horizon. Our military escort didn't know what to make of this.
It's possible they suspected bourgeois decadence in such talk. It's
possible they were right to be suspicious. Certainly the sky con-
trasted very sharply with the iron and stone of the city: grey and
silver and rust. The eye was inevitably drawn to the frozen rage of
sunrise. Such colours. We were on our way to meet Comrade Stalin
himself, in person, and all of us feeling almost as honoured and
excited as we did terrified. Then Sergei, as perverse as ever, tried to
get the whole carriage singing patriotic songs, but the soldiers didn't
join in.

A smashed motorcycle was lodged in the fork of one bare tree.

An indication that this trip was something special came when
one of the soldiers distributed American cigarettes. *American* cigarettes! We all smoked. The air inside the carriage, which had had
the night chill still in it, began to warm and blur. The soldiers
loosened their manner, became chatty.

'They weren't so badly touched here,' said one of them, waving his hand at the window. 'They complain, but compare this with the rest of the Motherland! Compare this with the *west*.' He made a *pssshh* noise with his lips. 'Hardly any damage, here.'

'They should see the Volga,' said another. 'I'm not only talking about Stalingrad, but the whole countryside round there.'

'I fought at Stalingrad,' said Sergei Pavlovich Rapoport.

That killed the conversation.

We arrived at a small station in the middle of farmland. As we disembarked, Sergei said, 'And where will our next train take us?' He said no more, but his meaning – that he was expecting us all to be shipped off to the Gulag – was clear enough. The soldiers escorting us decided to find this hilarious – fortunately for us.

Our further transport took the form of three mule carts. Adam Kaganovich, giddy (I suppose) with the fear and the excitement, pretended to take offence at this. 'Carts! Donkeys! You cannot expect us to put up with such rusticity, comrades! Comrades, remember that we are *science fiction* writers!' 'That you are science fiction writers,' said the Lieutenant, in charge of us, 'is precisely why Comrade Stalin wishes to see you.'

2

When we arrived at the dacha everything happened very quickly. We were taken through into a large room, with tall windows of uncracked glass and excellent views across the low hills. The ungrazed grasses, high and feathery, fuzzed the distant fields. One flank of the landscape was a blue-green, almost the colour of sky.

The room was under-furnished: a few chairs, nothing more. Over the mantelpiece was a large photographic reproduction of a group of revolutionary heroes. I recognised Molotov, Mikoyan, Kalinin and Comrade Stalin himself. In the middle was Lenin, with that expression on his face you often see in photographs of him – that sly narrowing of the eyes, his tight little beard bunched up around his upturned mouth, as if he is richly enjoying a joke that he has not chosen to share with anybody else.

A samovar was brought in and we all drank tea, smoking nervously the whole time. And then, without preliminary or preparation, in came *Stalin himself*, in the flesh, flanked by two aides. We all stood, of course, straight as iron railings, all in a line; and he came over and greeted us one by one, shaking our hands, and looking each of us in the eye. It was immediately evident that he knew our writings, that – indeed! – he was an enthusiast for science fiction. When he got to him, Frenkel dipped his head and said, 'Ivan Frenkel, comrade.'

'Ivan,' said Stalin. 'Ivan Frenkel. Not – *Jan?*' And he laughed. Frenkel, a Slav, had been born Jan, of course, but had been publishing under the name Ivan since the thirties. 'It's more patriotic,' he had once explained to me. 'It's a more patriotic name.' But what did Comrade Stalin mean by drawing attention to *Jan?* The expression on Frenkel's face was ghastly – smiling, but ghastly. Was Stalin saying: *Do not pretend to be Russian when we all know you to be a Slav?* He did not explain. He moved along the line with a jovial expression.

You will want me to say what my impression of him was. I can do little better than say to you that what most struck me, meeting him in the flesh, was how very *like himself* he looked. It is a foolish observation, I daresay, but that's what most struck me. You must remember that his image was ubiquitous in the Soviet Union at that time: and the strong features, the thick black hair and moustache, the sheer physical *heft* and presence of the man, were exactly as you would think they were. It is true that he looked old: but, after all, he was in his late sixties. There was a degree of pallor and slackness to his complexion. Little red broken veins embroidered the corners of his nose. His eyes were each surrounded by an oval of puffy flesh. But his gaze was unwavering. I had heard it said that when encountering Stalin the crucial thing was to *meet his gaze*. Any shiftiness about the eyes, any apparent avoidance of looking directly back at his gaze, could provoke mistrust, rage or worse. Only a few things about the physical proximity of Stalin surprised me. One was his height – for he was considerably shorter than I had expected. The other was his smell. A tart odour combined of tobacco and sweat. Also (this, I do not think, has been reported) his feet were very large in proportion to the rest of his body. I could see this as he moved along the line.

He shook hands with Sergei Rapoport, Adam Kaganovich, Nikolai Asterinov and myself, one after the other. When he met Asterinov he chortled. Visibly plucking up his courage, Asterinov said, 'Funny, comrade?'

'Oh, Nikolai Nikolaivitch,' Stalin said. 'I am only thinking that they were making a film of your *Starsearch*, and I ordered the production stopped! And yet I admire the novel very much!'

'Thank you, comrade,' said Nikolai Nikolaivitch, his voice pitched rather higher than was normal for it.

'Isn't that funny, though?' said Stalin.

'Very, comrade.'

Finally Stalin settled his tun-shaped body in a chair by the windows, and lit a cigarette. Adam Mikhailovitch sat. The rest of us remained standing. Adam glanced around anxiously and leapt back to his feet. 'No, no,' said Stalin, 'sit down, all of you.'

We all sat.

There was a single bird somewhere outside in the garden, chirruping over and over, like a squeaky wheel.

Stalin was quiet for a long time, staring into the smoke produced by his cigarette as if answers to many mysteries were written there. Then he coughed heartily and said, 'Comrades, I imagine you are curious why I have sent for you.'

We, of course, said nothing. Each of us vied with the other in adopting the most solicitous posture; sitting forward in our chairs, leaning a little, putting our heads to one side.

'I have learnt many things in my time,' said Stalin. 'And there is one thing I have learned above all. Nothing is so efficacious in advancing the cause of universal Communism as *struggle*. When the people have an enemy against which to unite, they are capable of superb heroics. When they lack such an enemy they become slack, they fall prey to counterrevolutionary elements, and generally backslide. The Great Patriotic War has surely taught us this above all! We all here remember the thirties – do we not?'

We murmured in agreement. Each of us, I am sure, trying hard to make our murmurs as non-specific as a murmur might be. Remember the thirties? The difficulty was not remembering the thirties. The difficulty was ever being able to *forget* the thirties.

'It took the most strenuous efforts by the politburo to hold the country together during those years,' Comrade Stalin said, smilingly. 'Enemies without and traitors within, and the people loose, loose like a – like—' He gazed out the window, as if searching for a suitable simile. Eventually, he went on. 'Loose. I had to be stern, then. I'm a naturally loving man. It's my nature to be loving. But sometimes love must be *hard*, or the loved ones become themselves weakened. Severity was the only way to preserve the revolution. But the war – the war gave us a *proper* enemy. Gave us something *to unite against*. Hitler's declaration of war saved Communism. And now we have won the war.'

'Hurrah,' said Sergei, but not in a loud voice.

Stalin's smile widened. 'Victory was a necessary result of the advanced Soviet science of war, and of the fact that the high command,' and he dipped his head, and we all understood he was referring to himself, 'the fact that the *high command* more thoroughly understood and was able better to apply the iron laws of warfare, the dialectic of counter-offensive and offensive, the cooperation of all services and arms, that modern warmaking requires. But most of all. Most of all … with the Nazis we had a threat against which the entire country could unite. Now, I ask you, is there a similar enemy *now* against which we may continue to preserve that unity? I ask you.'

And it seemed he was genuinely asking us, for he paused. My throat dried at this. Did he expect us to answer? Eventually Ivan Frenkel spoke up. 'America?' he hazarded.

'Of course,' boomed Stalin. 'Of *course* America! Only yesterday *Zvezda* reported that the American government machine-gunned workers in New York. Killed hundreds. *Of course* America. But I do not find that America *unites* the people in hostility, the way the German threat did.'

We said nothing. Nikolai Nikolaivitch fumbled a new cigarette from its box, and by doing so made it clear how trembly his fingers were.

'Besides,' said Stalin, with force, 'I give America five years. Do you think that defeating America will be harder than defeating the Germans? The Nazi army was the most modern and best equipped in the world, and we made short work of *them*. And now our weapons are even stronger; our troops battle-hardened and our morale high. I can tell you, comrades, that America will fall within five years.'

'Tremendous news,' said Sergei, in a loud, brittle voice.

'Indeed,' we all said. 'Excellent. Superb.'

'But it is my duty,' said Stalin, 'to consider longer-term futures than a mere five years. It is my duty to ensure that the revolutionary vigour is preserved long into the future. And this is where you can help me. Yes, you, science fiction authors. Once the west falls, as it inevitably will, and the whole world embraces Communism, where *then* will we find the enemies against which we can unite, against which we can test our collective heroism? Eh?'

This was a tricky question – tricky in the sense that it was not immediately obvious which answers were liable to provoke official displeasure. We pretended to ponder it. Fortunately Comrade Stalin did not leave us to stew.

'Outer space,' he said, in a low voice. 'Space will provide the enemies. *You*, comrades, will work together – here, in this dacha. All amenities will be provided. I myself will visit from time to time. Together we will work upon the story of *an extraterrestrial menace*. It will be the greatest science fiction story ever told! And we will write it collectively! It will inspire the whole of the Soviet Union – inspire the whole world! It is, after all, the true Communist arena. Space, I mean. Outer space is ours! That is your task, comrades!'

He got to his feet. He moved slowly, but with force. 'I have to go,' he said. 'But I shall return shortly, and I look forward to hearing what you have come up with! Soon, my friends, I shall return to you!'

3

That, naturally, was the last we saw of Stalin. We were left to our own devices, more or less, except for Malenkov, a senior party figure who stayed for a week or so to ensure that we did nothing foolish. By *foolish*, he told us, he meant 'anything liable to disappoint Josef Vissarionovich'. We were as eager as was he to avoid this possibility.

At that evening's first evening meal we chattered excitedly, and drank too much. It was the drink that meant we talked more freely than otherwise we might have done. Several military personnel, and of course Malenkov, were there the whole time, watching us, listening to what we said.

'Do I understand?' said Sergei. 'Do I understand what exactly we are to do? Presumably this work we are to compose is to be more than just a story.' He was appealing to Malenkov, but that man only smiled and said, 'General Secretary Josef Vissarionovich explained this to you himself, did he not?'

'Well, yes—'

'Then surely you have all the information you need.'

'More than just a story,' said Nikolai Nikolaivitch. 'A story, yes, but obviously not *just* a story. Comrade Stalin made it plain that what we decide will act as a social glue – that people, in short, will *believe* it, and organise on a mass scale to make it real.'

'There is one great merit in the idea,' I said.

'Come, Konstantin Andreiovich,' said Sergei, wagging his head, 'only the *one*?'

'The plan has very many merits, of course,' I said, hurriedly. 'But I am struck by one in particular. To unify the people against a human enemy – against Germans, Americans, Jews – necessarily involves us in a form of *in*humanity. For these enemies are human beings, after all.'

'Germans?' said Rapoport, disbelievingly.

'All human beings are surely capable of being brought within the healthy body politic of a Communist collective,' I said.

'The perfectibility of humanity,' said Frenkel, sourly.

'Not Germans,' insisted Rapoport.

'But against *this* threat – a perfectly unhuman enemy – the whole of humanity could unite. We would have that,' I paused, for I had been about to say *paradox*, but instead I said, 'that dialectical synthesis: a *fully peaceful* world that is simultaneously united in a great patriotic *war!*'

'Peace,' said Sergei. And then, in a high-pitched voice, 'Comrade, will there be a war?' And then, rapidly, in a lower voice, 'No, comrade! But there will be such a struggle for peace that not a stone will be left standing.' He laughed at his own joke. It was an old joke.

'I think that Konstantin Skvorecky is correct,' said Kaganovich. 'We have the chance to perform a massive public good. And what have we ever actually achieved, as writers? What are we ever likely to achieve? As *science fiction* writers? Escapist junk, mostly. Missions to other worlds? Sentient comets? Clouds of black spores that soak into the atmosphere and make the trees come to life and walk around on sap-filled tentacles? Junk, all of it. This, however, *this* could be something *worthwhile*.'

'I have a problem,' said Nikolai Nikolaivitch Asterinov, getting to his feet. 'I have a problem, that I wish to share with this, our science fiction writers' collective. We are to concoct a race of aliens against which humanity can unite. Spacefaring aliens, no?'

'Yes, of course.'

'Then this is my problem. We know the party line. The philosophy of the party has always been that capitalistic Western fantasies of launching rockets to other planets will always be doomed by the internal contradictions of the competitive inefficiency of capitalism itself. *Only* the combined and unified effort of a whole people would be able to achieve so monumental an achievement as interstellar flight. No capitalist race could ever achieve something as sophisticated as interstellar flight; only communists could do this. Now, how can it be that these evil aliens are able to build spaceships and fly across the void? Surely they are not communists?'

'Sit down,' said Sergei. 'You're making a fool of yourself.'

'In *Three Who Made a Star*,' said Nikolai Nikolaivitch, still standing, the – what were they called?'

Three Who Made a Star was one of my novels: an alternate history in which World Communist Revolution had taken place in first-century Judea. I spoke up. 'What do you mean?'

'The aliens they meet, in that novel. The ones with the three legs, and the spaceships made of spittle?'

'The Goriniks.'

'They. They were a socialist race, were they not? And you, Frenkel, in your Arctic story, the beings who live under the ice . . .'

'Stop this,' said Sergei, loudly. 'Sit down, Nikolai Nikolaivitch. You're making a fool of us, before our distinguished comrades.'

Asterinov looked around him, settled his gaze on Malenkov, and settled back into his chair. 'I'm sorry,' he said. 'Too much wine. Too much wine.'

One other thing I particularly remember from that first evening together, as the alcohol was drunk, was how clearly the grandiose nature of our ambitions manifested. Were we despised writers of pulp science fiction? *By no means:* rather, we were the inheritors of Pushkin and Tolstoy, of Homer and Shakespeare. 'We shall write a new *Iliad*,' announced Nikolai Nikolaivitch. 'We shall write mankind's greatest epic of war!'

'We have just finished a war,' I pointed out, in a glum voice.

War never finishes,' said Frenkel. 'How could war finish? What is there apart from war?'

The unspoken answer to his question rubbed a silence into the conversation like salt in a cut. Eventually, after a long pause, Frenkel went on. 'Life is war, life is struggle, we all know that.

And hard as the last war was, can we honestly say it was harder than the thirties?' He was so drunk that, despite the fact that Malenkov was still sitting in the corner of the room eyeing us thoughtfully, Frenkel essayed an impression of Stalin himself, purring his rs like a Georgian. 'Surely, comrades, you remember the thirties?'

Kaganovich laughed. Nobody else did.

'It is in the nature of Marxism itself,' said Frenkel, in a heavy, yokel voice, 'in the very fabric of dialectical materialism, that life *consists* of conflict, of enemies all about us who cannot be appeased and who must be destroyed. After war comes – not peace, but more war. And we are gifted here! Gifted by historical necessity! Gifted by the news that we shall be the ones to shape this new war. This next war! It will be ours! War and *war*!'

'I had thought,' I said, 'that the next war was to be against the Americans? To correct you, comrade, on one small point: we are planning the war *after* next.'

'War and war and *war*,' said somebody. With an alcohol-delayed jolt, I realised it was Commissar Malenkov. He was getting, slowly, to his feet, an unreadable smile on his face. Bluster as we might, we were all intensely aware that it would require only one phone call from this man to turn us all into corpses before the sun rose. All of us stared at him. All conversation stopped dead. 'Goodnight, gentlemen,' he said, with a curiously old-world courtesy. That I didn't like. That none of us liked. And he left the room.

After a space of time Kaganovich said, 'Jan Frenkel, your mouth will be the death of us. *Jan*. Jan.' And Frenkel blushed the colour of spilt blood, and looked furious, though he said nothing.

4

So our new phase as writers of science fiction began. We were in that dacha, like a high-class barracks, for months. We fell into a rhythm; working as one group or separating into smaller groups during the morning; then a long lunch, and perhaps a sleep. Then late afternoon and evening, working further. The soldiers guarding us brought us some of what we asked for: paper; pens; cigarettes (Russian cigarettes, alas).

Our mornings began with a gathering in the dacha's largest room to discuss, and make notes. Lunch would be our larger meal, brought to us by a surly battalion chef called Spiridinov. We worked and worked; mostly I made notes in a succession of notepads, and Nikolai Nikolaivitch typed them up on an enormous nineteenth-century typewriter that clattered like a rusty machine-gun.

In the evening, soup was brought in, straight from the oven and still in its copper pan. This was settled on the windowsill, where the sunset polished red gleams from the metal.

Sometimes we were supplied with vodka, sometimes not. In that respect it was like being back in the army.

We discussed and planned the nature of the alien foe that would threaten the whole of humanity. We decided that their weaponry would be atomic – very up-to-the-minute, this, for the mid-1940s. You must remember that there had been no official notification of the American atom bomb attack on Japan; our version of atomics was that of science fiction from the 1930s. But Comrade Malenkov personally approved this part of our design. We could imagine why; that such a threat would justify the Soviet Union in the accelerated development of its own atomic weaponry. We wrote pages and pages of human interest material, heroic exploits by soldiers of the Global Soviet; wicked traitors to the cause of humanity (Jews and homosexuals and the like); scene setting. We spent nearly a week on a set of stories about children encountering aliens. 'And yet we have not decided on the nature of these aliens!' Nikolai Nikolaivitch declared.

Grey rain fell all day. The sound of an endless flurry of wings behind the glass.

The weather cleared. The view from the glass doors was of hills, rising, sinking, and in places were hollows or sockets, grassed over but pooling the shadow until noon.

We wrote detailed accounts of alien atrocities. We had them villainously blowing up a city – New York, as a first choice. This was Rapoport's idea; that the main island upon which New York stands (what was its name? we wondered. Nobody had the courage to ask Malenkov to supply us with an encyclopaedia that might answer such a question – *Brooklyn Island* said Kaganovich, *Manhattan Island* said Asterinov, *Long Island* said I) would be exploded by a diabolic alien death ray. Then we had second thoughts, for such a stunt, we reasoned, would be hard to fake; and if the Red Army were actually to bombard New York into dust and shards then we would have been the authors of mass death. So then we toyed with the idea of aliens attacking Siberia; some remote and inaccessible place where the story could not easily be falsified. But Asterinov voiced the obvious objection. 'Our brief is to unite humanity against this monstrous alien foe!' he said. 'Why should humanity care if these aliens blow up a few trees in Siberia?'

'We need a compromise,' I suggested. 'Somewhere close enough to civilisation to be threatening, but not so close as to be easily falsified. Eastern Europe?'

'Germany,' said Rapoport. 'Let us have them erase Germany entirely. Turn that portion of central Europe into a blasted desert of polished and scorched glass.'

'A little impracticable, in terms of faking the scenario,' said Rapoport.

Nikolai Nikolaivitch only scowled.

'Somewhere else,' I suggested. 'Ukraine, maybe. Latvia, perhaps. Let's decide that later.'

'The Ukraine has been almost depopulated,' agreed Frenkel. 'What with the famine, and then the war. Let us have the aliens blow up some portion of the Ukraine. That would be the best option.'

How could we plan such monstrosity so very casually? This is not an easy question to answer, although in the light of what came later it is, of course, an important one. Conceivably it is that we did not believe, even in the midst of our work, that it would come to anything – that we felt removed from the possible consequences of our planning. But I suspect a more malign motivation. Writers, you see, daily inflict the most dreadful suffering upon the characters they create, and science fiction writers are worse than any other sort in this respect. A realist writer might break his protagonist's leg, or kill his fiancée; but a science fiction writer will immolate whole planets, and whilst doing so he will be more concerned with the placement of commas than with the screams of the dying. He will do this every working day all through his life. How can this not produce calluses on those tenderer portions of the mind that ordinary human beings use to focus their empathy?

6

The house had electricity, but the supply was intermittent. We worked in the afternoon in groups of two or three, or off by ourselves; and then we worked as a whole group in the evening by the light of oil lamps, tulip-shaped bulbs of brightness, orange as summer blooms. There would be three or four lamps placed upon the table, hissing quietly as if in disapproval of our work.

In the mornings there was a spring quality to the sunlight; a freshness. On one such day I walked in the garden with Nikolai, the two of us smoking earnestly. The brightness coming through the trees freckled the lawn with paler greens. Nikolai found a wooden soldier, a foot tall, in amongst the unmown grass, over by the shrubbery. It had once been bright with blue and yellow paint, but its time out in the open had blistered and stripped most of its colour off, and the wood beneath was damp and dark and crumby.

'I wonder who left this here,' I said. 'I wonder for how long they wept for their lost toy! I wonder if it was quickly replaced.'

'I wonder if they're still alive,' said Nikolai.

He tossed the thing into the foliage.

'Konstantin,' Nikolai said. 'I have something to tell you.'

'Yes?'

'I have not written anything in a decade. Longer.'

'Nonsense,' I said. '*Dark Penguin. The Grasshopper Lies Heavy. The Vulture is Moulting*. Superb books. And what about that series about the man who could breathe under water?'

'A French book, little known, and, I think, illegal here. *L'Homme qui peut vivre dans L'eau*. I simply translated it into Russian, purging it of bourgeois details and adding a few standard Russian touches. The same with the others. Though those were American, rather than French. I changed the titles, of course; and I was secretive. Who would want to be discovered in possession of an American novel?' He shrugged. 'I am a fraud. I can't pull my weight.'

This was strange news. 'Don't worry', I said, a little uncertainly.

'I am very afraid of disappointing the Comrade General Secretary. I was in the army. I understand how … *unmerciful* authority … needs to be.' His hand, I saw, was shaking as he lit a new cigarette.

'I was in the army too,' I said. 'We were all in the army, Nikolai.'

'Where were you posted?'

'Moscow. Then Latvia, Estonia, the west.'

'Moscow?'

'I,' I said, with a little tremor of remorse in my heart, 'know.'

'I suppose,' he said, in a slow voice, 'somebody had to be stationed in Moscow. Were you on the general staff?'

'God, no. I was a regular soldier. Like you. And I saw plenty of fighting too, later on. In Latvia. The Nazis fought like hounds. Their lives at stake, of course. All my friends died; and then I made new friends, and they all died, and …' I stopped. The wind moved between us and around us. The sun glared at us out of a petrol-blue

16

sky. The shadows of the trees shuddered. 'Well, you know all about that,' I said.

'Yes.'

We sat in silence, smoking.

'When I was a young boy,' I told Asterinov (I was telling him something I had shared with nobody since), 'I saw a red-haired man selling chestnuts in a market square.' Asterinov looked at me. 'I thought that red-haired man was Death,' I said. 'I still do. I still think that Death is a red-haired man.'

'Isn't he supposed to come in a black cloak and have a skull for a face?' This, of course, was how Asterinov's imagination worked; and it was how most people's imaginations work. They tap into the general well, which sometimes we call cliché. It is a weakness, but in another way it is a greater strength than any to which I have ever had access. It was what he had summoned his courage to tell me, I suppose, that day: my imagination is the *common* imagination, comrade, he was saying; and I have drawn on the imaginations of others to write my books.

'You're quite right,' I said. 'A skull. Not a redhead. I was a foolish child, I'm afraid, and I have carried this foolishness into adult life. Death – a red-haired man?'

We sat in silence for a further minute, or so.

'Comrade,' I said. 'There is no need for the General Secretary to be bothered with any irrelevant details.'

'He singled me out, that first day, to tell me how much he liked *Starsearch*.'

'He said he'd blocked the motion picture.'

'But he liked the novel! What if he pays close attention to me – to my contribution? What if he finds out?'

'Comrade,' I said. 'Calm yourself, please. Find out what? This is a collective project. Literature,' I went on, 'has always been a collective activity. Writers adapting plots from other writers, sharing ideas and characters and images, all the way back to Homer. Shakespeare didn't invent a single one of his plots. You have nothing to be ashamed of. Your works have been an inspiration to the Soviet people in the great war. And, and,' I stopped. '*Starsearch* too?' I asked, in a sorrowful voice.

Asterinov took a deep breath. 'No, that was one of mine.'

I could not explain the strange feeling of relief that passed through me when he said this.

A bifurcated cloud the shape and colour of a walrus moustache muffled the sun, with others following. Soon it began to rain, a drizzle drifting like spindrift, and we hurried indoors.

7

The next day we spent writing. The story we were assembling was growing; the particulars of the aliens – a very horrible, insectoid race, implacably individualist and implacably hostile to social animals such as human beings. To begin with, our aliens were something like giant ants, but the objection was made that the idea of a ruthlessly individualist ant was a contradiction in terms. 'That's the horror,' Sergei Rapoport insisted. 'Horror depends upon some substantive contradiction, some paradox that outrages our sense of nature! A live man, or corpse, neither is horrific: but a living corpse – *that* scares us!'

'You're talking nonsense, Sergei,' said Ivan Frenkel. 'Ants live in big collective groups. Ants are communists. We need a solitary insect – a spider.'

'Spiders are not insects,' retorted Sergei.

'Corpses can be scary,' said Nikolai Nikolaivitch. 'Not – living corpses,' he added, and I realised he was not making a suggestion, but was instead wrapped in the coils of memory. 'Dead ones.'

'I propose we do not call our aliens insectoid,' said Ivan, calmly. 'We call them arachnoid.'

'Yes, *Jan*,' said Sergei. 'Let us do that, *Jan*.' Frenkel coloured.

'I have a better idea,' I said. 'Let us disembody them.'

'Ghosts?'

'Radiation aliens. Sentient emanations of poisonous radiation.'

The others contemplated this. 'A little insubstantial, perhaps?' offered Nikolai Nikolaivitch. 'To be really scary, I mean?'

'But they would have *machines*. As we have tanks and planes, they would have robots and killing machines; but inside – they would be only waveforms of poisonous radiation.'

This met with a general agreement.

We sketched their culture, the reasons for their assault, the nature of it. One sticking point was whether we confined the battles to space – announce to the world that Soviet rocket ships had been launched into orbit and were fighting off the foe up there; or whether we should report that aliens had landed.

'We have agreed to blow up the Ukraine,' Frenkel reminded us.

'I assumed that would be a blast from space down to earth,' said Asterinov.

'No, no,' insisted Frenkel. 'People will not unite if the enemy is too far away. They won't believe the threat. They must land.'

'Like H. G. Wells' Martians,' said Kaganovich. 'That would be better.'

'Gherbert George,' said Sergei, pouring himself some vodka. 'Gh-*hh*-herberr Gyorgi.'* But nobody laughed.

'Comrades, remember,' said Kaganovich, holding up his hand. 'Everything we do must ring true! The whole world must believe it!'

'We will need props,' said Frenkel. 'Artefacts. Perhaps theatre professionals, or film makers, can construct devices that would pass inspection as alien technology. We must have film of the fighting.'

'In the future,' I put in, 'who knows what advances there may be in the creation of specialised filmic effects.'

'And, uniting all the evidence, our narrative of the ongoing struggle.' Frenkel was heady with the possibility.

'Cut up and sear together portions of flesh from various animals,' suggested Kaganovich, eagerly, 'and present them as slain alien bodies.'

* The Cyrillic letter Г, sometimes transliterated into the Roman alphabet as 'Gh' and sometimes as an aspirated 'H', is idiomatic Russian slang for 'shit'.

'You forget,' chided Sergei. 'We have agreed our aliens will be incorporeal beings'

'How are we to kill them if they are incorporeal?' said Kaganovich.

'That's easily arranged,' Sergei insisted. 'Make them . . . manifest, from time to time. Say they are linked to their machines, such that by destroying their machines we destroy them. Have them . . . possess certain individuals.'

We jotted it all down, and Asterinov typed it all up, and we filed it away in files.

8

We ate together, but the conversation did not flow naturally or easily. Often the only sound – I have heard it many times in my life and I have never encountered any other sound *quite* like it – was of people scraping metal bowls with spoons so as to leave no atom or morsel of edible material behind. We were civilised men. We had survived the Great Patriotic War, the severest and most heroic martial test ever endured by human beings. Because we were civilised we did not go so far as to lick our bowls, like dogs. But because we had lived through the war we knew to make the most of our bowls of stew, and not leave scraps or particles of food to waste. Therefore we scraped assiduously.

As he lit a cigarette Sergei said, 'I will tell you what I think the cause of the uneasiness here is. Mistrust.'

We were all smoking. 'Some of us are old friends,' said Ivan Frenkel. He did not say this as if contradicting Sergei, but rather by way of confirming what he had said.

'I'd like to suggest that we put the mistrust on one side,' said Sergei. 'I believe we have all been through – similar experiences. I, for instance, spent half a year being,' and he took a long draw on his cigarette, 're-educated.'

We all looked at him. None of us asked 'What was your crime?' But the question was implicit.

'I wrote a story. It was a simple enough story. There is a peasant called Aleksandr, and his wife, and their six children, and they live in a hovel. And one day Aleksandr meets a witch-spirit in the forest, a creature that takes the form of a great bird with wings of foliage and a green beak. But understand that this is a *good* witch-spirit. And anyhow, the witch-spirit promises Aleksandr that he will have wealth beyond measure if only he performs certain tasks for her – I'll spare you the various specifics, and the ways I folded over the narrative to make it an appropriate length. Build her a walking house, catch her a talking fish, that sort of thing. Suffice to say, bold Aleksandr successfully performs the tasks, and is told that his fortune is waiting for him at home. Wealth beyond measure, and it's waiting for him back at home. As he walks through the forest he contemplates all the things that the money will buy him, a fine new dress for his wife, a new house. He thinks, now I can feed and educate my children! Now I am free from worry! That sort of thing. Oh, I had a long passage on this walk through the forest, with some nice Gushenko-style descriptions of the trees reaching up into the sky all around him like limbs of hope, and so on. Anyway he gets home and, instead of finding a pile of gold, he discovers that his peasant wife has given birth to a seventh child. He is about to go crazy in his grief at this betrayal, when he suddenly realises. The witch-spirit has been true to her word, and so on, and so forth, for there is no greater wealth in this world than children. This story was printed in a literary journal called *Gorky*.'

'A fine story,' said Asterinov, twining his fingers in his black beard and tugging at the hairs.

'Six months in prison, that tale,' said Sergei.

'Was it the witch?' I asked 'I never know where the Party stands on issues of the supernatural. In one sense, clearly, any ghost or spirit at all is contrary to the principles of dialectical materialism. So putting one in a story could be asking for trouble. But, then again, ghost stories have a rich proletarian tradition. So perhaps *not* putting one in a story could be seen as bourgeois affectation, and insulting to the people.'

'I'm guessing it wasn't the spirits,' said Adam Mikhailovitch Kaganovich in a confident voice. 'I'm betting you couldn't keep the sneer out of your voice when you were talking about the peasant children. Did you call them brats? Did you *imply* that they were brats?'

'The emphasis on the importance of having children for the greater glory of the Motherland was, I thought, the *most* politically correct part of the whole thing,' Sergei replied, dourly. 'That was how I hoped to curry favour! The tale was, in effect, an exhortation to breed. What could be more patriotic? But, no, it wasn't that. It was – understand, I don't know for sure, I heard this at second- or third-hand, but – it was the walk through the forest. Apparently I was just that bit too convincing in my representation of a poor man's yearning for money. Money, comrades? Do we need money? No, comrades.'

'Money's no good without a life in which to spend it,' said Adam Mikhailovitch.

'Six months,' said Sergei. 'I spent as long as that on a military punishment detail.'

That pulled us up short. Prison is one thing; but military punishment quite another.

'I was fighting on the Volga,' said Sergei, 'at Stalingrad. And in one engagement we surged forward, we the Red Army. I had a rifle, but I lost it. Rifles were very precious, comrades, and to lose one was a sentence of death, no question. To go out with a rifle and come back without one? Cowardice. Criminal incompetence. Orders were very clear. But I lost it anyway, when my group was trapped in a street by machine-gun fire. A thousand hammer-claws pounding out at my vulnerable body. I ran. But then my wits came back to me, and I thought about what would happen if I went back without a rifle. So I loitered in the battlefield, and tried to pick up another rifle. It wasn't easy, because some of the troops had been sent in without any weaponry at all, and they were looking for guns too. So I struggled with two other Russian soldiers like rats over a piece of meat for the rifle held in the hands of a dead boy. No more than nineteen, I'd say, that boy. But dead, so I suppose you could say he was very old. I suppose nobody gets any older than dead. He was missing a portion of his head. There were three of us, and I was a fierce fighter but one of the others was fiercer yet – you must understand, this took place in the very midst of the battle, bullets screeching, mortars exploding to the left and right, great spurting clouds and rushes of dust and screaming and the horrible thunder-noise of planes overhead. The Germans milled that town finer than flour. A building was blown up, not far from us, and I got pieces of brick in my flesh; I was still picking out shards of tile and brick a month later. There were,' he stopped and stared at the light. 'Lots of bodies,' he went on, shortly. 'Anyway, this other soldier took the weapon and ran off with it, and I chased him. I was a little insane. There was a masonry dust all over us, so that we were white figures, pure white all over, clothes and skin, and with every step I put down as I ran white clouds like ectoplasm spouted from my boots and my trousers and my jacket. Anyway, this other one tripped over something, and fell and in falling he dropped the rifle. I picked it up, and when I looked behind me I saw that he had not tripped. I saw on the contrary that he had been shot. So I thought, maybe Providence wants me to have this rifle. After that I met up with some other soldiers, and fought with them for a while. I killed Germans. And when we fell back, I had my rifle with me. But, you know what? The boy, from whom it had been taken, the boy who had been lying on the ground with a portion of his head missing, had been called Sergei. Just like me! The same name! It is as if he were my alter ego! So. Do you know how I know this? How I know what the boy's name was? Because he had scratched his name on the butt, SERGEI. Providence, indeed. My captain saw this, and was outraged. The rifle is not your personal property, Sergei Pavlovich Rapoport, he said. Defacing Red Army property? Trying, selfishly and counter to Soviet war aims, to hoard military equipment for your own exclusive use? I was sentenced to a punishment detail.' He shook his head. 'Better than being shot, I suppose. But, hard. Hard, hard.'

None of us felt like talking after that. 'War,' said Frenkel, in a grumbling voice. 'Do you know what Tolstoy would write if he were alive today? Not *War and Peace* but *War and War*. He would write *War and War and More War*.'

9

We had assembled the overarching superstructure of our story, and had filled in many of the details. We were, I admit, proud of what we had constructed. And then one morning Comrade Malenkov walked in upon us, accompanied by half a dozen armed soldiers. My heart clattered in my chest as vigorously as a man who has been pushed downstairs by the secret police. I was, suddenly and overwhelmingly, certain that we were all going to be shot.

'Comrades,' said Malenkov. 'It is over. You are no longer going to sit around here, idling at state expense enjoying the best food and free vodka! Back to real work for the lot of you.'

I could see, at the corner of my vision, Asterinov blushing with anger, his face red behind the black of his full beard. I had spent so much time with him now that I knew what he was thinking, down to the very words: *Comrade! I protest! We have not been idling, but instead labouring hard and diligently fulfilling Comrade Stalin's personal order!* But of course he said nothing.

'Nobody must ever know about what you have done here,' said Malenkov.

I was conscious of my breathing. I daresay we all were. We were, all of us, stricken with the thought that these breaths would be our very last.

'You are to forget everything you have done here,' said Malenkov.

I breathed out then, because this meant that we were not to be killed.

'Everything. Comrades, understand me: it is a matter of supreme importance to the Soviet Union that you tell nobody of your time here. You did not write these elaborate stories. You did not discuss this matter. You never met Stalin. This sojourn never happened. Do you understand?'

None of us spoke. But he didn't need us to speak. It was self-evident.

'How does your science-fictional narrative open?' he snapped.

I looked from face to face. 'The Americans launch a rocket to explore space. The aliens destroy it with a beam of focused destructive radiation.'

'Start with a bang, eh?' Malenkov nodded. 'Good, yes. I like the way you begin with a smack aimed at the Americans, too. I like it. Then?'

'Then the aliens blow up a portion of the Ukraine, and poison the ground with radiation.'

'Good! Good. But I never want to hear it again. If I hear of it again, I shall take time from my busy schedule to put bullets in the back of *all* your skulls quicker than mustard. Yes?'

'Yes,' we said, in one voice.

'Back to real life for all of you,' said Malenkov, briskly. 'And none of this happened. But be clear: I shall be keeping an eye on each of you, personally. If you use any of the material you have invented here in your own stories – if you try to recycle any of this material – I shall know about it. The sentence will be ten years without the right of correspondence.' This was a euphemism, of course; it meant that we would be shot. 'If you so much as mutter about this dacha in your sleep, and your sweethearts, or whores, hear you, I shall know about it, and I will take measures to ensure you do not mutter any more. Yes?'

'Yes, comrade,' said Nikolai Nikolaivich.

'Good. As long as we understand one another.'

None of us was so foolish as to offer up, as it might be, 'But why, comrade?' or 'But all our work, comrade – wasted?' or anything along those lines. That would have been a suicidal gambit. This manner of sudden reversal was nothing new to us. Perhaps Stalin himself had suddenly cooled on his plan; or perhaps our work had been unsatisfactory; or perhaps there were hidden unseen reasons. It hardly mattered. All that mattered was that, given the choice between killing us to tie off the knot of this enterprise, and letting us all go with this injunction to secrecy, the powers had decided on the latter, even though the former was less messy. Malenkov didn't need to tell us twice to keep this secret. His parting shot was, 'And if you gentlemen should meet up, as is perhaps not inconceivable, in the future; not even then will it be acceptable to talk about this time together.'

With a sly smile, Frenkel looked straight at Malenkov. 'Comrade, I have no idea who these people even are.'

CHAPTER 2

1

That was that. We all went our separate ways and, I suppose, got on with the business of living our various lives. Speaking for myself I did what I was told: I forgot all about our elaborate narrative; about the radiation aliens and their designs upon planet earth; upon their strange spaceships and artefacts. Forgot *all* about it. I lived in Moscow. I carried on working as a writer, for a short time, although the late forties were hard years and I did other jobs to supplement my income. The fact that I could speak English got me a job working on translations of Western documentation for a governmental ministry. I married somebody who worked in that same ministry, but she had previously been in the Red Army and she found it impossible to acquire the habits of peacetime. She woke in the night often, screaming. She could not walk down a city street without seeing the bloodied and decaying spectres of all her dead friends, or of all the enemies she had killed. One time, when I came home from work, she thought me a German and ran at me with a knife. Ours was not a relaxed relationship. Then one rainy autumn day, when the Moscow trees were bleeding their red leaves in clotted clumps and the air was cool, she fell in front of a tram and died; and though I have often thought of it, I have never settled in my head the most likely explanation for her stumble. Perhaps she threw herself. Perhaps she indeed fell by accident. Perhaps she was trying to run away from a street full of zombies. I don't know.

I drank more than most Russians. That, I am perfectly well aware, is quite a boast.

The fact that I could speak English, which had previously obtained for me a relatively comfortable governmental job, now brought me under suspicion. I was arrested and sent to a camp, and for eighteen months I helped lay a railroad across northern swampland. It was an unpleasant place. It did little for my health.

Eventually, however, Stalin died. Afterwards, although long enough afterwards for my spirit to have been effectively broken, I was released back into Muscovite society. A broken bone mends, although sometimes it sets awry. This same is true of a broken spirit.

I worked at a variety of jobs, but did no more writing of science fiction, or anything else. I married again, and fathered upon my young wife two children, one a daughter and one a son. That my wife remained with me as long as she did amazes me only marginally more than the fact that she agreed to be with me in the first place. I was a horrible man. I did horrible things. Eventually she left me and took the children and I rarely saw her or them afterwards.

So I lived alone. I ate little. I used to perform a malign conjuring trick with the vodka I drank: putting it down my throat clear and then drawing it back *up* my throat bright pink-red. I smoked all the time, without cease. For a time I made a point of buying the more expensive brands of vodka, and better brands of cigarette, but this was a charade that I could maintain only for a while. I did this, I think, to try and convince myself that I was a sophisticated connoisseur of adult pleasures, rather than a mere drunk. But eventually I embraced the inevitable. When you *are* a mere drunk, three bottles of the cheapest vodka are always better than two bottles of classier stuff. Soon enough I was drinking anything at all, no matter how rough. I smoked Primo cigarettes.

Death is a red-haired man.

Then, one winter's day, something important happened. Let us call this a *turning-point*.

I was sitting in my flat, alone as ever. It was lunchtime, and I was lunching, as was my habit in those days, on vodka. I remember that particular day very well. The sunlight was washing through my uncurtained windows very strong and clear, as bright and astringent as alcoholic spirit. The light printed a block of brightness across my table top. I had just finished the bottle on my table, and was staring at this shape of light. I was marvelling, in a soggy, half-conscious way, at the beauty of it, at the way it stepped down from tabletop to floor. *Marvelling*, there, perhaps looks overstatement, but it is precisely the right word. Spirits and spirit. Spirit and spirits. The vehemence of the way the gleam launched itself from the table. The two-tier step down from the table onto the floor. These things amazed me.

I tucked a cigarette between my lips and fiddled with the tricky metal nipple on the top of the lighter.

The next thing I knew I had been translated into an idiom of pure bright light and pure bright heat. I sat there dazzled, momentarily. I sat there *spiritually* dazzled.

It didn't last long. Almost at once, like smelling salts, I was stung back to the mundane by the stench of burning hair going up my nose. Then I felt the scorch of pain on the skin of my chin and cheeks, and my eyes began watering.

This is what I had done: I had been drinking sloppily, and dribbled some vodka into my beard. Subsequently I must have flicked the lighter flame in a careless manner, such that the stem of the fire had brushed my face. My beard went up in a great buzz of light and fire.

I got to my feet. My eyes were closed now, but I would have seen nothing but brightness had I opened them. I took a step forward. I took another step forward. I remember thinking, but distantly (as if I were eavesdropping, telepathically, upon the thinking of some third party) that I was moving remarkably slowly for somebody whose face was on fire. My right foot went forward, and then my left, and my knee banged again the wall. I reached up with my right hand and – in perhaps the luckiest conjunction of body and object in my life – my fingers fell on the latch to the window. Had I not found that I would surely have stood at that window as my head burned, and the flesh roasted away, and the marrow cracked out of the skullbone. As it was, really without thinking about it, I pushed down and the window swung away. Then all I needed to do was bow down. I bowed, like a gentleman, to the winter sky, and the prospect of Moscow's bridal chill. My face went down into the snow that lay a foot thick on the windowsill outside.

I stood like that, uncomfortably bent over, for long seconds. The next thing I remember is that I was no longer standing, but was instead slumped with one arm stuck out through the windowframe and the other trapped behind the lukewarm radiator. I suppose I must have passed out. I couldn't tell you for how long. The snow against my face was giving me more authentic experiences of burning than had the flames.

I was sober enough to get myself to the hospital, and drunk enough not to panic on the way. The doctors treated me in that weary manner they employ upon the drinkers who throng their hospitals with idiot injuries, although they were impressed, I could tell, at my foresight in chilling the burns so effectively at the site of the injury. After a few days I was discharged to tend my bandages at home, alone. The nurse who helped me get my clothes back on and shuffle to the ward exit had a face white and pinched as any skull; and close-cropped red hair. He grinned at me. Away I went.

This was my turning point.

Now: I continued drinking through this period of convalescence, but only because I reasoned that drying myself out would require greater physical strength than a sick man possesses. I was right, too. And, true to my resolution, *I stopped* drinking as soon as my skin had puckered itself into its taut and tucked version of its former self – the face I wear to this day. I can speak without vanity and say that I do not, in fact, look too bad: my chin possesses a strange texture, and my beard now only grows on my neck (which I shave), but otherwise I mostly escaped this adventure without blemish. There is one exception, and that is the end of my nose. The skin on the end of my nose was burned raw, and the doctors covered its exposed gristle with a not very delicately handled skin graft: a circle from the inside of my forearm, skin of a very different texture to the normal skin of a nose. It looked, and looks to this day, as though I have something stuck to my nose. Strangers sometimes tell as much – 'Comrade, there's a sticking plaster on your ... oh, I'm sorry' – 'Friend, is that a shred of tissue paper caught on the end of your ... ? My apologies.'

Without alcohol to pass the time, or to distract me from the idiocy of my friends and companions, I fell into a different mode of living. I became, I suppose, grumpier and more reclusive. But at least I approached my sixtieth birthday alive. That was more than Rapoport had managed, for he disappeared into a camp in the wilderness under the rubric of 'political dissident', and was never heard from again. Adam Kaganovich died of a heart attack at fifty-seven. He had managed to stay out of trouble with the authorities, and had maintained his writing career; although it would be more precise to say that he had *preserved* his writing career by dedicating it entirely to staying out of trouble with the authorities, and none of the watery propaganda pieces he generated throughout the fifties and sixties are worth the cheap paper upon which they are printed. By the early eighties, though, his sheer longevity meant that he began to be celebrated by Russian fans of science fiction. There were conventions at which he was the guest of honour. When he died (in a Kiev hotel room, guest of honour at another convention) the papers ran complimentary obituaries.

As for the others: I lost all contact with Nikolai Nikolaivitch Asterinov. He was a fellow Muscovite, and therefore I might have expected to encounter him around or about the city, so perhaps the fact that I lost contact with him meant that he was dead. Of course, Moscow is a large city. But there are reasons, on which I shall touch later, for believing him dead all the same. As for Frenkel ... well, in the camps, where gossip is the freest currency prisoners possess, I sometimes heard news. I heard that 'Jan Frenkel', the name under which he had been charged, had been sent to a camp in the furthest Siberian east. Some months later I heard he had been transferred to a specialist prison in Moscow. Some months after that I heard that he had been executed, on Stalin's personal orders. So that was that.

2

But that wasn't that. The gossip had got it wrong, for I met Ivan Frenkel, by chance, as it seemed, one winter morning early in 1986, walking along Prospekt Vernadskovo. More to the point he met me, for I (my eyes not being what they were) didn't recognise him at first. He had aged well; his figure was still trim and muscular, and his face not excessively lined. He was dressed in a calf-long and expensive-looking black coat and was wearing a hat of bright blue fur. He was walking along in the company of a tall young man whose fur hat was a more decent white colour. And there he was, in the flesh, in the material mundane flesh, yelling out in a fierce voice:

'Konstantin Andreiovich Skvorecky! As I live and breathe!'

Then I remembered him. 'Ivan?'

He clasped both my shoulders and looked straight at my face. 'By all that's astonishing, comrade, I can hardly believe that I have met you here, on this day! What a strange luck to bring us together like this, by chance, after all these years!'

Even from the beginning I registered the strangeness in him emphasising the *chance* of our meeting at such length. But I only said, 'I heard that you were dead.'

He took me to one side, out of the hearing of his tall young companion. 'Comrade, you understand that gossip isn't always a reliable thing.'

'Indeed.' I nodded at the other fellow. 'And?'

'Professional acquaintance.' Frenkel nudged me a little further away from him, and then whispered, 'It's the most extraordinary chance meeting you like this. Konstantin, listen to me. I work for the government now.' I understood then that the tall man in the

32

white hat was by way of being a guard, or jailer, or minder: that his job was keeping an eye on Frenkel. Whichever government department would employ Frenkel, in whatsoever menial capacity, might well want to keep an eye on him; he had after all been in the camps.

'Really?' I said.

'In a minor ministry, a minor position.' He came closer to me. His breath did not smell pleasant. 'Listen!' He lowered his voice. It was the most extraordinary pantomime of secrecy. 'Do you remember our time in the dacha? After the end of the Patriotic War, do you remember our meeting with Stalin?'

'I remember very particularly being told *not* to remember it.'

'Ah, how could we forget, though?'

'I understand that vodka is one popular method.'

'Those were great times!'

'I try to resist parcelling time into good and bad. After all, from a scientific perspective one minute is exactly like another minute.'

'Rapoport and Kaganovich are both dead, you know,' said Frenkel. 'As for Asterinov – nobody's heard from him in years. He's probably dead too. You and I are the only ones left.'

'Really?'

'What do you think of that?'

'I suppose it's a salubrious mental discipline to reflect upon mortality,' I observed. 'I believe the philosophers recommend it.'

'You don't understand! You don't understand what I'm saying! Listen – didn't you *hear me* when I said I worked for the government?'

'Yes.'

'Never mind that! Say I'm lowly. But perhaps I have stumbled across . . . something remarkable.'

'When a governmental employee says something,' I observed, 'it is usually a good idea to check whether you're supposed to listen or not before hearing it.'

'That story we concocted,' said Ivan. 'You remember?'

'It was a long time ago, comrade,' I said, wearily, feeling suddenly sick of the whole conversation, and Frenkel's peculiar eagerness – and, I suppose, of life itself.

'We could be the *only two people left alive* who remember it!'

'Or,' I offered, 'we could be two more of the great mass who have *no idea about it.*'

'You don't understand!' He glanced over his shoulder once again at his minder. 'You don't understand what I'm saying! Let's say I've happened to become privy to a certain secret, state secret. It has to do with the particular department in which I clerk. Let's say I am – privy – to one of the most secret of state secrets.'

'If you are, then please don't tell me.'

'What if I were to say to you . . .

'Putting every sentence you utter in the conditional mode like this,' I interrupted, 'inoculates neither of us from potentially evil consequences.'

'That story!' he burst out. 'That fiction we worked on, and that nobody else but us knows. No other human being upon the entire world knows this fiction was even written, let alone knows all the ins and outs of it, all the specifics.'

'No fiction was ever shrouded more effectively in unknowing,' I conceded.

'Friend, *it is starting to come true.*'

The late winter sky overhead was all cloud, and had the quality of a vast marble wall reaching up to eternity, flecked with blurry specks of grey and black set in a ground as white as bleach. Moscow was lidded. The row of buildings on the far side of the road seemed crammed close against this wall. The few intervening cars moved sluggishly under its influence.

'What do you mean?' I asked, wearily.

'I mean exactly what I say. The things we plotted. That we buried. The story we wrote. It is starting to come true. In the real world. It's all coming true.'

'That doesn't entirely sound,' I suggested, 'possible.'

'No! You're right! It's perfectly impossible! But it's *true*, none-theless. It's true!'

That's how I met up with Ivan Frenkel again.

3

I am not trying to trick you. The purpose of this memoir is not trickery, or sleight-of-hand. There are no secrets in this book. I might go so far as to say: the purpose of this book is the very opposite of secrecy – it is drawing your attention to that which is hidden in plain view all the time. I am writing it to record the most profound change in my life; nothing less than a translation from one manner of existence into another, from something grossly physical into something – let us say, *spiritual*. You might call it ethereal, or radiative, or at the very least *other*. It all has to do with meeting the alien, and overcoming my cynicism. For I can confess I had fallen into a cynical, an ironic mode of life.

The great change happened in the year 1986, which was in itself a year of many changes. The Soviet Union was changing, with perestroika and glasnost and a number of suchlike words we are proud to have exported to the rest of the world. Then on 9 January – which was a Thursday – the American space-rocket *Challenger* was launched. I watched it, after the event, on a friend's television. The news footage was played over and over in Russia: the rocket lifting itself on the blowtorch tail of its own blast. The spacecraft shrinking as the camera followed it up, dwindling to a white dot in the dark blue, shimmying from side to side as the camera juddered slightly on its windblown tripod. Then, without preparation, the axe descending, with its immaterial blade, and cleaving through the whole length of the spacecraft from nose to exhaust and cutting it, with a great puff of magician's smoke, into two. The footage was silent, but, trained up by cinema, you heard the explosion anyway. One coral-like billow of white cloud suddenly blooming at the end, and two new tendrils of smoking white spiralling away in opposite directions. After that, just the endless hairy meteor-trails of debris coming back down.

No science fiction writer, even a *former* science fiction writer, could watch that and be unmoved.

To be honest, the mood in the USSR was a curious mix with respect to the *Challenger* disaster; for we envied the USA and desired to be like her to almost exactly the same degree that we loathed the USA and wished ill to befall her. It was a heart-clenching and rather contradictory occasion, that exploding rocket. Good Russians tried to kindle some national pride from the fact that, the following month, the space station *Mir* was launched without mishap.

The truth is that our country, having limped through a terrible century, was in a poor way. In that same February the papers were full of the news of the *Mikhail Lermontov*, a very large ocean vessel that ran foolishly aground near New Zealand. Our whole union was symbolised in that hulk. And what else did 1986 have in store for the USSR? Death throes. The Chernobyl disaster. The collapse of the Soviet system. The rise of the Moscow Mafia. And through it all, me picking out a precarious living interpreting between people who spoke Russian but no English and people who spoke English but no Russian. Turning *Ya ne panimayu tibia* into '[I don't understand you, and *Uspekhov*! into '[Here's to our success!]'

That day, when I chanced upon Ivan Frenkel again in the street, being monitored by his white-hatted official guard, he was enormously keen that we discuss this matter further. Our strange heated science fictional fantasy was coming true! We must talk about it, my friend. It must be talked about!

'It seems a strange development,' I noted. 'And by strange I suppose I mean – impossible.'

Frenkel winked at me.

This is what I deduced: Frenkel presumably worked in some monitoring station – which was a safe guess, of course, since almost all of the business of government is monitoring. His days were filled with inconsequential chatter, overhearing the mild quotidian treacheries and betrayals of Soviet citizens kvetching and complaining. Given his history in the camps he would not be trusted with classified information. Perhaps it gnawed away at him, his unimportance. Perhaps he dwelled on the day when Stalin himself summoned him – him, Ivan Frenkel, science fiction writer! – to do top secret work of the greatest importance. Perhaps, being old, he blurred together that glorious past and this degraded present in some mental construction. Perhaps he interpreted something he overheard, or read, or came across as evidence that the radiation aliens were massing overhead and readying themselves to come down.

Another man might have felt some pity for an old friend, and indulged him. But I am not another man. I only wished him to go away. I had no interest in his fantasies. The question I ponder now, from my present elevated situation is: Had I known then what I now know – that Frenkel was in effect speaking the truth – would I have been so dismissive? It's always possible, you see, that I would have been.

Frenkel pulled an official-looking notepad from his breast pocket and scribbled an address on it. 'This is where I'm working now. There are several good places for lunch in the area.'

'Your workplace is indeed very central.'

'Write *your* address on this piece of paper.'

Not wanting to prolong the scene I scribbled something down.

'Lenin hills?' said Frenkel, examining what I'd written. 'That's a *very* nice area.'

'Not bad,' I said.

'That's a very nice part of town *indeed*,' he said, looking me up and down.

I had written down my ex-wife's address, not mine. I wanted rid of the man, and his peculiar official guard, or monitor, or superior. We embraced, and went our separate ways. I hoped never to see him again. Moreover I can say, as a science fiction writer, that in some alternate reality, some different branching timeline, I never did see him again. You'll permit me, I hope, the indulgence of pausing here to imagine that eventuality – my consciousness sliding, frictionlessly, from choice to choice, veering left and right at the branching nodes of a billion quantum choices and into a world in which Frenkel and I never met again, and I lived out my life in peaceful, blissful boredom. A world in which I did not endure the sufferings I endured in *this* timeline. A world in which I didn't die in Chernobyl.

PART TWO

'The party proceeds from the Marxist-Leninist proposition:
History is made by the People, and Communism is a creation of
the People.'

*From The Programme of the Communist Party of the Soviet Union,
adopted by the 22nd Congress of the Party 1961*

CHAPTER 3

I shall stand before you now, as narrators used to do in old-fashioned fiction, to relate how the consequences of this story worked themselves out. We had written these aliens, and now they were coming true. You will want to know: *But were they truly?* And not wishing to deceive you I shall say: Yes, they were. (Of course they weren't! At least, either these stories were literally coming true, or they weren't. There's no third option.) In order to explain how this could be, I need first of all to relate two episodes. The first is a meeting I had with two Americans. The other sees me sitting in a restaurant being stung on the neck by a mosquito. It may not be immediately clear to you why these two episodes are so important; but you must trust me that they are, and that if you read on you will understand how and why.

Moscow.

The very cold winter of 1985–6 was on the cusp of changing into a very cold spring, and I was still in the process of getting on with my solitary life. I was queuing for hours every day outside dusty understocked shops, because I had no wife or girlfriend who was prepared to queue on my behalf. I was picking up work where I could find it: jabbing an accusing forefinger over and again at my typewriter to generate, slowly, the Russian version of some foreign document for *Izvestia*; sitting in an airless room with junior trade functionaries and a doleful-looking Cuban factory owner whose

English, though execrable, was nevertheless better than his Russian, on a day when no Spanish translator could be obtained. Much of the time I had no work.

One day I was called in to the Office of Liaison and Overseas Exchange; an annexe of government for whom I occasionally interpreted. It was a dusty, frozen day. I walked into town to save the price of a Metro ticket. An east wind pushed its icy palm against my face, and poured chill down my collar. The sun was shining very brightly. I might describe its light as *sarcastic*.

The Office of Liaison and Overseas Exchange was housed in an enormous concrete carton of a building on Leningradsky Prospekt. The glass of all the windows on its ground floor was covered in speckles of grit and dirt, as if they had caught grey measles. Its main entrance was an off-the-street alcove that trapped and turned over the wind most effectively. A miniature flurry of airborne jetsam seemed endlessly to be circulating in that space. Antique cigarette ends buzzed at my ankles like cardboard midges.

In I went.

I signed in, and rode the lift to the top of the building where Comrade Polenski himself met me. 'A real stab in the arse with a dagger, this pair,' he said.

'UK?'

'American.'

I was impressed. I said so. If I had known what was coming – I mean, what these Americans would mean for my life, and for the saving of my nation – I would have been more than impressed.

'Since Gorbachev,' Polenski was saying, 'my desk is *clogged* with Americans eager to visit Moscow.'

'What do these Americans want? Trade?'

Polenski stopped. He was twenty years my junior, and exactly my height; but since I had been considerably shrunken by age, he appeared somehow more condensed and solider than I. He certainly possessed more pugnacity. 'What do *they* want? Let me tell you something, you scorch-face bastard. Don't you worry what *they* want. Worry what *I* want. I'm the one you should worry about.

And one of the things I want is for you not to jab me in the arse with a dagger. All right? It may be that you have friends who enjoy being jabbed in the arse, but I am not your friend, and that is not how I choose to spend my time. Yes?'

I looked at my immaculately cleaned and clipped fingertips. 'Not the arse, comrade. I understand.'

He glowered at me; and then, abruptly, beamed. 'This must be why I continue to call on your services. Skvorecky,' he said. 'You are at least *droll*. You know how many people in this building are droll?'

'Is there a sub-department in charge of the production of drollery?'

'Droll isn't really our governmental style,' he said. 'Is my point.'

'Dictatorship of the drolletariat,' I said.

His scowl was back. 'See, sometimes you're amusing,' he said, 'and sometimes you go out of your way to jab me in the arse with a dagger. Come on.'

He took me through to a small windowless room, the walls of which were painted an unpleasant algae-green. Inside was a table, and four chairs, and two of the chairs were occupied with – exotic! – *American* bodies. I was introduced to Dr James Tilly Coyne, US citizen, and also to Ms Dora Norman, US citizen. Had this latter individual been cut into two portions with a horizontal slice at her waist, hollowed out and laminated it would have been possible very comfortably to fit the former individual *inside* her, afterwards replacing the upper element. '[I am pleased to meet you both,]' I said, in English. '[My name is Konstantin Skvorecky.]'

'[It's *indeed* a pleasure to meet you, sir,]' said Coyne, shaking my hand. I met his eye. Within twenty-four hours I would be staring at his corpse, lying on the ground wry-necked and with blood coming out of its nose. Poor James Tilly Coyne!

His frame was both short and slight, and his houndlike face was woodgrained with vertical age-lines down his brow and both cheeks. These wrinkles looked, rather mournfully, like the erosion lines of decades of tears. Yet his eyes were lively, and he smiled often.

43

Had I been asked to guess I would have put his age in the sixties; old enough, easily, to be Dora Norman's father. Despite his age his hair was very dark, though visibly thinning. It lay across the pronounced knobbles of his skull like the lines illustrators carve into metal plates to indicate shading in their engraved pictures.

'[I am afraid I have exhausted my guidebook Russian on your colleague,]' said Coyne, with a smile.

The four of us sat down around the table. '[He's no colleague of mine,]' I said, in English. [I am not a member of this ministry.]'

'[A civilian?]'

'[A translator, only. I have no official standing.]'

At this point, Dora Norman intervened. '[Mr – Koreshy?]' Her prodigious jowls quivered as she spoke. '[Excuse me, but . . .?]'

'[Skvorecky, madam.]'

'[Excuse me,]' she said again. '[But – you have something stuck on the end of your nose. I think it is a piece of paper tissue.]' She reached out, her hand remarkably small and dainty on its ponderously conic forearm, and brushed the end of my nose with forefinger and thumb. '[If you'll permit me,]' she said, and had another go at brushing the end of my nose. Her voice was high pitched, but melodious and indeed rather attractive. The bulk of her frame gave her soprano tone the merest hint of a sensual underthrum.

I took hold of her wrist and guided her hand away with as much gentleness as I could. '[Madam,]' I said. '[You are kind, but mistaken. It is not paper. It is a small tab of scar tissue. The mark of an old wound. An unfortunate place to have such a thing, I know.]'

'[Oh my word, I'm sorry,]' she said, in an alarmed voice. A blush spread across the silk expanse of her neck, passing as rapidly as pink tea suffuses boiling clear water, over the humps of her two chins and spilling colour upwards into her cheeks. This was really quite a pretty effect. '[Gracious I'm so *sorry*,]' she gushed.

'[It is perfectly all right.]'

'[I'm *so* sorry! God, em*bar*rassing! God *how* embarrassing! I'm such a fool!]'

'[Please Mrs Norman, think nothing of it,]' I said.

'[Oh God!]'

['Really, I insist.'] I was starting to become embarrassed at her embarrassment.

'[No – how ridiculously stupid of me. I'm the world's biggest fool.]'

'[Believe me,]' I said, forcing the least convincing smile imaginable from my tight face, '[you are very far from being the first person to make that particular mistake. It is after all an unusual place to have scar tissue.]'

'What are you two saying?' said Polenski in a suspicious voice. 'Don't exclude me. Why is she stroking your face? Are you two flirting, Konsty, you goat?'

'She mistook the scar on my nose for a piece of tissue paper.'

'Ha,' grunted Polenski. 'Ha!' He went on in his intermittent, bolting manner of laugher. 'Haha! Ha! Did she? Ha!'

Polenski's reaction deepened Norman's blush. '[I apologise, I can't apologise enough,]' she said, looking from him to me. '[I really am the world's biggest fool.]'

'What's she saying now?' Polenski wanted to know.

'She says she's the world's biggest fool,' I reported.

'She's certainly got the world's biggest arse. How *do* these Americans get so fat?'

'It certainly contrasts severely with the universal slimness of our Russian women,' I said.

Polenski decided to take offence at this. 'Are you really going to compare Russian woman and American?'

'[Amerikanski,]' said Coyne, brightly, in English. '[I know *that* much Russian, at any rate.]'

Polenski beamed at him. 'That's right, I said *American*, you fucking little sewer-rat,' he said, in a warm voice. 'You'd like to be awarded the Soviet Order of the Turd for your linguistic expertise, is it?'

Coyne looked expectantly to me. '[Comrade Polenski,]' I said, '[is saying how important it is for the Soviet people that good relations are maintained with the American people.]'

'[I couldn't agree more,]' said Coyne. '[That's precisely why we're both here.]'

'I will concede,' said Polenski, to me. 'Maybe some of our babushkas get a little plump. *I like* plump. You ever fucked a really skinny woman, Skvorecky? Your hipbones bang together like a spoon on a pan. No, no, no, *plump* is one thing. But this?' And he angled his smile again towards Dora Norman. 'It's ridiculous. It's like a – tent. A tent pumped full of jelly.'

'[Is he asking me a question?]' Dora Norman asked me. '[He's looking at me. Is there something he wants to ask me?]'

'Tell her I wouldn't stick my stubby little prick in her mouth for fear she'd swallow me whole,' said Polenski, still smiling broadly and nodding.

'[Comrade Polenski is saying how rare it is for a man in his position to have official dealings with a beautiful woman,]' I said.

Her blush went from rosé wine to burgundy. '[Gracious! Hardly! I hardly think – I am certainly no *beauty*!]'

'[Russian men,]' I said, '[appreciate the fuller-figured woman, Mrs Norman.]'

She fixed her gaze upon me. '[Miss,]' she said.

'[I apologise,]' I said.

'[Oh,]' she said, eagerly. '[I'm not rebuking you, Mr Svoreshy! Not at all! Only I wouldn't want you to get the wrong idea.]'

'[I shall strive,]' I said, bowing my head a little, '[not to get the wrong idea.]'

'Can we get on?' growled Polenski. 'I have work to do. And judging by the way you're eyeing her up, you presumably wish to take Madame Tub here to a hotel room and give her some private lessons in the Russian tongue.' He laughed at his own joke. 'Ha! Haha! Ah.'

'[Comrade Polenski,]' I translated, '[is eager to press on.]'

'[As are we,]' said Coyne.

'Tell him to make his pitch,' growled Polenski.

'[Mr Coyne?]' I said.

'[That's my cue, is it? Well, I represent an American religious institution, the Church of Scientology. We are interested in establishing a Scientological centre here in Moscow.]'

I translated for Polenski. 'A *church*?' he returned. 'Does he want me to quote to him what Marx said about religion? I will, you know. Marx said you can stick religion up your arse. Tell him that.'

'[It is not official Soviet policy to invite in missionaries from religious organisations,]' I told Coyne.

'Marx said it was the opium of the people,' Polenski growled.

'He also said it was the heart of a heartless world,' I put in.

'Fuck off, Konsty.'

'[We appreciate that. Please relay to Mr Polenski that the Church of Scientology is not an ordinary religious organisation. As you can tell from its name, it is based on the laws of science. Our interest is not in converting Soviet citizens to our belief-system, but rather in undertaking mutually beneficial and officially-sanctioned research.]'

'[What sort of research?]' I asked.

'[We have a number of ideas, and of course would need to discuss possibilities with the authorities. But for example, we in the Church of Scientology are very interested in the science of human personality. In trauma, and the effect trauma has upon the healthy development of the human mind. We have, by the same token, grave reservations about the so-called science of psychiatry, as it is practised in its post-Freudian mode; reservations we believe largely shared by the Soviet authorities. There are,]' he concluded, '[a number of areas in which we could work; and with your sanction we would like to purchase a Moscow site to function as our Russian base in order to continue this work.]'

I began the process of translating all this for Polenski's benefit, but he interrupted me after a few moments. 'Wait, wait. Scientific research?'

'[Scientology] from [science], science,' I said.

'Then it's not my problem!' He beamed enormously at the two Americans. 'Fantastic! They can go bother the Office of

International Scientific Coordination instead! I need never see their ugly faces ever again!'

Both Coyne and Norman seemed delighted at Polenski's big smile. '[Comrade Polenski,]' I told them, '[is genuinely delighted by what you say. The Soviet Union is always interested in legitimate scientific exchange and research.]'

'[Well that's really excellent news,]' said Dora Norman.

'Tell them both to fuck off,' said Polenksi.

'[Comrade Polenski,]' I said, '[will forward your request to the Office of International Scientific Coordination.]'

'Tell them, I hope I never see their grotesque faces again as long as I live.'

'[He will be in touch soon,]' I said.

And that was that. We all stood up; Dora Norman apologised once again for trying to flick away the scar tissue from my nose, and I left the room, not expecting to see either of the Americans again.

CHAPTER 4

In the lift going down I buttoned my coat and settled my hat over the worn carpet-texture of my hair, preparatory to making a dash through the entrance hall under the severe, disapproving gaze of the massy worker in the heroic mosaic on the far wall. I ducked past the doorman's booth, scurried along and out through the main doors, and into a flurry of wind.

Collision awaited me on the open street. I was keeping my head down to avoid the breezy debris, and ducking round the corner in that posture I didn't at first see whom it was I bumped.

'Konstantin Andreiovich Skvorecky!' declared this stranger, in a theatrical voice. 'Once again we meet! It must be fate!'

'Ivan Frenkel,' I said. 'I am just leaving.'

'Going? No no, I won't *hear* of it,' said Frenkel, gesturing peculiarly with his arms. 'It is destiny that we have met again. You and I – just the two of us.' He had the manner of a not very good actor overplaying a role. At the time I assumed this was merely his personal style.

Standing a little way behind him was the looming presence of the tall man; his bodyguard, or perhaps his chaperone. 'You *must* come with me,' said Frenkel. 'Just round the corner from here is an excellent Russian restaurant. We *must* have lunch.'

'Isn't it a little late for lunch?'

'Afternoon snack. Early supper. Come anyway! Have a little vodka with me.'

'I don't,' I said, 'drink vodka.'

'Not drink vodka!' He made pebble-eyes at me. It was all stupidly self-conscious and actorly. I wanted to say to him, *Please don't put yourself to all these theatrics on my account*, but he was in spate. 'Is this,' he addressed the street, or the front of the building, or the world at large, 'the Skvorecky I used to know? *He* could drink vodka! He could have represented the Soviet Union at the vodka Olympics!'

'I was drinking too much,' I said. 'I stopped.'

'Coffee then!' He again addressed himself, or so it seemed, to an imaginary audience. 'Surely he can't refuse a cup of coffee!'

'Frenkel, you're acting very peculiarly.'

'I have,' he said, putting his reeking mouth close to my ear and speaking in a more confidential tone of voice, 'something of the utmost importance to convey to you.'

'I have a pressing appointment.'

'Nonsense. You're chaffing me. Come along!'

I screwed my courage to the sticking point. Or, at least, I licked the back of my courage and pressed it against the sticking point in the hope that it would adhere. 'Not today, Ivan. Another day. I'm afraid I really must go.'

I jinked round him and made a little dash for freedom along Leningradsky Prospekt, but I ran straight into another obstruction. Frenkel's minder, the huge individual with the military bearing and the Easter Island face, was standing in my way. The sheer muscular bulk of this individual was remarkable.

'You remember Trofim?' Frenkel said, from behind me. 'From when we chanced upon one another before?'

'Of course,' I said. 'Good afternoon, comrade.'

'Comrade,' he nodded.

'Come and sit with us,' said Frenkel, strangely excited. 'I promise not to make you late for . . . for you next appointment.' His minder,

Trofim, took hold of my elbow with a grip of remarkable force. I almost squealed.

I stood there, under a sky the colour of tooth-enamel. It was a cold afternoon. 'I suppose it would take me no more than a few minutes,' I said, 'to drink a coffee.'

'Excellent!'

And so the huge fellow Trofim steered me along the road and down a side street towards a restaurant frontage. Upon the window pane was a poorly painted representation of a fat white O – a life buoy, I think – with the words Дары моря, indicating that it was a seafood restaurant. Beneath this, sitting on the dusty inner shelf behind the glass, was a dried, spiny-looking and almost heroically unappetising fish about a metre long, and looking like it belonged in a paleoarcheological museum.

We bundled in through its narrow tinkling door, all three of us, to find the interior wholly deserted of customers. A pained-looking young woman was standing by the kitchen hatch. Frenkel, practically dancing on his toes with excitement, selected a corner table and sat himself down. The waitress came over and he shooed her away; then he called her back and ordered black bread and coffee.

So began the second meeting, the one I mentioned above – where I was bitten by a mosquito. It was also, as you shall see, strangely important.

I sat down, and Trofim squeezed himself into one of the chairs across from me, somehow fitting his enormous legs under the lid of the little table. Frenkel said, 'I'm *so* delighted to have chanced upon you again, my old friend.'

'It is a wonderful coincidence,' I said, deadpan, looking directly at Trofim.

'So what were you doing in the ministry? Translating, was it?'

'Indeed.'

'I'm going to leave you now,' Frenkel said.

I transferred my gaze to him. My day was going from odd to odder. 'Well, goodbye.'

'Just for a moment, you understand. I just have a quick phone call to make. I'm sure they have a phone here?'

'I've no idea,' I replied. 'You're the one who chose this place.'

'That's right we did! A sleepy little place! Right in the middle of town! A sleepy little place! Sleepy!'

And off he went, leaving me under the unflinching gaze of brother Trofim. I puzzled my brain momently with wondering whom Frenkel might be calling, and what he might be saying. (*I've got him, he's here, we captured him!*) But it was more than I could fathom. And, to be honest, I found it hard to care one way or another.

There was a very strange atmosphere in the place. I couldn't quite put my finger on what it was about the place that unnerved me. I felt a huge weariness, perhaps a regular exhaustion, perhaps an existential ennui. I could barely move my limbs. A sleepy little place, I thought. A sleepy little place.

A mosquito bit at the back of my neck.

I slapped at it with my hand, and this action occasioned a very strange expression to bloom very slowly, like some creature of the deep seas, on Trofim's face. I remember thinking to myself: A mosquito? In Moscow *at this time of year*? Spring was not far away, true, but winter nevertheless had the city in its grip, and it was still very cold. Nor was it particularly warm inside the restaurant. *A Scarf Of Red* was playing on the radio. Except that there was no radio. I was imagining the music. Or it was playing next door. The sound had a distorted, unsettling quality. Perhaps it was playing next door, and the sound was coming muffled through the wall. Something like that.

There was a very strange atmosphere in the place. I brought my hand back round to the front, and saw only a miniature Moscow-shaped splatch of blood in the exact centre, like a stigmata.

Something was wrong. Something was not right.

I couldn't put my finger on what was wrong. The restaurant was deserted, but even though I could look round and see that it was empty I somehow got the sense that it was simultaneously *crowded with people.* Clearly that couldn't be right: either a place is empty, or else a place is full. I tried to wrangle the excluded middle. It wouldn't budge. It occurred to me that the place might be haunted – I might have picked up on the spectral presence of the dead, still thronging that place. But I don't believe in ghosts.

I looked at Trofim. Trofim looked at me.

'So,' I said. 'Trofim, is it?'

'Comrade?'

'That's your name?'

He nodded once.

'I am Skvorecky,' I said.

He nodded again, as if to say, This, I know.

I looked around. I was acutely, suddenly, uncomfortable. I felt utterly out of place. Time to leave, I thought. Like a schoolboy caught out of school, I measured the chances of being able to make a run for it, dashing past Trofim to the door and away. But I was old and frail, and Trofim young and fit-looking. It was unlikely I would even reach the door. Besides, there was some kind of obstacle in the way, something invisible, or visible (one of the two) that interposed between the door and myself. Perhaps this was only my mind rationalising a disinclination to move.

The back of my neck stung from where the mosquito had bitten me. The strangest little conversation with Frenkel was not taking place.

Trofim, on the other hand was staring at me with a weird intensity.

'Comrade,' he said, eventually, with the air of somebody who has been weighing up an important question in his mind. 'Your nose?'

'My nose,' I said.

'Your *face?*'

'Like it, do you?'

'What is *wrong* with your face?'

'It too accurately reflects the state of my soul,' I replied.

His eyes went a little defocused at this. 'Comrade,' he said, in an uncertain voice.

After a little while he said, 'What I mean is.' But getting this much out seemed to exhaust him. There was a long pause.

I smiled at him.

'There are scars on your face,' he said eventually.

'And my face is just the part of me that you can see,' I agreed.

Frenkel was back. 'Sorry about that,' he said, sitting down. The waitress brought over two cups of black coffee, along with some slices of bread and shavings of cheese. He smiled at her, less unconvincingly than she smiled at him. She retreated to a back room.

'Konstantin,' Frenkel said urgently, when we were alone. 'Did I tell you which ministry I work in?'

'You said you were very junior.'

'I did? Well, yes, that's true. Indeed mine is not a well-known or powerful section of government. It is concerned with UFO sightings.' He poured the coffee. 'UFO sightings,' he said again, as if perhaps I hadn't heard him the first time.

'People who have seen UFOs,' I said.

'Indeed. We're a busy little ministry. Though minor.'

'Are there many such sightings in the Soviet Union?'

'Many! More than *you'd* believe. Oh, it's the United States that gets all the attention, of course, with their fifty-one areas and their triplicate Close Encounters. But more UFO sightings are reported in the Soviet Union, year by year, than in the USA. Did you know that?'

'I had no idea.'

'We keep it secret,' said Frenkel. He shrugged. 'We're good at secrecy, in the USSR. The Americans have no talent for secrecy. They try, believe me; they get their CIA involved in all the sightings, black-suited men. But the USA as a nation simply leaks secrets.'

'Their lack of secrecy is evidently a symptom of national degeneracy,' I said.

Frenkel took me at my word. 'It is! Certainly as far as UFOs are concerned, it's a shocking lapse. *All* their sightings end up in the press. Few of ours do.'

'And why are our UFOs a matter for secrecy?' I asked, ingenuously.

At this Frenkel looked at me with frank astonishment. 'It is one of the jobs of my branch of government to keep track of UFO sightings,' he went on. 'Not all of them merit a great deal of attention of course. Indeed, few of them do. But those few ...' He shook his head, and once again we were back in the realm of awkward theatrics.

'Petrazavodsk,' said Trofim, as if prompting.

'Do you know what happened at Petrazavodsk?' Frenkel asked me. 'September 20th 1977? Do you know?'

I shook my head.

'Aliens – described by eyewitnesses as *radiating pulsating beams of light*. One witness called them *huge jellyfish of light*. Thousands saw them.'

'I don't remember it being in the newspapers.'

'Of course it wasn't in the papers! We had orders to keep it all quiet. But Andropov sent an order to the KGB and the whole Russian army – watch the skies! Seven and a half million men, watching the skies! They were scared, you know. Scared. I personally interviewed Captain Boris Sokolov, who was right at the heart of the encounter.'

I looked at Trofim. He was staring at me.

'Konstantin,' said Frenkel, leaning forward. 'Do *you* believe in UFOs?'

'You'll need to frame the question more precisely,' I replied.

It took Frenkel a second or so to process this, and then he laughed briefly and unconvincingly. It sounded like a horse sneezing. 'I see what you mean, of course,' he said, his face serious once more. 'My question is ambiguous between, *Do you believe UFOs are a feature of contemporary culture?* – which of course they are – and *Do you believe in the literal reality of UFOs?* Am I right? So do you believe in the *literal reality* of UFOs?'

'Somedays I'm not sure I believe in the literal reality of literal reality,' I said.

Trofim's brow crinkled, and his small eyes became an even smaller portion of his big face. They were like an umlaut over the fat U of his nose. The jaws of his mind chewed over this indigestible statement. He did not look happy.

'I'll tell you what I think,' Frenkel said. 'I think you *don't* believe UFOs are real. Am I right?'

'A rhetorical question?'

'I'd hazard the guess,' Frenkel persevered, 'that you're a *materialist*. Right?'

'Do you mean a dialectical materialist?' I returned, affecting an innocent expression.

'Comrade Frenkel wants to know if you ...' boomed Trofim; but Frenkel's hand was on his forearm.

'Don't worry too much about what Comrade Skvorecky says,' he advised the fellow, and I found myself wondering about the exact nature of their relationship. What *was* Trofim to Frenkel? His bodyguard? His minder? His *jailer*?

'Ever since I've known him,' said Frenkel, 'Comrade Skvorecky has been an ironist. That's a fair description, no?'

'It has an ironic aptness,' I replied, trying to scratch an itch inside the scar tissue on my face.

A mosquito had bitten me on the back of my neck.

It was the strangest thing.

Something was not right about that bite.

'But even an ironist may have sincere beliefs about *some* things,' Frenkel was saying. 'He may, for example, harbour a suspicion that the cosmos is so vast – so unimaginably vast – that humanity cannot be the only sentient creature to inhabit it. Skvorecky here used to write science fiction,' he added.

'As did you,' I reminded him.

He flapped his right hand. 'Keep that to yourself, please,' he said. 'That's not something I like to boast about. Particularly in my present job. But you haven't answered my question! Put it this way: do you think there's a *reasonable possibility* that UFOs *might be* – real?'

'Do you?'

'That's just it! If you'd asked me a decade ago I'd have said *no*. I mean, I'd have said: If you sift through all the sightings, and you filter out the hoaxers and the fantasists, the sleepwalkers and the drunks, the over-imaginative people who go to bed having watched *It Came From Jupiter* on the television, filter out the suggestible and the idiotic, the people who can't tell the difference between a commercial airliner and a spacecraft from Sirius Minor, then there would only be a few left, and those few could be described as honestly mistaken. But ... But! But!'

'But?'

He lowered his voice. 'Something major *is happening*. We're right in the middle of it. It's happening now. I'm no UFO cultist. By nature I'm a sceptic. But things have been passing over my desk that can't be explained away. There's been *proof*. It's more than just long-distance lorry drivers seeing lights in the sky outside Irkutsk. It's – it's real.'

'How exciting,' I said, in an unexcited voice.

'I don't expect you to believe me right off, of course,' said Frenkel. He sat back in his chair. 'I shouldn't be telling you at all. It's highly secret. It has galvanised the highest levels of government, I can tell you that. It's big. I, personally, have spoken to the General Secretary himself about it.'

'How exciting,' I said again. 'To meet the General Secretary,' I added, for the benefit of Trofim's scowling expression.

'Now, just listen for a moment,' Frenkel said. 'You're the only person in the entire world I can have this conversation with. Do you understand that? Because you and I have shared a unique experience.'

'Does Comrade Trofim know our secret?'

'I trust Trofim,' said Frenkel. Trofim sat up more straightly in his chair. But Frenkel immediately added, 'Comrade, would you mind going and standing over by the door?'

'The door?' replied the huge fellow.

'Just for five minutes. I have something personal to discuss with my old friend.'

A little awkwardly, Trofim extracted his treetrunk legs from beneath the café table and stood. He made his way ponderously to the door, turned, and stood motionless beside it.

'He's well trained,' I observed.

'Listen!' said Frenkel, urgently. 'If I were to say to you that I have *proof* that aliens are amongst us, that would be a big enough secret. But if I were to say to you . . . the aliens are here, *and* I have proof, *and* they – they – they are appearing exactly as we wrote them, in that dacha in the 1940s on Comrade Stalin's express order – what then? Because *only you and I*, in the whole world, know about that fiction!'

'If you were to say that?' I observed. 'And if *I* were to find it hard to credit?'

'But it's *true*. How would you explain it?'

'I'm not sure what you're asking me to explain.'

I glanced at Trofim, by the door. He stood unnaturally still, like a robot with the power supply switched off. The three of us were the only people in the restaurant; a fact which struck me, for the first time, as very peculiar. A central Moscow restaurant, at the end of a working day? Shouldn't it be crowded with people? The windows were black, as if the sun had given up on the day and sulked off. The clock on the wall showed four in the afternoon, but it felt much later. I felt suddenly exhausted. Ready for bed. This tiredness gave me a little push of inner annoyance. 'This whole conversation,' I announced, 'is most idiotic.'

'The truth sometimes is.'

'Let's be clear,' I said. 'The six of us *concocted* that story of space aliens.'

'We did.'

'We didn't base it on anything factual at all. We invented radiation aliens. Crazy, really. I don't believe a single one of us even approximately understood the physics of radiation.'

'That's right.'

'It was fiction. It was *our* fiction. We made it up. It's not real.'

'Fictional and unreal are not synonyms,' said Frenkel, smiling as if he had articulated a piece of profound wisdom.

'Ivan, you're saying that the story we invented is somehow, I don't know, *happening* in the real world? That there's proof that radiation aliens are invading?'

'There is! There's evidence!'

'Then the evidence is hoaxed. It is fictional. Maybe somebody has found out about our plan, and is going to the trouble to reproduce it in the real world.'

'But why should they?'

'I've no idea. I've really no idea.'

'More to the point, *how* could they *know*? Only you and I know, in the whole world!'

'As to that,' I said. 'I assume somebody kept a record. It must be filed somewhere.'

'It isn't.'

'How can you be sure?'

'I know because I've looked. I have access to those sorts of files, and it's not there. And anyway, who would file it?'

'Malenkov?' I suggested.

'Him? He didn't keep records of anything at all! Secrecy was his *whole life*. He didn't even keep a diary. No, not him. And none of us, none of the writers concerned, we wouldn't have the chance, even if we wanted to. No records!'

'Then no records were kept. It's only in our memories, yours and mine. And therefore, unless we are capable of shaping the real world with our mental fantasies – perfectly unconsciously, in my case – any resemblance between our story and the real world is merely coincidental.'

'I have proof!'

'Jan,' I said. 'You've come across certain reports of UFO activity, and you fancy a resemblance between those reports and that ridiculous story we concocted years ago. But its coincidence. It must be. The resemblance is pure chance.'

'Radiation aliens,' he hissed. 'Listen: do you remember the American spaceship that exploded?'

'Last month, you mean? That was in the news. What was it called?'

'[*Challenger*,]' he said in English. Then: 'It means *Aggressor*!'

'It was a launchpad malfunction, I believe.'

'That's what they're saying, of course that's what they're saying. But I have seen top-secret reports that it *wasn't anything of the sort*. I have seen the reports! The craft was hit by a beam of concentrated radiation energy in flight!'

'I find that hard to believe.'

Frenkel was positively bouncing in his seat now, like an excited child. 'Everything is about to change,' he said. 'Our government is talking to the Americans at the highest level, with a degree of openness never seen before. Détente is the watchword. It will be the end of Communism – Gorbachev is planning it, I'm certain. He's planning an alliance with America to fight the space threat together!'

I looked over at Trofim by the door. 'Jan, it's—'

'Ivan!' he snapped.

'Ivan, of course. Ivan: it's been a *pleasure* meeting you again, but . . .'

'Think *through* what we planned. The aliens would attack power stations, remember? Long Island, do you remember that? The Long Island disaster we planned? That power station that went into meltdown?'

'I think we got the wrong name for the New York island.'

'We planned they would explode an American rocket on launch, remember? They would—'

'Coincidence,' I interrupted, 'Launching rockets is an inherently risky business.'

'But the *aliens*?' he hissed. 'The aliens themselves? You think they're not *here*? Right now – in this place?'

This made an unpleasantly insectile sensation scutter along my spine. It chimed with my sense of there being something wrong in that place. Ghosts in the room. Goosepimples on my forearms. But of course – nonsense. I said so, and speaking the word solidified the fact of it: 'Nonsense.'

'I have *met* them!' said Frenkel, with disconcerting intensity.

'You have?'

'I was driving,' he said. I can't express how little I wanted to hear this particular confession, but he was in spate. 'My engine died. I saw a light – and it came right down to earth. It landed in a field beside the road I was on.'

'Right next to the stable containing the baby Jesus?'

'I'm serious! It was a sphere, a metal sphere, the size of a cottage. It came right down.'

'Like H. G. Wells predicted. Did it make a crater?'

'No! It descended in silvery light, and hovered a metre or so above the earth. I got out of my car and I walked through the mud – it was muddy, you know. The mud clung to my boots like cold treacle. When I got within twenty feet the thing came to life. It was so smooth and silvery I could see my reflection in it! A silver sphere five metres across. The whole field was reflected in it, distorted after the manner of convex mirrors. And then it grew legs.'

'It grew legs?'

'They sprouted from its belly. There was something insectoid about it. It was like a robot-insect. Great tail legs.'

'Three legs? Like H. G. Wells's tripods.'

'Two legs.'

'So more like Baba Yaga's house?'

'They were nothing,' he said, in a serious voice, 'like chicken legs.'

'I'll tell you one thing I do remember from that time in the dacha,' I said. 'I remember we called Wells Shit-Shit-Wells. I remember that. It wasn't very respectful to our great ancestor, really.'

'It came after me. Great loping strides. I was terrified. I tried to make it back to my car, but ...' Frenkel slapped both palms onto the table. 'It got me!'

'Got you where?'

'Got me inside its sphere – a metal tentacle came out, and yes, before you say it, that's like Shit-Shit-Wells too. Except that *these* were disembodied, radiation creatures; they weren't the octopoid aliens Wells predicted.'

'Did the aliens in Wells's *War of the Worlds* have eight legs?' I pondered. 'I don't believe they did.'

'I wish you'd take me seriously!' said Frenkel.

And he evidently did wish that.

He told me the whole incident. The details piled up. The silver globe wasn't real. Or it was real, but only the obtrusion into our material dimension of something far greater, a massy transcendentally-furnaced battleship – or something. 'The radiation aliens,' said Frenkel, for the half-dozenth time, such that by sheer force of repetition the word began to acquire familiarity and therefore reality in my mind. 'They don't communicate using material means, you see. They possess a form of telepathy, I suppose. They probed my mind, and as they did so I caught glimpses of their plan. They – probed me – very fully.'

He stopped and looked up. I became aware of Trofim looming over the table. 'Comrade Frenkel,' he said. 'I need to visit the toilet.'

'Can it wait?'

'Not really, comrade.'

Crossly Frenkel waved him away. 'Go on, then. Hurry.' As the big man's back receded across the café floor I thought again about making a run for it. But, as before, something in the room prevented me. Except that there was nothing in the room. There is either something in a room, or there isn't something in a room; it can't be both at once. Why didn't I run for it? You will perhaps think: did I believe that the radiation aliens were in the room? But I didn't think that. It was something else. I wasn't sure what.

'Wake up!' Frenkel said. 'Daydreamer!'

'What?'

'Wake up! Wake up!'

'Look,' I said. 'I really must be going.'

'Put yourself in my position for a moment,' Frenkel advised me, with a queer expression on his face. 'Imagine that you had become convinced that this story we invented was coming true. How would you explain it?'

'I'd assume I was dreaming,' I said, after thinking about it for a moment.

He glowered at me, and then, oddly, he started laughing. 'Pinch myself on the cheek!' he chuckled. 'And wake up! Wake up! Wake up! Very well; let's assume we tried that, and it had no effect. Assume you decide you're awake, and it's still happening. What then?'

The next thing I remember I was outside on the street. It was late. The buildings, towering in the dark all around looked as granite as giant tombstones, punctured in a few places with rectangles of yellow illumination. Above, in the spaces above the rooftops and between the buildings, the sky was black-grey, with the strangest tints of violet and mauve and an unnatural pink or pale green glow to the west. The streetlights burned fuzzily, a line of alien eyes glowering down upon the road. A car passed.

Another.

A small-engine motorcycle buzzed past with a mosquito sound. Mosquito? I reached round to feel the back of my neck. There was a lump.

I don't have exactly clear memories of getting out of that place. I suppose I said goodbye to Frenkel, once and for all, and got to my feet and simply walked away. Yes: now that I express my supposition I can locate that memory in my head. *There* it is. I said goodbye; I got up; I left. That is the way memory works. It follows supposition.

I started walking along the street, passing the Office of Liaison and Overseas Exchange; shut up now and dark. There was a taxi parked outside the main entrance, and as I walked past the driver got out onto the pavement. He was a medium-sized, middle-aged man. 'Taxi for Comrade Skvorecky?'

'I beg your pardon?'

'I was told to wait here for Comrade Skvorecky.'

'How do you know my name?'

'The fare has already been paid.'

'Paid?' I asked. I was surprised, but I overcame that feeling rapidly enough. I'll confess the thought of being chauffeur-driven home appealed rather more than joining the evening crush on the Metro.

'I am,' said the fellow, with a rather prissy exactitude, 'a licensed taxi driver. My name is Saltykov.'

'Do you always introduce yourself to your fares, Comrade Saltykov.'

'No.'

'Well – all right. A taxi ride home, then.' I told him my address, and climbed into the back of his vehicle. It did occur to me to wonder whether accepting Frenkel's paid-for cab was in some sense compromising myself. But I decided that I was too tired to bother my head with untangling his motivations for spinning so peculiar, and improbable, a story – or for seeking me out, as he evidently had, after so many years. There would be time to think it all through the next day, I thought.

The taxi pulled away from the kerb. I settled myself into the back seat as forcefully as if *I knew* that I was destined to spend several days in that taxi. But, of course, I cannot have known that I was going to spend days on that very seat, inside that very taxi. I could not see the future. Time doesn't work that way. Time goes from A to B, and not the other way around. Time runs forward. Or it runs backwards. One of the two. But it must do one of those two things, and there cannot be a third thing it does.

CHAPTER 5

I peered through the passenger window and at an unfamiliar neighbourhood. 'Comrade,' I said, as the taxi slowed down, 'you appear to be parking.'

'We are here, comrade,' said the driver. He applied the handbrake with an unusual precision. 'This is the Pushkin Club.'

'The what?'

'The Pushkin Chess Club.'

'I do not live in a club,' I pointed out. 'I was hoping to go home.'

'As a member of the club,' he said, 'I invite you to regard the Pushkin *as* home.'

'That is indeed generous of you,' I returned. 'But I no longer possess the mental clarity to play chess effectively.'

'Then you shall not play chess!' He spoke with the magnanimity of a benefactor. Then he got out of the car, came round, and opened the passenger door. I looked up at him from inside. 'This feels rather,' I confided, 'as if you are abducting me.'

His eyebrows went up. 'Certainly not!' he said. 'Abduction implies the forcible removal of an individual. You are perfectly at liberty to walk down the street – the Metro is a little way in that direction. I, however, am going into the club. I *invite* you to accompany me.'

I swung my legs out of the car, and levered myself with the awkwardness of old age into a standing position. The driver shut the passenger door, but then seemed to have some difficulty locking his cab: he fiddled the key in its lock, and fiddled it, and fiddled it. Eventually he secured his vehicle. 'My name,' he said, with peculiar dry precision, 'is Saltykov. That is my *last* name.'

'You already told me your name,' I said.

'I did not tell you my *first* name. It is Ivan.'

'I am pleased to meet you,' I said, somewhat puzzled.

'Would you like to know my patronymic as well?'

'It's not necessary, thank you.'

He seemed to take this in his stride, and nodded. 'I drive taxis at the moment,' he said. 'But my training is in nuclear physics!'

'How interesting,' I observed, ironically.

'Imagine! A trained nuclear physicist, reduced to driving a taxi for a living!'

'It's work, comrade,' I said, in a tone of voice like a shrug. Then, perhaps touched by a sense of similarity in our respective plights, members of the intelligentsia reduced to menial occupation, I decided I had been rude. To demonstrate courtesy I held out my hand towards him. He looked at this, in the streetlight, and the expression on his face caused me to look at it as well. The artificial illumination gave the skin a silvery, rather alien-looking sheen, which perhaps explained his disdain.

'You,' he said, as if working it out, 'are offering to shake my hand? Do not be offended that I decline to do so. I prefer to avoid physical contact with other men.'

'You do?'

'It is not personal to you,' he said. 'I have only the highest respect for your writing.'

You know my writing?'

'Of course! If it were in my nature to shake hands, or embrace, or kiss any human being, then you can rest assured that I would do all three with you. But I shall not.'

'That's a relief,' I said, uncertainly.

'I suffer from a certain syndrome. As a result I find physical contact with other men repugnant.'

'A – syndrome?'

'Indeed. The syndrome from which I suffer was first identified by an Austrian psychologist.'

At this moment the door to the club opened and another man burst onto the street. 'Here you are!' he boomed, with evident excitement. 'We're all inside! Leon Piotrovich Lunacharsky!' This man, Lunacharsky, evidently had no qualms about physical contact with other men, for he embraced me, clasping me to his chest with enough force to knock the wind from me, and leave me wheezing. 'Delighted! At *last*! And come through – please do.'

So I was burlied through the door and down an ill-lit stairway, which led into a basement so filled with people, and so malodorous, it resembled the hold of a slaveship. Leon Piotrovich Lunacharsky gave me a friendly shove, and I stumbled down the last few stairs to find myself standing in the midst of a pack of crowded tables, hemmed in to the extent that my hips were touching two sim-ultaneously. I couldn't at first get my bearings. It all seemed rather overwhelming: smoke; hubbub; confinement; smell. It was warm. Indeed it was rather overwarm.

'Welcome, comrade,' said Lunacharsky, in my ear, 'to the Pushkin Chess Club. In the Pushkin you can [push king].' He said the last two words in English. 'It's my little joke,' he added, hastily, perhaps mistaking the look of disdain on my face for noncomprehension. '[King] is the English for king, and [push] for moving a chess piece. It's an interlingual joke, it makes humour between English and Russian.'

'You speak English?' I said.

'You'll have to up the volume!' he laughed. 'It's *loud* in here!'

'You speak English?' I repeated, more forcefully.

'A little. I am in the process of translating the poetry of Robert Brownking, the celebrated Englishman. It is good poetry, with a commendable awareness of the proletariat consciousness.'

'Browning,' I said.

'Exactly.'

'You said, Brownking.'

'Exactly.' Lunacharsky's eyes made little darting movements, left to right. 'You know him?'

'Yes,' I said.

'You speak English too?'

'Yes.'

'[It's perfectly cricket, jolly-chap old-chap],' he boomed, perhaps in the belief that this was an idiomatic Anglophone expression.

I stared at him. The whole scenario had a peculiar and dreamlike feel. My neck still smarted from where the mosquito had bitten it.

'[I work as a translator,]' I said. '[And have rendered several English writers into Russian, Browning amongst them.]'

'[Brownking,]' he said, darting his eyes left and right. 'I only meant that he was [king] among poets, ha, ha-ha. King Robert the Brown! That is all that I meant by ha, ha-ha.'

A cellar space large enough for half a dozen tables had been filled with a dozen, and around all of these were crowded many hunchshouldered men. Some of these customers were indeed leaning over chessboards; but on most of the tables there were only bottles, glasses, and colourless fluid distributed unequally between the two.

'This way,' said Lunacharsky, guiding me from the door into the centre of the room on a path that involved some near-balletic contortions on my part to squeeze through the crush. 'We'd best make a start.'

'A start?' I repeated, with a sense of apprehension.

On the far side of the room the ceiling dropped vertically three feet, turning the remaining space into a wide, low alcove. The right angle of this ceiling feature had been decorated with a line of dour-coloured tassels. Lunacharsky ushered me between the tables, and as I made my way I came close enough to see that this line was not of tassels, but rather an unbroken set of mould-stalactites. On every wall condensation glittered like toads' eyes in the electric light.

'Friends,' Lunacharsky announced, stopping abruptly with his hand on my shoulder. 'Our special guest is here! Long promised –

now here he is! The noted Russian science fiction writer and expert on UFOs, Konrad Skvorecky!'

'It's Konst*urgh*,' I said, as an elbow impacted with the small of my back. The elbow had been pushed out to enable the owner to clap his hands vigorously together; and as I contorted my body to avoid further blows my ears were assailed by applause rendered more thunderous by the enclosed space.

When the noise had died away Lunacharsky announced, 'We're all aware of the excellent science fiction stories that our friend has written. But until recently I was not aware that he was also one of the great scholars of the UFO experience.'

'I'm not,' I said, but my words were drowned by another flurry of applause.

Silence again. Everybody was looking at me expectantly.

'So,' I said. 'This is neither a chess nor a science fiction club? You are, rather, UFO enthusiasts?'

The silence seemed to emanate from the walls themselves. Finally somebody in the far corner spoke. 'You have a sense of humour, comrade!'

At that, several people laughed.

The reality of the situation was starting to dawn on me. 'You have all assembled here to hear me talk?' I said.

'Of course!' bellowed somebody from the back with a voice of which a Cossack would be proud.

'You are,' said Lunacharsky, grinning in fear and shimmering his eyes furiously from left to right, 'our *special* guest. One of the most respected scholars of the UFO experience in all the Soviet Union!'

'No I'm not,' I said.

'What's that?' somebody called from the back of the little room. 'Speak up!'

'I am no expert in UFOs,' I announced. 'I fear you have been misinformed about me.'

'You are privy to the secrets of Project Stalin,' said a voice.

'My taxi driver, Saltykov, told me—' I started.

'I read your *novels*,' shouted someone else. There was a clamour of excited voices.

'Stalin briefed you personally!'

'You were present at the Kiev excavation!'

'You know! Tell us!'

'Comrades, comrades,' shouted Lunacharsky, rolling his shoulders and flapping his hands in front of his chest. 'One question at a time. Comrades! Friends! Fellow seekers-for-the-truth! Let him speak! Let him speak! I present to you: *Konrad Skvorecky!*'

'Not *Konrad*,' I said, crossly, 'my name—' and the applause swarmed up locustlike to devour my words. I cleared my throat. Eventually the applause died away. I looked quickly from table to table: many faces in the smoky dimness, and all staring at me with an intimidating eagerness.

'Well,' I said, croakily. I coughed again. 'The first thing is that my name is Konstantin, not Konrad.'

This was greeted with perfect silence, and the several dozen pairs of eyes focused an intense attentiveness upon me. I glanced over towards Lunacharsky, but he too was nothing more than a pair of staring eyes. I began to find the sheer momentum of the room's anticipation oppressive.

'The second thing,' I said, 'is that I have no expertise whatsoever where UFOs are concerned.'

This pebble made no ripple on the smooth surface of the room's eager attentiveness. It occurred to me that my audience might be taking this as nothing more than a polite gesture towards modesty on my part, like an Englishman's demurral. 'Really,' I said. 'I have no knowledge about them. I'm afraid there's been a misunderstanding. I have made no study of the phenomenon, nor do I believe that such devices even exist.'

I paused. Somebody gulped in the dark, perhaps taking a drink.

'There are no such things as UFOs,' I tried.

This did not break the stillness either.

'If you believe in UFOs,' I said, 'you are deluded.'

'Comrade!' said somebody from a table nearby. 'Comrade, we understand what you are saying.'

'You do?'

'Certainly. We understand your need to *express yourself* in this manner.' There was a murmur of agreement.

'KGB!' somebody hooted.

'Wise! Be indirect! Good thinking!'

'I don't think,' I said, 'that you have properly understood what I am saying.'

There was an expectant hush.

'There are *no such things*,' I enunciated clearly, 'as UFOs.'

A murmur went from table to table, but not of dissension, or outrage, but rather of dawning comprehension. Somebody clapped.

'No,' I said, becoming annoyed. 'You are deliberately mis-understanding me. Do not transpose my negatives for positives. I am not speaking ironically, or in code; I am stating a simple truth.'

'The truth *is* simple,' somebody boomed, from the back of the cellar. 'It is the attempt to cover up the truth that is complicated! That cover-up forces complications upon us!'

'That's not it,' I said.

'Well *said*, Comrade Skvorecky,' said somebody else. 'No! – we must hold fast to the dialectical! We *must negate* the official version!'

'That's not – look,' I said. 'There's little point in inviting a speaker to come if you ... look, you're not *listening* to me!'

The murmuring ceased; and I was greeted again with the spookily attentive silence. 'Don't close your minds!' I said. As soon as I said this I understood that it was exactly the wrong note to sound. Everybody clapped, as if I were a fellow brother and martyr. When the noise had died down I tried again.

'There are no UFOs!' I cried. 'Nobody gets abducted by them! They don't hover over fields in Georgia shooting silver beams of light at farmers!'

'Comrade?' called somebody from over to the right. 'Comrade! Comrade?'

'What is it?'

'Your face . . .' he said.

'My face is—'

'It is *burned*? Those are *burn scars* on your face?'

'Indeed. The story behind those scars is . . .'

'Radiation burns,' boomed somebody else. 'It's a common side-effect of abduction!'

The room erupted in noise, and my piping denials were wholly swallowed up. There was a prolonged hubbub. Finally, when the noise had settled a little, somebody else cried out, 'What was it like inside the craft, comrade?'

'I was never abducted,' I said.

'Did they undertake a physical examination?'

'What *colour* were they, comrade?' somebody else shouted.

'Were you stripped naked, comrade?'

'Child-sized, or were you touched by some of the tall breed?'

'I,' I said, and my voice collapsed into a rubble of coughs. It was very smoky in that subterranean space, and a lifetime of smoking had left my lungs in a poor way.

'The tall breed can be as high as three metres,' somebody declared.

'They like to probe the rectum!' shrilled somebody, with a squeaky but penetrating voice. 'They like to probe the *rectum*!' he repeated.

'Comrades,' I said, getting my voice back under control. 'Comrades, please listen to me.'

'Was it a *Moscow* abduction?' somebody demanded.

'When Stalin himself ordered . . .'

'Not only advanced technology was discovered in Kiev, but the entire *history of humanity* . . .'

'Petrazavodsk! I was there!'

'They like to *probe* the rectum!'

'How long were you away? Time dilation can mean—'

'They like to *probe the rectum*!'

'The case of Andrei Kertész,' he was gone for six months, although *he* thought that only a few hours had passed . . .'

'When,' boomed somebody above the roar, 'spaceships travel close to the speed of light . . .'

'Rectum!'

'To *map* the incidence of abduction *across* the Soviet Union is *to realise* . . .' screeched somebody.'

'Ghost rockets!'

'Radiation burns!'

'They like to *probe!*'

'The correlation between abductions and sunspot activity . . .'

'Project Stalin!'

'A properly *dialectical* understanding of the UFO phenomenon . . .'

'Comrades,' I tried again, but I was immediately drowned out by the high-pitched voice of rectum-man, who seemed, indeed, very insistent that the room hear what he had to say: 'They like to probe the rectum! They like to probe the rectum! They like to probe the rectum!'

'*Friends*,' a voice bellowed, commanding the crowd in a way my raspy throat could not. It was Lunacharsky; standing beside me, with both his arms up. The ceiling was so low that this meant he was touching it. 'Silence! Comrades, be quiet! Please!' And the noise gradually sank back down. 'Comrades,' said Lunacharsky. 'I think we'd all like to thank our friend Konrad Skvorecky for his insights . . .'

Applause filled the little space like expansive aural foam. It was the concrete manifestation of my own impotent annoyance. I nodded my head like an idiot. Feeling oddly powerless in the face of this public approbation, I turned to find the stairs with the thought of getting away and finding the nearest Metro. The taxi driver, Saltykov, was standing between the exit and me. 'It was a very interesting talk,' he said.

'Thank you,' I said. 'I have to go now.'

'I insist that you come and meet my friend.'

'No thank you.'

'I insist, and so does he. He is American.'

'I'd prefer to go.'

'He's your friend too. That's what he says.'

In the noise and dark I wasn't certain I'd heard this correctly. 'I'm sorry? I don't know any Americans.'

'His name,' said Saltykov, gesturing towards the deepest corner of the basement bar, 'is James Tilly Coyne. He represents the Church of Scientology.'

A little disoriented, I found myself threading through the crush of humanity two steps behind Saltykov. There was a table fitted snug into an alcove. 'Please sit down,' said Saltykov. He nudged me, and I ducked my head to fit under the alcove. In the furthest corner of the recess, nursing a bottle of beer without a glass, sat Dr James Tilly Coyne, US citizen. He beamed at me. 'An excellent performance,' he said. In some sense, a way in which I could not quite understand, the disorientation of finding this individual sitting here, in this bar, was connected with the disorientation of sitting with Frenkel in the restaurant earlier that day. They seemed to be aspects of the same disorientation.

Let us say that science fiction is a kind of conceptual disorientation of the familiar. Of course if that were true, you'd think I'd be more comfortable with the sensation.

CHAPTER 6

I sat down. 'Mr Coyne,' I said.

'And how pleasant to meet you again,' he said.

'Your Russian is very fluent,' I said.

'Thank you!' he said. 'But I am poor with contemporary idiom. I like to come to places such as this. This club for example. In part I mean to acquire contemporary idiom. Such things, one cannot learn out of books.'

'It is almost,' I said, 'as if you have no *need* of an official translator.'

'That business at the ministry?' he said, pinching a simulacrum of remorse from his squinnying eyes. 'I am sorry. I am sorry about that. Will you forgive me?'

'Is there something to forgive?'

'We were detained by the authorities,' he explained. 'I've come to the USSR many times, toing and froing between here and the USA. It is an occupational hazard of such travel that occasionally the authorities become suspicious and detain me. In such circumstances I have learnt it is best to ... *pretend* to be less knowledgeable than actually I am.'

'I understand.'

'Wise, wouldn't you say?'

'But if you are asking about wisdom,' I said, 'you are asking the wrong man.'

Saltykov had reappeared, carrying three bottles of beer. 'Here you are! I am content to drink beer,' he added, a little mysteriously. 'I hope you are too?'

'I am not thirsty,' I said. 'Forgive me if it appears ungrateful on my part.'

'I drink one beer a day,' Saltykov explained, seating himself. 'Always between the hours of six and nine in the evening. Never at any other time, never more than one, and never anything stronger.'

'I prefer not to drink alcohol at any time.'

'Mr Konstantin!' said the American. 'Are you [teetotal], my friend?' Then, to Saltykov he added, 'That's the English word. I don't know the Russian equivalent.'

'There is no Russian equivalent,' I said in a level voice. 'It is a concept alien to, and corrosive of, the Russian tongue. But yes, I do not drink. I used to do so. I found myself with a choice: continue drinking; continue breathing. I chose the latter.'

'You do not drink beer?' said Saltykov in his prissy voice. '*Or* vodka?'

'Sometimes I touch tea.'

'I do not drink vodka either,' said Saltykov. 'It is unpleasant stuff. I drink very little, in fact, although I permit myself, as I explained, one bottle of beer between the hours of six and nine.

'I do believe,' said James Coyne, beaming, 'that I am sitting at a table with the only two [teetotallers] in Russia.'

'Mr Coyne,' I said. 'I think I'd better go. I have had a tiring and, indeed, rather confusing day.'

'Please don't go just yet,' said Coyne, sitting forward with a sparkle in his eye. 'I'm here for one reason only, and that's to meet with you.'

This, of course, made no sense at all. 'You've come to Russia to meet *me*?'

He laughed again, with pleasant warmth. 'That's right, sir. I've come to Russia to meet you.'

'And so it is that my day gets odder and odder,' I said. 'I am a nobody, Mr Coyne, I assure you. I live in a very small flat. I know nobody of any importance, and actually hardly anybody of *any* kind at all. As the English say, [I eke out a living] as a translator. There's no reason for my neighbour to cross the hall to meet me; certainly no reason for an American to cross the world for that purpose.'

'It is a matter of the very greatest importance,' he said.

'You *are* a baffling human being,' I said. 'And so are you,' I added, looking at Saltykov.

'Me?' Saltykov returned, looking hurt. 'Why say that *I* am baffling? You ought to be more understanding. I,' he added, 'have a syndrome.'

'Syndrome,' I repeated. 'What is it?'

'Do you mean, *what is* a syndrome,' he asked. 'Or do you mean, what particular syndrome do I have? It is important to be precise.'

'I am guessing that precision *is* your syndrome,' I said.

He put his head a little on one side, no more than five degrees. 'Do you know what? That is quite a good way of putting it! Yes, yes, I like that way of putting it.'

'I'd say,' said Coyne, after sizing me up and down, and with what at the time I took for extraordinary prescience (though now, of course, I understand how he was able to know so much about me), 'that you have a syndrome too, [Mr] Skvorecky.'

'Do you think so? Not precision, surely.'

'Not that. I don't mean to presume.'

'Presume all you like,' I said.

'You were in the war, I suppose?'

'The Great Patriotic War,' I said, nodding. 'But you might guess as much about me from my age.'

'In America we observe that many survivors of war suffer from a condition called [post-traumatic stress disorder]. You understand the English?'

'I've heard of this disorder,' I said. 'I'm surprised you think I suffer from it.'

'What?' asked Saltykov, blinking. 'I didn't catch the name of the syndrome.'

'After-trauma stress syndrome,' I translated.

'It is often diagnosed in soldiers who have survived a war,' said Coyne.

'The war was four decades ago,' I pointed out.

'But it was an unusually savage war,' he returned. 'It laid its imprint upon you when you were very young. One's [thetan], which is to say, one's soul, is more impressionable when one is young.'

'That is one English word I don't know.'

'It is a piece of Scientological terminology.'

'After-trauma stress syndrome,' mused Saltykov. 'But I have a question. Why is it that some syndromes are named after individuals – scientists, say – and others not? My syndrome, for example, is named after a notable Austrian doctor, Dr Hans Asp—'

'[Post-traumatic stress disorder,]' I interrupted, speaking English. '[It's *possible* I have been touched by this, I suppose. But if so, then surely the whole of Russia has been suffering from that. After the trauma that was the Great Patriotic War.]'

Coyne nodded, and replied in Russian. 'Or the trauma we call Stalin.'

I was made a little uncomfortable by the closeness of his gaze. Saltykov looked left and right. There was a little hole in the conversation, and he filled it. 'I have another question,' he asked both of us, or neither perhaps. 'Why cannot *colour* shock the sensorium in the same way that electricity or collision can?'

I looked at him. 'What?'

'Do you wish me to repeat my statement?'

'No, I heard you. *What* was short for what on earth are you talking about?'

Saltykov took my question seriously. 'I am making an observation about the world: extremities of touch are shocking, as with a blow. Extremities of taste likewise – chili, acid – or of smell, and the same with smell, as with smelling salts.'

'Smelling salts,' I repeated, trying to keep hold of the wriggling thread of his thought.

'Exactly. And of course, extremities of sound are painful. The earsplitting din, the panic shout. These can, of course, be literally intolerable. As for sight, well the photoreceptive layer of the retina is divided into rods and cones. Rods are easily overstimulated by illumination – the intense glare of light that blinds – but cones, responsible for colour vision, do not seem to work this way. In a normal eye, there is no intensity of colour (as opposed to of brightness) that is *actively painful*, or intolerable, after the fashion of these other things. Since colour is indeed perceived in terms of varying intensities, it is very strange that the intensity doesn't seem to have an upper level. I wonder: is this the only portion of the human sensorium that works this way?'

Things seemed to have reached a moment of pure absurdity. A mosquito had stung me. Saltykov was a mosquito, buzzing in my ear. I started laughing. 'You are a philosopher!' I said. 'A philosopher!'

'In a sense I am,' said Saltykov, with prim outrage at my reaction. 'But I do not see why that fact occasions hilarity.'

'I'm sorry, comrade,' I said, getting to my feet. 'Comrade, I apologise. I implore you, take no offence. Please blame my reaction on exhaustion and old age. I bid you both good night.'

'Shall I drive you in my taxi?'

'If it does not offend you, I shall take the Metro.'

'[I hope you don't mind if I accompany you up the stairs,]' said Coyne, in English, also getting to his feet. I wanted to tell him not to bother himself, but instead I found the laughter bubbling up again. Frenkel had been abducted by aliens! The far-fetched story we invented, for the benefit of Stalin himself, *was coming true*. Every Moscow taxi driver was a secret philosopher who took their passengers to the Pushkin Club rather than to their actual destinations. The world was insane. 'Come along then, my new American friend,' I said. And we picked our way through the tables of the Pushkin, crammed with faces now scowling and hostile where before they had been eager and welcoming, and made our way up the stairs and out in the cold.

CHAPTER 7

We were on Zholtovskovo Street, and it was very late in the night. 'Will you walk with me?' Coyne asked. 'My hotel is not far from here.'

'Which hotel?'

'The Marco Polo. It's just off the Tverskaya Ulitsa. Do you know it?'

'That's a little close to the Militia headquarters for my taste,' I said.

'Oh but it's opulent, the Marco Polo. It's new, you know. It's a symbol of the coming Russia. Of the coming, opulent Russia.'

'It sounds too expensive for the likes of me,' I said.

'The hotel?'

'The new Russia.'

He coughed. '[Expense,]' he said in English, adding a word that I did not recognise, but which might have been a reference to Smolensk. 'I'm American!' he beamed. 'I have a reputation to keep up! Come back to the hotel and I'll show you. Perhaps a drink of vodka before we turn in for the night?'

'I don't drink vodka.'

'I forgot. You and Saltykov, the only two adult human beings in the entire Soviet Union who don't drink vodka. But perhaps you'll have a coffee? Or a glass of water?'

'People seem strangely eager to press hospitality upon me today.'

'A testament to your sociability! Or perhaps they are trying to win you to their cause?'

'An unlikely supposition. You forget that I'm a nobody.'

'But you are *not*!' said the American, earnestly. 'You are a *very important* person. You have the opportunity to save the lives of millions.'

'What?'

'You and I need to have a conversation, my friend. It may be the most important conversation you ever have in your life.'

I digested this. 'I take it, this is the opening gambit by which your Church converts people to its faith.'

Coyne laughed, easily and fluently. '[You're droll,]' he said, in English. Then, in Russian: 'Nothing like that. But the truth is almost too alarming to express. The future of – well, millions of lives, certainly. It's probably not too much to say: the fate of the world.'

'The fate of the world?'

'I'm not [bullshitting],' he said. 'You know that term?'

'I'm familiar with many of the varieties of Anglophone shit.'

'Well, believe me that what I'm telling you now is not [bullshit]. It's a threat to millions of lives. It's a threat to the whole world. I am not talking metaphorically. It's real.'

'So: you wish to have a conversation with me about a threat to the whole world, that I am uniquely positioned to avert?'

He laughed. '[Yes, that's about the up and down of it.]'

'[Both up *and* down? What a paradoxical man you are.]'

'[Perhaps. But I am truthful.]'

'If you say so.'

'I do. My religion is about uncovering the truth, and speaking the truth is of course a necessary part of that. I *am* here, in part, to test the waters for a possible Scientological base in Moscow. Just as I have told the authorities. But – the truth is I'm not here *primarily* to do that. Despite what I said in the ministry earlier. Well, the *truth* is I work in nuclear power. I have a degree in nuclear physics. I work in the States as a safety consultant for nuclear power stations.'

'Saltykov claimed something similar.'

'Hey! That's right!' We walked under the light of a streetlamp, a dunce-hat-shaped cone of brightness sitting on the pavement in the black night. He stopped me, and I looked at his face. The bright overhead illumination worked a strange etcher's trick upon the lines on his face, scoring them deeper, and shining waxily off the portions in between. 'I'm about to tell you something top secret. Top top secret. Do you understand?'

'I understand. Understand and believe are two different words.'

'[I couldn't talk with you about it in that club. And I won't be able to talk about it in the hotel room, which is probably bugged. Strike probably, insert certainly.]'

'And here outside,' I said, 'it's just you, me and comrade street-lamp here.'

He slapped the metal pole amiably. The light was pouring down upon him, as if in a shower. And then, perhaps believing that what he had to communicate to me was better uttered in the decent darkness of the space in between the streetlamps, he took hold of my arm at the elbow and walked on. 'Top secret.' He repeated.

'I'm agog.'

'Ms Norman and I flew into Moscow from Kiev,' he said.

I stopped and bowed my head. 'I shall keep this profound secret in my innermost heart, and undertake never to tell a soul.'

'That's not the secret,' he said, with a sharper tone, tugging harder on my arm as he walked on. 'Unless you realise *why* we were in Kiev?'

'Perhaps you were visiting the celebrated Kiev opera?'

'No no,' he said. 'Like I said, I'm a safety inspector. I'm part of a top-secret exchange programme between the Soviet and American governments. I bring my expertise in nuclear safety to a number of Soviet reactors. That's how I know Saltykov.'

'You knew him before his taxi-driving days?'

'[Oh he knows a *tremendous* amount about nuclear power,]' said Coyne, reverently. [That's his training. That used to be his career. He's fallen out with the administration over some footling nonsense, dissent or something. But he *knows*. I've had dealings with him before, and there's nobody whose knowledge of nuclear power I respect more.]'

We were walking now in the dark between streetlamps. Indeed, I noticed that the next streetlamp along was not illuminated. A broken bulb, I supposed. Twenty metres further down the street the next light along hovered in the air like a beacon. Then the strangest thing: just as I was looking at this it suddenly went out. All the lamps along Zholtovskovo, to that point where the street bends through ninety degrees, snuffed out.

Buzz, buzz. One by one, clicking off into darkness.

Though the night was moonless, things were not completely black; many of the windows in the buildings were illuminated, and there was a glow over the rooftops from the Garden Ring, one block behind. But it was pretty dark, for all that. 'Localised power failing,' I said.

Again: that weird miniature crescendo of a mosquito's buzzing.

'[Power,]' said Coyne, in English. '[A word with many meanings. I visit Soviet *power* stations. The Soviet authorities get the benefit of my expertise in beefing up their security. The American government gets to feel it has an agent inside the Soviet system, checking up on an enemy state's nuclear capacity. Of course I'm only ever allowed inside civilian installations. But it's a mutuality thing,]' and he switched to Russian. 'It's a sign of the increasing thaw between our two nations. It *is* dark, though, isn't it?'

Directly above, between the architectural margins of the two lines of rooftop, a few stars were visible. One, winking at me as if to take me into its confidence, slid steadily along the sky. A plane.

'Is this the top secret thing that you wanted to tell me?'

'*That's* not the top secret thing,' said Coyne. 'Or, to speak precisely: that *is* top secret — it's [classified], as we say in the States. But that's not what I want to talk to you about. I have something more important to tell you. All that jabber, back in the chess club. UFOs? You believe?'

'I like to think of myself as a rationalist,' I said. It was cold, and

I crossed my arms and hunched my shoulders beneath my coat.

'Quite right. Most of those UFO stories, they can be dismissed. But there are a few that are hard to dismiss, no? A small proportion, granted. But consider any phenomenon in the world, I mean, for instance, natural phenomena. Most phenomena in the world are mostly chaff, with a small proportional kernel of truth. Ask yourself this: What if a UFO were to provide us with *hard evidence?*'

'That would clear up some of the uncertainty on the subject,' I conceded, not really very engaged with the conversation.

'Agreed. And that would be good, no?'

'Certainty may be preferable to uncertainty,' I said, unsure where Coyne was going.

'The only question then,' he said, speaking more rapidly, as if excited by his own words, 'is: What constitutes evidence? An alien craft? Some alien pilots? Embalmed alien bodies to stick in the Smithsonian behind perspex? A chunk of alien machinery in the Moscow Polytechnical Museum, yeah?'

'That would be something.'

'[But how would we *know* it to be alien?]' he went on, slipping into English. '[Might it not be, say, a prop? How will we know? How will we know, in this reality or another reality? By its *effects*, that's how. By their fruit shall ye know them. Not something that looks like a raygun, because you might have taken that from a film set. But something that actually shoots destructo-rays.]'

'[You have one of those rayguns about your person?]' I asked. '[Now that the lights have gone out, I find myself become alarmed at the prospect of muggers.]'

He stopped. '[Really?]'

'[Not really, comrade. There are no thieves in Russia, because Communism provides for all needs.]'

'The effects, not the artefacts,' said Coyne, more slowly, in Russian. 'No? That's what I want to talk to you about. Imagine they had a weapon that could lay waste to eastern Europe, western Russia.'

'They?'

'You know whom I mean by they.'

'Scientologists?'

Humour slid past him. 'No – no – aliens. Imagine it! They might – what's the word, [brandish] it . . .'

'Brandish,' I said.

'Sure, exactly. Say these aliens brandished their weapon, and world leaders said: I don't believe you, you're bluffing. OK? Now, what if it was actually *used*, the weapon was fired and Europe and Russia were devastated – you couldn't argue with that, could you?'

'Stop for a minute,' I said. 'I need to catch my breath.' We stopped. I panted. My lungs are not those of a young man; and neither are they the lungs of a non-smoker. 'Let me just see whether I understand you correctly,' I said, when I had the puff. 'Hostile UFO aliens have a weapon that will devastate Europe and Russia. They plan to use this weapon.'

'That puts it very well.'

'And you *believe* in these aliens?'

He didn't answer for a few moments. Finally he said, 'The business of surveying nuclear reactors is an immersive business. You know? You go around inside these reactors, and your attention is very minutely focused on the internal details: pipes and cladding; spent fuel pools; reactor cores. But every now and then I put my mind out from the inward details, and picture the whole system of nuclear reactors – all of the reactors in the world, spread out beneath the sky, all round the curve of the earth. Hundreds of them. I imagine myself soaring suddenly high in the sky, looking down. Do you know how that makes me feel?'

'Vertiginous?'

'Worried. *Vulnerable*, that's how it makes me feel. If I were an invading alien force – well, I would be looking down upon a spread of fantastically powerful bombs, that my enemy had thoughtfully arranged right in the heart of his territory, just waiting for me to trigger them.'

We started walking again. Eventually he spoke again. 'How well do you know Kiev?'

'Kiev?' I shrugged, and folded my folded arms more tightly against the cold. 'I passed through there during the war. There wasn't much to see.'

'It's been rebuilt. There's a lot of rebuilding there. Digging and filling in. Uncovering the past. Building tends to involve that. *Reitarskaya Street*. Is that an address that means anything to you?'

'No.'

'No matter. Did you know that there's a power station not far from Kiev?'

'I should imagine there are power stations not far from most large cities. Cities need power, after all.'

'The one near Kiev is called Chernobyl. Have you heard of it?'

'I never did well,' I said, 'in my Memorising the Names of Soviet Power Stations class at school.'

'Well well,' he said. 'Quite. Chernobyl, anyway, means [worm-wood], in English.'

'Chernobyl,' I repeated.

'[Wormwood,]' he said, speaking English now, [is in the Bible. It's in the Book of Revelation. Do you know it?]

'[The Apocalypse of St John,]' I said. '[The end of the world, and so on.]'

'[Precisely! Wormwood – the Bible says that a bomb will fall like a gleaming star, and destroy millions of lives, at—]'

Then things happened very suddenly. Trying to remember the sequence of events afterwards I was struck by how staged it seemed, right from the start. This may have been because the first thing to happen was the sudden glare of an arc lamp directed down upon us, as if we were indeed inside a theatre and not out on a cold dark Moscow street in the middle of the night. I heard the click of the light being switched on, and the fizz (I'm sure) of its filament heating up. I was blinded, of course; the light was sudden and intense. It was also from directly above, as if somebody had leaned out of a top-floor window and shone a lamp downwards. I felt a weird twist in my stomach. Light, light, light. Buzz, buzz. I blinked. Coyne had cried something out, in his surprise, but I couldn't tell you what it was. His bony hand darted out, like a cobra-strike, and seized my shoulder. I blinked. I blinked again. Out of the ammonium wash of the sudden light, the shape of the building to my left was starting to become discernible.

The sense grew stronger of a fizzing sound, or a sub-rumble, or some strange almost inaudible yet powerful and unmistakable *sound*. It made the watery marrow inside my bones tremble, whatever it was. It made the hairs on my skin shiver upwards. I didn't know what it was.

I blinked.

Then there was a second sound, and this one was unambiguous: a high-pitched whistle, or soprano songnote, like tinnitus.

I was screwing my eyes up. I could see Coyne standing next to me, the colours of his clothing bleached by the ferocity of the light. I squinnied some more, and his face became visible. He was not standing, his feet were not on the ground. His head was floating. I looked again, and saw that his whole body was above his head; and that his head was upside down, on a level with mine. His face looked – alarmed. I daresay mine did too.

His arm was out and his hand was gripping my shoulder, such that when his body jerked upwards and made as if to fly into the sky, it was this grip that, initially, held him back, though it nearly hauled *me* off my feet. His face was still level with mine, although now bulging and red, but his feet were ten feet up in the air. His fingers clawed at the fabric of my coat. There was a heave, and his grip failed and then he was gone.

I stumbled. I looked up, but looking up stung my eyes and I could see very little; except that, there in the very heart of the glare, was a wriggling figure.

It was a very impressive show.

The tinnitus-whistle grew in volume, and the rumbling sub-bass seemed to grow too; my stomach swirled and swirled, and my scrotum tightened so hard it was painful. I felt a sensation I had not experienced since I was a child immediately before Christmas. It was partly excitement, and the numinous sense that something extraordinary was about to happen; but this feeling – you know it, of course; the feeling I'm talking about – it is in the nature of this feeling that it was also flavoured with alarm. Or terror.

Something snapped.

Afterwards, when trying to explain it to the Militia, that was the phrase that came back to me. It was not quite the *sound* of something snapping; not a rope giving way for instance. It may actually, on reflection, have been an absence rather than a presence; not the *sound* of something giving way, but the consciousness that the sub-bass thrum had ceased, the apprehension that a sound was lacking.

I started to breathe in. You know that kind of breath. It is a breath of wonder. Quite a show! Really, *quite* a show!

The breath was a third drawn when the whistling stopped, and the light changed quality. I heard a new noise: a rapidly crescendoing whiffling sound, and I had the sense that something was coming down. And with a heavy crunch Coyne landed on the pavement directly in front of me. He came down head first, and a long snake curled down through the air after him to tumble onto his body.

I jumped back, startled, but even as I jumped I understood what had happened. So having jumped onto my left foot I launched forward again, and went down on one knee beside him.

He was still breathing, and still capable of movement. He had fallen on his front, but he was using his fingers, scraping them against the ground and drawing them back into a fist, and scraping them outwards again, to push a sheet of dark paper out from underneath him and to slide it along the pavement. But it wasn't paper, it was fluid. He had fallen on top of, and broken open, a bottle of artist's ink, and that was now spreading its stain along the floor. His head was turned to the left.

Coiled on his back was a silver rope. I reached forward and touched it, and it felt warm. It was no thicker than a finger. It coiled and coiled, and it was tethered to Coyne's ankle.

There was no rope.

'Coyne,' I said, leaning over his ear. He wasn't moving. His back was not rising or falling. Of course it was not *ink*, spilling out from underneath him. I wanted to say something to him, but my mind was perfectly empty. I had no idea what to say. What could I say? What ought I to do?

Coyne spoke. 'React!' he told me, in a raspy voice.

And the whole unrealness of the experience burst pressed itself upon me. Of course it was a show! A show for my benefit! Of *course* I ought not to be frozen there. I ought to react. When you put on a show, you expect your audience to react.

'What?'

'*React!*' he ordered.

'I don't understand what you want me to do. Laugh? Clap?'

He rolled his eyes.

'You want me to, what?' I said, growing angry, and conscious for the first time of how rapidly my heart was beating. 'What, burst into applause?'

He seemed to be nodding. 'Or—' he started to say, his lips working as if he were chewing the pavement.

'Or what?' I snapped at him. My startlement was converting itself into anger. How *dare* he scare me like this? 'Or how else am I supposed to react to such an absurd performance? Or what will you *do*, exactly?'

As abruptly as it had switched on, the light went out. The darkness was everywhere. I blinked and blinked, and only very slowly did his body start to become visible to me again. There was a sudden movement of the rope, a repeat of the whiffling sound – or perhaps it was a broken, gaspy breath from Coyne's lungs, squeezed from his broken ribcage. In fact, the more I consider it, I wonder whether this wasn't exactly the sound of the *death rattle*. I had read about such a thing as a death rattle, though I had never heard one in life before. I leant further forward, pulling off my right glove to place a finger on the artery in his throat. Touching his neck was an uncanny thing, and not pleasant. His felt like a sack of knucklebones from a butcher's, not a neck. There was no pulse at all. The last of his breath whiffled out of him.

'Four,' he said, very distinctly.

The streetlights came on as I sat back. I could see that I had been kneeling in his blood, and that my trousers were marked with it. And as I looked up I could see two Militia officers, guns out, *running* along the Zholtovskovo, running with furious haste and towards me.

CHAPTER 8

They put me in a basement cell with no windows. There was an electric light bulb in a wire cage on the ceiling. The blank walls were covered with tooth-sized white tiles. I sat on the bench. After a while I lay down on the bench. It being a Militia cell the bench was long enough for me to lie upon. Had it been KGB the bench would have been too short, and set into the wall at enough of an angle to threaten to roll me off it and onto the floor, so as to make sleep harder. But the Militia are ordinary police, and a fair amount of their work involves locking drunks away and letting them sleep themselves law-abiding. The KGB, conversely, prefer a sleep-deprived prisoner. A prisoner is more useful to the KGB exhausted.

In another reality, perhaps, I stayed awake and plotted my escape. But in *this* reality, I fell asleep. A couple of hours at the most.

I woke at the sound of footsteps outside, and then the door sang its hinge-scraping song – a pure, soprano tone. Two officers roused me and led me upstairs, both of them as tall and broad and impassive as Klaatu himself. One was carrying handcuffs; but he took one look at me, elderly and shuffling as I was, and evidently concluded they were superfluous.

It was the small hours of the night, and the station was quiet. Decades of cigarette smoking had imparted a warm, stale quality to the declivities and crevices of the building. The smell was a mixture of tobacco, body odour, upholstery and a metallic quality hard, precisely, to identify: gunmetal, perhaps. I was sat at a table in an interrogation room and left to my own devices for perhaps quarter of an hour. The table, no larger than a statue's plinth, was crowded with enamel mugs: white sides, blue-lipped as if with cold, I counted nine of them. Some were empty. Some held inch-thick discs of cold, oily-looking coffee, as black as alien eyes. I pondered why they had sat me down at this table, with all these used mugs, but my brain was not working as smoothly as would have been good. It was the dead of night. I am an old, tired man.

Eventually a young officer unlocked the door, gathered all the old mugs onto a tray and carried them away without saying a word. The door closed and the key turned with a noise like a blown raspberry; and then, without pause, it blew another raspberry as it was unlocked. The door swung open again.

'My name,' said the officer, sitting himself down opposite me, 'is Zembla.' He put a tape recorder on the table between us.

'I'm pleased to meet you,' I said.

'Are you prepared to assist us in our enquiries?'

'By all means.'

He peered at me with two midnight-coloured eyes. The cloth of his uniform creaked as he shifted in the chair. On went the recorder. 'Officer Zembla, interrogation February 20th 1986. Suspect to state his name.'

'Konstantin Skvorecky.'

'Occupation?'

'I work as a translator.'

Zembla looked hard at me. 'As it might be, foreign languages?'

'As it might be.'

'In particular?'

'The English particular. I speak a little French too.'

'That's a job?'

'Doesn't it sound like one to you?'

'Just speaking a language?' said Zembla. 'Not really. You speak English? But isn't England full of people who speak English?'

'True,' I said. 'But not many of them speak Russian.'

'Why go to England for that? The Soviet Union contains *millions* of people who speak Russian!'

I looked closely at him to see if he was joking, but he seemed to be serious. 'You make an interesting point, comrade,' I said eventually.

'Anyway. Never mind that. So. You were present at the crime scene?'

'I haven't been told what the crime is.'

'James Coyne, an American citizen, was discovered dead on Zholtovskovo Street by two officers. You were discovered kneeling next to him. This is a serious matter.'

'Death is rarely otherwise.'

Zembla switched the tape recorder off. 'The *Americanness* of the deceased is serious,' he said, with a poorly repressed fury. 'Death is absolutely fucking ordinary and everyday in this job, comrade. You understand?'

'I think so.'

'*Death* is not serious. Death is fucking *comedy*, as far as I'm concerned. Death is the jester, yeah? He—' Zembla turned his hand over and back in the manner of an individual searching for right words. 'He, he does whatever it is that jesters do.'

'Juggling balls?' I suggested.

Zembla's face stiffened. It possessed, in repose, a really quite impressive sculptural quality: massy and stone-coloured. Then his lips started working, and eventually words came out. 'I'll cut off *your* balls and juggle them *in the air* you fucking little *cock-end*. You understand?'

'Perfectly, comrade.'

'Don't fuck me around.'

'No, comrade.'

The tape went on again. 'Describe how you came to be beside the deceased.'

'I was walking with him along Zholtovskovo Street when he was killed.'

'You killed him?'

'Certainly not.'

'You knew him, though?'

'I met him for the first time today. Or perhaps, yesterday. If it is now past midnight.'

'How did you meet him?'

'I was working as a translator in the Office of Liaison and Overseas Exchange. Mr Coyne was there, together with a Miss Norman, discussing—'

'Wait!' Zembla took out a notepad. 'Also an American?'

'Yes.'

'Spell her name.' I did so, and he wrote it down, tracing out large letters like a child with a crayon. 'His wife? Mistress?'

'I've really no idea, comrade. They were both representing the American Church of Scientology with a view to establishing a cultural exchange in Moscow.'

'That's what they said?'

'Yes, comrade.'

He leered at me. 'You believed them?'

'It seems to me that the business of an official translator is to translate,' I said. 'Not to believe or disbelieve.'

Zembla's chunky thumb went back to the tape recorder. Off. He leaned forward. 'You remember what I said about your balls?'

'Juggling them, you mean?'

'You *remember* that? Do you have *memory problems*, old man? Or do you *remember*? You think, perhaps, that was just a figure of speech? It *wasn't* a figure of speech. I will *literally* cut off your testicles and throw them about this room. Do you think I've never done it before? Do you think I've never cut off a man's balls?'

'I'd imagine there's a considerable loss of blood.'

He glowered at me. 'Loss of blood!' he said. 'That's *right*. Not to mention the loss of *balls*. That's *another* loss. That's a more *significant* loss. Blood can always be transfused, can't it? But there's no hospital in the world will transfuse you new *balls*.' He let me

95

ponder this medical undeniability for a moment. Then he said, in a gloating tone, 'Do you think we didn't *know* about Dora Norman? Well we did. We know all about Coyne, and his business here. You don't fool us.'

'Comrade, I'm honestly not trying to fool you.'

'When I got you to spell her name just then,' he said, 'I already knew it! It was a *trick*. We'll soon have Norman Doriski in custody. Very soon.'

'Dora Norman,' I said.

He narrowed his eyes. 'Think of your ballbag,' he said. 'Think about it long and hard. Give your ballbag careful thought. *I* would, if I were you.'

'You would?'

'Yes.'

'You'd think about my ballbag?'

'The tape recorder isn't king in here,' he told me, his eyes going from side to side. '*I'm* king in here.'

'I had always assumed that the optimum interrogation strategy was *nice cop nasty cop*,' I said. 'Not *nice cop confusing cop*.'

He opened his eyes very wide at this, but didn't say anything. Perhaps he couldn't think of a retort. Instead he pointed his forefinger at my face and gave me a severe look. Then he jabbed his meaty thumb at the tape recorder. The spindle-wheels of the cassette again began turning again. 'How did you come to be walking with Mr Coyne along Zholtovskovo Street after midnight?'

'I encountered him quite by chance.'

'By chance? You didn't *arrange* to meet him again?'

'No. I went to the Pushkin Chess Club, and he happened to be there.'

'You went to the Pushkin Chess Club?'

'Yes.'

He turned off the recorder again. 'Big chess fan, are you?' he sneered.

'The club has a social function in addition to the playing of chess.'

'Ever played chess with your own *balls* instead of the kings? Eh? Have you? Because I can arrange exactly that sort of game. I'll cut them off myself with my penknife, and you can use them as the two white kings. Understand?'

He turned the tape recorder on again. I'll confess I was finding his one-note attempt to intimidate me strangely endearing. 'There's only one white king,' I said. 'One king per player in a game of chess.'

He jabbed the tape recorder off. 'I know that!' he snapped. He poked his thumb at the machine, turned it on, turned it off again, perhaps by accident, turned it on again. 'Don't fuck with me, little man. You seem to *enjoy* being disrespectful to me. Do it once more and I won't cut your balls off, I'll fucking *rip* them off with my own right hand.'

I considered telling him that he was recording this tirade onto his cassette, but elected, after a moment's consideration, not to. It was his machine, after all. 'Fair enough,' I said.

'OK. We're going to proceed with the interview in a moment. I'll ask questions, and you'll give me the answers I want to hear, OK? No more disrespect, or your balls will no longer be attached to your body.'

'OK,' I said.

'Good.' He pressed the cassette button, turning the machine off. He seemed to believe that he had turned it on.

'So, comrade. You met Mr Coyne in the Pushkin?'

'He was there, yes.'

'And you didn't expect to see him there?'

'Certainly not.'

'Why not?'

'For one thing, I assumed he couldn't speak Russian.'

'Why not?'

'Well, I suppose I reasoned: if he spoke Russian, why had he needed my services as a translator in the ministry, that afternoon?'

'Why indeed? So he *did* speak Russian?'

'Fluently.'

'Why, then, *had* he asked for an interpreter at the ministry?'

'I've no idea, comrade.'

'You can't guess?'

'I suppose he didn't want the ministry to know the extent of his Russian knowledge. As in a game of poker, one keeps certain cards hidden from the other players.'

'So he was playing poker?'

'Metaphorically, yes, I suppose so.'

'What *was* he playing, though?'

I thought for a moment. 'Poker?' I hazarded.

The thumb jabbed at the tape, switching it, as he thought, off; although in fact he had turned it on. 'You fucking little shit, you testicular idiot. Don't fucking backchat me, all right?'

'No, comrade.'

'You *know* what I meant when I asked that question?'

'The poker question?'

'No! No!' He seemed genuinely to be losing his temper. 'I asked *what he was playing at*. Answering poker is just, fucking – what's the word – *facetious*. It's glib. If you're fucking *glib*, I'll remove your testicles. Yes?'

'I understand,' I said gravely.

'You haven't forgotten what I said about your testicles?'

'I don't think I'll ever forget it.'

'Then perhaps,' he said, 'we can proceed. Or we'll be here all fucking night.' He pushed the switch on the tape recorder again, and the little wheels stopped turning. '*For* the record,' he said, leaning back in his chair. 'What was Mr Coyne *actually* doing in Moscow?'

'You're asking my opinion?'

'Yes.'

'I don't know.'

'That's not an opinion.'

'I'm sorry.'

'All right, all right. Look. Tell me how you came to be walking down Zholtovskovo Street with the deceased.'

'He said he wanted to have a word with me. About something important.'

'You were talking Russian?'

'Mostly. Occasionally we'd swap to English.'

'And what did he want to talk about? Wait! Wait! Shit, shit, shit.' Zembla lurched forward and peered at the tape recorder. 'The little wheels aren't going round. Is it broken? Piece of shit.'

'I believe it is turned off.'

Gingerly, Zembla tried the REC button. The spindles began to turn. He switched it off and they stopped. I watched, as realisation kindled in his big face. 'I've been doing it the wrong way round,' he said. 'Turning it *off* during the interview, and turning it *on* during the ... ah, the interruptions.'

'It looks that way, comrade.'

'Shit!' he said, with real panic in his voice. 'All the stuff about balls is on tape!' His gaze, when it came up to meet mine, was imploring. 'I didn't mean it,' he said. 'I didn't mean any of it. All that stuff about cutting off your balls. I would never *actually* do anything so brutal.'

'I believe you,' I said.

'It was just a strategy! It was just jabber, to get you talking! Really, I'm a gentle-hearted man.'

'Your gentleness shines through.'

'The captain is going to be *peeved*. He won't like it.' Fumblingly he pressed the rewind button. 'Maybe I can just erase the whole thing? Start again? How does one erase these fucking little cassettes anyway?'

'I'm not an expert with such machines,' I said.

'Oh, and shit. Shit and oh. The captain is going to be *annoyed*.' This prospect really seemed to alarm him. He stopped the rewind and pressed play. Tinnily his own voice sounded out, *fucking little shit, you testicular idiot. Don't fucking backchat.* He jabbed it off. 'Oh dear. Oh,' he said. 'Dear. Oh no.'

'We can start again,' I offered.

But Zembla picked the machine up and burlied his way out of

the interrogation room, leaving the door open. For a while I simply sat there, looking through the open door at the stretch of corridor outside, and wondering what the likelihood was of my being able simply to walk out of the Militia headquarters. I didn't move. It recalled to me my strange experience in the restaurant the previous day: staring at a door, thinking about walking through it, but not doing so.

Buzz buzz.

Soon enough, another officer came through, carrying a different cassette tape recorder. This man was older, and wore a more worldly-wise expression. 'Comrade Skvorecky,' he said, and if the spirit of a million cigarettes could have been gifted a voice it would have rumbled and creaked exactly as his voice did.

'Yes, comrade.'

'Officer Zembla has been called away on urgent police business.'

'I understand.'

'My name is Liski.'

'Officer Liski.' I nodded.

He settled the machine on the table, turned it on, and reached into his pocket for a packet of Primos. He offered me one, then took one himself. His lighter ticked to life, the flame like a painter's brush painted fire against the ends of each of the white tubes in turn. We both inhaled at the same time. 'Now,' he said. He expelled smoke the colour of a summer sky as he spoke. 'If you please, tell me about your last encounter with the deceased.'

'Comrade,' I said, feeling calmer for the cigarette, 'do not think me disrespectful, but may I ask: he *is* dead, then?'

'He is.'

'It all seems,' I confessed, 'somehow, unreal.'

'It is, nevertheless, very real and very serious. An American citizen, found dead on the streets of Moscow, and you the only person in the vicinity. You comprehend why you have been taken into custody?'

When put like this, my situation seemed graver than I had

previously realised. 'I am not responsible for Mr Coyne's death,' I said.

'Why don't you tell me how it happened?' said Liski, settling back in his chair. It was obvious that he was a dedicated smoker, both from the deep vertical creases that marked his face, and from the fact that those wrinkles visibly lessened as the tobacco relaxed his muscles.

'As I was explaining to the previous officer,' I said, 'I had met Mr Coyne for the first time that day. Then by chance I encountered him again at the Pushkin Chess Club. At the end of the evening he asked me to walk with him a little way, as he made his way back to his hotel. He said he had an important thing to tell me.'

'Why you?'

'Why me?'

'What I mean is: what was it about *you* that made him want to confide these things?'

'A good question, comrade. I can't really answer it.'

'And what were these things he had to tell you?'

'They concerned alien life.'

One heavy eyebrow defied gravity. 'UFOs?'

'Precisely. Perhaps that is why he wanted to talk to me. There had been some discussion in the Pushkin on this subject. I had been represented as being an expert.'

'You are an expert on UFOs?'

'No, I'm really not.'

'Then why were you so represented?'

'A long time ago,' I said, 'I used to write science fiction stories.'

'Like Zamiatin?'

'I met him once, actually,' I said. 'Although the stuff I wrote is feeble indeed compared to his genius.'

'What,' said Liski, 'did Mr Coyne want to say to you about UFOs?'

'He said they were a great danger to the world.'

'I see. Did he specify this danger?'

'It had something to do with nuclear power stations.'

'Any particular power station?'

'He mentioned one in the Ukraine. He said there was a prophecy concerning this station. In the Bible.'

Liski finished his cigarette. 'To be clear: he claimed that the Bible contains a prophecy that UFOs will attack Ukrainian nuclear facilities?'

'When you put it like that, comrade,' I said, 'it does sound a little . . . far-fetched.'

'You're sure he wasn't joking?'

'He seemed very earnest.'

'He *actually* believed in these UFOs?'

I thought about this. 'I believe he did.'

'And do you?'

'Believe in UFOs?' I said. 'No. I don't. Or—'

'Or?'

'I don't want to be evasive, comrade. Doesn't it depend on what you mean by UFOs? If you are asking me whether there are actual metallic saucers that have flown here from Sirius to snatch up a long-distance lorry driver outside Yakutsk and rummage around his lower intestine: no, I don't believe that. But there is a – phenomenon. That can't be denied. A cultural phenomenon. Many people believe in UFOs. So many that UFOs possess actual cultural significance. We might say that my individual unbelief in God doesn't wish away the Catholic Church.'

Liski looked enormously uninterested in the particularities of my unbelief. 'So what happened?'

'What happened?'

'After Coyne told you about the imminent UFO attack on Ukraine?'

'Then,' I said, trying to get the order of events straight in my head. 'Then.' But it had been so strange a sequence that sorting it out in my recollection was harder than you might think. 'What followed is very strange, comrade. I can't think you'll believe it.'

He was motionless in his chair. 'Try me.' His voice a purr.

'First there was a power cut. The streetlights on Zholtovskovo Street all went out.'

'Just on that street?'

'Yes. The lights were still lit on the Garden Ring; I could see the glow over the rooftops. And some of the windows in the buildings were still lit. So, yes, just the streetlights. And then – well then somebody turned a spotlight on us.'

'A spotlight?'

'Like in a theatre. Or a prison camp.' I stumbled over this latter phrase, with an unpleasant sensation in my spine that I shouldn't have made that particular comparison. It was dawning on me, I think, that my chances of being released from criminal captivity were very small. An American had been killed, and I was the only individual at the scene. 'It was,' I said, resolving to tell the police the truth, howsoever strange it might be, 'shining straight down upon us, from directly above. It must have been a very powerful bulb, because the light was blinding.'

'Could you see who was shining this light?'

'I couldn't see anything apart from the light.'

'Was it mounted on the roof? Was somebody leaning out of a window with it?'

'I don't know.'

'I see. And then.'

I paused. 'What happened next was that Coyne flew up in the air.'

This didn't seem to faze Officer Liski. 'Straight up, was it?'

'Actually, yes. He flew upwards, and tipped upside down. I knew he was upside down because he grabbed hold of my shoulder.'

'He was in mid-air, and he grabbed your shoulder?'

'Exactly; and his face was about on a level with mine. Except that his face was upside down.'

'Unusual.'

'Very. Might I have another cigarette?'

Carefully, with the reverence of a true believer, Liski retrieved two more white cylinders from the packet and lit them both. He passed one to me. 'Carry on.'

'It sounds incredible, I know, but somebody must have snagged Mr Coyne with a rope. A rope around his ankle, I think, and they were trying to haul him upwards. He grabbed my shoulder, and that interrupted his upward progress for a moment, but then they yanked harder and he disappeared up into the light.'

'You saw him?'

'I suppose my eyes,' I said, 'were becoming accustomed to the brightness. I looked up and saw him, weightless as it were.'

'As it were? Or actually?'

'He was actually dangling from a rope. But I could not see the rope from my perspective. He hung there for a moment, and then he fell back down. I assume it was the fall that killed him.'

'So whoever was holding him up let go of the rope?'

'I suppose so.'

'Do you think he let go by accident? Or was this a deliberate attempt to kill him?'

'I couldn't say, comrade. But he came down, and the rope came down with him.'

At this, Liski sat forward. 'You saw this rope? You examined it?'

'My primary concern,' I said, 'was attending to Mr Coyne, to see if he was hurt. But I suppose I did notice the rope, yes.'

'Can you describe it?'

'It was rope,' I said. 'It was a pale colour. It may, actually,' I added, trying to pull the memory out of my brain, 'have been a steel cable. It may have had a silver colour. Colour was hard to judge. It was warm and smooth to the touch.'

'You touched it?'

'Yes. It was warm and soft, but it didn't feel like rope. Perhaps a synthetic cable? I'm surprised you're so interested in the rope.'

'No rope was found at the scene,' he told me.

I thought about this. 'You're sure?'

'Indeed. There's no indication on the ankles of the deceased that he had been suspended from a rope in mid-air. No rope burn or marks on his legs. And no rope was found.'

'I would assume, therefore,' I said, 'that the rope must have been retrieved.'

'You said it fell down on top of Coyne?'

I thought about it. 'I think it did,' I said. 'I'm not sure.'

'Did you see somebody come out onto the street and retrieve the rope?'

'No.'

'Militia officers were at the scene very quickly. They found no rope.'

'I can't explain why you didn't find the rope.'

Liski looked at me. 'You checked Coyne's body yourself?'

'He was still alive,' I said. 'It was all so startling, so unexpected, that I half thought it was all an elaborate practical joke. He was still breathing, although I noticed very quickly that blood was seeping out from under his body.'

'His neck was broken in the fall,' said Liski. 'He landed on his left arm. His wristwatch was metal, and it cut through the flesh into his ribs. But it was the breaking of his neck that killed him.'

'I see.'

'Did he say anything?'

'He did. He— This is the strangest thing. He told me to respond.'

'To respond? To respond to what?'

'I didn't know. I assumed, in the moment, that he wanted a response to the acrobatic display he'd just put on. Applause, for instance. He told me I'd better respond, or else.'

'Or else what?'

'Just or else.'

'Was he,' Liski asked, 'speaking Russian, or was he speaking English?'

I cast my mind back, but on this subject it was a perfect blank. 'I don't remember. I'm sorry comrade, I honestly don't. The two of us had been speaking Russian, and then switching to English, and back to Russian. His last words might have been either.'

'Humph,' said Liski, dropping his cigarette to the floor and toeing it dead.

'It's a strange thing,' I said, 'but I just can't remember. I mean, I suppose, given the shock, that he'd be speaking English. Wouldn't he? Wouldn't the surprise and the shock jolt him into his mother tongue? But then again, he was very fluent in Russian. And we'd mostly been speaking Russian as we walked. Do you think it's important?'

'Is that all he said?'

I thought. 'He said four,' I added.

'Four what?'

'Just four.'

'The number four?'

'The number four.'

Liski stared unblinking at me. 'Four o'clock?'

'Maybe.'

'Four roubles? Four assailants? Four what?'

'Do you know what?' I said, abruptly. 'If he was speaking Russian then it would be four. If he was speaking English, however, it might be *for*. It could, in other words, have been a connective, as if he was going on to say something else, except that death intervened.'

'In sum,' said Liski, sitting back in his seat, 'the victim's last words were *Respond – or else! For* . . . and then he died.'

'It does sound odd,' I conceded.

'Perhaps he was saying: *Respond! Or else four* . . . as it might be, *Respond, or else four men will attack.*'

'Respond or else,' I repeated hesitantly.

'Respond – or else four space-aliens will visit you? Respond – or else four nations will be attacked with alien space-bombs?'

'I don't know,' I said. 'I'm not sure.'

'It would be helpful,' said Liski, 'if you could remember whether he was speaking Russian or English.'

'It would.'

'Come along,' he said, turning off the cassette machine and getting to his feet. 'Back to the cells with you. Enough for tonight.

We'll talk some more tomorrow. Maybe your memory will work better in daylight.'

'I can't imagine,' I said, getting to my feet with a rickety series of popping noises in my joints, 'that a lot of daylight penetrates down here.'

CHAPTER 9

I was taken back down to the same cell as before, but now it was no longer empty. Sitting on the bench, staring forlornly at the wall, was Ivan Saltykov, former nuclear physicist and now Muscovite taxi driver. 'You!' he called when I came in. 'You've been arrested?'

'Perhaps you think,' I said, nodding at the Militia officer who was escorting me, 'that I am here as a translator? To translate your gibberish into Russian?.'

'No jokes! None of what you think are jokes! I'm not in the mood.' Exactly on the word *mood* the cell door slammed heavily shut. 'I am very *un*happy,' Saltykov said, in his peevish, old woman voice. 'How could I be happy when I have been handled?'

'Handled?'

'Touched,' he said. 'Touched! I explained to the arresting officers that I did not like to be touched by,' he almost hissed the word, 'men, and furthermore that such touching was unnecessary, since I was content to come along with them and be no trouble. But they *handled* me anyway.'

'I can only commiserate,' I said.

'It is important to me to – now, now, please don't *interrogate* me on the whys, Skvorecky ...'

'I wouldn't dream of it,' I said, puzzled.

'It is *important* to me to lock, and unlock, and relock, and unlock and relock my car every time I leave it.'

I looked at him. 'Really?'

'I must lock it *three times*.'

'What self-respecting taxi-driver could do more?'

'I am under no obligation to explain myself to you,' he said. 'It is simply a matter of settling my mind. I lock, unlock, relock, unlock and relock my car and then I can walk away from it. My syndrome is such that . . .'

'Ah yes' I said. 'Your syndrome.'

'Anyhow. Anyway. I explained this to the arresting officers, but they would not permit it. Can you imagine such a thing? I could *lock my car*, they said, but *any further nonsense*, they said . . . can you imagine, they described it in those terms? . . . *Any further nonsense* they would confiscate the keys.'

'Such language,' I said, deadpan, 'amounts almost to assault.'

'It's the American, isn't it?' Saltykov said. 'They won't tell me what he's done. They've rounded me up simply because he is a friend of mine. I am a nuclear physicist! I was educated at the Institute of Novgodnokorsk! I received one of the best educations in nuclear physics in the world!'

'The American,' I said, 'was a friend of yours?'

But it was not easy to divert Saltykov when he was in spate. 'My syndrome is often associated with high intellectual capacity and a rigorous and logical mind. Such things are *assets* for intellectual pursuits!' To the extent that his dry, old-maid manner permitted it, he was working himself into a considerable lather. 'I do good work for the Soviet Union! Then the KGB say they *want a word*. I answer all their questions in a logical and intellectually rigorous manner! And the result is a year's internment!'

'You were interned? Where?'

'Where? Here in Moscow. But a year! I had done nothing wrong! And now, simply by virtue of my friendship with James Coyne, I am in prison again. And – *handled!*'

'I'm sorry to be the one to tell you this,' I said, 'but James Coyne is dead.'

'I end up having to drive a taxicab around Moscow for a living.

And my education in nuclear physics is world class! Dead, did you say?'

'I'm afraid so.'

'That makes me sad,' said Saltykov, in a voice that sounded, on the contrary, rather self-satisfied. 'It is a shame.' He looked at me. It struck me then that his was a face with a very limited range of expressions in its portfolio. A default blankness of feature gave him an oddly prissy, and indeed complacent appearance. He processed this news. 'How did he die?'

'There is some mystery associated with that,' I said. 'Which is to say, he died because he fell from a height, and broke his neck. But as to the how, and who, I am in the dark.'

'Oh dear,' said Saltykov, in a distracted voice. 'A great shame. You must not think,' he added, distractedly, 'that I am unconcerned about this news. My syndrome does not predispose me to many friendships, but the American was a dear friend for all that.'

'The way you refer to him by his nationality alone, rather than his name, suggests as much,' I said.

His brow puckered. 'You are suggesting – wait. I do not know what you are suggesting. Is that a joke? I am not good with jokes.' His brow cleared. 'I think I understand. You mean to imply that, were I a close friend, I would refer to him as Coyne, or perhaps James Coyne.'

'Or just James, perhaps.'

'My syndrome is such that I rarely understand jokes,' said Saltykov. 'Nor, I must say, do I see that a man's death is an occasion for joking.'

'We all deal with bereavement in our different ways, I suppose.'

'I can see that. So, poor James died under suspicious circumstances? It would not surprise me if it transpired he *had* been murdered. He had powerful enemies.'

'It does all feel very,' I said, rubbing my raspy hair with the palm of my hand, '*peculiar*. Not just that there is a conspiracy at work, but – I don't know. An *idiot* conspiracy. An insane conspiracy. A conspiracy by cretins. Perhaps I am becoming paranoid.'

'Things are not as they seem, eh?'

'You could say that.'

Then, from bickering like a child, Saltykov switched modes, in a manner I began to see was characteristic of him, into philosophy. 'Our first apperception is that things are not the way they seem. That is simply what it means to be human, it is our first experience of life, as children. Later we may finesse this into a grounding belief that *we are being lied to*. This in turn may develop into an entire metaphysics, which we call paranoia. Do you know what Theodor Adorno says?'

'I don't even know who he is.'

'Oh, he was a philosopher. A great Marxist philosopher, although not one in favour with the current administration. He says, "The whole is untrue." That's a lesson too difficult for most to learn. Nothing is so comforting as paranoia! Nothing is so *heartening* as *depression*. Imagine what it would be like if things *were* the way they seem! Intolerable!'

'It is something to ponder,' I said.

He was about to speak further when the door opened, singing the song of its hinges. Two guards came in and hauled Saltykov to his feet. I got to observe at first hand his reaction to being touched. His face instantly became radish coloured, and seemed even to swell a little; his eyes closed up and his voice came whistling through the slit of his mouth. 'Leave me alone! Don't touch! No touch! Do not touch me!'

'He's perfectly pliable,' I said, trying to intervene. 'He simply has a phobia about being handled by men. If you leave him alone, he'll come along very placidly.'

But the two policemen ignored me. Saltykov's reaction had pressed the button of their training, and they responded with a display of how to control an uncooperative prisoner. The red-faced spluttering fellow found his arms tucked behind him, like a skater on the ice, as handcuffs were fastened on his wrists. 'No!' he squeaked, 'No! Touch! Not! Men! No!'

The two men then hooked him under his armpits and lifted him from the floor, leaving his legs to wriggle in air. They swept him smoothly through the door and away. The door slammed.

I lay myself down and tried to sleep. Half an hour passed, but sleep kept slipping from my mind like soap evading slippery fingers in the bath. Then the door sang, and a trembling Saltykov returned. The reason for his trembling was rage, not fear. 'Handling me as if I were meat!' he said. 'Their fingers were right on my flesh.'

'Surely your clothing interposed?' I suggested.

He looked at me as if I were some sort of monster.

'I apologise,' I said.

'I must wash! I need to wash myself! Oh, but there are no facilities here. I *need* to wash!'

'What did they want to know?'

'I'll tell you what they *didn't* want to know, however many times I told them. They didn't want to know that I suffer from a syndrome recognised *internationally* by medical science. They *didn't* want to know, having handled me, that I need to wash myself in a shower all over my body with my left hand once, my right hand once, and my left hand again. That's what they didn't want to know. I ask you! If one of their prisoners suffered from diabetes, would they deny him insulin?'

'But what did they want to know about the *American*?'

Saltykov was not to be distracted, however, until his fribbling fury had worked its way through his system. He railed against his captors, and walked around and around the cell, always in a clockwise direction. Eventually his fury abated, and although he did not stop fidgeting awkwardly, he at least sat down.

'They wanted,' he said, a quarter-hour or so after I had asked the question − for this was also characteristic of him: you thought he had simply ignored what you had said, when in fact he stored it in a queue inside his brain and addressed it when he had worked through more pressing psychopathological matters, 'to know about my relationship with the American. They asked many questions about last night in the Pushkin. Was Coyne there, were *you* there, and so on.'

'And what did you tell them?'

'I told them the truth,' he said. 'Of course.'

'Of course. Comrade Saltykov, let me explain my position. I was walking with Coyne when he was killed. I met him for the first time in my life yesterday; I never met him before in my life. *You* knew him.'

Saltykov turned to look at me. 'But wait for a moment,' he said. 'Why should I trust you?'

'Trust me?' I repeated. 'But what do you mean?'

'You might be a plant. The authorities sometimes work that way. They put one of their own, in disguise, in the cell with the accused, and hope thereby to continue the interrogation by surreptitious means.'

'I am no plant!'

'But can you prove it?'

'For all I know,' I countered, '*you* might be the police agent working in disguise.'

He opened his eyes wide at this, as if the notion had not only never occurred to him but *could not* occur to any sane man. 'Do not be ridiculous,' he said. 'That is ridiculous. How ridiculous a notion!'

'No more ridiculous than accusing *me*.'

'On the contrary! *I* am a trained nuclear physicist!'

'You are a taxi driver,' I retorted. I confess I was growing angry.

'It is respectable work,' he countered.

'For most men, yes. But *you* are the taxi driver of doom.'

'Such abuse is merely unbecoming.'

'I boarded your taxi-car in the understanding you would take me home. *Had* you taken me home, I would presently be asleep in my own bed, with no other worries in the world. Instead you took me, against my will, to the Pushkin Chess Club, where I became entangled in the death of this American. I hold you responsible for the fact that my life has taken this dire turn!'

'Pff!' he said. He turned his face away.

'I shall probably go to prison for the rest of my life,' I said. 'And it will be your fault.'

After this little outburst we sat in silence for a long time. We were brought breakfast on a tray (black bread, thin-sliced cheese, milk in enamel mugs) by a young Militia officer, with little plugs of shaving cream tucked into his ears like hearing-aids and nicks on his red-raw chin and cheeks. He blinked at us, yawned oxishly, and went out again.

Saltykov began eating at once. The food seemed to thaw his ill-humour. 'Eat, comrade,' he said.

'I'm not very hungry,' I said, truthfully; for lack of sleep leaves me feeling rather nauseous. 'I believe I shall skip breakfast.'

'Ah,' said Saltykov, 'that is one thing you cannot do!'

'Can I not?'

'By definition, whichever meal you next eat will break your fast. Do you see? It is in the nature of the word.'

This did not dispose me to conversation with the fellow. I folded my arms and put my chin on my chest. For a while there was only the sound of Saltykov's munching and chewing.

'So,' he said, eventually. A full belly had put him in a much better humour. He tried for a smile, but managed only a sort of crookedness of the lower face. Then he winked. I was surprised at this. He was acting, indeed, for all the world like a child attempting to insinuate himself into the confidence of an adult. 'So. You were the *last person* to see the American alive?'

'A dispiriting thought.'

'And what did he say?'

'Say?'

'Come come, don't be coy. You can tell me.'

'I am not usually remarked upon for my coyness.'

'Then out with it!' He tried the weird face-stretching exercise once again, and once again failed to manage a smile.

'What did he *tell you*? He was very interested in,' and Saltykov, I am certain with perfect genuineness, glanced back over his shoulder, as if to check that there were any eavesdroppers nearby, 'a certain *project*, initiated by a certain *dictator*. A certain, now *deceased*, ruler of all the Russias. You know that of which I am talking.'

'I would answer your question if I understood it.'

'Walls have ears,' Saltykov said brightly. 'Or is it: walls *are* ears? I forget. The latter would imply that we are inside a gigantic ear. Either way it would be foolish of me to blurt out a name like Project Stalin, or to mention the impending alien attack upon Chernobyl.' He stopped. A troubled look passed over his face. 'I have,' he said, 'said more than I meant.'

'Remembering that you are a member of the Pushkin Chess Club, your credulity ought not to surprise me.'

'Credulity?'

'Concerning UFOs.'

'Psshh! Not so loud. Not *out* loud.'

'I shall be more circumspect, and adopt your cunningly impenetrable code.'

'But what did Coyne say?' he asked. 'Had he found out whether it is truly to be Ukraine? We only suspected. But is it? And *which* of the reactors?'

At this, belatedly, and with a piercing sense of my foolishness for not comprehending earlier, I finally understood what Coyne had been saying as he died. I opened my mouth, and then shut it for mere foolishness.

At that exact moment we were interrupted. Singsong, the door turned on its musical hinges.

'Comrade,' declared a voice, forcefully. It was Officer Liski. 'You are free to go. The people of the Soviet Union thank you for your assistance with the investigation of this crime.'

'Me?' I said.

'No, comrade. The other one.'

Saltykov bobbed to his feet, like an amateur debater. 'I object. I wish to make official complaint. I have been brutally handled by your men, despite suffering from a syndrome that makes such contact odious to me. I deeply resent such treatment.'

'Resent it all you like,' Liski said. 'But resent it *outside*.'

'Do-on't!' said Saltykov, his tone changing from brittle annoyance to wailing apprehension, as Liski advanced upon him, as if with the intention of grasping him by the arm and hauling him through the door. 'Do-o-on't to-o-ouch *me*! No *touching*! No hands *touching*!' He had backed his small body so hard against the cell wall it was as if he hoped to topographically transform himself from a three- to a two-dimensional being.

'Comrade,' I said to Liski, from my seated position. 'He dislikes being touched. He will go, with no need for coercion, if you simply tell him to.'

Liski stopped. 'Prove what this prisoner says,' he told Saltykov. 'Go.'

'Reactor Four, Saltykov,' I said, as clearly and distinctly as I could. 'That's the answer to your question.' But the look on the man's face made my spirit sink; for it seemed inconceivable that he would comprehend my words. Terror was seated in that face, and his mouth was as round as a drainpipe's end. 'No!' he said, flapping his hands in the air in the direction of the uniformed man.

'Reactor *Four*,' I said again. 'Saltykov!'

'Get him out,' said Liski to one of his officers.

'O-o-o-o-o,' replied Saltykov, cringing, and dancing round the uniformed man like a crab. 'O-o-o,' he added, as he darted through the open door. Doppler shift nudged the tone of his wail downwards a notch as he ran up the stairs outside.

Liski sighed, and returned to the door.

'And what of me, comrade?' I asked. 'When can I look forward to my release?'

'You?' he said. 'If we constellate the severity of the crime, the length of sentence likely to be passed upon you, and your advanced age, then the likelihood is – never.'

'With respect,' I put in. 'You must include my *innocence of the crime* in your constellation.'

'You are our prime suspect,' Liski said in a flat voice. 'To be honest, you are our only suspect. You have a criminal record. You were, we discover, in the camps for many years.'

'As a political!'

'Nevertheless. You were the last person to see the deceased alive.

You admit you were walking along the Zholtovskovo with him. Then one of two things happens: either he is snared by a rope and hauled upward, or else you and he quarrel and fight. The latter seems more likely, to us, than the former. Either way, the next thing, the American is lying on the ground with a broken neck.'

'Look at me!' I said. 'Note my physical decrepitude. Do you think I have the strength of arm to break a man's neck?'

'The crime is being investigated, comrade,' Liski said, pulling the door closed as he went out, 'and perhaps other leads will emerge; but as it stands – I'd advise you to cultivate patience.'

He slammed the door behind him. I lay back on the bench. There didn't seem to be much more to do.

I slept, I sat, I slept some more. Many hours passed, although in that windowless space I could not gauge exactly how many. Eventually I was removed from the cell by two militia officers and marched up the stairs into a room with windows, which at last gave me some sense of the time of day. It was now late afternoon. It had been raining in the day, and the wet rooftops were lacquered yellow by the low sun. Light came in shafts through the windows. I was led through to the captain's office. I was not offered a seat.

The captain, seated behind his desk, looked up at me with a fauvist face rather startling in the severity of its primary colours: choleric red skin, intensely blue eyes, and white smoothed-back hair.

'I have yet to be charged with a crime,' I said. 'I believe that under the law I must be officially charged, so as to know the crime of which I have been accused.'

'Konstantin Skvorecky,' said the captain, in a voice simultaneously deep and buzzing. 'We've had interventions from higher authorities. From high up in the government no less.'

Perhaps I was a little drunk with lack of sleep. 'You misunderstand the nature of government, comrade,' I said, in a tone of polite correction. 'It comes from the people, from the ground up. No altitude there.'

'Believe me, friend,' said the captain, signing a document. 'You have no cause for levity.' He coughed, but when he spoke again the wasp was still in his voice box. 'We are releasing you into the custody of the KGB.' He said this as he might have said *May God have mercy on your soul.*

'KGB?' I repeated, with some alarm.

'Indeed. You are still under arrest, of course. There, signed and completed.' This last, I understood, was addressed not to me, but to somebody standing behind me. 'He's yours now.'

'Thank you, captain,' said a familiar voice. It took me a moment to place it.

'We would appreciate,' continued the captain, 'if you could keep us informed of developments. The murder of an American, you know . . .'

'Oh, I'll undertake personally to keep you in the loop.'

I turned. The first person I saw was the vast frame of Trofim, tall as Andre the Giant. And standing beside him, zoo-keeper-like with his gorillan charge, Ivan Frenkel. 'Hello again, Konstantin,' said Frenkel. And then, with a slow distinctiveness, he smiled broadly.

CHAPTER 10

Frenkel and Trofim led me away. They did not even handcuff me. Like the Militia, they clearly thought there was no point in restraining so elderly and broken-down a figure. 'You told me you were a lowly employee of an obscure ministry,' I remonstrated with Frenkel mildly.

'Did I? I don't remember that.'

'You certainly didn't tell me you were KGB.'

'You are upset that I kept my membership of the KGB secret from you,' he observed. 'Perhaps you are unaware of the fact that the KGB is a secret organisation?'

Trofim's huge hand was on my shoulder as we stepped through the main entrance and onto the street. The afternoon was in the process of burning coldly into the deeper blue of evening. The streetlamps had been lit. The sky over the roofs was a garish lamination of yellow, salmon, lime and – higher up – dark-blue and black. Light shimmied and shifted on the wet pavement, like an untrustworthy thing. There were puddles in the gutter in which vodka, or petroleum, mixed oily rainbows. A large black auto was parked at the side of the road, and into this I was shuffled, Trofim's enormous hand on the top of my head to make me duck.

The driver, sitting up front, was a gentleman I had not previously met: a skinny fellow with red hair trimmed close over the back of his head, and a hard-edged, freckled face. The cut of his hair swirled like rusty iron filings on a magnet. This is the fellow who, in a matter of some few months, would shoot a bullet from his standard-issue Makarov automatic pistol right through my heart. I don't mean to confuse you: but it seems fair to give you, the reader of this memoir, a glimpse of my future; and the glimpse is of a bullet bursting from the end of his pistol and going directly through the heart in the middle of my chest – out the other side, too.

We'll come to that in due course. I suppose I am saying, at this point in the narrative, keep an eye on this red-headed man.

Trofim got in the front passenger seat; which is to say, he somehow folded himself small enough to squeeze into the front passenger seat. Frenkel sat himself down next to me. 'Off we go, lads,' he said.

The car growled as a dog growls when somebody menaces its bone. It pulled smoothly away, and into traffic.

Frenkel sat in contemplative silence for a while before addressing me. 'It was one day in the 1950s,' he said in a serious voice. 'I had occasion, on account of my work, to look at an atlas. It struck me then – there was Russia. I put my hand,' and he held his broad hand up in front of me, 'over Siberia and the east. Let's not concern ourselves with them, I thought. Russia, Georgia, Ukraine, that's enough. And here was Germany, East and West, so small. The Mammoth and the Polecat. Goliath and David. Excepting only that Goliath was us, and Goliath won. Germany, such a small place, so underpopulated – compared, I mean, with us. Then I thought: We were so joyful about winning the war! We thought *we* were David and *they* were Goliath. But it was the other way about ! We were much bigger than them. Defeating them was as inevitable as Josef Vissarionovich constantly claimed in his wartime speeches.' He shrugged. 'It was a shock, you know? Realising that.'

'Tell me, Jan,' I said. '*Were* you abducted by space-aliens? Did that really happen to you?'

'You're not listening to me, Konstantin Andreiovich,' Frenkel replied, sternly. 'My revelation? It was the Force of Necessity. There's nothing else in the cosmos. You know science fiction.'

'Not for many years. I haven't kept up.'

'You know one of the main varieties of American science fiction? The alternative history. And you know the most popular form of alternative history?'

'I've no idea.'

'They call it Hitler Wins. It's that mode in which the Nazis are victorious in the war. Dozens of novels about what the world *would* have been like. Imagine!'

'I imagine things would have been rather unpleasant.'

'Here's my point: Soviet science fiction writers never write that sort of story. Alternative history has no pedigree in Soviet science fiction. Do you know why? Because we understand necessity. Russia could not have lost to Hitler. Postulating what things would have been like had he won is meaningless to us.'

'The moral of this story?' I prompted, feeling light headed. I had not, you see, eaten during my Militia captivity.

'The moral is Necessity. You'd do well to accept it. Necessity.'

The car pulled from the slip road to accelerate smoothly along the main ring. Other cars, I could see, were pulling over to permit us to pass. A car so large, so modern, so unrusted, could only be KGB.

'You and I,' he said to me. 'We're old men.'

'I can hardly deny it.'

'The Soviet Union is *our* place. This is where we belong. It is the *country* for old men. Communism is the *system* of old men. All those antique statesmen standing on their balcony watching the May Day Parade. Old, old men. Men like Chernenko. You knew where you were with Chernenko.'

'In Gaga-grad,' I said.

'Oh he wasn't as senile as people now say. You see, I *knew* him.' He considered this statement. I realised then that, although Frenkel might put great energies into lying and deception, he was nevertheless oddly punctilious about the truth of all matters pertaining to the dignity of the Communist Party. I say *although* and *nevertheless*. Perhaps I should say *because* and *therefore*. 'Well,' Frenkel added, 'it wouldn't be quite accurate to say I *knew* him. I worked with him, or worked *under* him. I sat in meetings that he chaired, for instance.'

'I'm impressed by how elevated your position truly is.'

This clearly annoyed him. Perhaps he thought I was rebuking him for boasting. 'I'm only saying that Chernenko was not senile. I'm only saying that I should know.'

'Comrade, I'm not criticising,' I said. 'For the whole of the 1970s I had no better employment for my brain than as a filter for several hundred gallons of vodka, like an old sock used for straining moonshine. I believe I have only two memories from that entire decade. I'd never claim the right to criticise others for senility.'

Ivan stared at me. 'Comrade,' he said, coolly. 'I shall be frank with you.'

'Franker than you usually are?'

This was the wrong thing to say.

'You fucker,' he snarled, suddenly furious. 'One thing I hate in this world and you are fucking *it*. You are an ironist.'

'An ironist?'

'Fundamentally, you take nothing seriously. You believe it is all a game. It was the same in your novels; they were never serious. They had no heart. That wasn't *my* way. For me, as for Asterinov, literature was a high calling. A serious business. One story, not the ludicrous branchings of possibilities and ironic alternatives. But *you*, you don't really take anything seriously, do you, comrade?'

I thought about this. I can be honest, now, and say that I had not previously considered the matter in this light. 'There may be something in what you say, comrade,' I conceded.

'Understand,' Frenkel added, his fury draining away a little. 'I do not exactly denounce you for this. Some human beings are ironists. Others take the business of the world very seriously. The worst that could be said,' he went on, his voice acquiring a slightly portentous edge, 'is that *revolution* is not achieved by ironists.' I thought of all those pictures of Lenin; those myriad images of him smiling at his own private joke, squinnying up his eyes in amusement at the absurdity of things. But I held my peace. Frenkel was still pontificating. 'Revolution is a *serious* business. Changing the world for the better is a serious undertaking.'

'No doubt.'

'Chernenko was old, it is true. His mind was perhaps ... less *flexible* than comrade Gorbachev's is proving to be. But – and I do not speak out of disloyalty—'

'The idea!'

'It is *not* disloyalty to Gorbachev to say this,' Frenkel snapped, over-insistent, 'but General Secretary Gorbachev wants to institute *change*. He wants to change the way the Soviet Union is run. Perestroika and so on. But Chernenko – you see, *he* was born before the Revolution. That meant he understood change in a profound way; understood in a way somebody like Comrade Gorbachev never can. Chernenko lived through that time when change was the idiom *of the whole world*. Gorbachev can never understand change in the same way, because he was born after 1917.'

'So was I,' I pointed out.

Frenkel rubbed his bald head. 'You miss my point. You do so on purpose.'

'In itself, perhaps, a definition of irony.'

'Communism,' said Frenkel, as if explaining to a stubborn and unlikable child. 'Communism is *government by old men*. Capitalism is different. Under capitalism things are run by the young, the thrusting, the violent. You know how it is in New York.'

'To be honest I don't really know how it is in Moscow,' I said. 'And I live here.'

'Don't be obtuse. You know what happens on Wall Street. It's gangsters in suits. It's teenagers high on their own piss and testosterone. They're the ones who make all the money, and who have all the power. Capitalism is the jungle. In the jungle the top gorilla never gets to grow old, because there's always some young psychopath ready to brain him with the,' and he stumbled a little. I noticed that two frogspawny spots of spittle had accumulated in the corner of Frenkel's mouth. He was getting worked up. 'The jawbone of an ass,' he concluded, unexpectedly.

'*Ass*, comrade?'

The tone in which I said this increased Frenkel's fury. He reached across and put his thumb against my chest, digging it into my sternum. It made me think of army basic training – it gave me, indeed, one of those vertiginous feelings of a deep memory surfacing abruptly and unexpectedly – when we had been taught how to stab a human being with bayonet or knife: to press the thumb in amongst the corrugations of the ribcage, to find the ossified knot at its base and then slide the blade underneath.

Though as old as me, Frenkel was considerably more muscular, and in much better health.

Trofim stirred in the front seat, readying himself to intervene if it proved necessary. He was not, of course, preparing to intervene on *my* behalf.

'Comrade,' I said, mildly.

'You're *still* not listening to me Konstantin Andreiovich,' he said. 'You're not listening to me because you're too busy trying to fuck with me. Don't think I don't understand what you're about. You're trying to commit suicide. The traditional Russian method, the vodka, takes too long. Setting fire to your own cranium was too shocking a method to proceed with. Am I right? Am I right?' He took his thumb away, and I relaxed the muscles across my back. 'Fucking idiot. You, Konstantin Andreiovich, I'm talking about *you*. Do you understand?'

'You have a very eloquent thumb,' I said. My ribs were sore.

'That's what I mean by an ironist. You can't take the direct route. The direct route would be a rope around the neck and jump off the table, but you won't do *that*. You exist in a haze of possible paths through life. That's not the way!'

'Or a leap from a bridge,' I said.

'Because you're incapable, you want *me* to do your dirty work. The question is: *Why?*'

'Or in front of a train.'

'The question in other words is: Why *me?*' Frenkel leered. 'We go back a long way, I suppose. You and I stood in line and met comrade Stalin *in the flesh*. How many people can boast that?'

'Since boasting requires breath,' I said, pretending to calculate an answer, 'and since meeting Stalin usually preceded the confiscation of that very quality ...'

'Fuck you, Konsty. *I'm* not your enemy. Don't make *me* out to be your enemy. You could help me, if you chose to. You could perform a life-saving service for the Soviet Union, if you'd only work with me and stop fighting me.'

I looked at him. I felt enormously weary. 'I've decided,' I said.

'Yes?'

'Jumping off a bridge in front of a river cruiser with a rope around my neck,' I said. 'To make assurance doubly sure.'

'Fucker,' said Frenkel.

'Shakespeare,' I corrected.

Suddenly, and unexpectedly, Frenkel began laughing. 'Do you know what, Konstantin? Do you know what?'

'*What* is only one of a great many things I do not know.'

'I'm not used to this. I'm a senior figure, comrade. I'm KGB, you understand? When I talk to people they're almost always polite and deferential.'

'*Almost* always?'

He waved this away. 'Oh, sometimes I speak to my superiors. They're usually curt. But this ... bantering! It makes a change, I can tell you.'

'I don't think you're right,' I said.

'What?'

'About Communism being government by old men. Revolution is a newness coming into the world. Revolution is a continual youth, the resurgence and eternal youth of mankind.'

'Comrade,' he said, and again his hand came up, only this time it was to my shoulder. '*You're* an old man.'

'So are you.'

'Exactly! Who knows better how to run a country? The young

have crazy ideas. They have absurd, destructive energy. But the *old* have – wisdom. Which quality is better for governance? Don't answer, I'm being rhetorical. Besides, you misunderstand the logic of Revolution. Revolution is the manifestation of historical necessity. It is the coming-into-the-world of inevitable historical consequences. History is old. History is an old man. What's older than history?'

'Death,' I said.

But Frenkel wasn't in a mood to be metaphysical. 'History is the oldest man there is. That's what Communism says. That's what Marx says, if you boil him down. He says: You can't escape history. You can't *avoid* him, or trick him, or *bribe* him. He rules. That's all. The capitalists think they've overthrown history, they think history has come to an end and there *is no* history. They think there's only money. But they're fooling themselves. History can't be escaped. History doesn't care for youth, or money, or fancy clothes. History is the tyrant that makes rulers like Stalin look weak and benign.'

'Speaking personally,' I said, 'my interpretation of Marx sees him as being more dialectical and less monolithic.'

At this Frenkel laughed loudest of all. 'Your personal interpretation of Marx!' he repeated, and I was unsure whether he was amused by the fact that anybody actually read Marx, or by the notion that it was possible to have a personal perspective on a figure so marmoreal.

The car pulled up by the side of the road. Frenkel shifted in his seat the better to look straight at me. 'Tell me what he said,' he said.

'Who?'

'I will ask you the question once,' said Frenkel. 'I shall even ask it twice. But thrice I will not ask.'

'"Thrice"?' I repeated, unable to keep the incredulous tone from my voice.

'Quiet! You hear? Be quiet! I want to hear you *answer* the question, not banter with me.'

'I understand, comrade. Nevertheless, as one writer to another, I must query thrice.'

'Trofim – put a gun in his ear.'

The huge fellow swivelled, a little awkwardly, in his seat at the front of the car, and glowered at me. He did not look comfortable. 'I'm not sure I can manage the ear, sir,' he said in a slow voice.

'What?'

'Unless Comrade Skvorecky turns his head? Otherwise the angle is not correct. Perhaps the eye?'

'The eye then! I don't care! *Menace him*, you idiot!'

With an impressively fluid gesture for so large a man Trofim unholstered his pistol and reached round the back of the seat in which he was sitting. His left hand grasped my neck and held it in place; and with his right hand he pressed the end of the muzzle against my left eye. Naturally I tried to flinch backwards, but Trofim held me firm, with an insulting ease. His reach was long enough for this to be no effort for him. He possessed arms a gorilla might have envied for length, muscularity and, I daresay, hairiness. My head was pressed against the upholstery of my seat, and the gun was digging against my eye. This was very far from comfortable. I put my hands up, on reflex, and wrapped my fingers about Trofim's left wrist, where his hand had fixed my neck, but it availed me nothing. He was much too strong for me.

'Now that we have your *attention*,' said Frenkel. 'You fucking ironist. You went for a walk with Coyne. The American. You are now going to tell me *exactly what he said to you*.'

'Gladly, comrade,' I said, in a slightly strangulated voice. 'I have just given the Militia a complete transcript, and am happy to do the same for the KGB.'

'Fuck you, Konsty,' said Ivan. 'What did you tell the police? I'll have Trofim scoop your skull out and feed your brains to your wife.'

'My ex-wife,' I said. 'She might be less distressed by the scooping than you imagine.'

'Quiet! Fucking *be* quiet!'

The pain in my eye was sharp, like a migraine. 'I'll be quiet.'

'What did you tell the police?' Frenkel was yelling at me. 'You fucker, what did you *tell* them?'

'I told them what happened,' I gasped. 'I was walking with Coyne. That's what I told them. He seemed to think I was privy to a plan, although I assured him I wasn't. That gun is hurting my eyeball.'

'Where? Did he tell you *where?*'

'He said aliens were going to attack a nuclear reactor,' I said. 'I'm starting to worry I'll lose the sight in that eyeball.'

'Yes, yes, yes, but did he tell you *where?*'

'Lithuania,' I improvised. 'He said it was connected to the ghost rockets after the war. I think he believed it, too.'

Frenkel, I was relieved to see, accepted this. 'Better!' He sank back into his seat. 'I like you when you're cooperative, Konstantin Andreiovich. You can do one more thing for me, to prove that you are in a properly cooperative mood. Or perhaps I should let Trofim squeeze the eyeball right *out* with his gun.'

'That wouldn't be my preference.'

'Tell me where the woman is. The American woman.'

Suddenly the gun was taken out of my eyeball, a very relieving sensation, although it left my vision scattered and lanced across with weird neon cobwebs and blobs of light. I rubbed at the eye with the heel of my hand, which didn't help particularly but seemed the thing to do. Trofim had reholstered his weapon.

'Where is she?' Frenkel asked me again, sitting forward to be able to turn his head and look properly at me.

'I don't know.'

'Don't *know?*' This answer infuriated him. He flung himself back against the seat and bounced forward. The car rocked on its suspension. 'Give me the pistol! Give it to me, Trofim.'

The weapon was handed back.

'Open your mouth, you fucking idiot,' he ordered.

I opened my mouth. So, I noticed, did Trofim, although he snapped it shut soon enough when he realised that his superior had not been addressing him.

The barrel went between my teeth. I tasted the distinctive, slightly marine flavour of gunmetal.

'No more nonsense,' Frenkel declared, in a tone of businesslike savagery. 'You know where the fat woman is hiding. You are going to tell me. If you tell me, and if you are not lying to me, I shall lock you away. If you *don't* tell me, or if you *lie* to me, I shall pull this trigger, here, now, in this car.' He yanked his hand up, hinging the pistol downwards against my lower teeth. 'And here's a KGB trick: I'll shoot you *down* your throat. That way I don't get your fucking brains all over the interior of my car. It will have the added bonus of causing you to die slowly and in great pain from internal bleeding. Do. You. Understand?'

'Gghhah,' I affirmed.

'It is possible,' he went on, 'when one has a prisoner in this position, to shoot so that the bullet goes right through the gut and exits through the anus. But it is much more painful, and less messy, if I angle the trajectory slightly so that the bullet goes into the inside of your thigh. *Where is she?*'

'Ghaah ghg ga-gahh, ghhah geh-h-ho gughu,' I said.

There was a silence. In a low, controlled voice, like a bomb disposal expert about to remove a vital component from an infernal device, Frenkel said, 'I'm going to slide this gun out of your carious mouth, Konsty. When it is out you can repeat what you just said. If it is a wisecrack, or if you say that you don't know, then these will be the last seconds of your mortal life.'

He pulled the gun barrel out of my mouth. I wriggled my tongue against the inside of my mouth. 'Thank you, Jan,' I said.

'Where,' he asked, in a low voice, 'is she?'

'I don't have the address, just a telephone number,' I said.

Frenkel pondered this. 'Write it down,' he told me. He pulled out a small piece of card and a pencil stub from his pocket. I scribbled my ex-wife's telephone number on the card and handed it back. My jaw ached. My eye was still spooling out luminous patterns into my brain. I couldn't see properly.

Frenkel took the card, and pencil, back from me. 'Then this is what we are going to do,' he said, calmly. 'Nik' – this to the driver – 'take us to the Heights.'

The car scraped to life, and we pulled away from the kerb. Nik, the one with the cropped red hair, did not signal, or even look where he was going. One car was forced to swerve, and several others to brake, but nobody sounded their horns, or shook their fists. Ordinary Muscovites had no desire to tangle with official business.

'Trofim, you are to take him to the safe room,' ordered Frenkel.

'At the top of the building?'

'Of course at the top of the building, you ox!' The car slowed, turned a corner, and then accelerated. 'Take him up there, make him phone the fat woman. *You*,' he said to me, 'will tell her to go to – I don't know, somewhere a tourist would know.'

'Red Square?' I suggested.

'Yes. Tell her you'll meet her in Red Square. She'll be able to find that. Tell her to wait outside the GUM. Tell her to go *straight there*: to get a taxi, and go straight to the GUM side of the square. Tell her that you *must meet her*, absolutely and straight away. Are you listening to this, ox?'

'Sir,' said Trofim.

'Make *sure* he says all that. If he says anything else, or tries any nonsense, kill him.'

'Sir.'

'And if you do have to kill him, remember to put him in the chute.'

'Sir.'

'The chute, you hear? Don't just leave him lying there. Yes?'

Trofim had coloured. 'Sir.'

'In fact, the best thing would be to take him to the chute, put his head in and shoot him there. Please, I'm asking you as one civilised man to another, *please* try not to get too much mess on the furnishings. Yes?'

Trofim nodded. Nik, the driver, was chuckling quietly.

'Don't break anything, no?'

'No, comrade.'

'And no blood on the carpet this time?'

'No, comrade.'

'I must say I hope there will be no need for the chute,' I said, in a worried voice.

'Do as I tell you and there may not be,' said Frenkel, complacently. 'Konsty, you can still be of use to me. You can be of use by delivering us this woman, obviously, but perhaps beyond that as well. You may still have a use, and usefulness is your best bet at extending your lifespan. There may be a future for you after all.'

'As a science fiction writer,' I said, 'I have a particular interest in the future.'

CHAPTER 11

The car pulled up outside a tall block, in a uniform and fairly clean street of tall houses. Trofim clambered and lumbered out of the car, unpacking himself, as it were, from the front seat. He opened the door for me.

'Trofim will look after you,' said Frenkel.

'An ambiguous phrase,' I noted.

Frenkel laughed. 'Upstairs with him, Trof. Take him to the room. The first thing he does is make the call. After that, settle him in. If he differs by so much as a thread from what we agreed – settle his final account.'

'His account, sir?'

'Kill him, you idiot.'

'Comrade,' said Trofim, meaning *yes*, and snapping to attention on the pavement. I realised this about Trofim: that, when in his military mode, he used that word as a universal signifier. The other thing I realised about Trofim, as he ushered me through the main entrance to the building, was that he really was enormous. He would have stood six foot six in his stockinged feet, excepting only that it was impossible to imagine him ever removing his boots, or going off duty. He appeared to have borrowed, or more likely to have been issued by the authorities with, the musculature of a much larger animal than a human: a bear, say. Or a Grendel. His neck was thicker than his head. Indeed, his neck was thicker than my waist.

We were at the foot of the stairs. 'Is there no lift?' I asked.

He shook his head. 'Yes,' he added, as an afterthought.

'Yes there is a lift? Why do we not avail ourselves of the lift?'

He stared at me as if I had posed a metaphysical conundrum.

'It's not working?' I prompted, after long seconds. 'Is that it?'

'Comrade,' he said to me, tipping his chin to the stairway.

I peered up the stairwell. 'How many flights?'

'Seventh floor.'

I sighed. 'I'll warn you now, comrade, I am not as fit as once I was.' He greeted this news with his default, meaty impassivity. His general bearing was somewhere between *I don't care* and *I don't understand.*

'Off we go, then,' I said, gloomily.

We ascended one flight of stairs, half a floor, before my lungs began complaining. Another flight and I was gasping like a cracked steamvalve. Comrade Trofim walked moodily on and I followed, but by the time we reached the second-floor stairwell landing my breath was positively hooting. 'I need to rest, comrade,' I gasped.

He loomed over me. 'Your lungs, is it?'

'An expert diagnosis, comrade' I said, between breaths. 'Old model, you see. Early revolutionary design. Single cylinder, two-stroke lungs. They're noisier than the newer models.' I saw his huge face touched, distantly, with puzzlement. 'I just need to catch my breath,' I said. 'An old man's lungs are not as efficient as a young man's.'

'Comrade,' he said; meaning, *ah!*

I dragged two breaths in. A third. Trofim was breathing silently, and without apparent motion of his chest.

'So,' I tried, to fill the silence. 'You were in the army?'

'Comrade,' he said in the affirmative.

'Afghanistan, is it? Why aren't you there now?'

'I needed medical attention,' he said, with a slow, offhand deliberateness that implied multiple bullet wounds.

'Really? What for?'

He pondered this, and then said, 'Because I was wounded.'

'Obviously,' I said. 'But how?'

'A tooth,' he said, and a dark look passed over his face.

'Nasty,' I said. 'Impacted, was it? In the jaw?'

'Skull,' he said.

'I've often thought they're more trouble than they're worth, molars.'

'Oh no,' he said, looking at me as if I were some kind of a simpleton. 'It wasn't *my* tooth.'

'Your skull, though?'

'Oh yes.'

I thought about this. 'Were you *bitten* by one of the mujahadeen, comrade?'

'Oh no,' he said, clearly surprised at my obtuseness. He pondered for a bit, and then said, 'The landmine disassembled him pretty thoroughly, comrade.' He pondered further. 'He wasn't in any state to bite anybody after that,' he said.

I gave this some thought. 'This individual was blown up, and you were blown up with him?'

'No,' said Trofim, looking even more puzzled. 'I was nowhere near that mine.'

'I am stumped.'

'One of his teeth,' said Trofim. Then he added, 'Flew. The doctors said that. Like a bullet.'

'I see,' I said. 'Shall we go on up?'

I made two more flights without much difficulty, and another two with a quantity of rasping and wheezing; and we stopped again. It became evident that Comrade Trofim had been pondering matters during this, for me, tortuous climb. 'How did you know I was in the army?' he asked.

'You have a military bearing,' I panted.

This pleased him. 'Comrade,' he said, standing a little straighter.

I blinked and blinked, but my left eye, where the gun had been forced, was still filled with luminous chaff. I could not see properly out of it. 'I suppose I would assume,' I added, 'that, perhaps, you were flown back for hospitalisation in Moscow, and that your exemplary war record and, uh, personal attributes brought you to the attention of Comrade Frenkel, who seconded you to his personal team.'

If Trofim had been amazed at my stupidity earlier, he was now, clearly, amazed at my insight. 'Comrade!' he said, by way of articulating his astonishment. Then after further thought, he added, 'Did Comrade Frenkel tell you so?'

'The Comrade Commissar and I don't have that sort of relationship,' I said.

Puzzlement descended again. 'Commissar?'

'My little joke,' I said. 'Shall we press on?'

We made two more floors before I stopped again. 'Only one more to go,' I said, sucking air.

'Your lungs are bad, comrade,' he said.

'You think?'

'Oh yes, comrade,' he said, earnestly. He peered vaguely through the landing's grubby window; a view of housetops, flanked on either side by the elephant-leg grey of two tower blocks. 'Asthma is a disease of the lungs.'

'I had not realised that a medical education is part of basic army training.'

'But you're mistaken, comrade,' he said. 'It is not.'

'Asthma is a disease of the lungs,' I said. 'Emphysema also. But in my case I think it is merely that I am a man in my mid-sixties who has spent over half a century smoking Soviet cigarettes.'

'Soviet cigarettes are the finest in the world,' said Trofim, on a reflex. The phrase *Soviet x is the finest in the world* had evidently been etched into his brain for, I would hazard, any value of x. Indeed, I daresay he believed that Soviet alphabets contained the finest xs in the world.

'You're not a smoker,' I observed.

'Oh no,' he agreed.

'Wise,' I said. 'Soviet lungs are the finest in the world, brought up breathing the pure air of the Motherland. We have a duty not to pollute them.' But speaking ironically to Trofim was precisely as effective, in terms of communication, as speaking Mongolian would have been. 'It must be a little demeaning,' I offered, 'for a warrior such as yourself to be given the mission of escorting an old fart like me up some stairs.'

He considered this for a very long time. Eventually he said, 'You remind me of my grandfather.'

'He was an ironist too?'

'Oh no,' he said. 'He was from Tvov.'

'I daresay,' I said, rousing myself for the final set of stairs, 'that comrade Frenkel has told you *why* this American woman must be located and killed?'

'Comrade,' he said, his best effort at stonewalling.

Finally, with a sense of achievement that Sir Edmund Hillary, that New Zealander, would have recognised, I reached the top of the staircase. Trofim brought out a key and opened the door, and I stepped in. It was a perfectly ordinary suite of rooms, left over from the Romanoff era, although in a recognisable state of dilapidation: two settees on wooden claws, clutching golfballs of wood with arthritic intensity. Two wooden chairs. An empty bookcase. A stained rug. Near the curtainless window was a table on which the telephone sat: a skull-sized chunk of bakelite. Two doors, both of them closed, led through to other rooms. There was a musty smell. There are, in point of fact, very many different varieties of musty smell. Some, as in old bookshops, are even actively pleasant. The smell in this room was not pleasant.

Trofim nodded at the table and, as I made my way, breathless, over towards it he locked the door behind him and pocketed the key.

'Make the call, as Comrade Frenkel instructed,' he said, balancing his thumb on the stock of his holstered pistol.

'I'll just,' I panted, 'get my breath back.' To show willing I picked up the telephone receiver.

Trofim came towards me, trying to look stern rather than just stupid. 'No funny business,' he reminded me. 'Precisely as Comrade Frenkel instructed.'

I took a breath. 'As he instructed.' I took another breath.

'Are you ready?'

'In the army,' I asked him, 'they trained you to kill?'

'In,' he said, lowering over me, 'dozens of different ways.'

'To kill the enemy. Also to disable him?'

'In dozens of different ways,' he repeated.

'I daresay,' I said, 'that these are skills you don't forget just because you've left the army?'

By way of reply, he flexed his meaty right hand into a fist, and then unflexed it.

I held the telephone receiver in my right hand, and my left was upon the dial. In as smooth and forceful as motion as I could manage, I heaved with both hands. The trick, I knew, was to mean the gesture completely. The trick was not to think *I'm old, I won't have the strength;* but to think rather *I'm still twenty.* To think *I'll brain the fucker.* To put myself into it completely.

The receiver went hard into Trofim's left eye; the body of the phone cracked against his right cheekbone. He took a step back, more in surprise than pain I'd say. The electrical cord had come cleanly away from the wall. I threw the entire set at his face. He was alert enough to bring up his arm to shield himself from this projectile, but I had already grabbed the chair, a hand on each side of the seat. With the high back facing away from me I angled the whole thing forward, and jammed it upwards with as much force as I could gather. The top of the chairback went in under Trofim's chin, making contact with his throat and cracking his head up. It made a sound like a butcher's cleaver going into a rack of lamb. Unbalanced, the big man tumbled. He banged the back of his head hard enough against the wall to leave a dent in the plaster. Then, like sprawling Goliath, he was on the floor on his back, and his enormous boots were jerking up and down. I leapt forward, the chair still in my hands. I came down hard upon his torso, the chairback resounding as it impacted. The breath went entirely out of him. The chair was on top of him, and I was on top of the chair; and my hip had knocked painfully against the edge of the seat.

For a second time I wedged the top of the chairback under his chin.

'You were in the army,' I said, gaspily.

His face was darkening, turning if not quite blue then certainly losing its usual fleshtone. He gurgled something.

'I was in the army too, comrade,' I said.

'You have hurt my windpipe,' he scraped. His right arm was clutching ineffectually at the chairback. His left arm was trapped beneath his enormous body.

'My military service was a while ago,' I panted. 'But it was a longer tour of duty, and incomparably more toughening than a couple of months in fucking *Afghanistan*.'

'Comrade, I think,' he gasped, 'you've broken my rib.'

I was, in truth, in a rather delicate situation. He was a strong young man, and I a weak elderly one; and, broken rib or not, I worried that my getting off him would be quickly followed by him getting to his feet and repaying in kind. On the plus side, simply squatting on him like the figure of nightmare from that old illustration, leaning all my weight onto the chair, enabled me to recover some of my puff. Although this was not something that could happen quickly.

He face was a colour that would have indicated rude health in a cheeseplant.

'Like my – sweet old,' he wheezed, incredulous, 'grandfather.'

'Like many young people,' I observed, breathing in and out as leisurely as I could manage. 'You have a mistaken notion about the elderly. You project sentimental notions onto my generation. Appearances aren't everything, you know.' I was chattering like this because I was trying to think what to do. 'And, especially with respect to my generation, you ought to consider that we have drunk more vodka, had more sex and killed more people than you – ever –

will. But tell me one thing, Trofim. Tell me this one thing. Do you *believe* all this stuff about aliens?'

'Of course,' he rasped, weakly. 'Yes.'

'Really?'

'Mngnaow,' he creaked.

'I think I might have wet myself a little, in all the excitement.' I tried to peer down at my trousers, without taking any of my weight off the chair.

'Mngnaow,' he repeated, in a weaker voice.

His face now was purple as a plum, and his eyes bulged like sloes.

I glanced about the room with an eye to locating something with which to immobilise Trofim: I pondered tying him up, but there was nothing but the telephone cord, and such cord has too little friction to tie well. I considered removing his pistol from its holster and using that to control him, but I was not at all sure that I could unbuckle the holster and remove the gun without taking my weight from the chair. My fear was that, given the chance, Trofim would simply toss me aside. Then it would be the chute for me.

I decided to try reasoning with him. 'Comrade,' I said, 'I will remove my weight from your throat in a moment.'

He did not reply. There was not so much as a gasp. His face was now a rather fetching deep dark mauve. His eyes had a lifeless cast to them. I could not feel motion in his chest. I weighed up in myself whether he might be shamming, but my options were limited.

I climbed off him, and waited to see if he burst into life. But there was nothing. Perhaps I *had* murdered him. This was not a comfortable thought, for all that I did not doubt his willingness to ram me in the chute.

I put my skinny, mottled hand into his right trouser pocket, and found the keys. Then, with a mighty creaking inside my own complaining bones, I got to my feet and went over to the door. I was holding a dozen keys on a metal ring. The first I tried did not fit the lock. The second fitted the hole, but refused to turn. My left eye, where the muzzle of the gun had compressed the eyeball, could not focus, and was still buzzy with shiny hallucinogenic flashes and skeins. I held the fourth key close in front of my right eye, and inserted it into the keyhole.

Behind me Trofim drew a huge, beast-like, shuddering breath into his lungs.

'Infamy!' he croaked, and then, with a huge phlegm-heavy cough, he spoke the word again, much more distinctly and with rather startling volume. 'Infamy!'

'Perhaps,' I muttered aloud to myself, as the fifth key failed to go into the keyhole, 'I should have removed his pistol when I had the chance.'

I could hear him getting to his feet. I did not need to look behind me; the sounds he was making were enough. The sixth key would not turn. My face was close to the door, and my compressed retina span odd, insubstantial, neon blue-white spirography upon the wood; my eye, evidently, still complaining at the treatment it had received in the car.

'Skvorecky!' Trofim bellowed

I believe that I had, finally, broken through his ox-like placidity and made him angry.

The seventh key, with a nice sense of its own numerological pedigree, rotated through the full three-hundred-three-score degrees, and the bolt slid back. There was not a moment to lose. I yanked the key out, opened the door a foot or so, slipped through, and closed the door behind me. I shuddered the key back in the lock on the outside of the door with a trembly hand. As I turned, and whilst the bolt was in the process of sliding across, the handle suddenly shook with poltergeist ferocity under my hand.

But the lock was engaged.

Something exploded: splinters flew. Smoke billowed through a new hole in the doorway. The detonation echoed in the hall.

'Open this door,' yelled Trofim, separated from me by a thin panel of wood. I thought of the size of his fists, and the bulk of his musculature. Then I thought about the flimsiness of the door. It was not a comfortable thought.

'You have damaged the door!' I cried out. 'You have damaged the furnishings!'

'I'll kick the door down with one swing of my *boot*,' boomed Trofim, like the wolf from the folktale. Or as the wolf might have sounded had he been wearing military boots.

'What did Frenkel *tell you* about damaging the furnishings?'

'I'll wring your neck, Skvorecky!' he boomed; and with a noise of splintering wood the toe of his boot appeared through the lower panel of the door.

'Remember Comrade Frenkel's commands!' I cried. 'He gave you *a direct order*!'

There was another crash, and a whole panel of wood smashed free. Clearly reminding him of Frenkel's orders was not going to stop him. I looked about me. There was a cast-iron bootscraper on the floor to the left of the door, black but speckled all over with strawberry-coloured rust. 'You'll never catch me, Trofim,' I shouted. 'I may be old, but I can run faster than the wind!'

'I shall kill you!' boomed Trofim, from behind the rapidly dis-integrating door.

I kicked the bootscraper, and it clattered down the stairs. Hard to say whether the sounds it was making were actually like those an old man would make hurriedly descending a staircase. No time to worry about that, because with another smash the door flew open. Trofim came out like a freight train. No: like a *military* train, filled with high explosives.

I stuck my right leg out, and straightened my toes in the shoe like a ballerina. Trofim tripped. It was a schoolyard trick to play upon him, I suppose; but I shall say this. It was not my outstretched leg that was the enemy. It was Trofim's own bulk, combined with the velocity with which he came hurtling through the door.

He moved through the air, and his momentum took him, like a ski-jumper, head-first downwards, following a line parallel to the staircase. There was the sound of a stick trapped in the spokes of a freewheeling bicycle, overlaid with a raging roar, and then his head smashed through the plaster of the wall of the half-landing.

He lay there, as if decapitated: visible only from the neck down on the landing, his triffid-thick legs trailing back up the stairway behind him.

I started down the stairs. My legs were trembling a little, making it important I placed my feet carefully so as to avoid falling. I do not know whether they were trembling with fear, or exhaustion, or simple old age. As I reached him I paused over his body, partly to see if he were still alive. He had his pistol in his right hand, and I bent down to retrieve it from him. As I did so he stirred. I recoiled: clearly not dead.

I was a flight down when I heard Trofim speak again. 'My head!' he boomed.

I was almost at the bottom of the second flight when I heard him again, a little less distinct: 'I'll put *your* head through the wall.' There were the sounds of somebody large moving about above, and the small smashes and bashes of chunks of plaster falling and scattering.

I was three floors down when I heard him bellow, and get to his feet.

I hurried my gait, and was at the main entrance to the building as I heard the thunderous thumping of Trofim's boots coming down the stairs above me. I don't know where I thought I was going. Trofim was moments from catching me. But my instinct was to run. So I hobbled on.

I went outside, down the stone steps and onto the pavement, turning my head left and right in a desperate attempt to decide which way to go. Neither path looked promising. With the timing of a dream, a taxi pulled up, the door opened of its own accord, and, without even thinking, I climbed inside. Indeed, I was *pulled* inside, and bundled across the lap of somebody already on the rear seat. But I hardly paid attention to that.

As the car pulled away I looked back to see the red-faced,

bulging-eyed enormity of Trofim bursting from the building's main entrance, plaster dust smoking from his bashed-up-looking head.

The car swung away, and I saw Trofim recede in vision as he shook his hands in impotent fury, those terrible, man-killing hands.

I was too surprised to be relieved.

I was not alone in the taxi. Sitting beside me was Leon Piotrovich Lunacharsky from the chess club. 'Lucky we were here, comrade,' he beamed. '[Jolly luck of the Irishmen,]' he added in English. '[Or is it that it should is,]' he added, getting tangled in his excitement. '[Jolly luck of the science fictioneers?]'

'What?' I stuttered. 'What?'

'It took me a little while to process what you told me,' said the driver. 'It is a function of my syndrome that sometimes mental processing takes a little while. But I usually *will* process mental information, given time.' The driver, of course, was Saltykov.

'Saltykov,' I said.

'Reactor Four,' Saltykov said, without looking round. 'The American had found out not only the location, but the reactor number, too. He got the information to you before he was killed.'

'Bless him!' sang Lunacharsky. 'Bless him for an American saint! He will save many lives!'

'And you trusted me enough to tell me, too! But I was distracted,' Saltykov went on in his implacable, unpassionate voice. 'The policemen were attempting to lay hands upon me, even though my syndrome renders such contact intolerable.'

'We waited outside the police station,' said the bubbling Lunacharsky. 'Then we saw the KGB take you away in your big car. We *followed* them. We thought you were as good as dead!'

'As good as,' I confirmed. 'Since 1958.'

'When that ape took you into that building . . .'

'Leon Piotrovich Lunacharsky wanted us to drive away,' said Saltykov, proudly. 'I insisted we stay.'

'And I am very grateful indeed that you stayed,' I said.

'And now,' said Leon Piotrovich Lunacharsky, like a radio continuity announcer, 'we shall take you to Dora Norman, the American.'

CHAPTER 12

I had previously only encountered Lunacharsky in the darkness of the Pushkin Chess Club, and it was a strange thing to see him by the light of the day. He seemed, somehow, less robotic. He had a broad face, with wideset eyes, slightly downward-pointing at their outside points. There was a streak of white in his thick, black broadbrush mane of hair, like a badger. His moustache lay languid, like a black odalisque, across his plump upper lip. Forty years of age, or thereabouts, I would guess.

Saltykov's taxi crossed into a right-hand feeder lane and turned into a new road. It blended with the dusty, rusty mass of Moscow traffic and swept passed a series of industrial buildings.

'I'm more excited than I can say,' Lunacharsky bubbled. 'To be in the same car as the great Skvorecky!'

I was having difficulty with my breath.

'Oh dear,' said Saltykov, from the driver's seat.

My nerves were enormously jangled. 'Oh dear?'

'I have come the wrong way,' said Saltykov. 'That was an incorrect turn.'

'What?' I snapped. 'Saltykov, where on earth are you going?'

He became, as far as his buttoned-down manner permitted it, annoyed. 'It is because you have distracted me by talking! You should not distract the driver of a vehicle!'

'Don't distress yourself, my friend,' said Lunacharsky, whose mood was perfectly irrepressible. 'I see where we are! We need to turn right again and make our way back onto the ring road.'

'If you *talk* to me,' Saltykov said, with a mosquito whine curled into the words, 'then I will be *unable* to concentrate properly upon the driving.'

'Don't upset yourself, my friend. Take the right turn that is – never mind, you missed it. There's another right turn, up here. Take *this* one and ...'

'Could you please,' I said, 'tell me what is going on?'

'I shall explain everything!' boomed Lunacharsky.

An open-topped lorry, trailing a huge conical sleeve of dust like a crop-spraying plane, thunderously overtook the little taxi. Our car shook monstrously in the wake. 'Speed up!' I bellowed.

'I am driving at the optimal speed for fuel efficiency,' retorted Saltykov in no placid voice.

'Come, my friend,' Lunacharsky told him. 'Simply circle round, circle round. We need to get back on the correct road. Mademoiselle Norman is waiting!'

'Yes! Yes!' Saltykov peeved, as another car swept past, its horn howling. 'Do not talk to me, or expect me to talk to you, because if you do so I will be unable to concentrate upon the driving!'

'He suffers from,' said Lunacharsky, turning in the seat to face me, 'a particular syndrome ...'

'I gather,' I replied.

'But he is an expert man! He knows *everything* about nuclear power stations!'

'Comrade, I would be obliged if you could tell me,' I said, as the car slowed, turned, and accelerated again, 'what on earth is going on?'

'I shall explain everything! By the time we arrive at our friend Saltykov's flat, where Mademoiselle Norman is sequestered – by the time we arrive there, everything will have been explained to you! You will know *everything*. And therefore you will understand how high are the stakes.'

'At the moment, I am completely in the dark,' I said. 'So there is a lot you need to explain.'

'You underestimate the extent of your knowledge,' he replied. 'You know more than you think. You know Frenkel, for example. You understand the nature of the threat we face.'

'I knew him a long time ago.'

'I meant to say how much I admired your attitude in the chess club yesterday,' gushed Lunacharsky. 'Negation! When we threw questions about Project Stalin at you, you simply *negated* them. It was *more* than denial, because when somebody denies something it always bears the imprint of its opposite. If an official denies something it is tantamount to an admission! But you – you *negated*. It was gloriously dialectical. In this, I assume science fiction has prepared you. Because the worlds created by a science fictional writer do not deny the real world; they antithesise it!'

'You are,' I said, a little uncertainly, 'complimentary.'

'Indeed! You see, that is also the *nature* of the UFO phenomenon. It is *dialectical*. In the club the other night, you stated the thesis. *You* could do this, because you were personally involved, with Frenkel, in the original project. Your thesis is: there are no UFOs, we are alone in the cosmos. The antithesis was advanced, often foolishly, by the other members: yes there are UFOs, they visit us nightly! But without the thesis to counter this antithesis, there could be no synthesis. And the synthesis is . . .'

'Is what?'

He looked down his long nose at me, with a twinkle in his eye. 'It is a mistake to assume that extraterrestrials must be material. Or immaterial. What if they exist in a dialectical superposition of the two conditions?'

'And if you spoke the same sentence in Russian rather than gibberish?'

He beamed at me. 'My dear friend, I am being too *general*. Let me fill you in on specifics. The American, and his lady friend, entered the Soviet Union at Kiev. Now, there was a *reason* why they entered the Soviet Union via Kiev. A crucial reason.'

The motion of the car slowed. We stopped.

At this point my conversation with Lunacharsky was interrupted. Saltykov had stopped his taxi at a red traffic light. Somebody, outside the vehicle, was shouting. It was a pedestrian who was yelling. Then, startlingly, the door was hauled open, with the result that the noise from outside spilled in. Lunacharsky turned, and began to say, 'Comrade, this taxi is already full ...' but the shouting drowned him out. *Out of the car! Or I shall shoot*, swam into focus.

I recognised the voice; hoarse, but distinct. And glancing across I recognised the meaty fist. It was holding a pistol, and the pistol was pointed in through the open door.

'Saltykov,' I bellowed. 'Drive! Go!'

'The traffic light is red,' said Saltykov.

'All of you!' Trofim was yelling from outside. '*Out – of – the – car—!*'

His huge hand, with its monstrous reach, came snaking into the back of the cab like Grendel reaching for prey; or like the octopus in *Twenty Thousand Leagues Underneath the Oceans* trying to winkle submariners from the *Nautilus*.

Lunacharsky was trying to remonstrate through the open passenger door: 'Comrade, it is a misunderstanding, comrade, please put the gun down.' He had, I noticed, planted one of his feet against the inside of the car, next to the open door. A great force was hauling at him and trying to draw him out. Trofim shouted at us to get out of the car.

'Never mind the fucking colour of the light,' I yelled. 'Go! Accelerate! He has *a gun* on us!'

'It is against the rules of driving. More to the point it contradicts common sense, to drive through a junction when the light is red,' said Saltykov. 'Other cars would collide with us, and immobilise the ...'

'*Weave* through the traffic, you idiot – weave – just *go now*. He'll kill us all!'

'This is the KGB! Out of car!' shouted Trofim. He had thrust his huge, troll-like left hand inside the taxi, and had taken hold of Lunacharsky's lapels. 'Let go!' Lunacharsky yelped, bracing both his feet now against the frame of the car's door. I could see Trofim levelling the pistol with his other hand.

'Go!' I shrieked at Saltykov. 'What are you doing? Press your foot onto the accelerator!'

'The traffic light is red,' insisted Saltykov.

'I don't care! Go! Go!'

'The traffic light is green,' said Saltykov.

With a noise from the tires like a soprano's top note, and a rush of acceleration that yanked me back against the seat, the taxi roared away.

The strain on its engine was such that the exhaust backfired deafeningly.

For a moment Trofim's arm was still inside the vehicle as we moved away; but then the huge hand lost its grip and slipped out of view. I looked back to see the giant KGB man rolling ponderously in the gutter.

The passenger door slammed to, bounced open again, and slammed once more. I reached over Lunacharsky to grab the handle and heaved with all my might. From being a ridiculously cautious driver, Saltykov was now driving with absurd abandon. We swerved, spun sharp left, and zoomed away. 'The engine backfired!' he hooted.

'I heard it,' I replied, speaking loudly enough to be heard over the roar of the engine. Relief sparked into rage. 'What were you *playing* at?' I shouted. 'Why did you just sit there? That was Trofim. Did you drive past exactly the same place you picked me up?'

'I took a wrong turn,' he replied, peevishly. 'Because you insisted on *talking to me* as I drove! Both of you. I was distracted from the concentration necessary to drive an—'

'So you took a wrong turn! Surely you didn't need to retrace *exactly the same route* to get back on track?'

'My mind is methodical,' he insisted. 'That was the only way I knew.'

'Your mind is insane,' I yelled.

'If you had left me alone and not talked to me,' he wailed. 'If you had left me alone to drive, instead of pestering me with questions, I would never have got lost! It's your fault.'

Lunacharsky seemed uncharacteristically silent. But I was still full of outrage at what Saltykov had done.

'You drove *directly* past the house in which they'd been holding me,' I said, slapping the back of the driver's seat with my fist in petty rage. 'Trofim was still *standing there*! Exactly where we left him! And then you stopped the car!'

'Stop slapping my seat! That is distracting to the driver! Please do not distract the driver!'

'Of course he was still standing there,' I said. 'He's an ox. Where would he go? And you drove along the same road, and then you *stopped the car*. Right in front of him!'

'The traffic light was red!'

'And if it was? You could jump the light. People have been known to jump red lights. Have you never seen a *film*?'

'I was of course conscious of the need to make a rapid escape,' he insisted, 'but I was, equally, conscious of the danger of collision with another vehicle were I to drive through the red light. How could we make good our escape in that circumstance? What if we were injured, or killed, in the collision? How would that serve our purpose?'

My attention, now, was distracted by Lunacharsky. He was staring at me with a unpleasant intensity. I returned his gaze. 'Your car did not backfire.'

'I heard it distinctly. I like to keep my engine clean. It's a clean machine. I may need to service it. The diesel available in Moscow is inferior quality.'

'Your car,' I repeated, 'did not backfire.'

Saltykov's flat was part of the Gorky Estate, an accumulation of tottery-looking towerblocks in a concrete park, from the very peak of the tallest of which, if you stood on tiptoe, you might be able to see some of the treetops from Gorky's more famous park. The blocks all stood on fat concrete legs, and Saltykov drove his taxi in underneath the belly of the nearest. He parked beside the pillar. There was space, here, for a hundred cars; but only half a dozen were parked. The rest of the space was taken up with metallic rubbish bins, like huge oil-drums, overfilled and spilling their waste onto the floor. A black-faced tractor, blushing with rust, sat beside a large heap of mechanical bits and bobs.

Saltykov killed the engine, and for a while we two sat in silence. 'You are certain he *is* dead?'

'I fought in the war,' I said. 'I saw enough dead bodies then. I know a dead body when I see one.' We sat for a further moment in silence. 'Believe me,' I said, shortly, 'I'm sorry to say so.'

'It is very regrettable that he has been killed,' Saltykov replied. 'I am sad. You must not think otherwise. You may think otherwise, because my syndrome interferes with my capacity to express emotion.'

'Your syndrome,' I said, in an unfriendly tone, as I fiddled a cigarette out of its pack.

'This death is regrettable in many different ways,' said Saltykov, in a precise voice. 'For one thing—'

But I interrupted him. 'Please do not itemise the various ways in which it is regrettable. We can both agree it is regrettable. You are not a machine, after all.' I lit my cigarette.

'In many ways, there is something machine-like about the processes of consciousness that characterise my syndrome,' said Saltykov, with, I thought, a hint of smugness. 'Nevertheless, we have to decide what to do now.'

'We have to get out of Moscow,' I said. 'It's not a difficult deduction. The KGB are looking for us. Trofim may be an ox, but he'll be able to remember the registration of this car. We need another car, or we need to find another mode of transport, but either way we need to remove ourselves from the city. We need to go a long way away.'

'I do not possess another car,' said Saltykov. 'As to removing ourselves, that was precisely our plan. And do not forget Mademoiselle Norman.'

I had indeed forgotten her. 'Where is she?'

'In my apartment. But first we must do something with Lunacharsky, or to be precise, the deceased body of Lunacharsky.'

'Yes, yes,' I said, unable to stand it any more, and yanking open the door of my side to stumble out of the car. 'Let us dispose of Lunacharsky.'

I stood in the shadow of the vast building's underside whilst Saltykov fussed from rubbish bin to rubbish bin, each almost as tall as he. From one he retrieved a torn sheet covered with the chocolate brown patches of dried blood (from what, who knows) that he laid on the ground beside the passenger door. Onto this we pulled Lunacharsky and wrapped the cloth about him, and in this undignified and dirty toga we heaved him up and into a bin. It was a sordid business. Then I smoked another cigarette whilst Saltykov fussed, like an old maid, at the back seat of his car. 'A little blood has pooled in the space between the back of the seat and the base of the back,' he reported, in a quasi-scientific tone of voice.

'*Why* did you not drive through the red light?'

'I reasoned,' said Saltykov, in what was indeed a reasonable tone of voice, 'that were I to do so I would involve my taxi in a collision with a car coming through the junction from another direction.'

'I still can't believe,' I pressed, 'that you retraced *exactly your previous route* in order to find your way back to the correct road.'

'What you need to understand about my syndrome,' he said, indistinctly, his head inside the car, 'is that . . .'

'I have heard enough about syndromes,' I reported. 'Let us all agree the death is regrettable.'

'Yes, we can agree that.' He stood up, and ran, like a chicken, to the nearest bin to rid himself of whatever cloth he had been using to wipe away the blood. His knees came up almost to his chest when he ran. Then he went round to the boot of the car and drew out of it a perfectly clean, folded blanket. This he arranged fussily over the back seat. 'Dora Norman,' he said, 'has been very distressed at the death of her American friend, Coyne.'

'Understandably,' I said.

'Perhaps for her to learn of the death of Lunacharsky would only augment her distress?'

'I don't suppose she needs to know.'

'Then let us go up. We must collect her, and we must leave Moscow.'

'Collect her?'

'We can hardly leave her here!' said Saltykov. 'I am a registered taxi driver. The authorities have my address and details. The KGB will come to this address and detain her. To leave her would be to condemn her to death.'

'*Collect her* makes her sound like a piece of luggage.'

Saltykov locked his taxi. Then he turned the key again to unlock it. Then he locked it once more. Unlock, lock. Unlock, lock. 'Now,' he said, 'we are ready to go up.'

We crossed to the main entrance. When we opened the main door we let a Moscow breeze inside, and litter rustled and moved over the entrance-hall floor like paper wildlife. We waited beside the pockmarked steel doors of the lift. There was nobody else around.

'We must go straight away,' I said. 'Who knows how quickly the authorities will put two and two together, and raid this address?'

'To be precise,' he said, 'it is a question of how easily the KGB can retrieve details from the Militia. It may not happen rapidly.'

'That is not a reason to be dilatory.'

The lift door creaked open, and a fantastically shrunken and wrinkled old woman shuffled out, carrying a string bag bulging with provisions. Her head was located in the space directly in front of her torso, as if her neck fitted into the centre of her sternum rather than between her shoulders, and her black hump traced a curve of mathematical purity. We waited until she had gone by and stepped inside the lift. The inside was urinous.

'Our deceased comrade and friend,' I said, as the doors wheezed shut, 'was about to tell me what on earth is going on.'

'He was?'

'He promised me a full explanation.'

'He did?'

'He did. But then he was shot dead. Perhaps you could provide the explanation instead?'

'I'm afraid I cannot,' said Saltykov. 'I am not apprised of the complete picture. Comrade Lunacharsky was apprised of the full picture.'

The sinking sensation in my stomach was only partly a result of the lift's motion. 'You are making a joke?'

'By no means. I knew James Coyne, a little, through professional contacts. I would have called him friend. It was Coyne who introduced me to the Pushkin Chess Club, and to Comrade Lunacharsky. I understand only a few indistinct elements of the larger picture. They, I believe, saw the whole thing.'

'They saw the big picture. You never saw the big picture?'

'I am a recent recruit to their commendable plan.'

'I see.'

The lift doors wheezed open. Standing on the landing was, I would have been prepared to swear, exactly the same old lady as we had seen exiting downstairs: the same woody deep-wrinkled face, the same low-slung head and black hump, the same string bag. She shuffled into the lift as we stepped out onto the fifteenth floor.

Saltykov's tiny apartment was as minimalist as I would have expected it to be: sparsely furnished and ferociously neat. The worst that could be said of it was that it was a little dusty, and that the windows could have done with a wipe; but everything inside was certainly carefully arranged. The books were arranged (by the colour of their spines) so tightly on the bookshelves they effectively formed laminated blocks. I did what any lover of books would do: I checked to see what volumes Saltykov had upon his shelves. Most of these books were novels by the English writer Agatha Christie – in Russian, of course – although there were several technical manuals relating to nuclear power. Apart from the books, the tiny apartment was undecorated. There were no photographs on the wall, no knick-knacks, no distractions. A narrow settee was arranged exactly in the centre of the living room; and exactly in the centre of the settee was the ample frame of Dora Norman: as large as life. Larger, indeed, than most lives.

She looked exactly as I remembered her, although her face bore signs of grief, and those, rather surprisingly, suited her. Her ample features appeared dignified and, even, beautiful in their sombre repose.

She saw me, and smiled. '[Mr Koreshy!]' she said. ['Oh how pleased I am to see you again!]'

'[I am delighted to meet you again, Ms Norman,]' I said. '[And my name is still Skvorecky.]'

It looked for a moment as if she might cry. '[I am sorry,]' she said, bleakly. '[I am struggling to get the hang of Russian surnames.]'

'[There is no need to apologise.]' Feeling awkward standing over her, I sat myself on the corner of the settee. '[I was sorry to hear of the death of your friend, Mr Coyne.]'

'[He told me, you know,]' she replied.

'[He?]'

'[Jim. He said it would be dangerous. He warned me he could die. I pooh-poohed him.]'

'[You,]' I asked, after a pause, '[did what?]'

'[I dismissed what he said.]'

'[Ah!]'

'[But he was right! Oh, the poor foolish man.]'

'[Please accept my commiserations.]'

She looked straight at me. '[I have been sitting here in wonderful Mr Saltykov's flat, just thinking and thinking about it. Do you know, I barely knew Jim? I knew him a little from the Church, of course. But I was never very close to him. And now he is dead, I find myself more upset in principle than in actuality. Does that sound heartless?]'

'[Of course not,]' I said.

'Remember,' said Saltykov, coming into the room, 'don't tell her about the death of Lunacharsky. If she discovers that Lunacharsky is dead, she could go all to pieces.'

'[What's that?]' she said, looking up. '[What was that about Mr Lunacharsky?]'

'You idiot,' I snapped. 'If you didn't want her to hear about Lunacharsky, why did you mention Lunacharsky.'

'She does not speak Russian!' Saltykov objected, in a surprised tone of voice.

'You may be surprised to hear,' I retorted, 'that the English for Lunacharsky is Lunacharsky.'

'[What are you saying about wonderful Mr Lunacharsky?]'

'[Ms Norman,]' I said. '[Mr Lunacharsky is unable to join us right now.]'

'*You* mentioned his name!' objected Saltykov. 'What are you doing? Are you telling her that Lunacharsky is dead? I told you not to tell her that Lunacharsky is dead!'

'[I have only picked up a few words in Russian, I regret to confess, in my time here,]' said Dora, in a low voice, '[but doesn't *smertz* mean *dead*?]'

'[I'm afraid so, Ms Norman,]' I told her, glowering at Saltykov. I essayed a mournful face, but my face is not a very flexible organ.

'[How dreadful! Your friend!]'

'[It is regrettable, yes,]' I said. '[But he was hardly my friend. I met him for the first time yesterday.]'

'[Oh.]'

'[Our situation is precarious, here in Moscow, and I'm afraid we must get out. I do not seek to alarm you. But you ought to know that not only the police but also the KGB have become involved.]'

'[Oh my,]' she said.

'What are you saying?' said Saltykov, hovering awkwardly by the door. 'What are you telling her?'

'I'm saying we need to get out of Moscow.'

'And so we must,' he agreed. 'Just as long as you're not telling her that Lunacharsky is dead.'

'[Kiev,]' said Dora. '[It must be Kiev.]'

'[I would prefer to take you to the American embassy here in Moscow, my dear Ms Norman,]' I said.

'[We entered the USSR via Ukraine. The terms of the visa are very clear. I won't be allowed out from Russia – only from the Ukraine.]'

'[Going to the Ukraine, Ms Norman, will not protect you from the KGB. Only last year President Shcherbytsky reaffirmed the close bonds between the Ukraine SSR and the Union of Soviet Socialist Republics. The jurisdiction of the KGB is ...]'

'[Nevertheless, I must get to the US embassy in Kiev,]' she insisted. '[Can you do that?]'

'[You are quite sure that is what you want?]'

'[I'm serious, Mr Koreshy. If you leave me in Moscow, the Russians will block my leaving the country on the grounds that my travel permit was for the Ukraine only. They will request I be handed over to their law enforcement officers.]'

'[The American embassy here would never hand you over!]'

'[Perhaps not. But I could spend *years* sitting around the embassy building. Get me to Kiev; I'll be on a jet to New York in a day. Please!]'

'What is she saying?' Saltykov wanted to know.

'She wants to go to Kiev.'

'But of *course* we must go to Kiev! Where else would we go?'

'What on earth do you mean? Why not Finland, or the Crimea?'

'Kiev! Of course Kiev! Didn't Coyne explain to you?'

'[Is it far?]' put in Dora. '[Is it too far to drive?]'

'[It is about as far from here as Madrid is from Paris,]' I told her. '[Which is to say, in American terms ...]' But my knowledge of American geography was too rudimentary for me to call to mind a comparison. '[Well as far as between any two American cities that are as far apart from one another as Madrid is from Paris,]' I concluded lamely.

'You and I *are* going to Kiev,' said Saltykov emphatically. 'Let us take her too.'

'And why are you and I going to Kiev?' I asked him.

'Didn't Coyne *explain* to you?'

'He did not.'

'Because we are the only ones left,' he replied.

'Left to do what?'

'The others are dead,' he said. 'If we don't get to Reactor Four at Chernobyl it will be exploded, and many millions will die. Which would be a regrettable turn of events.'

'Regrettable indeed. You're *sure?*'

'Of course!'

'I thought Lunacharsky knew the details, and you did not.'

'Oh I know about the attack on Chernobyl. I know about *that!*'

'Who is going to attack it?'

'The aliens.'

'I see. And *why* are they going attack this nuclear facility?'

'That,' said Saltykov, 'I don't know. Presumably in order to make war upon humankind'

'And Lunacharsky knew all about this?'

'Oh yes. And so did Coyne.'

'[Chernobyl,]' said Dora. '[You're both talking about Chernobyl, aren't you? Did James discover which reactor was going to be the target?]'

'[Her told me,]' I replied. '[Four.]'

'We must go straight away!' said Saltykov. 'Immediately! Immediately *after*, that is, I have voided my bladder into the toilet. We must go to Kiev!' He repeated this phrase as he made his way across his little hall to his toilet. 'We shall go to Kiev!' Then he closed the toilet door behind him, and Dora Norman and I waited for him. The silence between us was a little awkward; and was punctuated only by the faint sound of a stream of fluid striking porcelain.

CHAPTER 13

Thirteen. That unlucky number. In this thirteenth chapter we travel to Chernobyl, where I shall be blown up and exploded and destroyed.

Unlucky enough.

We went down in the lift and out through the hall like outlaws, glowering and looking all around. But of course we *were* outlaws. Dora had no luggage; all her belongings, including her passport, were in her hotel room, and there was no possibility of returning to retrieve them. We would have to make do without these things. She was more anxious about lacking her toiletries, and a change of clothes.

'[I apologise,]' she said to me, as we made our way to the car. '[I have been in the same clothes for two days now. I'm afraid I must not smell good.]'

'[By no means,]' I replied.

'[I *must* smell. And it's only going to get worse. I must smell.]'

'[Your smell is delightful,]' I said. '[Believe me. Your scent possesses an intoxicating femininity and delicacy which fills my nostrils with joy.]'

She looked at me quizzically. '[Do you have a good sense of smell? I only ask because, if you're pardon me saying so, your nose is a little – scarred.]'

'[I have almost no sense of smell at all,]' I said, smiling.

'[My scent receptors were all burnt out when my face was scorched.]'

She looked at me again, and then burst into birdsong-like laughter. '[How comical you are!]'

'[Others have noted my ironical nature,]' I conceded. To smile broadly was to stretch the skin of my face uncomfortably, but I smiled to the extent that I was able.

'[All that blarney about my lovely smell, and you can't smell anything!]'

'[The smell is in my heart, beautiful Ms Norman, rather than my nose. A nobler organ, I feel.]'

She laughed again. We were at the car.

'I shall drive,' Saltykov announced. 'I shall listen to the radio. You,' he said to me, 'must sit on the back seat with Ms Norman.'

'Ms Norman,' I replied, 'would surely prefer to have the back seat to herself.'

'Because of her bulk?' Saltykov said.

I believe he meant nothing offensive in saying this; it was merely the weirdly blank straightforwardness of his manner. I looked at her, as she, all unwitting, smiled back.

'For shame!' I said, to Saltykov. 'Why must you be so rude? I meant simply that, as a single woman, in a strange country, I am certain she would prefer her own space. I am certain she would rather not share the seat with an ugly, old Russian man she barely knows.'

'You need not accuse me of discourtesy,' said Saltykov. 'She cannot speak Russian.'

'Nevertheless.'

'Besides, *you* are making assumptions about her. Should you not ask her?'

'[Ms Norman,]' I explained, '[We are discussing our seating arrangements in the car. Saltykov wishes to have the front entirely to himself. I am insisting that I sit up front and that you be given the rear seat to yourself.]'

'[Because I'm so heavy,]' she said, with a slightly mournful tone. She tried to add a trilling laugh to this, but it gurgled into nothing.

'[No!]' I said, rather over-insistently. '[Not at all! No no!]'

'[It's quite all right,]' Dora said.

'[Please, Ms Norman,]' I insisted, with old-style Russian courtesy. '[I insist upon it.] I shall sit up front.' I said this last in Russian to Saltykov, speaking with finality.

'Nonsense,' said Saltykov. 'You cannot sit in the front passenger seat. It would distract me. It would make for unsafe driving.'

'You are an absurd and rather childish fellow,' I said.

'I am neither! But we must get on quickly, and I am resolved to get on safely, so I must have no distractions as I drive. Driving,' he added, with a spurt of sudden energy in his voice, 'is a *complicated* process. I must concentrate wholly upon it.'

'Much of the process is governed by the autonomous nervous system,' I offered.

'Nonsense,' said Saltykov, as if this were the most absurd notion he had ever heard. It dawned on me then that perhaps he was not like other men when it came to driving cars. Perhaps he had to distil every atom of his concentration into the process of operating all the various levers and pedals that make a car move forward. I was, at any rate, disinclined to contest the point. 'I shall inform Ms Norman of your intransigence,' I said, stiffly.

I relayed Saltykov's insistence to her in English. As I did so, I became conscious of the possibility that she, unable to understand Saltykov's Russian, might suspect me of inventing his peculiar insistence as an excuse to place myself near her. As I thought this I blushed, and even stammered, for it filled me with a strange and sudden anxiety. As I chattered on in English, that strange vocalic language, I ran through the following sequence of thoughts in my own head. First I tried to reassure myself: she would not assume that a man as old as I could have sexual designs upon a woman as large as she. Then I thought, But she is a woman, for all that, and young, and single. Why might she not assume sexual predation as my motive? For all she knows, I prefer bulky women to the skinnier kind. And then, as she acquiesced heartily enough in my request, '[Of course you must sit on the back seat! It wouldn't do to distract the driver!]', I felt a counterflush. For as she smiled I was gifted a glimpse past the apperception of an anonymous spherical quantity of human flesh; and into the individual. Her eyes were very beautiful. Her eyes struck me. When she smiled, the extra flesh on her face dimpled, and this had the effect of spreading the expression more widely, really for all the world as if her whole face, and not just her mouth, were smiling.

I found an unexpected joy kindling inside me at this smile. I found myself wanting to do something to make the smile re-emerge. For a glittering moment, the veil lifted just enough to give insight past the external epiphenomena of Dora Norman and into her soul. And then she pulled the rear car door open and climbed inside, or rather she tackled the job of climbing inside, leaning forward and hauling the various fleshly components of her mass through the opening and rearranging them into a sitting shape, and the spell was broken. I was, once more, blind to her, and I saw only her bulkiness. She ceased, indeed, being a human being, for that portion of time that I was unable to uncloud my view of her.

I got in next to her. Conscious, I suppose, of my inner failing, and self-aware enough to be a little ashamed, I was excessively polite to her.

'[It's extraordinarily kind of you to permit this,]' I said, like a genteel character from a Dickens novel.

'[Don't be silly!]'

I promised not to be silly.

We made our way quickly through the outskirts of Moscow, and soon enough we were on the almost deserted highway heading southwest. In those days, in Russia, few people drove, and nobody but delivery drivers and truckers drove between cities (things are very different now). From time to time another vehicle would pass us in the other direction, or a tractor would appear in front of us, scattering scales of mud from its dinosaurian rear wheels as it grumbled along the road at fifteen miles an hour. If the road were perfectly straight and perfectly empty then Saltykov might overtake such an obstacle; but if there were the merest reason to be cautious, then Saltykov was cautious, and we crawled behind the tractor until it turned off the road into the field of some enormous farm.

We drove all afternoon. At some point, with the sun low and elderly in the sky, Saltykov turned off the highway and made his way into a village to try and buy some diesel. The place possessed one solitary petrol station, and its owner told us that he had none to sell. He directed us to a second village. So we left the village, and Saltykov manoeuvred his taxi very slowly along a one-track road whose surface was suffering the tarmac equivalent of psoriasis. It was thirty minutes before we rolled into the next village along: a set of concrete cubes and boxes distributed upon and amongst cold green fields. The petrol station there was shut, and nobody seemed to be about. We bought some sausage and bread from a shop owner. When I asked for directions to the nearest petrol station the owner offered to sell us some diesel himself. In a yard at the back of the store he had a pile of jerry cans, and after sniffing at the uncapped mouth of one of these, and insisting a portion of the stuff be poured into a cup for him to inspect, Saltykov agreed to the purchase.

We drove back to the main road, Dora and I eating bread and sausage quietly on the back seat, and Saltykov – who seemed to need no solid sustenance at all – complaining peevishly about the quality of the diesel he had just bought. 'It is making my engine knock.'

'Is it distracting you from driving?' I asked.

'It's distracting the engine from functioning optimally.'

I dozed for an hour or so. When I awoke we were still in motion, and the sun was going down in rural splendour, laminating the horizon with two dozen shades of alien reds and beetle-iridescences, and aqua-yellows and Jupiter-oranges. There are no sunsets finer than those in the level country of western Russia.

The road ran along the edge of a vast forest, and for a long time we skirted the gloom.

'[I can't sleep,]' said Dora. '[I keep thinking about James.]'

I couldn't think of anything to say to this, so we sat in silence for a while. The sky deepened, and grew darker: thrush-coloured; crow-coloured; then finally an ice and transparent blackness.

'[The stars!]'

I craned to peer through the glass. '[There they are,]' I agreed.

For a while she was silent, and then she said, '[I've been trying to find a way of raising this subject.]'

'[What subject?]'

'[I hope you won't mind. But James said that you are a science fiction writer.]'

Now it was my turn to bark with laughter. '[Indeed! I used to be.]'

'[You have not mentioned the fact. Perhaps I trespass upon your privacy by talking about it.]'

'[By no means. It is simply that I have not written science fiction for a long time.]'

'[Might I ask?]' she said. '[Why did you stop writing it?]'

'[I,]' I started. But I did not complete the sentence.

We rolled along the road. Saltykov was humming something to himself in the front seat. The radio was playing, but the volume was turned down so very low that I hardly believed he could hear it.

'[I apologise,]' said Dora. '[I feel I have touched upon a tender spot.]'

'[It's not that, it's not that,]' I said. '[I simply have not thought about it for a long time. My life seemed to—]' But again the sentence fell away. I had been going to say *die*, but that seemed an absurd and melodramatic thing to say. I tried again. '[Science fiction was my passion when I was young. Because science fiction is about the future, and when we are young we are fascinated with our future worlds. That's natural, since when we are young we possess no past, or none worth mentioning; but we possess an endless future stretching before us. But I am no longer young. When we are old, the future vanishes from our life to become replaced with death.

Accordingly we become intrigued, rather, with the past. We have the same escapist urge we had as youngsters, but it takes us back, into memory, instead of forward into science fiction]'

'[You're not so old,]' she said. I was about to contradict her, scoffingly, when I realised that her words were intended not as a statement but as a reassurance to me. So instead I said. '[Do you read science fiction?]'

'[I love it,]' she said, gazing through the glass at the evening sky. '[Those stars ! Who would read about ordinary things when they could read about extraordinary ones? Of course, I am a Scientologist.]'

'[I confess to my ignorance about your religion.]'

'[Sometimes it is mocked,]' she said, '[Because people don't understand it. And because it is a relatively new religion. But it is rooted in the faculty of humanity to unlock our imaginative potential. The founder, our leader, is, was, a writer of science fiction. That's not a coincidence.]'

'[The truth is,]' I said, feeling the urge to confide in Dora – an urge I had felt with nobody for many decades. '[The truth is the war bashed the science fiction out of me. The war and after the war. The things that happened. The imagination is like any other part of the body; it can be healthy and strong, or it can be broken, or diseased, and it can even become amputated. Science fiction is the Olympics Games of the imaginatively fit. After the war I was too injured, mentally, to partake.]'

'[Like an amputee?]' she said, looking at me. '[But it need not be like that. I mean, if we were talking about another sort of writing, then of course I would see what you mean. But science fiction …]'

'[I'm afraid I don't follow.]'

'[I only mean – it's science fiction! If your science-fictional imagination is broken, you can rebuild it with imaginary high technology! If your writer's soul is amputated, then *because we are talking of science fiction* you can fit it with a robotic prosthesis! You can write again, and write better, stronger, as a cyborg.]'

'[Wonderful,]' I said, my face aching again as I tried to smile. '[I have not previously considered it in that light.]'

We drove through the darkness. 'Shall I take a turn driving now?' I said to Saltykov.

'Do not distract me!' he snapped.

'I am only offering to ...'

'Talking to the driver! Distracting the driver!'

'You may be getting tired. Why not let me drive for a few hours whilst you sleep?'

'You are distracting me!' he complained. 'I told you not to distract me! Do not talk to me!'

I gave up on that approach. Instead Dora and I talked about Scientology. She explained aspects of her faith to me, and I sat meekly and listened. Then we talked a little about science fiction, and the contrary impulses in the human spirit; to dedicate itself to the past, which is to say (because the past is by definition dead and gone) to death; or to dedicate itself to the future, and to possibility, and to a better world. '[Communism,]' I said, '[is the same desire. For the future. For a better future.]'

'[Communism is science fiction,]' said Dora, gravely.

'[And vice versa.]'

'[I can think of many American writers of science fiction who would be insulted to think so.]'

'[Perhaps they do not fully understand the genre in which they are working.]'

Eventually we both slept, or tried to. I dozed uneasily at first, in the back seat with Dora. I sat facing forward and simply closed my eyes; she moved her bulk with a surprising grace and ease, almost felinely, to settle herself into a more comfortable position. Saltykov was humming: he still had the radio on at low volume, and the intermittent wash of band music, folk music and the occasional Western song formed a fractured lullaby. I drifted in and out of sleep.

I was aware, in a half-awake manner, that the motion of the car had shuffled me along the back seat a little, and that the side of my head was now resting on Dora's well-fleshed shoulder. It was fantastically comfortable; it was really astonishingly comfortable; there was a rightness about it that brought me a sense of peace and sweetness. I suppose I was also conscious of a certain unease at the unbidden and unsought intimacy; but only very distantly, a more quiet sound than the radio playing in the front of the car. After all, she was asleep, and her shoulder was, quite simply, extraordinarily comfortable. I slipped away into deeper sleep.

I experienced that unconscious muscular spasm that occasionally accompanies the drift into sleep, and which is known to the medical profession as the myoclonic jerk. I lurched forward and smashed against the back of the driver's seat. This was enough to wake me.

I had not experienced a myoclonic jerk.

It took a moment to go through the mental manoeuvres to understand what had happened. The car had been in a collision. We had crashed. We were stopped, slewed across the road. The sky outside was cold grey, mixed with a quantity of purple-blue.

'What?' I cried, pulling myself upright. 'What? What happened?'

'We hit something,' said Saltykov from the front, in a tight voice. He did not look round.

'What did we hit?'

Dora had been rolled over by the collision, and was face down in the footwell. She got herself upright with some effort. '[What happened?]'

'We hit something,' I said to her, automatically speaking Russian. And then, in English: '[We hit something.]'

'A deer,' said Saltykov, in his same tight voice.

'[We hit a deer,]' I said.

We all opened our respective doors and tumbled from the car. The sky was underlit, a perfect dark grey concavity above, paling only slightly at the horizon. There were stars above us. To the east, back along the road we had been driving, the darkness was beginning that slow dissolution into warmth, as if the horizon line were an electric filament beginning the process of heating up.

To the right and the left of us, flanking the road, shapes loomed: darkness solidified. Forests.

'Where are we?' I asked.

'A little way from Bryansk,' he said. 'I think.'

'We've made good time,' I said.

'I have damaged my taxi,' he said, in a strangled voice. 'My taxi is my livelihood. Who will want to hail a taxi with a distorted or tangled front portion?'

'It is not so bad,' I said, peering. 'It is all right, really.'

'It is not all right. It *is* so bad.'

'[The poor deer!]' said Dora, going over to the side of the road. An imperfectly bundled-up roll of brown carpet lay there: the victim. I went to stand beside Dora. The creature's neck was bent impressively backwards; one of its eyes was black, and the other a mess of red. Its horns were nothing more than spring buds bulging from the top of its head, furred like catkins. I took hold of its rear hoofs and pulled the carcass fully off the highway, to deposit it amongst the bushes at the roadside. When I climbed back onto the tarmac Dora was standing, head back, gazing upwards at the spread of stars still visible in the predawn sky.

'[So many,]' she said to me.

'[Rather more than is absolutely necessary, I've always thought,]' I replied, in a sour voice. I wiped my hands on the inside of my jacket, but doing this made my hands feel no cleaner, and only seemed to spread the sense of deathly contamination onto my clothing.

'[Necessary for what?]' Dora asked me in a voice of child-like surprise.

'[Don't you think the sheer number is a little vulgar?]' I asked.

She began to laugh, a gorgeous little trickling laugh. '[Your grumpiness, because it is not heartfelt, but only a sort of act you put on – your grumpiness is charming!]'

This wrongfooted me. I found myself smiling. '[You're the first person to say so, or think so,]' I said.

'[That profusion,]' she said, lifting her right arm to gesture at the sky, '[it means life.]'

'[You mean that amongst so many stars there must be some with planets upon which intelligence has evolved.]'

'[Four hundred million stars in our galaxy,]' she said. '[A billion galaxies. Of course there is life. That is precisely what profusion means.]' She was talking with a tone of awe in her voice; but then I considered her religious affiliation, and understood that such awe was strictly religious.

'[We're surrounded by life above,]' she said. '[And canopied over our heads with life. But not below us ... below us is only rock.]'

'[Surely there are moles?]'

'[All right,]' she said, '[I concede the moles.]' I was experiencing the peculiar sensation of the smile again in my cheeks.

'We must go on,' insisted Saltykov. 'We have to be at Chernobyl today or it will be too late. We have no time to lose. Please, re-enter the car.'

The car groaned on along the road as the sun rose and licked the sky clean of stars. Dora and I talked together. I told her about the radiation aliens; which is to say, the story of their creation. She expressed polite astonishment, and seemed genuinely involved in the tale. Halfway through this dawn conversation I was, with sudden insight, able to put my finger on the unusual and slightly uncomfortable sensation in my torso: it was happiness. I had not felt that for a very long time.

The only true ground for amazement is rarity. Consequentially, amazement is always a *relative* judgement. She was like no woman I had met before. Of course it is also true to say that nobody who has suffered prolonged periods of hunger, indeed of starvation, as my generation of Russians has done, could ever find too *skinny* a woman attractive. Such women are, for people who have lived through the times I have lived through, the icons of a world that seeks to deny us nourishment. Dora was the very opposite of this. This is my roundabout way of saying that, as the sun came up over western Russia, on that nearly deserted road, I found myself struck by the thought that Dora was a beautiful woman. You don't have to look so surprised that I would say such a thing. It was a belated realisation, yes, that's true; but my brain was old, and battered, and scorched, and could not make the rapid connections and realisations that had marked my youth. The important thing is that I got there in the end.

CHAPTER 14

We arrived at the Ukrainian border a couple of hours later. There were wooden sheds and a barrier, but the barrier was raised and nobody seemed to be, about. '[We are, after all, all members of the one glorious union of soviet republics,]' I explained to Dora.

Twenty minutes into the new country we drove into a town. Saltykov found a source of diesel: a garage tucked into a small alcove behind a café. We waited whilst a tractor driver filled the tank of his machine, and then watched as he clambered onto the seat and drove it away: its Oo wheels leaving four parallel blotchy lines of mud on the tarmac. Then Saltykov filled his tank; and Dora and I walked about to stretch our legs. There was a café overlooking the macadamized square, but it was closed, and to judge by the thickness of dust on its inner windowsill, and the number of dead flies behind the glass, had been closed for some time. We walked a little further, up a narrow street of lowering yellow-plaster housefronts, the windows tiny, inset holes each blocked with a single fat vertical iron bar. We discovered a bakery where we were able to buy some new bread, and some milk.

Back in the car we drove out of the town and munched the bread and drank the milk as we travelled. 'I had a conversation with the woman at the pumps,' said Saltykov.

'Really?'

'She asked what the registration of my car was. I explained it was Moscow. She said she didn't know how long it had been since a Moscow registration had filled up at her fuel pump.'

I waited to see where this story was going, or what the punchline was going to be; but this seemed as far as Saltykov wanted to take it.

'Well, that's very interesting,' I said.

The road took us through other towns and through countryside and finally into the suburbs of Kiev; a great many low concrete buildings, and then, as we came closer to the centre of the city, larger high-rise concrete buildings. '[I don't see any older buildings,]' said Dora, peering through the glass.

'[Not much survived the war,]' I said.

It is an attractive city despite all that: wide boulevards lined with many chestnut trees, or cherry trees, both of which were just starting to bud into blossom. Trams clanked and swayed down the middle of the larger roads; and their electrical cables ruled as-yet unwritten musical scores against the sky. There was an air of mid-morning bustle. It seemed busy, after so much vacant countryside.

'[And where is the American embassy?]' Dora asked me.

'[I don't know. I shall ask Saltykov.]'

But this conversation did not go well. '*I* don't know where it is!' he snapped at me. 'How should I know?'

'Well I don't know either. We need to ask somebody. Find a policeman.'

'We can hardly address a policeman!' Saltykov said. 'Are you insane? How insane are you? Is that the form your insanity takes – drawing a policeman's attention to us?'

'The policeman need not know who we are,' I said.

'Driving a Moscow car? Asking for the American embassy? How could this not draw attention? Perhaps I should add that I am a qualified nuclear physicist, and that you are on the run from the KGB?'

'There is no need for sarcasm,' I suggested.

'If you persist in—' Saltykov began, and then he jerked the

steering wheel. Saltykov, it seemed, had been compelled to swerve to avoid colliding with a small motorcycle. The tyres sang like sirens, and with a cumbrous shudder the car moved sideways, slid a little, and stopped. Immediately, from surrounding morning traffic, a symphony of horns rang out.

'You distracted me!' gasped Saltykov, in outrage. 'Did I tell you not to distract me when I was driving? And *yet* you distracted me! I very nearly collided with the two-wheeled vehicle.'

He seemed to be in a very bad mood. I have no doubt that this, of course, was in part to do with his lack of sleep.

'Move the car,' I urged, from the back seat. 'We are blocking the junction.'

'Do not tell me what to do. And do not distract me,' said Saltykov.

'All right – but move the car.'

'That is telling me what to do! I asked you not to tell me what to do! You deliberately told me what to do after I told you not to tell me what to do! I need *hardly* tell you how distracting it is to tell me what to do when I have previously *told* you *not* to tell me what to do!'

I put my teeth together, behind my lips, and tried counting, silently to ten; in Russian, then in English. I still felt the urge to pound Saltykov with my elderly fists. I tried again in French. At *huit* Saltykov had calmed down sufficiently to restart the engine and move the car.

We drove through the streets of central Kiev in silence. Eventually, Saltykov drew his car to a stop outside a row of shops. He turned the engine off and withdrew the key. 'You may go into one of these shops,' he told me, 'and ask about the embassy.'

'Very well,' I retorted, clambering from the car in a fury.

The first shop sold clothes and, although there was very little by way of stock, there was of course a queue. I contemplated joining the queue, although I would have been queuing not to buy anything but only to ask the way to the American embassy. This, I decided, would be a ridiculous thing to do. So I came out of the shop again, and went into the shop next door: a bookshop. The shopgirl was fitting blocks of volumes into the shelves like a bricklayer; I asked if she knew the whereabouts of the American embassy, and she expressed her perfect and complete ignorance. Coming onto the street again I stopped a passerby: a bearded individual in a black overcoat with a bundle of wooden dowels in his hand. 'American embassy?' he said, with a puzzled expression. 'In Kiev? There's no American embassy in Kiev. You want Moscow. That's where the American embassy is.'

'Comrade,' I pressed, in a crestfallen voice. 'You are sure?'

'What should Ukraine want with an American embassy? Kch, kch, kch.' This last was a strange little scraping-gulping noise he made in his throat, something I took to be an expression of disapproval. 'You know, you should know about the embassy being in Moscow,' he added, his face creasing further from puzzlement to suspicion. 'You have a Moscow accent.'

'Thank you, comrade,' I said, stepping away.

'Have you come *from* Moscow *to* Kiev to look for an American embassy?' he called after me, pointing at Saltykov's Moscow numberplates. 'Why would you not simply go to the American embassy in Moscow?'

I hurried back to the car. The man stood on the pavement staring at us. 'Drive away,' I told Saltykov.

'Did that individual give you directions?'

'There's no American embassy in Kiev,' I snapped. 'Just drive away, before he flags down the Militia and we are all arrested.'

'No American embassy?' said Saltykov in his implacable voice, pointedly not starting the engine of his taxicab. 'But that is not good news.'

I explained the situation to Dora. '[Oh no!]' she said, her flawless brow creasing with dismay. '[What can we do? Oh no! And we came all this way!]

'[It would be terrible to think that the deer died in vain.]'

'What did she say?' Saltykov wanted to know.

'She considers it unfortunate.'

'Indeed. Of course, on the other hand, it was *necessary* for us to come to the Ukraine, embassy or no embassy. So it is not entirely unfortunate.'

'Necessary?'

'I have already explained,' said Saltykov. It is crucial that we make our way to the nuclear facility at Chernobyl, not far from here. It must be today. Tomorrow would be too late.'

'You are sure about the date?'

'I am sure of what Coyne told me.'

'We can hardly take Ms Norman to the nuclear facility.'

'Indeed!'

The man on the pavement was still there. He had tucked his faggot of wooden dowels under his arm and had taken out a notepad and a pencil in order to write down the registration number of Saltykov's taxi. 'We must go,' I said. 'That man is writing down your numberplate.'

'Get out and remonstrate with him,' Saltykov told me.

'You do it!'

'But I have a disinclination to interact with strange men, on account of my syndrome. You must do it.'

'Certainly not.'

Making unhappy noises, Saltykov started his car and drove away. 'The situation cannot be helped,' he said. 'We must take Ms Norman to a hotel. We must book her into a hotel, and then you and I must drive out to Chernobyl.'

CHAPTER 15

Ukraine: so here we were. The countryside was one of low hills, but as the road fell into line alongside a lengthy stretch of water, more like a Scottish loch than a normal lake, a vista opened up to the west of open fields. The sky seemed showy, a projection rather than a reality: large irregular flint-coloured clouds against a shining grey expanse. The clouds looked as if painted upon a vast transparency that was being slid slowly from left to right along the backrail of the horizon.

We were driving to Chernobyl, Saltykov and I. Dora Norman was settled into a pleasant room in a downtown Kiev hotel room. Saltykov's taxi was not quite the same after its collision with the deer as it had been before. It creaked and rolled awkwardly when taking corners; never a rapid machine, it appeared to have less capacity for velocity now. But it was still working.

'The question,' I said, 'is what we do when we get there.'

'There is a conspiracy to blow the facility up. We must find the bomb. Where exactly in the facility the bomb will be – that is the real question.

'The real question,' I countered, 'is whether we will get there at all, in this galvanised lizard cock of a car.'

'That is a question on nobody's lips,' Saltykov replied in a peevish voice. 'That is a ridiculous and insulting question. Do not, by talking, distract the driver.'

The car creaked, and the engine continued making the sound of a man continually throwing up, and slowly, slowly, we followed the road round, and the blocky profile of Chernobyl nuclear facility rose up amongst the trees, shouldering the low hills aside and pushing its roofs towards the sky as we approached.

Though the guard at the gate was young – no more than eighteen, at a guess – he was nevertheless completely bald. It made him look, oddly, vulnerable. First of all he peered at us through the glass of his little hut. Then he stepped outside, fumbling with his hat, fitting it over his egg against the chill of the early spring air. His face looked like something drawn in felt-tip pen upon an elbow. 'Pass?'

'Pass,' repeated Saltykov intently.

It occurred to me that we ought to have foreseen this eventuality. But the guard seemed disproportionately impressed by Saltykov's response.

'You're with the others,' he said. 'I don't need to see your badges?'

His inflection was such that it took me a moment to understand that he was asking a question. 'That's right,' said Saltykov, quicker on the uptake than I.

'Go in, comrades. You want to go left at the end there,' he stuck his arm out, 'and park in Car Park One.'

'Reactor One *is* where we're going,' I said, as my elderly brain caught up. 'To join our colleagues.'

The guard stepped back and raised the barrier, and we drove through. I turned my head as we drove off, watching him scurrying back inside his little booth. Saltykov followed the road left and drove past the hangar-shaped enormity of the first reactor. 'But we don't want Reactor One,' I said.

'No. We want Reactor Four. So you said.'

'I only know what Coyne told me.'

'His dying words.'

'How do we tell,' I asked, 'which reactor is which?'

'Are you asking,' he growled, as we drove past the ranks of parked cars, 'whether the reactor buildings have large numerals painted upon them? If you are, then the answer is: no they don't.'

'I can see that they don't.'

'Then perhaps you would limit yourself to useful questions?'

'I would ask a useful question,' I said, sourly. 'But I wouldn't want to distract the driver.'

We exited the far side of the car park and drove along one-track tarmac, round a bend and between two separate huge cubes of architecture. 'That's *One*,' I hazarded, tipping a thumb behind us, 'so this must be Two.' The road turned again, flanking the second reactor, and past a fumble of low buildings. We passed a second, less crowded car park. The road went through a copse of trees, and then ran alongside a pond. 'That pond will supply cooling for the reactors,' noted Saltykov.

'Won't that make it radioactive?' I asked.

'Everything in the world is radioactive,' said Saltykov, with a humourless chuckle in his throat, 'to one degree or another. You learn that when you are educated about nuclear power, as I have been. There's no getting away from radiation.'

'There are, I assume however, degrees.'

'Indeed. A little radioactivity is fine. A lot is not fine.'

I peered at the pool with suspicious eyes. The water, perfectly still, looked like mahogany in the grim light. We were moving slowly enough for me to note that carp were crowding the pond. A single fin was unzipping the surface of the water.

'Radioactive fishes,' I said.

Then we turned again and Reactor Three filled our windshield, like a grey iceberg. We drove round it and yet another huge shed loomed into view.

'That one, then,' said Saltykov.

We followed the road round until it decanted us into another car park. It was almost wholly unoccupied: a few cars, but then nothing more than the white-painted sets of IIIs and Es on the ground, like a giant practising his lettering. Saltykov parked, and we got out. I rubbed life back into my stiff old legs. Saltykov was spryer than I.

'So here we are,' I said. 'Reactor Four. It's hard to believe.'

'Things are either believable or they're not,' said Saltykov, pursing his lips. 'Belief is not something that admits of degree.'

'How true. For example, *I believe*,' I said, 'that you are the single most annoying human being on the planet. I also *believe* that you're quite mad.'

'By no means! My syndrome is a thing apart from insanity.' He locked the driver's door, and unlocked it. Then he locked it again, and unlocked it. Lock, unlock, lock. 'Perfectly sane,' I agreed.

As we walked towards the main entrance, I said, 'It is strangely deserted.'

'And why should it be crowded? Didn't you hear the guard at the gate? Everybody is with our colleagues in Reactor One.'

'Whoever our colleagues are.'

'Whoever,' agreed Saltykov.

'And you, as an expert, will tell me it's safe to leave a nuclear reactor untended like this?'

'These things run themselves,' said Saltykov. 'The best thing to do is leave them alone. The last thing you want is some foolish operator tinkering with the controls.'

The reactor building itself loomed over us as we approached. The air was colder in its shadow. I felt a tingle of dread. More than a tingle: a tang. 'It looks,' I noted, 'like a pastiche of an aristocratic country house. Two wings, one on either side. A main entrance. But all in *concrete*, and with hardly any windows. And so much bigger – it must be ten floors high. Like a country house built by giants as a satire on bourgeois wealth.'

'It sounds,' said Saltykov, 'as if you are groping towards a description of the Revolution itself.'

'How do you mean?'

'Come! Revolution is a *giant* enterprise. A giant construction. A satirical reworking of bourgeois life on a larger scale.'

'Just when I think you're some kind of idiot savant, comrade,' I told him, 'you surprise me with a sudden perceptiveness.'

'I am highly intelligent,' he said blandly.

There was nobody at the entrance; although there were two porter's lodges immediately inside the door, one on either hand. We stepped into a capacious hallway, battleship-grey walls and linoleum underfoot. Despite the cold of the morning it was, inside, warm as a Crimean summer. There was a curious, not unpleasant odour. I couldn't place it.

'So where now?'

'We need to find the main reactor pile. If somebody has planted a bomb, that's where they will have done it.'

'Perhaps,' I said, displaying again my characteristic belatedness, 'we should have armed ourselves? What if we surprise the bomber in the act of planting the bomb? Wouldn't a gun be useful?'

'I do not possess a gun,' said Saltykov. 'Do you?'

'No.'

'You accuse me of insanity, and then rebuke me for not bringing something neither of us possesses.'

It took us fifteen minutes of trying doors (some locked, some not), of ascending and descending stairways, of pausing for me to catch my breath, of making our way along corridors and through rooms before we found ourselves back where we had started.

'I thought you *knew* about these reactors,' I snapped, crossly.

'I know the science,' he retorted, crosser than I. 'Not the individual architectural layouts. I know how the machinery works, that is all.'

We tried again. This time we spent out energies climbing an endless series of flights of stairs. I began this process resting at the top of each flight, to regain my breath; but after half a dozen flights I was driven to sitting on the stairs halfway up as well as at the top of each flight, puffing. Finally we reached a lengthy corridor, and along this, slowly, Saltykov increasingly furious at the delay represented by my exhaustion, we went. There was a door about halfway along with MAIN REACTOR posted above it.

'At last,' I growled.

And through we went.

There was no doubt that we were indeed inside the main reactor hall. It was huge: a four-storey-tall open space, longer and wider than a football pitch. Despite the chill outside, and the prodigious size of this interior space, the air here was warm. It smelt, oddly, if faintly, and in a metallic way, of honey.

Saltykov took it all in. 'We're looking down upon the top of the reactor,' he said, pointing to the left at an inset grid that stretched from wall to wall. And over there,' he said, pointing to two Olympic-sized swimming pools away to the right, 'are the spent fuel pools.'

'And where is the bomb?'

'How would I know?'

'Imagine you're a terrorist. Where would you want the brunt of the explosion to be?'

'Comrade, a bomb, even a small bomb, set *anywhere* in here would cause catastrophic damage. The core is filled with uranium wands' – I remember distinctly that he used that term, *wands*, as if he were talking about a wizard's props – 'that have to be kept at *precise* distances from one another and cooled to a *precise* temperature, or they will go bababoom.'

'They will go what?'

'Baba,' he said, widening his eyes for effect, '*boom.*' And with the last syllable he threw his arms wide, to imitate the action of an explosion.

'That's a rather peculiar word to use, comrade,' I said.

'What?'

'*Boom* is enough to communicate what you wish to say,' I said. 'The baba is superfluous.'

'Nonsense,' he insisted, stubbornly. 'Bababoom is perfectly expressive.'

'It's decadent.'

'It's expressive.'

'Expressively *decadent.*'

'Why are you *chaffing* me?' he asked. 'Do not chaff me. It serves no purpose. We have a bomb to find. Concentrate upon that, instead of upon twitting me.'

'But to find it – how? You are saying it could be anywhere hereabouts.'

'Say rather: we are standing *inside* a bomb. The core? It is cooled by water injected through it. This water is steam, at a temperature of three hundred degrees. You can imagine the pressure such a thing puts on the pipes. Severing any of these pipes would result in—'

'Yes yes,' I said. 'Boombaba!'

'*Boombaba*,' he scowled, 'is just stupid. You say it only to chaff me. Why do you waste our time *chaffing* me?'

Directly in front of us, thirty feet away or so, was a gigantic concrete column that supported the distant roof. It was wrapped around with a spiral stairway like the snake on Asclepius's staff, and this staircase lead up to various massy and inconceivable gantries and platforms overhead. And down this stairway a man was descending: a sack-bellied comrade, unshaven and unhappy looking. His cream-coloured, lumpy bald cranium was fringed from left to right round the back with a strip of lank black hair that rather resembled a spread of galloons, or pompons, or tassels. There was a starmap of grease spots across the front of his overalls.

'I'm *going*, comrades,' he announced.

'Going?' I repeated. I had the notion that he was leaving in disgust at our bickering. But that was not it.

'I got the message,' he said. 'Same as everybody else.' He stepped from the stairs and started towards us across the floor. 'Was just finishing something up.'

'Message?' asked Saltykov.

'Don't worry, comrades,' he said, holding up his hands as he trotted forwards to display two palms like a gigantic baby's. '*I* work in a nuclear power station. I understand the importance of looking after your health. I *mean* to look after my health.'

'Of course you do,' I said.

'Don't worry about *me*,' he said again, approaching. 'KGB is KGB. Prying into the business of KGB is certainly worse for your health than radiation.'

'It's a view,' I said.

He passed us. 'Reactor One,' he said. 'Straight there. Did they send you to fetch me? That's like them. Go fetch Sergei, is that what they said? He's probably napping – was that it? Comrade, I was wide *awake*. There's work to do. I'm a skilled technician, I do more work than three of *that* lot together – yes, yes,' this last in response to what he fancied was a disapproving expression on my face, although in fact I was merely bewildered, 'yes comrade, I'm going right now. Off to join the jolly party. Reactor One, yes yes.'

He burlied out of the room. We two were now entirely alone in that cavernous space.

Saltykov and I looked at one another. 'Unmistakably KGB,' I said. 'Apparently.'

'You look more KGB than I do,' he observed, sharply.

'By no means.'

'Let us continue this demeaning, childish fight no longer,' he said, briskly. 'Please understand the urgency of our situation. To answer your earlier question: there are *half a dozen* places in this reactor where even a small bomb would result in disaster. Do you understand? High pressure superheated steam; a large quantity of active uranium, and a larger quantity of spent fuel, which though spent is still prodigiously dangerous. If this building goes up,' and he threw his right arm in the air, adding actorly emphasis to his declamation, 'then it will destroy the land for miles around. It will spread a plume of lethal radiation across the whole of Europe – Russia too, depending on the prevailing winds. It could, for an example, poison the Mediterranean for half a dozen generations. It might turn Germany and Belarus and Poland into wastelands. It might sweep back and swallow Russia and Georgia. It would depend upon the wind. Did you happen to notice the prevailing winds, as we were coming in?'

'I didn't.'

'Well, let's hope it doesn't matter. If I say millions of lives depend upon this, then I'm not exaggerating. Do you understand?'

'Comrade Saltykov,' I snapped, 'please stop asking whether

I understand. May we agree to assume, from now on, that I *do* understand? Can we take that as read?'

He looked at me. 'We have known one another for a very short space of time,' he said, in an exasperated voice, 'yet we bicker and snipe at one another like an old married couple.'

'We are the only two individuals in the entire USSR,' I said, 'who do not drink vodka. Ours is therefore a unique bond.'

'I'm going downstairs. If I were going to place a bomb, I would put it in one of the chambers downstairs abutting the reactor itself. For maximum damage. You – you just search about up here.'

'What am I looking for?'

'You were in the army, weren't you? A bomb! A bomb! Look for a bomb!' He stomped towards the door.

'I'll wait for you here then, shall I?' I said. 'I mean, we'll rendezvous here, shall we? In?'

'In!' he echoes. 'In? In!'

'I meant *in half an hour*, for instance,' I shouted, growing angry myself. 'That's what I meant. I meant, in half an hour, let us rendezvous again *here*.'

'Either here,' he growled, without looking round, 'or, if the bomb detonates, then in heaven. And *I don't believe* in heaven!'

And then I was alone.

CHAPTER 16

There was something uncanny about being the sole human being in so enormous an enclosed space. 'It's like a film set,' I said to myself. There was a continuous noise that was more hiss than hum, and a pervasive if hard to identify sense of pulse, or sentience, as if the entire reactor were alive. This was not so comforting a thought. I tried to put such thoughts out of my head.

I walked over to the nearer of the two spent fuel pools, and looked over the edge. It was a surprisingly unsettling perspective: four-storeys deep and sheer all the way down. The waters were of an unnatural turquoise blue, and possessed a hyperlucid clarity, like the water that might fill the lakes of a distant planet in a science fiction magazine's cover illustration. The view right to the bottom gave me a twinge of vertigo. Now, it is true that I have never liked heights; and this, I believe, is a common phobia. But I do not know many people who also experience vertigo at the deep end of a swimming pool, as I do. I suppose it is a deep-seated refusal to accept that an almost invisible medium is able to support my weight. Some part of my mind believed that, were I to tumble into that enormous circular pool, I would not float but would rather sink leadfooted all the way to that distant, uncanny, deathly bottom. 'Idiot,' I told myself. 'You've more to fear from the radioactivity. You can't *fall*. The water would hold you up. Falling isn't what's fearful here.'

The bottom of the pool was a ridged grid with a high-tech look to it; but the walls on all four sides were tiled exactly like a public swimming pool.

My eye ran down the vertical perspective and there it was: a black case, no larger than a suitcase. The bomb, of course. There was almost a sense of anticlimax about it; to stumble upon it straight away without even having to undertake a proper search.

It was three quarters of the way down the wall, suspended on a single cable. I squatted down, and gave the line a tentative tug. It did not feel too heavy. The thought crossed my mind that this might not be the bomb after all, but rather an ordinary piece of power-station machinery. I pulled again with the notion of retrieving whatever-it-was and finding out. In retrospect this was foolish of me, for of course the line could have been booby-trapped, but that chance did not occur to me. Given all that I know now, from my privileged perspective, looking down upon a completely different mode of existence, and with all the benefits of hindsight – of what we know about Chernobyl, and the precariousness of the cage that contained its nuclear dragon – it is hard to justify such a cavalier attitude. I could have hurried away to notify the authorities, of course; and they could have dealt with the threat in a comprehensive and knowledgeable manner. But all I can say, as far as that is concerned, is that it literally did not occur to me. I was singleminded. My only thought was to prevent disaster; and not wholly for altruistic reasons either, remembering of course that any disaster would mean my own death.

Up I tugged, like a fisherman hauling in his line. As the box drew closer to me it became apparent that it was a plain black suitcase; nothing more extraordinary than that. With a small splash it broke the surface. I laid it on the poolside. The wire was hooked around its handle. Water dribbled off it, and also squeezed, for several seconds, through the side of it in four curving wafers. It was, evidently, not a *watertight* suitcase.

Almost on a reflex I reached forward and pressed the dual latches that held the case shut. They both sprung free with a piercing double click, and my heart stopped – for only at that moment did it occur to me that such an action might have detonated it.

But it did not. Wheezing with the shock I lifted the lid.

Inside there was a cluster of fruit-sized black metal balls, like haemorrhoids; and a small black wallet-sized device. There was also a certain quantity of water. I took out one of the globes. There was no mistaking it. It was an RGD-5 grenade – standard Soviet-army issue. It looked like a small metal aubergine, with a metal ridge around its middle. The fuse looked as though somebody had buried a fountain pen halfway into its top. Its pin was a bald keyring of metal. The device was wet in my hand, and the water was warm. There was something repellent, almost organic, in this warmth.

So there I was, holding a grenade in my hand in the very heart of the active reactor of a nuclear power station.

I had to think what to do next. Clearly I ought to remove this suitcase from the power plant. There were five grenades in all; one in my hand, and four in the case. Perhaps the best thing would be to carry the whole kit outside; take it into the woods, where its explosion would do less harm. Very well: I needed to uncouple the case from its metal cable. I put the loose grenade down on the side of the pool. Then I closed the lid of the case, to get a better look at the handle, and the metal cable hooked around it. The cable was steel, heavy; as thick as my little finger. There was no way I could cut it. It was attached to the handle with a closed loop: the main body of the cable had been threaded through the cable's eye. It could not be undone. I laid the suitcase down next to the loose grenade. Then I looked again into the water. I could see that the cable was attached via a clip to a fastening point set in the side of the pool, no more than a foot below the water. It would be an easy enough business unclipping that.

'Saltykov!' I yelled. 'Saltykov, I've found it! I have the bomb!'

I lay down and reached with my right hand into the unsettlingly body-temperature warmth of the turquoise waters. A finger-twist with the clip and it came free. I had it by my fingertips, and then a nerve twitched in my arm, or I fumbled, or something happened, and I dropped it. The end of the cable fell away through the water.

This was clumsy of me.

I got to my knees and looked over the edge. There was something rather soothing in watching the leisurely fall of the cable through its medium; such a long way down. It unfolded in slow motion, and went taut. Then, with a slick inevitability, it continued its downward slide. The suitcase, no effective counterweight to the mass of dozens of metres of steel cable, slid across the tiles. My heart jolted, and I made a grab for the case, but my wet finger slid across its wet surface, and it went with a splash into the water.

I watched it sink for what seemed a very very long time. Part of me was convinced, irrationally perhaps, that the jolt of hitting the pool bottom would detonate the bomb. But it touched down, distantly, silently, and lay skewed across the griddle-iron pattern of the pool bottom.

'Saltykov,' I called out again. 'I *dropped* the bomb!'

There was still one single grenade. It was right there, on the floor beside me. Not knowing what else to do, I picked it up. I was conscious mostly of embarrassment. I suppose I thought, rather incoherently, that I might make small amends by taking away this single RGD-5. I could at least dispose of *that* in the woods, which – surely – would be better than nothing. The fact that there were still four grenades in a case at the bottom of Chernobyl's spent fuel pool was ... Well, there was nothing I could do about that. I got to my feet.

'You've dropped the *bomb*?' shouted Saltykov, outraged, from behind me. Of course he was angry. The process of turning round to confront him was also the process of registering that something strange had happened to his voice. It had deepened and broadened in a most peculiar and rather comical manner – in sum, it wasn't

Saltykov's voice at all. More, I thought that perhaps I *recognised* the voice. It sounded like Trofim's voice.

I turned, and there he was: with his oxen manner, and the same half-comprehending expression on his big Slav face as he had ever had. He was aiming his pistol at me.

I held the grenade in front of me. Trofim waggled the gun. 'Give it to me.'

I looked at the grenade. Since I carried no gun, it was the closest thing I possessed to a weapon. 'I'd prefer not to,' I said.

'Just give it to me,' he repeated.

'You don't want it, Trofim,' I said. 'It's sodden. It's not going to explode.'

'They're naval grenades,' he said, the crease in his brow deepening. 'They're water resistant.'

'Well,' I said, digesting this fact. 'Well, it's probably radioactive. It's more radioactive, down in that pool, than – Godzilla,' I said, rather at a loss for a comparison. 'You don't want *this* grenade. It'll give you cancer. I'm surprised to see you here, comrade.'

'*I'm* the one who is surprised,' said Trofim, possessively.

'Very well,' I said. 'I concede my surprise to you. You're welcome to it. I'm not surprised in the least to see you here. You planted this bomb – when, a few days ago? A week? It failed to detonate, and now you've come back to change it. Or change the detonator. Or something.'

'I am not permitted to disclose confidential data pertaining to my mission,' said Trofim, with the air of an amateur actor reciting his lines. He stepped towards me, the gun level at my chest the whole time. I held up the grenade. 'One more step,' I said, 'and I shall pull the pin.'

'Pull the pin *out*,' he said.

'Pull the pin, yes, means pull it *out*.'

'I'm telling you,' he said. 'Not asking.'

'I'm not sure you understand me, comrade,' I said. 'I *will* pull it out, if you come any closer.'

He took another step towards me. 'Do it.'

I thought about this for a moment. 'Perhaps you meant to say *don't* do it?'

'That's not what I meant to say.' He took another step, and was now standing no more than two yards in front of me. The pistol in his right hand was still aimed at my chest. His left hand was carrying his little briefcase.

'You're calling my bluff,' I observed.

'You're not bluff,' he said. 'You're the least hearty man I've met.'

'I,' I said, and stopped. 'What?'

'*Ironist*, that's what Comrade Frenkel said. He knew you, all right.'

'When I said bluff, I meant—' But I was distracted. 'Are you saying you *want* me to blow you up?'

'What I *want* doesn't come into it.'

'You surely can't want to be blown to pieces inside this power station?'

'I am not permitted,' he repeated, 'to disclose confidential data pertaining to my mission.'

'You do realise that if I pull the pin we will both die?'

He puffed his chest out. 'I'm a warrior,' he said. 'If dying is the only way to achieve my mission, then so be *it*.'

I coughed. 'Well, I'm not a warrior. I'm a science fiction writer.' I disengaged my finger from the ring-pull. 'I have no desire to immolate myself.' Catching sight of the expression on his face, I added: 'To blow myself up, you know.'

'Give me the grenade,' he said.

I thought about this. 'I will if you promise not to use it.'

'I *must* use it.'

I didn't like the sound of this. 'No promise, no grenade.'

A light went on in his eyes, as if the idea was only just then occurring to him. 'I'll shoot you and take it from your dead body.'

'It's like playing chess against a grandmaster,' I said, crossly. 'You have forced my move, Comrade Spassky.'

He stared at me. 'Don't you recognise me? It's Trofim.'

'Christ, *have* the stupid grenade.' I held it out towards him.

Still aiming the gun straight at my chest, he reached up to take the grenade with his left hand. But he was still holding his suitcase in this hand. For a moment his face bore the traces of a brain strenuously wrestling with a logic problem that was almost *but not quite* beyond his capacities (if I put the *mouse and the dog* in the boat, and leave the *cat* on the nearside bank, then paddle across to leave the *dog* on the far side of the river ...). He lowered his left arm. He put the suitcase on the floor and then reached out with his left hand, now empty. I handed him the grenade, and he took it. Then with as smooth a gesture as I could manage I reached down and picked up the suitcase.

Both of Trofim's hands were occupied: gun, grenade. 'Put that down!' he said.

'The suitcase?' I asked, as if requesting clarification. 'You want me to give it up?'

He straightened his right arm, bringing the muzzle of the gun up to my face. 'Give it up *right now*.'

Give it up? Or put it down?'

'Do it now!'

'Which, though? Up or down?'

'Put it *up*,' he said, becoming agitated. 'Give it *down*. Give it – *put* it down.'

'I'm a little confused, comrade, as to which direction you want me to move this suitcase.'

'Put it down or *I will shoot you* and,' he said, a flush starting to spread over his face, 'shooting you will *make* you put it down. *Then* it will be down. *You* will be down'

'All right, all right, I'll put it down,' I said.

With a single heave I threw the case. It fell with a surprisingly loud splash into the far side of the pool.

It took a moment for him to process what I had done. 'It's fallen,' he said, perhaps because explaining it to himself solidified the concept in his head. 'It's fallen *in the water*.' His voice was higher pitched than usual. Two steps took him to the edge of the pool and he peered down. 'I hadn't primed it! he said. His voice rose another semitone. 'You threw it in the water! Look! It's sinking all the way down.'

I took him at his word, and looked into the pool. 'You're right,' I said. 'At any rate, it's not sinking *up*.'

'You threw it in!'

'You said it was waterpoof.'

'But I hadn't *primed* it!' Trofim's capacity for petulance, like his musculature, was larger than a normal person's. 'I hadn't primed it! It's ruined now! How can I prime it now? You've ruined everything!'

'Look on the bright side,' I said. 'It wasn't your fault. If you take me back to Moscow you can put the blame on me.'

'We've got to retrieve it! We have to fish it up!'

'The best thing would be to go down like a pearl diver. Give me the gun and take your jacket off.' He looked towards me, and there was something almost heartbreaking in the way hope flickered in his eyes, for the second or so before he thought better of himself. His eyes narrowed. 'You're trying to trick me.'

'You're right,' I said. 'It must be thirty metres deep, that pool. You probably wouldn't be able to hold your breath under water for long enough.'

'You go!' He brought the gun closer to my face.

'Well I *certainly* couldn't hold my breath. You know how poorly my lungs function.'

A sly look, or what approximated one for Trofim, crept into his features. 'Aha,' he said. 'You're trying to trick me again, but I'm wise to you! *Your* lungs don't work *anyway*! You could go under the water without ill effects.'

I looked steadily at him. 'Could you explain your logic?'

'My what?'

'Your logic. The logic of that statement.'

'The logic is,' he said, 'that, and there is logic. It is *logically* the situation that since your lungs don't work in air, you won't need them under the—' He looked at me. 'Under the, um.'

'When you describe this as *logic* ...' I said.

His eyes defocused momentarily; but he snapped back. '*This* is my logic!' he cried, brandishing the gun.

'And it is a very persuasive argumentative tool,' I agreed. 'But it won't make my lungs work under water.'

Something gave way in his will. His shoulders sagged. His voice, when he spoke, was almost imploring. 'What am I suppose to do now?'

'Why don't the two of us get out of here?' I said. 'Go find a bar and discuss that important question over a drink?'

'Oh no,' he said. 'I can't leave. The mission. You were in the army, after all. You know the importance of orders. You understand the importance of completing your mission.'

'Having been in the army,' I said, 'I know how often commanding officers send honest soldiers to their deaths for no very good reason.'

But this didn't hit home. 'Comrade Frenkel is a great man,' he told me, stiffly. 'This mission is of the utmost importance for the continuing success and survival of, *survival* of, the Soviet Union.'

'I'd say the Soviet Union needs good men like you alive,' I said. 'I'd say you can serve the Soviet Union better alive than you could as a corpse.'

'I could at least shoot you,' he said, in a meditative voice.

'I'll wager those aren't your specific orders.'

'Oh no. I don't have any specific orders with respect of you. I don't believe Comrade Frenkel expected you to be here.'

'Well there you go.'

'But he's keen on his men showing initiative,' Trofim added, aiming the handgun at my head. His brow creased once again, and the redness rose once again in his cheeks. 'I wish you hadn't thrown the suitcase into the pool!'

'What can I say? I'm an impulsive man.'

He remembered then that he was holding the grenade. 'I could pull the pin,' he said, holding it up between us. 'And throw *this* in the water. It would sink down, wouldn't it. Plus, I'd have time to get out of this chamber, at any rate.'

'Come come, comrade,' I said. 'This is a nuclear power station. You are trying to *blow up* a nuclear power station. Or have you forgotten? You think a seven-second grenade fuse gives you enough time to outrun a nuclear explosion?'

Two fat worry lines wormed into the flesh of his brow. 'You're right of course,' he said, in a gloomy tone. 'Well, there's nothing for it then.' He aimed the gun again at the centre of my brow.

'Comrade,' I said. 'Think what you're planning! To blow up this power station – it would be like dropping an atomic bomb on the heart of the Ukraine! Have you any idea how many would die? Do you really want their deaths on your conscience?'

But this, I realised at once, was the wrong tack to take. The worry lines disappeared from Trofim's brow, and a rather vulgarly calculating expression passed across his eyes. 'But, comrade,' he said, 'Didn't you yourself fight in the Great Patriotic War? How many millions died then, defending Russia? How many is too many? Some thousands may perish in Ukraine, but they will be sacrificing their lives for a greater purpose.'

I felt my temper begin to stretch. Clearly the thing to do at that time, in that place, was to try and talk Trofim round; get him to holster his gun and put the grenade down. To persuade him to leave. Who better to do this than a man who has spent years as a writer honing his powers of expression? But I had had a long day. 'Oh, don't be idiotic,' I snapped. '*Purpose?* What plan could possibly justify such sacrifice of life?'

He looked almost gloating. 'It's secret.'

'So? You're going to kill me anyway!'

'Yes,' he agreed, slowly, as if the reality of the situation were only then dawning on him. 'I suppose I am going to kill you.' My stomach swirled.

'So, why not tell me?'

'Oh no,' he said, ingenuously. 'I was ordered to tell nobody.'

'Comrade, permit me to say, I believe you *will* tell me. What harm can there be in talking to a dead man? Dead men keep secrets better than anybody.'

'Orders.'

'You'd send me to my grave without knowing?'

This clearly troubled him. 'I do apologise, comrade. But there's really nothing I can say.'

I had to keep him talking. Perhaps, I thought to myself, Saltykov will come back in, creep up behind him and disarm him. I didn't want to dwell on the details of how he would do this: Saltykov's weakling-buffoonishness tangling with this slab of honed military flesh. If I had tried to picture the details to myself its impossibility would have impressed itself upon my mind and scorched my hope. But I wanted to hang on to the possibility. 'I shall try and reason with you, comrade,' I said, 'as one old soldier to another. Things have very clearly not gone according to plan for you, here in Chernobyl. You will have to explain to your superiors why you failed to complete your mission. Take me back to Moscow, and I will support your story. Any story you care to concoct. I am a writer after all, and good at concocting stories.'

'Stories of monstrous octocats from space,' he said, in an enormously mournful voice.

'Science fiction is the literature of the future,' I said, scratching through my brain to recall some of the vatic emptinesses of Frenkel's pronouncements on the genre. 'Science fiction *imagines* the future. It seeks not to reproduce the world, as have all hitherto existing literatures, but to *change* it. It is the Communism of literary forms. It is the literature of proletarian possibilities.'

'I am truly sorry, comrade,' he said. 'But I cannot report failure of the mission to Moscow. I must detonate the grenade.'

'Even though it will kill you.'

'It will kill you also.'

'That,' I said, 'is also an important consideration.'

'My father,' said Trofim, standing straighter as he gave vent to this small confession, 'was a soldier. He died of cancer. He said, in

195

hospital, that he wished he'd died on the battlefield. He said that dying on the battlefield was better than dying in hospital. If I have to choose, I know which one I prefer.'

'You omit the third option, which is not to die at all.'

'To complete the mission,' he said, holding out the grenade.

'Think, Trofim! You want to turn this premier nuclear facility into a radioactive crater? Think of the hundreds of thousands you will slaughter! Children – women—'

Then Trofim said the most extraordinary thing I ever heard him utter. In a clear voice, as if reciting sacred text, he said, 'We are not alone in the universe, comrade.'

It took me a moment to gather enough of my wits even to reply. 'What?'

'There are higher intelligences guiding what we do here.'

'What are you talking about?'

'Comrade, they are *radiation* aliens. If I detonate this grenade, and explode this nuclear pile, I will transform my grossly material consciousness into pure radiation.'

'No you won't,' I said.

'Yes, I will.'

'Seriously, Trofim, you won't.'

'Yes,' he repeated, articulating a credo too grounded in faith to be challenged, 'I will. My consciousness will move to a higher dimension.'

'Trofim, you don't sound like yourself.'

'It will not be death. I will be translated into a realm of pure energy. This blast will propel me, and I will face our sponsors face to face.'

I considered this, and tried to formulate the most trenchant criticism. There had to be a way I could make Trofim see its lunacy; some form of words that would persuade him. In the end I opted for, 'No you won't.'

'Yes I will.'

'Translated into pure radiation? Meeting radiation aliens? This won't happen.'

'Yes it will.'

'No it won't.'

'Yes it will.'

'No it *won't.*'

'Yes it will.'

'It *will not.*'

'Yes it will.'

This argumentative strategy was not having the desired result. I tried a different tack. 'If you explode the grenade, all that will happen is that you will exterminate your consciousness, and mine.'

'No I won't,' he said.

'You'll die.'

'No I won't.'

'Yes you *will.*'

'No I won't.'

'Yes *you will*!'

'I shall meet the radiation aliens,' he said, firmly.

'Comrade,' I said. 'Listen to me carefully. The radiation aliens – I *made them up*. Me! You're talking to their creator. Comrade Frenkel and I, and a gaggle of other science fiction writers, back in the 1940s. We *wrote* them.'

He was looking at, but not seeing, me. 'Comrade Frenkel ...'

'Comrade Frenkel has his own reasons for wanting to pretend this absurd narrative is real. But it is *not* real. Please do not *believe in* my ridiculous science fiction! I do not write science fiction for you to *believe in it*! For God's sake! For the sake of the Mekon himself – don't! None of us really understood what radiation even *was*, back then! It was all rumour, and conjecture, and wild stories about the American attack on Hiroshima. We didn't know! If you pull that pin, you won't be translating yourself into a higher consciousness; you'll be blasting yourself into sand and ash and scattering yourself in fine grained, radioactive form across the whole east of Europe.'

'Comrade Frenkel told me,' said Trofim, with a stubbornness

that was not aggressive, since it inhered simply, we might even say *purely*, in the very limitations of his own mind, 'told me that you were a slippery fish. A slippery fish, he called you.'

'You *can't* believe all this UFO mumbo-jumbo?'

'Of course!' he said.

'You've been brainwashed,' I told him. 'You've joined a cult.'

'Religion,' he said, as if considering the concept.

'Marx called religion the opium of the people,' I said, angrily. 'But at least opium is a high-class drug. UFO religion? That's the *methylated spirits* of the people. It's the home-still *beetroot-alcohol* of the people.' I was furious, of course, because I knew I had failed. This had been my chance to talk Trofim round – poor, dumbheaded Trofim. This had been my moment to overpower him with my superior wits, just as he would (given the chance) have overpowered me with his superior muscles. But if my supposed skill with words was not sufficient even to persuade an individual like Trofim, then what good was I? In retrospect I wonder if I wasn't being unfair to myself. It is of course easier to fool an intelligent man than a stupid one, for the intelligent man is in the habit of shifting his thoughts around and around, where the stupid one more often than not has fastened onto a single notion like a swimmer clinging to the raft that will keep him afloat. In retrospect, I suppose I could never have persuaded Trofim of the idiocy of believing that the middle of an atomic blast was the gateway to a higher mode of existence.

I fumbled in my jacket pocket and located a cigarette. It was, I knew, the last cigarette I would ever smoke – and so it proved.

'What are you doing?' said Trofim.

'I'm smoking my last cigarette,' I said, snapping back the metal lid of lighter and manoeuvring its knob of flame onto the end of the white tube. 'The last cigarette,' I added, 'that I shall ever smoke.' Sucking the smoke into my chest added a tincture of calm to the rattled choler of my body. My stress unnotched itself one belthole. I breathed out, lengthily.

'I believe that smoking is not permitted in here, comrade.'

'By all means,' I said, 'fetch a supervisor and report me.'

He stared at me. 'Smoking is very bad for your health,' he said.

'So is being caught at the exact heart of a nuclear conflagration.'

'Comrade,' he said mournfully, 'please do not be sarcastic.' There was a popping noise: Trofim was tutting. That would be like him – to tut me like a disappointed schoolmaster.

'I'll make you a deal,' I replied. 'I will abjure sarcasm for the remainder of my earthly existence, if *you* agree not to pull the pin on your grenade.'

'It's too late.'

I breathed in another long draw on my cigarette. Despite the absurd situation in which I found myself, relaxation was starting to spread through my muscles. 'This alien realm to which you will be transported. Will I get there too? Or will I be blasted to material atoms, even as you translate into radiation consciousness?'

'You don't understand, comrade,' he said.

'I'm trying to understand.'

'You don't *believe*.'

'Comrade Trofim,' I said, turning away from him to face the pool, 'if you pull that pin, then I shall lose all respect for you.'

'I have already pulled the pin, comrade,' he said, in a wavery voice.

That was what the popping sound had been. The fuse had been ticking down all those long seconds of chatter. I had, perhaps, a single second remaining of earthly life.

It seems very strange to me, looking back at that mortal portion of my existence, to think that I could, standing as I was on the very lip of eternity, give myself over to petty annoyance. But mortal humanity cannot ever *prepare* itself for death, for the very good reason that we can only prepare for events with which we are familiar, or which we can comprehend, and our own death is neither of these things. Until we are dead we will stubbornly believe, in some corner of our consciousness, that we will continue living; and once we are dead it is, naturally, too late to believe anything at all. As the mechanical fuse marked off the last remaining second of my life I was aware, of course, that I had failed. I found it was possible to bring all my consciousness into the focal point of the cigarette at my mouth. I drew a very last lungful of smoke. Of all the cigarettes I had smoked before, this may have been the most simply pleasurable. Previously I had either *been aware* that I was smoking, an awareness tinged necessarily with guilt at the harmful effects the foul stuff was having upon me, or else I had smoked from automatic, unconscious habit, as I concentrated upon something else, in which case I was hardly aware that I was smoking at all. But for that one perfect moment, on the edge of death, I could suck the tobacco into my lungs knowing that, since I was dying anyway, *it* could do me no harm. I began to breathe out a tentacle of smoke, and with the smoke blew away all my anger. It felt like a lifetime's anger. And, in that perfect moment, two thoughts occurred to me. One was the purest optimism, and it was this: *The grenade may be a dud.* The other, which seemed to spool naturally from that first, was: *I shall ask him simply to replace the pin, and he will do this.* As to why I believed I would be able to persuade Trofim to do this, I'm not sure. It came into my head as clearly, and purely, as a revelation. It was all I needed to do. I started to turn my head, saying, 'Com—'

I heard just the start of a roar; no more than a split second before it vanished entirely from my sensorium, or else before my sensorium vanished entirely. The material solidity of the space we were in was deconstructed and reconstructed as light, clear and bright and warm, alive and bright and warm. It was *pure* light. I did not have time to think, *the grenade has detonated, Chernobyl has exploded* – I did not, then, have time to think anything at all because there *was* no time at all. Time had evaporated. Instead of time there was the experience, filtered as if through memory, of white light and white heat, the rushing and beating upon me of great waves, monumental tides, of white light and white heat. A process of replacing every single one of the carbon atoms in my body with photons; and a reverberating pulse that swarmed upon the net of my nerves.

When I was a child, I had believed that death was a red-haired man.

Out of perfect whiteness and the perfection of the light a single point of sensual connection began to coalesce; one unsullied, soprano musical note, a musical note as pure as mathematics, like an angel singing, a spirit-entity heralding my arrival in a new place.

PART THREE

'Жить стало лучше, товарищи. Жить стало веселее.'

'[Life has got better, comrades! Life has become more joyful!]'

Stalin, speech to the Stakhanovites' conference,
17 November 1935

The clarity of this sustained, pure musical note was beautiful. Then it was insistent. Presently it became annoying.

I had been annoyed for much of my life. It occurred to me it made sense I would translate into the afterlife in the same state of mind.

'Have you never wondered,' somebody asked me, 'why tinnitus manifests as a *musical* note in that manner?'

'I have never wondered that,' I said. 'It has never occurred to me.' I wasn't speaking. The other voice wasn't speaking. This was a new mode of existence, a new form of communication. Thought to thought. I had been translated into pure radiation.

'It is, in effect, a malfunction of the inner ear,' said my interlocutor.

I was in a new sort of space. An endlessly busy hurricane of light, with roaring, and then the roaring abruptly stopped. White, or bright whiteness speckled with a billion scuffs of bright grey. The musical note emerged from it, as pure as before. As pure as before. The violin sound had modulated, surfed a sinewave, intensifying and shrinking alternately. Like a squeaky wheel turning over and over.

It was a bird, singing in amongst the foliage.

*

Yes, there was foliage. It was like a poem by Fet. I walked through the light and it gradually coalesced into strands beneath my walking feet. The strands were bronze-coloured, not white, and then darker-coloured, and clearly it was grass. Strolling over grass, a slight upward incline, a long July hill leading up into brightness. 'And now I shall meet the radiation aliens,' I thought to myself. 'I, who doubted their existence for so long!'

The upward slope of the hill invited me to keep walking. It was a peaceful rhythm, heatbeatlike; and it seemed to involve no physical effort. That was my first intimation that things were different. The sky above me was an intense yet milky blue, very bright, very *right*, and it did not hurt my eyes. The grass beneath my feet was the beer-coloured, though dry, central Russian summer pasture. The stems of the grass were soft as strands of hair. They reached to my ankles. It was an intensely pleasurable experience to walk through it.

I was coming up, in a leisurely way, to a dacha: exactly the same as the dacha in which I had spent those weeks, immediately after the war, with Sergei Rapoport, Adam Kaganovich, Nikolai Asterinov and the other person, whose name I could not then remember. But it was not exactly the same for, hovering above the low roof, very clearly visible against the bright sky, were two mighty letters:

SF

Science Fiction, of course! How tremendously, how *deeply* exciting! At last I understood. I was approaching the mansion of science fiction itself. The radiation aliens, who had received my energetic engram (or whatever had happened to me inside the reactor) were now bringing me, in a profound sense, *home*. Naturally, I grasped the rightness of this. It had been in an earthly manifestation of this house that we, the writers of Soviet science fiction, had concocted the aliens in the first place. And the aliens had turned out to be *real*! We had channelled, without realising it, the true nature of the cosmos. We had articulated actuality and we had thought we had

206

been writing fiction. We were hierophants of a hidden futurity, the pens that scribbled what they understood not. But in death – in *my* death – I had finally understood. The American, Coyne, *had indeed* been snatched up by aliens. There had been no rope. The rope had been a figment of my imagination, my way of rationalising the tractoring-beam of alien technology. My scepticism had corrupted my own experience, for the aliens were real. Trofim had not been babbling when he talked of them. And *here* they were! In this house! And I had invented them, or rather they had invented me. That last phrase made a trembly, hair-tickling, heart-thumping sense. They had written *me*, as I had written *them*. I had never stopped being a writer of science fiction, and the paradox of the phrase is that science fiction is living fact.

I quickened my pace. Naturally I was eager finally to meet the aliens, for I believed they would explain everything to me. The snake bites its own tail.

My excitement was such that it took me a moment to comprehend that there was something wrong with the floating signifier, the two holographic letters hovering over the roof of the dacha. I looked again, and saw that the S was twisted about. Something was wrong with it. It was proclaiming not SF, not exactly. I looked again.

ZF

It was no Z; the S was the wrong way about. This was a puzzle. Of course, I was looking at Cyrillic, not Latin, characters: which is to say, the 'S' was a C and it was the C that was mirror-written. The F (which is to say, the ф) was not inverted. It was the correct way about. Why would one letter be reversed and the other not? My brain buzzed, and lurched. Then it occurred to me that one property of the character ф is its mirror-symmetry, such that it looks the same from front as from back. From here, but slowly, as the most obvious things sometimes do occur, I reasoned that I was looking not at SF, but at FS *from behind.*

So I was coming up towards the back of the dacha – and indeed I was, because I recognised the slope, and the broad windows of the back room in which we had sat and talked decades before. Yet this was a puzzlement, because I could not understand what FS abbreviated. But I was at the house now, very conscious of the fact that I had believed myself to be approaching from the front. This unnerved me. Nobody wants to sneak up the back route when they can march proudly up the front. I hurried along the side of the building, a huge beige rectangle with two blank windows like eyeholes in a robot skull, and I kept glancing upwards as I jogged so as not to lose sight of the gleaming letters. It was clearer now. The building was labelled not SF but the reverse:

ф С

And then, with a second sense of foolishness at being so slow to realise, I saw that there were more than two letters. There were two *strings* of letters. Not individual signifiers, but strands like DNA encoding a more profound mystery. It was that I had not seen the other letters until I came round the front. But now I could see that the F was the end of one word, and the S the beginning of another. I was a little breathless now, and panting, an intimation that I had translated *some* of my earthly limitations into this new mode of existence – my shortness of breath, for example – and I stopped, gazing upwards, to get a good view of the legend. It was written in bold and unmistakable letters. I could not understand how I had not seen it fully before: shining script, each letter a metre high:

Иосиф Сталин

And from looking up I looked down, and he was there, standing on the porch. He was beaming at me. He was the most distinctive-looking human being I think I have ever laid eyes upon. Of course he was here, in this place. 'Josef Stalin,' I gasped, hurrying forward. 'Josef Stalin.'

'Comrade Skvorecky,' he boomed. 'Come up here! Come up to the porch! Let us *talk*!'

I was in my twenties again, and as nervy and callow as ever I had been in that decade. 'To find *you* here, comrade!' I kept babbling. 'To find you *here*!'

'You are surprised?'

But, as he asked that question, I realised I was not surprised. Surprise did not describe my state of mind. I apprehended inevitability as, itself, an emotion. Of *course* I would meet Stalin. Had I ever believed that Death had red hair? Death was not a red-haired man. Here I was.

He led me through the main door. The hallway inside was exactly as I remembered it. We went through to the back room: there were the broad windows, and their view over the rain-washed green of Russian hills.

'I am not surprised, comrade,' I said, bravely. 'I take it I am not alive any more?'

'Consider,' said Stalin, settling himself into a chair. I looked around: we two were in the familiar old room of the dacha. There was the same photo on the wall, although this time Stalin was surrounded not by Molotov, Mikoyan, Kalinin but by Rapoport, Kaganovich, Asterinov and myself. I was there in the photograph, scowling my twenty-eight-year-old scowl, and all the others were grinning. I thought: At least I am alive with my scowl. Much good their grins will do them now they're all of them dead. But then I realised I was dead too, scowl and all. Everything had changed.

Stalin sat there, looking up at me.

'Consider,' he said, lighting a cigarette and puffing it contentedly. 'You were inside the main reactor room of a nuclear reactor. You stood in that place at the precise moment it exploded. Do you think you could survive such a blast?'

'No.'

'Ah! But it was no *ordinary* blast! It is one thing to be blown up by high explosive, and quite *another* to be blown up by *radiation*. As the citizens of Hiroshima discovered! Radiation!' He beamed, and the strands of his moustache spread minutely. I fancied I could almost hear them rustling.

There were seats on the far side of the room. I picked my way over the bare boards of the floor and sat down. But I had no cigarettes. I was aware that I had smoked my last cigarette. I had stood inside the reactor building and smoked my last ever cigarette. That was all over, now.

'Radiation?' I said.

'Radiation,' he confirmed.

'Let me put it this way,' I offered, trying to master my sense of over-awe. 'For a long time I disbelieved the existence of alien beings, these creatures – you – from another star. I accepted that other people *did* believe. I simply did not share their belief. But is it the case that . . . I am now meeting the aliens?'

Stalin's face was capable of great sternness, but also of great benevolence. Such a warm and wide smile!

'Might it be,' I said, 'that I am not encountering you as you really *are*? Perhaps you are assuming a human shape, to facilitate interaction between us? You have been into my mind and pulled out this memory.' I cast my arms around. 'This memory of me being in this dacha. Of me meeting the original Stalin. Using that memory you have built this imagined space, in which you and I can talk. But you are not *truly* Stalin.'

'I am truly Stalin,' he said, his smile broadening further.

'But as a radiation alien,' I suggested, 'surely you do not naturally possess corporeal form? Surely not.'

'And what do you know about the radiation aliens?' Stalin asked me.

'I thought I knew,' I said. 'I thought I'd written you. I thought I had created you.'

'A common human mistake. You think yourselves Frankensteins, to have made monsters. But the monsters were always there. It was never needful for you to create them.'

'I did not think I had done it alone,' I said, nodding at the photograph.

'You *could not* have done it alone.'

'So it's not that we wrote you – is it that you somehow shaped *us*?'

Stalin puffed his cigarette. Light from the uncurtained windows made beauty in the unfolding curves and curls, shells and eels of smoke.

'Consider,' he said again. 'What is radiation? It is light. Does light not hurt us? Have you never been *sunburnt*, comrade?'

'Sunburn,' I repeated.

'Many people believe that aliens lurk in the shadows, hide away. That they only emerge at night, like vampires.' He chuckled. 'No! No! Aliens come from the stars, not from the darkness between the stars. We come precisely *out of the light*. It is simply our brilliance that is harmful to you. That's all. And who has been more harmful than I?'

'The malign star shining down upon us,' I said. 'The star worm-wood, the Chernobyl.'

'I was in full view! All the time! In the *centre* of the brightly lit stage. And look at you, with your burnt face!'

I put my hands to my face: I was no longer in my twenties. The skin had been scorched by age, and vodka, and tobacco, and above all scorched by—

He could, of course, read my mind.

'By light!' he said. 'Your face was scorched by *light*!'

'Light altered my form,' I said, running a finger over the thickened tab of scar tissue over the end of my nose.

'So.' Stalin gestured at himself, at his stocky, barrelled torso. 'Human form? Look at me. Remember what I did. Was I ever *human*?'

'You were inhuman,' I said, with a sense of dawning comprehension.

'Exactly so! I was *always* the alien. Always – it was always there. I fought the Nazis and killed a million of them, soldiers and civilians. Why did I fight the Nazis? To protect the Russian people?' Every time he made his expressive gesture with his right hand, a comet-tail of smoke trailed from the blood-red gleam at the tip of his cigarette, weaving a back-and-forth folding of silver-blue in the air. 'To protect the *Russian* people? But in 1933, and in 1934, when the people were starving, I confiscated their grain. How many millions died? Ten million? Try to *imagine* that number of people.'

'I cannot.'

'I can, because my mind does not work as yours does. I can imagine that number alive, and I can imagine that number dead, and the latter pleases me more. Do H. G. Wells's Martians joy in the destruction they cause humanity? Of course they do.'

'It's not as if you descended in metallic craft . . .' I began.

'What form of life am I?' Stalin demanded. 'Did I hide it? Did I ever *pretend* humanity? My name is steel, not flesh. Steel-built Joe.' And as I looked, I noticed, again belatedly, with a sense of my foolishness in not having noticed it before, that his flesh was harder and less yielding than ordinary flesh. 'I, robot Josef.' He chuckled. 'Did I ever show the *weaknesses* of flesh?'

I remembered what I had read of Stalin's youth. 'Your father beat you.'

He acknowledged this with a dismissive tilt of his head. 'He beat me because he was a drunk. He was angry with me, and with my mother, because I was not his natural child. My mother was promiscuous. My father knew me to be a bastard. People speculated as to who my actual father was: the merchant Yakov Egnatashvilli – a wrestling champion, no less! A strong and handsome man, that merchant. Or the priest, Father Christopher Charkviani. A police-man called Damian Davrichewy. All these names. Nobody realised who my actual father was because they were not looking in the correct place.'

'Where should we have been looking?'

'I ordered a million people to be shot during the Great Purge of the 1930s. Half a million died during forced resettlement. Two million died in the Gulags. I did all this. You need to ask yourself simply one thing. Is this what a *human being* would do?'

'In an important sense,' I agreed, 'no.'

'I did it all in plain sight. I did not hide. I came to the Soviet Union, an alien from a hostile world, and did as much damage as I could. Such was my mission. I was born December 1878. Do you know what was happening throughout 1878?'

'I would assume many things.'

He laughed like a blunderbuss. 'Of course many things! But I mean one thing in particular. X-rays. They called it cathode radiation, in those days. It had been discovered in 1876, and by 1877 and 1878 every scientist and physicist in Europe and Russia was building the equipment, firing out the rays, irradiating animals, people, objects, wild and promiscuous experiments – it was everywhere. There was a large laboratory at Gori, in Georgia. But there were such laboratories all over Europe. Think of that! Think of the *consequences* of that!'

I shook my head. There was a crudeness, a kind of pulp aesthetic, about this. 'But you weren't literally made of steel,' I said, haltingly. 'You were not actually ...' I imagined him replying: *And who got close enough to me to know?* But he wasn't speaking. He wasn't interested in my questions.

'The thing,' he said, 'that puzzles our souls about radiation poisoning is the way the very word contradicts its message. We are habituated to think of poison as a product of *darkness*, of dirt and putrescence, of secrecy and shadows. But radiation is a form of *light*, and it is hard for us to think of light as poison. Light can blind, of course; and it can of course burn; we *know* that. We comprehend that. It correlates to our sense of its essence. But *poison us*? What is more alarming than the thought that poison can *radiate*?'

'I don't understand.'

'Has there ever been a being like me? Before, in human history?'

'Adolf Hitler?'

'Oh, *him*?' He looked away. 'I'll tell you.' He leant forward. His cigarette was still threading the air with a silk-line of smoke. Either he had lit a new one, or he had somehow made the first one last a surprisingly long time. 'I'll tell you. Hitler was a human tyrant. He murdered millions, but he murdered those he considered *other*. He had his tribe, these Aryan humans, and he directed his destructiveness against other varieties of humanity. That's what human beings have done for hundreds of thousands of years. Hitler's particular distinction is to have effected destruction on a very large scale, and for that we have to thank the rapid advances of industrialisation. Me, however? I did not limit myself to a particular group, or scapegoat-crowd, or others. I waged war on the whole of humanity. I killed non-Russians. I killed Russians. I killed my opponents and my supporters. I killed Jews, Aryans, Slavs, black, white and yellow. I killed men, and I killed women. I killed my own army – in many of my battles I executed more of my troops than were killed by the enemy! I killed members of my own family. I killed my friends, my enemies, my political allies, my political opponents, my doctors, my generals, my party members. I used to send orders to Soviet cities that would read: *Draw up a list of a thousand names – exactly a thousand – and execute them all.*' He beamed at me. I peered at him more closely, as if for the first time. His moustache looked lacquered. His hair had the appearance of a single solid shape, like something carved from liquorish. He was a metal frame, with a plastic outer skin. He was an android, and yet we had not noticed it. His eyes twinkled – that kindly-old-uncle twinkle of his eyes. He had the look of a skilful and detailed *copy* of a human. He did not look like a human. He was not even made out of flesh. He was, of course, made of metal: polished, shaped, expertly fitted: and the very fronds of his moustache were wires of ore, and his skin was burnished. Steel-fashioned. SF.

All I could think was: how had I not noticed it before?

He could read my thoughts: 'You did not think of it. Nobody thought of it, I know, but you have less excuse than the others. You! A science fiction writer! Only consider: to invade a planet? A whole planet? To lay it waste – to devastate its population? H. G. Wells thought you needed armies of robot tripods and deathrays; that you needed to set your weaponry against the weaponry of the aborigines. But you don't need that. You can set *your enemy* against your enemy. You can infiltrate your enemy and set them bickering amongst themselves. What else has this century been, but humans striving with humans to destroy the world? What could give greater comfort to *us*?'

I could, perhaps, have asked: Who are you? Where are you from? Why are you so hostile? I could have asked: What is your civilization, your culture, your history? I could have asked: Are there others like you? Are all alien lifeforms manifestations of radiation, or are there corporeal beings out there too, like us? But I didn't ask any of this. Instead I asked: 'How were we able to write you?'

'You?'

'We science fiction writers. How did we *know*? Did we ... channel you?'

For the first time a wrinkle appeared in the taut, plump skin of Comrade Stalin's face; a wrinkle beside his left eye. 'Channel?'

'Did you infect our minds? Were you inside our heads? Is that what happened? Why did you inspire us to *write* you?'

'I think you have it the wrong way round,' said Stalin, yawning. 'You wrote *us*? I think you have misunderstood. All human conceptions are on the scale of the planet. They are based on the pretension that the technical potential, though it will develop, will never exceed the terrestrial limit. But if we succeed in establishing interplanetary communications, all our philosophies, moral and social views, will have to be revised. In this case the technical potential, become limitless, will impose the end of the role of violence as a means and method of progress.'

These words sounded familiar to me, but I could not place them.

Like summer clouds drawing away from the sun, light intensified in the tall panes of glass. It washed clean and perfect and blinding into the room. Light is a form of radiation.

*

You have a *duty* to make me understand, I said. Or if I did not say these words then I thought them. One of the two.

'It is a question of reality,' Stalin was saying, out of the light. It was all light now; I couldn't see anything else. 'Let's say we're here, all around you, and yet you cannot see us. Why might that be?' And then again: 'Some of you see us. We have been processing you, in ones and twos, for many years: it is millions now. Yet you are not sure it is actually happening, and even *they* are not sure, oftentimes. How can that be? *What* kind of radiation are we talking about?'

This seemed to me, then, to be a profound question. What kind of radiation *are* we talking about?

'Its not that we're one thing, and *then* another. That's why you find us so hard to see. It is as if you were to look at a frog and say: So, what are you? Are you a fish? Or a rabbit? It is as if you were to say: I can only *see you* if you are a rabbit, or a frog. I cannot see you otherwise.'

I couldn't see anything because it was so bright. Or perhaps I couldn't see anything because it was so *dark*. It was dark, and it was light, at the same time. Or, it was some third thing. What kind of radiation are we talking about?

I thought: If I am back in the dacha, and it is immediately after the war, then Frenkel must be here as well, somewhere. Where is he?

I could see Stalin again, surrounded by brightness.

'What kind of radiation are we *talking* about?' he beamed. The individual hairs of his moustache moved, as stems of grass move when the wind is on them.

And he stopped. A switch had been thrown, somewhere. A cord had been yanked from its socket. He stopped, like a manikin denied power.

He stopped.

A flashbulb moment, endlessly prolonged. Then it snapped off, and shrank away, as if I were rushing backwards away from a star and it was dwindling to a white globe, a circle, a dot, a point.

Don't you know who I am?

A different question. This last in a woman's voice.

The light had swallowed itself into a TV-dot, centred in blackness. Everything was black except for this dot. The dot held steady, bright. Then the dot moved, shining to the left, and to the right. It was shining in my left eye. 'Do you know who I am?' It was shining in my right eye.

'Josef,' I said. 'Josef.'

'Who is Josef?' This voice was a child's.

'Joe, SF,' I said. 'Sf, sff, ssff.'

'Hold still.' A child's voice, or a woman's.

'Joe-s-f Vissarionovich Stalin,' I said, with a great effort, as if forcing something from my chest.

'You are mistaken,' said the voice.

Then came the god Hypnos. You know him as Sleep. He came with skin as grey as exhaustion, and huge black slumbrous eyes, almond-shaped and ink-black, and he was the size of a child, because children sleep much more than adults, sleep being the proper realm of children, and so of course Hypnos is child-like. The proper realm. He flew through the air, as Hypnos may, and clutched about my head and my neck with elongated fingers. I wanted to ask him: but am I dead? Am I truly dead, or am I only transformed into an existence of pure radiation? But all he whispered, insistently, like a heartbeat – exactly like a heartbeat, with the thrum of the muscle and the afterhiss of blood slipping silkily along the arteries – was: Joe SF. Joe SF. Joe SF.

PART FOUR

'In many heads everything has become confused.'

Aleksandr Gelman, addressing the party assembly of the board of the
Russian Union of Cinematographers, 1986

'The main thing needed now is work, work, work.'

Mikhail Gorbachev in Khabarovsk, 1986

'Doctor Bello,' she said, again.

I was lying on my back.

This was a new voice. I had not heard this voice before, or I had. Either I had heard this voice before or I had not, or there was a third option.

'Doctor Bello,' she said again.

I contemplated this name for a long time. It seemed to have some mystery attached to it.

'Can you speak?'

'Of course,' I said. It was my voice. It was a little croaky, but it was perfectly functional. I was dead, or. I was either dead or I was alive or there was some third option.

I had no idea who I was. I could not think what my name might be, where I was lying, what had happened to me, or anything like that. The most I could remember was meeting Josef Stalin. But I had only the vaguest memories of what he had said to me. But – had I not *actually* met Stalin, once upon a time?

I was lying on my back, and I was lying in bed. Lying on and in at the same time. I was not at the dacha at all. Stalin was not there. I was in a hospital room. Dr Bello was a doctor, and she was standing beside the bed.

The quality of light was completely different in this place. It was subdued, filtered, and ordinary. Bearable, I thought. Light was coming through the window over in the far wall.

'Have you ever heard of Egas Monis?' the doctor asked me.

'It is a place on Mars,' I said, raspily, but with confidence.

'No, no. It is the name of a human being.'

'Is he a science fiction writer?' I asked. 'I believe I have heard of his name, and it is the name of a science fiction writer.'

'He won the Nobel prize.'

'Well then he cannot be a science fiction writer. No writer of science fiction would be awarded such a prize.'

'His was a prize for medicine. He was awarded it in 1949 for his work with the surgical operation called *pre-frontal lobotomy*. Why would you think he wrote science fiction? Why would you think such a thing?'

I considered this. 'Perhaps,' I answered, upping something from deep memory, 'because I am *myself* a science fiction writer?' Retrieving this was like pulling through my gullet and out of my throat a long piece of string I had, for some reason, swallowed. It was not, that is to say, pleasant.

'Really? How very interesting.'

'Do you read science fiction?'

'Not at all. Not ever. Science fiction is for adolescent boys and people who make models of aircraft from plastic and glue. I am a mature woman, which is to say, the opposite of a science fiction fan.' She considered for a bit. 'You science fiction writers write about the future, don't you?'

'Sometimes.'

'That may be a problem.'

'In what way?'

'What I mean is this: you may find it harder conceptualising the future in, ah, the future. Can you write about something else? The present, say? The past?'

'I could try.'

'That might be a good idea. One of the things Egas Monis discovered is that the frontal lobes of the brain are where we imagine the future. Where we plan and project ourselves imaginatively forward in time. Because the future makes some people anxious – what might happen, and so on – Monis discovered that destroying portions of this lobe reduced people's levels of anxiety. Do you feel anxious?'

'No.' And I really didn't.

'That's good.'

'Are you saying that you have performed a pre-frontal lobotomy upon me, Doctor?'

'*I* have not. Although such an operation, if it is going to take place, really *should* be performed by a medically trained professional.'

The curiosity I felt on this matter was of a generalised, rather pleasant sort. There was no urgency in it. 'Has some other doctor lobotomisied me?'

'As to the medical expertise of Leo Alexeivich Trofim, I cannot say.'

My memories of Trofim were bright and immediate. I knew who *he* was. 'Trofim! – I never knew his first name before! He is a Leo, is he? Like Tolstoy! For some reason that pleases me.'

'As your doctor I am pleased to see you pleased. You will recover more quickly if you have a positive mental attitude.'

'Is Trofim here?'

'He is not far from here. Although he is no longer in a state of coherent bodily assemblage.'

'Where is here?'

'Kiev.'

'In the Ukraine?'

'Is there another Kiev?'

'I mean: the Ukraine on the planet Earth?'

There was a few seconds' silence. 'As your doctor,' she repeated, shortly, 'I am pleased that you have not lost your sense of humour. A sense of humour will be helpful to you as you convalesce.'

'I meant the question,' I said, feeling momentarily confused, 'seriously.'

'Seriously has a different interpretation in the realm of science fiction, perhaps.'

There was a sort of mental spasm, another memorial regurgitation inside my brain, like a mamma seagull splurting half-digested fish through her beak for her young. 'I was in the Chernobyl nuclear facility,' I said.

'Reactor Four,' she said.

'The reactor exploded,' I said.

'Certainly not,' she said. 'Unless *the reactor* is your nickname for your young friend. He certainly was, according to the autopsy reports, a well-built individual.'

'Chernobyl is still intact?'

'It is generating the electricity that powers this hospital,' she said. 'So we must be grateful that your friend's grenade did not inconvenience it.'

There was a cut, as if in a film. The doctor was no longer there, and instead a nurse – a very tall, thin young man with a bald head and the podgy, ingenuous face of a child – was taking my blood pressure. I had been asleep, or time had slipped, or something else had happened. 'I was talking to the doctor.'

'Were you?'

'Doctor Bello.'

'That's her name.'

'She was the middle of telling me something? I think I zoned out.'

At this point I think I zoned out. I was alone in the room. The window was very tall and thin, and admitted a perspective across a courtyard to a flank of rectangles, like the grid at the bottom of the spent fuel pool, only arrayed vertically rather than horizontally at the bottom of the pool. It took me a while to recognise these as blank windows. There was a tree somewhere in the space between my window and these windows, for a broomstick of branches poked out from the right side of the rectangle. These branches were usually motionless protrusions into the field of view, rather jagged and unpleasant, but every now and again a breeze would insinuate itself down into the courtyard and elate the twigs to a flurry of waving.

Now the window was dark, and the only illumination was a nightlight above the door. It shone with a gorgeous jade-green light; delicate and dim.

The nurse was coming in through the door. It occurred to me that he unlocked the door before stepping through it, and relocked it when he was through. For some reason this action snagged my attention. He was carrying a tray. On the tray was a bowl of broth and a small boulder of bread.

'How long have I been here?' I asked, between sips, as he spooned the soup into my mouth.

'You know what I reckon about time?' the nurse replied. 'I figure that the passage of time is subjective. I don't know much about frontal lobe injury, but I know it can do strange things to your sense of the passage of time. Does it feel like you've been here for a long time?'

'Months.'

'Ha!' This pleased him. 'Two days – three now. Or *is* it months? A philosopher might be able to tell us the difference. And why, anyway, *should* we submit to the tyranny of the calendar? The clock? Days? Months?'

He broke off some of the bread, dipped it in the broth, and poked one end in between my lips. I disliked the texture of it.

'Which is it?' I asked, annoyed, or tried to. I wanted solidity. But he wasn't there anymore. I was alone in the room as the rectangular photographic print that was the window yielded the effects of the chemical wash in which it had been immersed and very slowly went from black to purple, to grey, to a yeasty paleness.

No.

Actually I wasn't in the room, I was on a trolley, flowing along the longest corridor in the world. Actually it wasn't a corridor, and those weren't lights set at intervals into the ceiling; it was a liftshaft and those were floors. I was falling. Actually I wasn't in a corridor, I was back in the womb, and the womb was a metal sac, like the interior of a toothpaste tube.

The doctor was helping me sit up in bed. I was in my room again. 'Did I have a scan? Was that what that was? I assume that is what has just happened to me.'

'As we discussed,' she said. But I had no memory of such a discussion. 'You used to be a smoker, I think'

'A smoker?'

'A smoker of cigarettes.'

And her words unlocked that whole storeroom of memory. I had been entirely oblivious to cigarettes until she uttered those words; and then, suddenly, I craved a smoke. I knew once again that stretched, physiological need for nicotine. 'Do you *have* any cigarettes?' I asked. 'I feel the need for one, right now, very acutely.'

'Smoking is not permitted in here,' she said.

That reminded me of something.

'It is obvious,' the doctor was saying, 'from even the most cursory examination of your body, that you have smoked far *too* much for far *too* long. But I knew you were a smoker even before I examined you. Do you know how I knew? I shall tell you. You had a cigarette in your mouth. When they pulled you out of the pool, at the plant, they said your lips were set fast about the stub of a cigarette.'

'I remember that cigarette,' I said, fondly.

'It played a part,' she said, 'in saving your life. There's an irony there, perhaps. As a medical practitioner I spend much of my working life telling people *not* to smoke. I spend a lot of time telling them that. Almost as much time as I spend telling them not to drink. But in this case . . .'

'That cigarette saved my life?' I said.

'It relaxed your muscles. Your friend, Mr Nuclear Reactor, your friend Leo-as-in-Tolstoy, *his* muscles were tensed tight. The shrapnel cut through him like snapping harpstrings. He went to pieces.' She chuckled, and then stopped herself. 'If you see what I mean. You, though, you were relaxed. Sometimes people come into the hospital here having fallen from, say, a high building. Adults, but also, sometimes, babies. The babies have a greater chance of surviving, because they don't tense themselves in anticipation of the impact. They don't know any better. They hit the ground as soft sacks, and so don't shatter.'

'I believe I have heard something of the like,' I said.

'Your muscles were slack, so some of the shrapnel passed straight through without causing too much damage. Pieces went through your legs, and arms, and there is a hole through your stomach and out the other side. It was a good job that none of the pieces had a trajectory that intersected your spine. A piece got stuck in your ribs, and another inside your head, but we were able to get both of those pieces out.'

I looked at my own left hand. I was wearing a stigmata. Turning the hand over, I saw the matching scar on the back. I flexed my fingers; they were stiff, and a little sore, but they worked.

'Is this how a grenade works?' I said, amazed.

She looked at me. Her face was a series of regular curves, regularly arranged, but there was a professional blankness in her expression that reduced what might otherwise have been beauty. 'Weren't you in the army?'

'I was in the army,' I said, with another internal wrench of memorialising regurgitation.

'Then you should know how a grenade works. It is usually a fatal device, a grenade. Don't misunderstand me. But, luckily for you, you were relaxed. And luckily you were blown into the pool, which extinguished and cooled your burns. You were partially in the pool. And a quantity of water had been blown about. There was much water in the air, and it rained back down upon you. So you didn't burn.'

'Thrice lucky,' I said.

'More than thrice. Your face was exposed to the blast, and your skin should have been badly burned. It was, in fact, burned. But your face has been burned before, hasn't it?'

'I can't remember,' I said.

'Your chin and cheeks, some of your nose and much of your brow is covered with old scar tissue. The scarring indicates what must have been a fairly severe prior burn.'

'I can't remember,' I said again.

'Scar tissue is in some senses weaker than ordinary tissue; but it has a higher concentration of collagen, which makes it *structurally* tougher.'

'I see.'

'There is, furthermore, another piece of luck here,' she said.

'I've lost count now,' I said.

'The grenade was fairly radioactive. It had been left in a radio-active environment for perhaps a week, and had become itself fairly radioactive.'

I considered this. 'That's lucky?'

'Normally, no. Normally that is no more lucky than smoking a cigarette is healthy. Normally the fact that this grenade was radio-active would be extremely *un*lucky. You had a fragment of this radioactive grenade stuck inside your skull for two and a half days. We have just operated to remove it. It entered through the left temple – *your* left, that is – so that's how we retrieved it; out through the hole it made going in.'

I put my hand up to my head, and felt, on the left side, the enormous fabric excrescence of a surgical dressing, clamped to the side of my skull like an alien facehugger that had missed its target. 'Don't fiddle with that,' said the doctor, severely. 'There's a tap under there.'

'Tap,' I said. I am not sure why I added. 'The American word is [*faucet*].'

'That's as may be. Our tap is designed to relieve intercranial pressure, and must not be meddled with.'

'Meddled with,' I repeated.

'Comrade Skvorecky,' said the doctor. 'Did you know you have cancer?'

'Cancer,' I said, as if leafing through the medical textbook of my memory. Most of the pages were blank. But I remembered this: 'Because I was in Chernobyl?'

'No no. Judging by its growth, I would say you have had cancer growing inside your brain for several years.'

'Oh,' I said. I pondered this. It sounded like news, but I couldn't bring myself to feel any anxiety. 'I may have known that. I may not. I can't remember if I knew or not.'

'Located on the border between the perifrontal lobe and the midbrain. Under normal circumstances I would describe such a growth as inoperable.'

'Oh dear,' I said. 'Does that mean I am going to die?'

'Everybody dies, comrade.'

'True of course,' I agreed. I felt remarkably placid about this news.

'You should ask: Am I to die *soon*?'

'Am I?'

'As to that, I can't say. We took out some of the growth when we were in your skull, but wholly to excise it would require us to remove more brain tissue than would be compatible with your continuing mental function.'

'Oh dear,' I said again, passionlessly.

'On the other hand, the grenade fragment was lodged in such a way as to be, in fact, in contact with the tumour.'

'Oh dear,' I said once more.

'Not oh dear, comrade. The grenade itself had been irradiated by, it seems, a week or more in close proximity to depleted uranium. It was itself therefore radioactive. It therefore itself irradiated the tumour for two days. We've taken the shrapnel out now, but there's little doubt that it has done you good.'

'Done me *good*,' I said, as if testing the word on my tongue. 'Good.'

'Cancer cells are more susceptible to radiation than ordinary cells. That, combined with the limited surgical excision, has, I believe, materially lengthened your life expectancy.'

'To be clear,' I said. 'By smoking a cigarette, inside a nuclear facility, whilst having my skull blown up by a radioactive RGD-5 I have *extended* my life expectancy?'

'A strange chance, indeed. You have months of convalescence ahead of you, of course. Your shrapnel damage amounts to having been shot in the body and head half a dozen times, in addition to being concussed and burned. I would be concerned about such injuries in a young, healthy man; but in a man of your advanced years and poor health it is much more alarming. How old are you, exactly?'

I thought about this. 'Old,' I said.

'When were you born.'

'I can't remember.'

'You fought in the Great Patriotic War?'

'I suppose so. I'm sorry but I can't remember precisely.'

'Well. There has been a degree of neural damage. It seems to be affecting your left brain – your right side – in particular. There has been additional scarring, and various other forms of superficial damage. But all things considered. All things considered—'

I felt quite remarkably calm. But a memory of standing in the reactor hall at the power plant, trying and failing to persuade ox-like Trofim to put the grenade away, flashed into my mind, and with it came the memory of full-strength anxiety. 'Chernobyl,' I cried. 'It blew up!'

'No no,' said the doctor, crossly. 'I explained this. It is true that somebody *had* conspired to vandalise the power plant – and true that the consequences would have been horrific. There was recovered, from the bottom of one of the spent fuel pools, a suitcase containing a number of grenades. Had *they* exploded, particularly had they been fixed to the wall that the spent fuel pool shared with the reactor ... well then there would have been serious damage. But the single grenade in the hand of your friend did not do so much damage. The other grenades were covered by thirty metres of water, and were quite untouched by the explosion. The reactor itself is shielded in dozens of metres of concrete, and it was fine. Almost all the force of the blast went upwards. There was, I am told, one piece of damage. Trofim was holding a gun in his right hand. The hand was blown off by the explosion, still holding the gun; and the gun struck the ground. The round in the chamber fired, and this bullet pierced one of the steam pipes, leading to a small reduction in pressure. But the staff have practised for that eventuality. They were able to restore pressure. The explosion, on the other hand, caused very little damage.'

'Luck indeed,' I observed.

'Or fate.'

'Thank you, Comrade Doctor,' I said.

'Comrade Colonel Doctor,' she said, and left the room, locking the door behind her.

I dreamt. I was in the dacha again, but the quality of the experience was not as *visionary* as it had been before. There was Stalin, except that his moustache was a mess of fine tentacles rather than hair, his nostrils were two teethed orifices, his skin bristled with pale warts, and his eyes glowed red.

I awoke with a sudden insight, brilliance igniting inside my head like fireworks. 'Christmas Day, 1917!' I cried aloud. 'The day of my birth!'

I was telling an empty room.

Death is a red-haired man: his skin is pale, and his eyes unusually dark. He smiles. He has every reason too. How he must haunt a hospital such as this.

I dreamed, and when I woke up the nurse was rolling me to one side to pull away the bedpan. 'There's a Militia officer here to speak with you,' he said.

I brought my eyes into focus, something that seemed to take me longer now than formerly it had. I don't know who I expected to see, but it was a uniformed policeman, sitting in a hospital chair, his broad-peaked cap in his lap.

'Good afternoon,' he said. 'I am Officer Pahulanik of the Ukrainian Militia. I am a policeman. Do you understand?'

'Good afternoon. I understand perfectly.'

'There are, it seems, protocols regarding the circumstances under which I may take you into custody.'

'Am I under arrest?'

'Your case seems complicated,' said Officer Pahulanik. 'You were arrested in Moscow with respect to the death of an American citizen. You were released into the custody of the KGB. According to the KGB, you are still in their custody.'

'They do not say they released me?'

'Nor that you escaped. Nor that you are dead. Accordingly . . . it is awkward. No policeman wishes to incur the wrath of the KGB, or trespass upon their proper ground.' He looked carefully at me for a time. 'Then there is this matter of attempted sabotage in the Chernobyl nuclear reactor.'

'I was endeavouring to prevent such sabotage. At risk of my own life, I tackled an individual armed with a grenade.'

'That would seem to be the case,' said Officer Pahulanik. 'And yet, it remains to be explained why you – a lowly translator from Moscow – chanced to be inside Chernobyl at the precise moment a saboteur attempted to explode the facility with grenades.'

'My memory is a little enholed,' I said. Then, since *enholed* did not seem to me a proper Russian word I stopped. I spent a few moments trying to remember whether it was, perhaps, an English word. When that didn't seem right I pondered, vaguely, about French. Then I said, 'I suffered a degree of injury of the brain. An irregular piece of metal was deposited in my frontal lobe.'

'So I hear,' said the policeman. 'Does this mean that you can no longer remember what you were doing inside the facility?'

I thought. Elements of the journey from Moscow flapped batlike through the cavernous spaces of my brain. There were no faces, and no names, in my memorious supply. I said, 'I'm afraid not. I am not memorious.' My memory refused to focus. Was *memorious* even a word? And there was somebody else, too, but I could not figure who, or what this person had been doing, or what my relation to them was. I could not remember how I had come to be in Kiev after being in Moscow.

'I was with somebody,' I said, in a slow voice. 'Or I wasn't. It must be one or the other.' I was not attempting to deceive the police; and I had the distinct impression that it was all there. But it was a great deal to process. Perhaps I should say, I *remembered*, but I was not yet used to having so many memories in my head again.

'Indeed,' said the policeman. 'It seems you were indeed with somebody. You were with a KGB agent called Trofim. Another agent, whose identity and present location is obscure, had gathered the entire staff of the Chernobyl nuclear station in Reactor One. He was addressing the staff in stern and, it seems, forbidding terms, although none of them seem very certain as to the exact content of his speech. But there he was, talking away. And now he has vanished. You, comrade, are officially still in KGB custody in Moscow. You certainly *were* there. Next thing we know, the KGB are in Chernobyl. And so are you. You didn't fly down, because we have checked all the passenger manifests. Nor did you come by train, because the stations were guarded. You do not, according to records, possess a car. Perhaps you might have stolen one, but all the cars in the Chernobyl car park have been accounted for. So how else might you have come there? What do you *think*?'

'Why should the KGB bring a prisoner all the way down to the Ukraine from Moscow?' I asked, genuinely. I asked the question because I wanted to know the answer.

'I find it best not to pry too closely into the business of the KGB,' said the policeman. In all this, he had not moved from his chair, nor approached the bed. 'It would be injurious to my career, and possibly to my life, if I attempted to arrest an individual who was already in KGB custody.'

'I see your dilemma.'

'Well, then, comrade. Perhaps you can help me. In the cupboard beside your bed – there – would you mind?'

He pointed, and, with some difficulty (for movement did not come easily to me, and was not comfortable), I opened the bedside cabinet and brought out an alien raygun. It was a long tube, with a handle, and a switch.

'That is a Geiger counter,' said the policeman.

'It is not an alien raygun,' I said, mostly for my own benefit.

'Indeed not. Please point it at you, and press the button.'

I did so. Immediately the device leapt to life with a ferocious crackling, like ten thousand dry twigs on a huge fire. 'That's not good,' I observed, placidly.

'Comrade, you have pressed the test button. That is there to ensure that the machine's speakers are operational.'

'If that were a reading of my radioactivity . . .'

'Then you'd be dead in half an hour, and I'd be very ill. Switch it off.' I did so. 'Press the trigger, on the front of the handle.'

I did this, and the device burped and snapped. It popped and was silent; popped twice and was silent again.'

'There,' said the policeman. 'It turns out you *are* radioactive.'

'Not badly?'

'Badly enough to prevent me taking you into custody, I'm pleased to say. You can turn it off now,' he said, getting to his feet, 'and replace it in the cabinet. Your nurses and doctors may need to avail themselves of it.' He got to his feet. 'Comrade, the Ukrainian Militia is content to leave you in this secure medical facility.'

I spent ten minutes manoeuvring my legs out of the bed, and another fifteen leaning against the wheeled crutch of my drip-rack, two fluid-heavy sacs swinging like an old man's pendulous testicles (*ballbag*? I thought; and understood that this was a memory too, although I wasn't sure how it related to the others). With infinite attention I made my way over to the window. My joints seemed to squeak. Or else the wheels on the drip-rack squeaked. It was one of the two, certainly. And here was the window. I looked through it. There was a courtyard, and standing in the courtyard, three floors below me, were three nurses: two female nurses and one male nurse. They were smoking, talking. One had her back to me: a plump and cornfed foreshortened torso, from my perspective, upon which the manmade fabric of her uniform stretched and wrinkled. This chimed, somehow, deep inside me. She had flame-coloured hair. The other female had hair the colour of black coffee, and a wide-faced, wide-hipped loveliness. She was laughing. And every now and again she threw a great bale of smoke over her left shoulder like a worker clearing spectral snow with an invisible shovel. As I watched, the male nurse – casually and with no reaction of shock or outrage from either woman – reached out and squeezed the breast of the brunette. His face was animated, but he was not looking at the woman he was pawing. Perhaps he was telling a story, and this was illustrating it. I was struck by how strange an action it was.

They finished their smokes and went in. There was nothing in the yard now except a stone bench, and some runty bushes, and a deal of litter on paving stones: spent cigarettes, old cartons, rubbish.

I looked over the roof at the sky: a cold-looking, hazed white. The sun was there, diluted by the cover of clouds. I looked and the sun seemed to be shivering in the sky. The motion disturbed me, because, after all, the sun is the stable point around which the world moves, and everybody knows that. And if we know that the sun herself moves too – as perhaps she does, on some larger galactic pavanne, then we need not trouble ourselves with it. But to *shimmer* in the sky? It was as if the sun was struggling in harness. Then I put my hand to my face and understood that it was my head that was trembling; and that when I looked down again at the courtyard with my trembly eyeballs it too seemed to quake like the terrors were in it.

'What are you doing?' said my nurse, in a sharp voice.

'I was watching you lark about downstairs,' I replied. Except that the words did not come out of my mouth coherently. My mouth did not seem to be working properly. I considered: it seemed likely I'd said nothing at all except inarticulate gurgles.

'What's that, old man?' said the fellow, kindly, taking my weight, sliding an arm under my right armpit. 'Come on, back to bed with you.'

I felt dizzy. There was a purple-edged tint to familiar things. I could smell a certain smell, and after a while I recognised it as the smell of a certain bunker where, in 1941, I had spent five weeks in close company with half a dozen men. It was the smell of male body-stink and cordite and dust. I could smell it now, although the only scent my male nurse exuded was one of soap. And although by the time I was back on the bed the smell had changed to one of roasting nuts. Not any old nuts, but particular nuts roasting on a brazier on the corner of Market Square, on a winter's morning in the days after the civil war. My grandfather was leading me along, and my breath was steamtraining out of my mouth in a most delightful way. I was a young boy, and it was a joy to me to pretend to be a steam train. My grandfather was telling me that the civil war was over, and how glad we must be. 'Our war is over now,' he told me, 'but in England it will shortly begin, and in all the other countries too.' 'Can I have some chestnuts?' I pleaded. I was, I don't know, ten years old. 'Will you go back to England now that the war is over?' I asked. 'I'm Russian now,' he said. 'I'm Russian as all Russia.'

The man selling the chestnuts was Death.

Alone of all the people in the busy square he was hatless, and he was pale as summer clouds, and skinny as unfleshed bones. He was selling chestnuts. His hair was red as firelight, and his skin was a blank, and his eyes were black, so that they looked deeper and deader than human eyes. As we made our way over I became scared. 'It's Death,' I told my grandfather. 'It's Death.' And grandfather, his accent becoming more pronounced as it often used to do when he was angry, rebuked me. 'Don't be silly. He's a respectable Russian selling chestnuts, and you'll not insult him with such childishness.' But I didn't want to go any closer, and held back, and tugged at my grandfather's coat.

'Come along old man,' said the nurse, and at his words, as at a magic spell, the hallucination vanished from my eyes and my nose. 'Come along old man, what you want to be wandering about for? You're as white as milled flour.'

I awoke, suddenly, and there was sweat all on me. It was cold on my skin. It was the middle of the night. I could not lie there. If there is one thing the Great Patriotic War taught me, it was not to lie there. The ones who lay down, though only to catch their breath, or only to rest their wound for a moment – those were the ones who died. You had to keep going. No matter what. No matter what. Not that it mattered. No matter what. Not, I told myself, that it mattered. I was not anxious about going on. It was a matter of simple will. I had to speak to – I couldn't remember who. She was somewhere in Kiev – I did not know where, but I must find her.

Her?

I had no memory of any *her*. And yet that lack of memory felt like a palpable absence, as if I should have such a memory.

I woke up again, with no memory of the intervening time. I did not feel very comfortable. I was sitting on the floor with my back to the wall. They were hauling me upright. *They* were hospital staff. It was daytime, and spring light was printing a sharp, new trapezoid on the wall beside my bed. There were two nurses, and they were picking me up, and tutting me. They fussed me back to bed, and reinserted the drip, and wiped me up and then the doctor was there. 'Mr Skvorecky,' she said. 'I must ask you to remain in your bed. If you persist in getting out of it, I really cannot be answerable for your recovery.'

'I should like to make a phone call,' I said.

'Follow your doctor's orders,' she replied, 'and in a day or two that might be possible.' She had the Geiger counter in her hand, and was running it over me. It tutted disapprovingly, although intermittently.

'Perhaps you could forward a message for me?' I asked.

'To whom?'

'I can't remember. I'm sorry.'

'That is going to make it hard to deliver the message.'

'I know – I appreciate that. I think there was somebody in the reactor with me. I wish I could tell you more about him, but I'm afraid I don't remember, exactly. Except that it is very important I communicate with him, for some reason.'

Dr Bello sighed. 'I shall be honest, Mr Skvorecky. The Militia seem curiously uncertain about your status, which is to say, as to whether they have or have not taken you under arrest. Although they are certain that they have further questions for you.'

'I understand,' I said, placidly. 'But he can tell me something I need to know. To fill in the holes in my ... in my ...' There was something else I meant to say, but it was sliding out from the speech centres of my brain, and playing peek-a-boo in other portions. A car. A deer. A man lifted bodily into the night air and dangling up there.

'Does Death have red hair?' I asked.

'What's that?'

'Do you think Death is a redhead?'

'Isn't he supposed to be a skeleton?' was the reply, and I didn't recognise the voice. It wasn't Dr Bello's voice; she was no longer there. It was a new voice. It possessed a breathy, underpowered quality that I didn't like.

'I've met you before,' I said, sitting up a little in the bed.

Here was a man, with red hair, sitting in the room's single chair, surveying me in bed. I did not like his smile. He did not work for the hospital.

He and I were alone in the room together. The light was on. Perhaps turning on the light had woken me up. I don't know.

He smiled at me. This was not a pleasant smile.

'You were Frenkel's driver,' I said. 'You drove us around, whilst Trofim was pushing his pistol into my eye socket. And then,' I added, for this memory had just that moment come back to me, 'Frenkel himself put *his* gun inside my mouth. And you drove the car. You work for Frenkel. You're KGB.'

'I am KGB,' he agreed.

'You've come to kill me?'

'I have come to kill you.'

I thought about this. It seemed a flavourless, angstless statement. The words had the quality of facts rather than emotions.

'It seems I am hard to kill,' I said.

'I'm sure I'll manage it.'

'And why are you going to kill me?'

His eyes said *I need a reason?* but his mouth said, 'Orders.'

'I suppose it has to do with poor Trofim,' I croaked. I thought about my meeting with the Steel-Stalin. 'I suppose I'm getting in Comrade Frenkel's way. He wanted to recruit me, in order to intensify the . . .' But I couldn't think of the word. 'To do,' I went on tentatively, curious in a dispassionate way, to see what words would come out of my mouth, 'something . . . for the creatures. The aliens. But whatever he hoped, I'm having the opposite effect.'

'Gabble gabble,' said the red-headed man. I knew I had met him before, but I couldn't recall his name. 'I'll give you this: you hide your fear pretty well, old man.'

I thought about fear. Shouldn't I be afraid? But if there was any sensation there it was, rather, the memory of fear than fear. I contemplated my situation. It seemed clear to me – mental clarity sometimes drew its ticklish bow across the violin string of my consciousness – that I needed to *get out of bed* if I wanted to save my life. I needed to *get up and lock the door*. I needed, however hard it might be, to rise from my bed and get to the door. If I could lock the door, I would survive. Did the choice really present itself to me so starkly? Death here, life there, a key in a keyhole the difference. I had the memory of an elongated chopstick of light shining through a keyhole and into a darkened room. Why was the room so darkened? What *was* the light on the other side of the door that spilled so promiscuously through the tiny hole? Where was it shining from? A chink of light. Then I thought to myself: Of course *the light is defined by the darkness*. I don't know why I thought this.

I moved my legs round until they dangled over the edge of the bed, like two sleeves of cloth. Then I pulled the wormy plastic tube from my arm and got, unsteadily, to my feet. Red-haired Death was sat in the chair, regarding me with a complacently predatory expression. I suppose he was wondering what I thought I was doing.

'After the first death,' I told him, with a grunt, 'there is no other.'

'Gabble gabble,' he said again. From a holster inside his jacket he withdrew a pistol.

Three steps, doddery, and I was at the door. This motion tired me out. I paused for a moment to breathe.

'Are you thinking of making a *run* for it?' he asked. 'A *stagger* for it? A *bumble* for it?' He was amusing himself. 'A *shuffle* for it?'

'I don't think I'd get very far,' I said. I needed to pause twice in the middle of this short sentence in order to catch my breath. There was a deep-bone ache in my legs. I felt nauseous. This was too much exertion for me. But at least I was at the door now.

'I've been involved in various pursuits of suspects in my time,' he said. 'This will be an interesting, if brief, addition to that body of experience.'

I opened the door an inch, two inches, and I reached an arm round to the outside. I could feel, without needing to look round, the pistol aimed between my shoulder blades. 'I think,' I said, groping for the key in the lock, 'you mis—' and there it was, and I fumbled it from its hole, '—understand.'

I pushed the door shut, and leant against it for a moment, to recover. But my labour was almost completed now.

'Get back in the bed, old man,' said the redhead. 'I have no objection to shooting you, but it might be simpler all round if I just smother you with a pillow.' He did not move from the chair. 'It'd be demeaning to have you lurching down the corridor at half a mile an hour. I'd shoot you in the back, you know. I have no compunction about shooting people in the back. You'd bleed out on a hard hospital floor. Wouldn't you rather die in bed? You're an old man. Old men always hope to die in their beds'.

'There,' I said, slipping the key into the keyhole on the inside of the door, and turning it round. 'A little privacy.' I pulled the key out.

Make no mistake: the physical effort this manoeuvre required, and, without wishing to sound vainglorious, the courage and application it entailed, was greater than any effort I had made for decades. But I was fighting for my life. And, without anxiety or fear, and without any strong preference for living over dying, I so fought.

'What are you doing?' the redhead demanded, a peevish tone entering his voice. 'Have you locked us in?'

I turned. One step and my knee almost folded. Another step. I didn't want to collapse in a heap on the bed; or, worse, miss the edge of the bed and tumble to the floor. That wouldn't do at all. It required a focus of effort. 'A little,' I gasped, 'privacy.'

'Give me the key,' he ordered, flourishing his pistol.

The final step and I paused. 'A moment,' I gasped. 'Let me get. Back into the bed.'

'Why did you lock the door?'

'A little,' I panted, 'privacy.'

I was standing with my hands down on the mattress. My intention had been to swallow the key straight down, but now that I had it in my hand it seemed far too large and jagged. I thought about taking a drink of water, but even so I could not see it going down the gullet. Things are often different in imagination to the way they are in reality.

I put my hip against the edge of the bed, and levered myself round into a sitting position, facing him. The mattress felt hard beneath me. Still in his chair, he was aiming the pistol directly at my face.

'Is this about delay?' he demanded. 'Come on, old man. You're a hero of the Patriotic War. Don't demean yourself.'

'You're right,' I said. Leaving the key tucked into my bedclothes I raised my right hand, empty, and put it to my mouth. With what I hoped was a convincing dumb-show I made as if to swallow the key.

'Hey!' said the redhead, leaping to his feet. 'What are you playing at?'

'Gah!' I said. Did that sound like somebody with a key sliding down his gullet? 'Gur! Gah! That *is* uncomfortable.' I leaned back against my pillows, and slid my heels along the mattress until my legs were flat. Then, perhaps too theatrically, I patted my stomach. 'The condemned man,' I puffed, 'can choose his last meal.'

'You've gone gaga!' said the redhead. Why'd you do that? You've locked yourself in a room with your assassin.'

'I decided against,' I said, slowly as I recovered my puff. I could feel the key digging into my buttock. 'Trying to run away.'

'I suppose I can go out the window?' the redhead said, and went over to look. 'Or, well that's quite a drop. I suppose I can just kick the door down.'

'You could easily kick the door down.'

'Why did you lock us in?' he asked.

'I thought it would be more fun,' I said, 'the other way around.'

'What's the other way around?'

'Me. Chasing you.'

'*That's* more like it,' he said, smiling broadly at the absurdity of the situation. 'That's the spirit that beat the Nazis! You're an old man. Unarmed. Walking three paces exhausts you. I'm a young, fit, KGB operative with a gun. I've killed dozens of people healthier than you. But *you're* the one chasing *me!* That is indeed the way to think of it. That's a better way to go.' He tucked his pistol back into his holster and beckoned. 'Come on then! Come get me!'

'When you say,' I said, reaching over for the bedside cabinet, 'that I am unarmed . . .'

I pulled out the Geiger counter.

Immediately he drew his gun again and held it two-handed, pointed straight at my head. 'Put that down,' he said.

'It's not a gun,' I said. 'It's a Geiger counter.'

There was a pause. 'Geiger-Müller tube,' said the redhead; but he kept the gun trained on me.

'Here's a funny thing,' I told him. 'The American President? His name is *Reagan*. You know what that means, in English? A literal translation into Russian would be *President Laser Pistol*. Isn't that funny?'

I pointed the tube at my own chest.

'Stop!' he barked. 'Is *that* a laser pistol? You said Geiger counter. Is it a laser pistol, though?'

'Tch! And where would I get hold of a laser pistol?'

'You and I both know where,' he retorted quickly. 'Who knows what weaponry *they* might dispose of, when it's no longer useful to them?'

This barely wrongfooted me. It might have given me pause, if I hadn't been so tired. I pushed on. 'Well if it's a laser pistol,' I said, settling the end of its plastic muzzle over the exact centre of my chest, 'and I pull this trigger, then I'll do your job for you. On the other hand, if it's a Geiger counter, all that will happen is that you'll discover how radioactive I am.'

I could see the fox-like process of calculation flicker in his eyes. He was starting to work out what I had done. He glanced over to the door. Then he took a step towards me, and then stopped. 'You've locked me in,' he said, in a low voice.

'It's not a question of me escaping from you,' I told him.

'You're bluffing,' he said. 'Bluffing is what you are doing.'

'Shall we see? Shall I press the button?'

'Bluffing,' he said.

'You know how one of these works?'

'Go on,' he instructed.

I pushed the test button, and the counter crackled and trilled to life. For long seconds he stood there, listening to the malign static interference sizzle and sizzle. Eventually he spoke. 'You've been here more than a week.'

I turned the machine off.

'If you're *that* radioactive,' he said, backing against the window. 'You'd have died long ago.'

'Are you concerned about *my* health?' I asked. 'Or your own?'

He swallowed. 'Is it *them*?' he said.

'It'd be better for my purpose if you came over here,' I told him. 'Get a fuller dose. Put a pillow over my mouth, and lean over me. Get a proper coating.'

'Did *they* make you immune, somehow, to radiation? Is that why you're still alive?'

'Never mind that. Are *you* immune to radioactivity, comrade? That's the question.' I was gathering my strength after my exertion;

such strength as I had. 'Because if you are, then feel free to stay here as long as you like. But if not—' I breathed in, and out. 'If not, then I'd advise you to get out as soon as possible. Really, there's no time to lose. Every second increases your cancer risk.'

'Christ,' he said. 'You're white hot. Christ you're a fucking *bomb*.' He pulled the window open and peered out. Presumably he thought: *too far to jump*, because he turned back to face me, and this was the first moment since his arrival in my room that I felt hope flicker in my brain. There was a panic in his eyes.

'That hairdo,' I said. 'You towel it dry after showering? That'll start falling out now, of course. Bright side: you won't have to bother about it anymore. No more tiresome *washing* or *drying* your hair. You can skip that whole portion of the morning routine. Think of the time you'll save.'

He raised his pistol at me, and then lowered it. 'Give me the key,' he said.

'As for that,' I said. 'Your options are: to get me to vomit it up. Or perhaps cut me open for it. You have a knife?'

'Give me the fucking—' He aimed the gun at me again. Then he reholstered it.

'Just cut me open and rummage around. Of course, it'll significantly increase your dose. But if you stay here too long then—' I started coughing at this moment, on account of all the talking I was doing and the dryness of my throat. But it succeeded in increasing the panic in the redhead's face. I took a sip from the glass of water beside my bed.

The redhead bolted suddenly for the door, and heaved with all his strength on the handle. 'Give me the key or I'll blow your alien brains onto the *wall*!' he shouted.

'My *alien* brains?' I said. 'I have to assume you're going to shoot me whatever happens.' I was fingering the Geiger counter in my lap. 'So your threat is hardly an incentive.'

He began kicking at the door. He was wearing comfortable leather loafers. 'Army boots would be more useful for that, comrade,' I told him.

He kicked, and kicked again. 'Bastard!' he grunted. 'Bastard!'

'You do not seem to be making much of a dent.'

He spun round and, once more, drew his pistol on me. 'I'll at least finish you off,' he told me.

'All right, all right,' I said, calmly. 'Hold on a moment. I'll *give* you the key! I'll cough it back up! I'll even wipe it on the bedclothes, to remove as much of my highly radioactive saliva as I can manage.'

It did not suit his face for his eyes to be as wide open as they were. He looked disconcerting. He levelled the pistol at my head, and then with a moan of frustration he span and fired into the door once, twice, and then a third time. The noise of the pistol was very great, and it struck my inner ear like a crashing blow, leaving me with a high, pure singsong note. There was the stench of burnt powder. I shook my head ponderously, and the whine vanished from my ear.

The redhead aimed another kick at the punctured door, and kicked right through it. Now he was compelled to hop on one foot, for the other had become snagged through the woodwork. He almost fell backwards, and then he pulled the foot free, and did a little staggery dance. He swore.

'The door opens inward, comrade,' I said.

The wood around the handle was splintered and frayed. He pulled his right arm into the sleeve jacket, and using the fabric as a makeshift glove to protect his skin from splinters, he took hold and hauled the door towards him. It gave way with a noise of snapping wood, and once again he almost fell backwards. But at least his exit was clear now.

In the open doorway he turned around to face me. 'They should keep you in a fucking lead-lined room!' he said. He aimed the pistol at my chest.

I did not experience any spike or fear, or excitement. My heart kept beating smoothly.

'Hey!'

This was my doctor's voice. I heard running footsteps in the corridor outside. The redhead turned and waved his pistol at them. 'KGB business,' he barked. 'KGB business.'

'Murdering my patients in their beds is *nobody's* business,' cried the doctor. Ah! But she was fearless, my wonderful Dr Bello. I learned afterwards that she was not alone; the banging and thumping had roused half a dozen hospital staff, and they had all come scurrying down to see what the fuss was about. I daresay the red-headed man contemplated gunning them all down; but it was not a likely calculation.

'Get out!' snapped Dr Bello. She had reached the door, now, and was looking with horror at the mess of splintered wood. 'Damaging hospital property? Breaking down doors? Threatening hospital patients with a gun? I'll call the Militia, KGB or no. I'll speak to your superiors! I'll take it all the way to the top. I know people.'

The redhead growled, and looked at me, and then he growled again. 'You want,' he said, speaking in a low tone, 'to put him in a fucking lead-lined *room*.' And he stalked away.

And then they all came hurrying into my room, and fussing about me, and reconnecting my drip. Dr Bello took the Geiger counter from my lap. 'Doctor,' I told her. 'You have saved my life.'

'It is a doctor's business,' she said, in a plain voice, 'to save the life of her patient.'

After that there was a great deal of fuss. The Militia came to see me again, and a guard was placed on my room. I was visited by a senior KGB officer. He was very old, and in uniform – a vast, stiff concoction of cloth and braid, upon which a great many medals clustered like bees upon a beehive. His face was prodigiously weathered by age, and lined with a series of deep creases in the vertical and the horizontal, giving him the appearance, almost, of crumbling brickwork.

'Comrade,' he said, in a voice like rust. He did not tell me his name.

'Comrade.' I nodded.

'You fought in the Great Patriotic War,' he said.

'As did you,' I replied, nodding towards his medals. 'And now, you are in the KGB?'

He smiled, and leaned a little towards me. 'Confidentially, now,' he croaked. 'As one old soldier to another.'

'As one old soldier to another.'

'People think the KGB is a unity,' he said to me. 'But it is not so.'

'No?'

'No. There are different ... sects, shall we say. Different tribes. Shall we say different tribes?'

'We can say tribes.'

He leaned back again. 'My subordinate will take a statement,' he said, shifting his weight in the chair, and groaning slightly, either with the effort of moving himself or else with the world-weariness of having to go through these formalities. Then he said, 'Colonel Frenkel is presently under investigation.'

'He's a colonel? I had no idea he was so elevated.'

'Between you and me,' said the senior KGB officer, 'and in confidence as one old soldier to another, he is not – universally liked.'

'You astonish me,' I said.

'I have seen the report on your war service, and I have seen the report on Colonel Frenkel's war service, and frankly yours is more glorious.'

'Yet he is a colonel in the KGB, and I am an out-of-work translator in a hospital bed in Kiev.'

'You were never going to get on in the world, once you'd decided to work as a translator,' croaked the senior KGB officer. 'Who can trust translators? Living in two languages? How can speaking like an American not corrupt the soul a little?'

'There may well be something in that,' I conceded.

'As one old soldier to another,' said the fellow again, wearily. 'Colonel Frenkel had been put in charge of a section, tasked with a certain highly secret long-term mission, by Chernenko himself. It is sometimes the case that, with the death of a general secretary, the missions inaugurated by that general secretary possess enough inertial velocity to . . .' But he seemed to lose his thread. He peered at the bright window, and then he yawned.

Everyone, it occurred to me, seemed very tired. I, of course, felt tired myself.

'Did this project have to do with UFOs?' I asked.

'It is secret business,' said the senior KGB officer. 'But as one old soldier to another? Chernenko certainly believed in aliens from space, like a credulous boy. This is, in fact, a matter of public record. Other general secretaries have shared this belief. A great quantity of military, and KGB, resource has been wasted chasing UFOs around the Soviet Union. Wasted.'

'You do not believe in UFOs?'

'Of course not. And neither do you. I require that you give a statement to that effect. Write this: James Coyne, the American, was murdered by people – do not say government agents, say counter-revolutionaries – in a crude attempt to make it appear he had been kidnapped by space aliens. Say that.'

'And we are certain,' I said mildly, 'that he was?'

'Of course he was,' said the senior KGB officer. When he became irate, his voice rose from a croak to the sound of a metal file rasping on metal. 'Hum hum! You told the Moscow Militia so! He was hauled up by a rope around his ankle, like a deer in a snare!'

'The Militia never found the rope.'

'What does that matter? You don't think it truly was *aliens*?'

I searched my mind. It had, before the explosion, been a cluttered and rather oppressive mind to live inside; but now it was clear and brightly lit: long elegant hallways and wide shining windows and order. I must concede it was an improvement. 'No,' I said, 'I do not.'

'There we are then! It's nonsense. Poisonous and decadent nonsense, imported mostly from the USA, with films such as *Warring Stars* and *Intimate Embraces of Three Different Kinds*, and other such pornography.'

'I have not seen these films.'

'Quite right. They are banned. Nevertheless dedicated groups of counter-revolutionaries stage illicit screenings.'

'Comrade,' I said. 'If I may? As one *old man* to another. This talk of counter-revolutionaries and so on – it is old-fashioned, you know. The Soviet Union is undergoing a process of reform and restructuring.'

He grunted at that. 'Make a statement: say that persons unknown murdered the American. State categorically that there are no such things as space aliens, and that no UFO hovered over Moscow that night. Do not mention the events in the nuclear reactor. That is still a secret matter. But it is important we issue assurances to the Soviet people that they are not being *menaced* by *UFO*s.'

'Very well,' I said.

'Do that, and you will be released from KGB arrest.'

'No charges?' I said.

'It is my belief,' he grumbled, by way of reply, 'that you attempted to *prevent* the traitor Trofim from detonating a grenade inside the nuclear reactor. For that all Soviet people are grateful. We express our gratitude by informing you that, if ever you make public what happened in that place, we will arrest and charge you immediately. But otherwise you will be free to resume your work as a,' and he chewed the word a little before speaking it, 'translator.'

He stood up. 'One thing we don't understand,' he said, 'is how you *got* to Kiev.'

'How did I *get to* Kiev?' He was asking me a question about memory, and my memory was still clumsy. 'How?'

'From Moscow. Somehow you slipped out of Moscow. Frenkel had men at the stations, and the airport, you know. Watching for you.'

'I drove,' I said, prompted to the statement by something. I couldn't have told you where the memory came from. Mumbling in the dark. I could smell fresh bread. There was somebody else there.

'You *drove*? You own a car?'

'I was driven.' The memory bulged against the membrane of my mind, and threatened to burst through. Then it receded. You've had that experience: where you think something is going to come vomiting up, but then recedes. 'Or did I drive myself? I can't remember.'

'Nobody *drives* from Moscow to Kiev. Don't be silly. What do you think we have trains *for*?' He fitted his hat more securely to his head and left the room.

I never learnt his name. His subordinate, also in uniform, came in as he went out; and I dictated a statement to the effect that there are no such things as UFOs. This, I signed. It was nothing but the truth, after all. There are no such things as UFOs. Except in the imagination of such people as science fiction writers.

How many days passed? I don't know, exactly. A number of days. The tap was removed from the side of my head, and a simple bandage placed there. My hair, where it had been shaved away, was growing back itchy and bristly.

I practised a great deal with my right side: moving my right arm, flexing my right fist. It felt stiff, as though with cold. But I could at least move it.

With the nurse's help I climbed from my bed. I walked to the window, and I walked back from the window. 'Very good,' I was told. 'You should have seen me,' I gasped, 'when I walked to the door to lock it. Now, *that* was a walk.'

'We are keen to discharge you,' said Dr Bello. 'A nurse or security officer must sit on a chair outside your room all day and all night. It is an onerous duty we have to discharge.'

'I can only apologise for being so difficult a patient,' I told her.

'Why waste energy on apologising that you could use getting well? Once you are well you can remove yourself from the hospital. Then you will cease to be our problem.'

'And, by way of after-care?'

'As for that, well you can tend for yourself,' said Dr Bello. 'That is to say,' she added, turning away, 'you can take your place in the supportive bosom of the united nations of Soviet peoples.'

'A comforting thought indeed,' I said.

'You could be more grateful,' said Dr Bello, mildly. 'You are lucky to have survived.'

'It is a convention of science fiction,' I said, 'that each reality is shadowed by alternate realities, every history has a variant alternate history. In such alternatives, I doubt whether I *did* survive. My alternate history stops at page number two hundred.'

'Page two hundred? And when did you meet me?'

'Round about page two hundred and twenty.'

'So your novel ended even before I met you. Still,' said Dr Bello, getting to her feet, 'I find the endings of novels to be the best parts; so an ending that comes more quickly is probably to be preferred.'

I gave three separate reports to Militia officers, and two, in total, to representatives of the KGB, but I fear these reports – filed, somewhere, I suppose, to this day – differ markedly from one another. I was not attempting to mislead the authorities, but my memory was gappy: bubbles of pure-lit clarity rising through a fog-coloured sea. Specific stimuli might trigger new memories to pop up, which would in turn leave me slightly bewildered.

'You just sit there and look at Trofim,' said Frenkel, leaning over me.

It was dark. Therefore it was night. I did not recognise his voice. I did not recognise his voice. Then, abruptly, I *recognised* his voice and I woke up with a jolt. 'But how are *you* here?'

He had a torch in his left hand and he threw the light from this into my sleepy eyes, as he might throw sand or dust. But I did not need to make out his features from in amongst the knot of shadows; I remembered his voice, and with his voice I remembered everything about him. 'I met a senior KGB officer,' I told him, 'who said you were under internal investigation.'

'Leo, keep *your* eyes on *his* eyes.'

'Nonsense,' I said, with a gummy mouth. Then I said, 'There's supposed to be somebody outside my door. I'm supposed to have a guard, day and night. I hope you haven't killed them.'

'I'm invisible. You cannot see me. Fast asleep,' said Frenkel. I remember thinking this was silly of him: speaking like a hypnotist. That wasn't going to do him any good. I have never believed in hypnotism. It's mere stage performance, like card tricks and sawing the woman in—

Sawing the woman in.

Sawing the woman. Something about the woman.

'Hold still,' said Frenkel, crossly.

There was something enormously important about the woman. What woman?

'You're going to kill me, obviously,' I said, distractedly. 'The guard on the door will be embarrassed when he wakes in the morning.'

'I'm invisible,' said Frenkel, in a soothing voice,

'To find that I was killed in the night, when they were supposed to be guarding me.'

I felt a dry hand on the back of my neck, as Frenkel reached round. An old man's parchmenty palm. The blaze of electric light filled my eyes. I couldn't see anything except the light. 'You are calm,' said Frenkel. I took him to mean: *in the face of your impending extinction.*

'The nature of the injury I have suffered in my brain,' I told him, 'is such that it has taken the anxiety from contemplating the future.'

'You haven't suffered your brain injury yet,' said Frenkel. This struck me as an oddly disconnected thing to say. I pondered the words, but as I pondered them I found I couldn't be sure that Frenkel had even said them. But if Frenkel hadn't said them, where had they come from?

There was a jab at the back of my neck. A mosquito bite.

I yelped, more in surprise than pain. I cannot say whether I believed that this sensation was that of a stiletto bursting in between my vertebrae, or only a mosquito bite.

'You won't remember,' said Frenkel.

This struck me after the fashion of a challenge. 'I'll remember if I want to,' I returned. The torch flickered in front of my face. I still couldn't make out Frenkel's face. Then, for a horrible moment, I thought I *did* see a face, but the face I thought I saw was Trofim's. Trofim's huge bovine face floating directly in front of me: as if he were sitting across the bed from me. I do not believe in ghosts, as I believe I have mentioned before; but this was startling. 'I can remember anything I want to!' I cried, in a wavery voice.

'You won't remember,' Frenkel said again. It was certainly Frenkel's voice. I could hear it very distinctly.

'I remember *you*,' I said, defiantly. 'I remember you exactly. I remember meeting Josef Stalin.' Did I remember that? In the dark I seemed to hear Trofim muttering *Joe-SF, Joe-SF.* There was a stutter inside my brain. 'I remember driving from Moscow in a car, in the back of a car with . . .'

'You won't remember,' said Frenkel for a third time, as if weaving a charm.

'That's no good you know, I don't *believe* in hypnotism,' I said, as forcefully as my reluctant throat muscles permitted. 'I remember driving in the car with . . .'

It came to me.

'Dora,' I said, in a voice of dawning wonder. 'Dora.'

And then, with something like a consummation, or a sense of arrival and rightness, Dora came into my memory. The thought of her, like air filling a gasping lung, made me blush; and blush with sheer pleasure of memory. It all blocked itself in, and then shaded with colour and solidity. I loved her. It was hard to think that I had forgotten that I loved her. But I was not anxious, because it was not that the love had gone away, but only that my mind, with mental grit thrown in its metaphorical eye, had blinked, and blinked, and for the moment not seen it.

The other man was still talking.

'I am going to come back in a minute,' he said. 'And we will continue our little talk. And you will forget all about what has happened here.' And the torch went out.

I sat in the dark for a long time. There was no further talk. He was not true to his word.

A strange dream.

There *was* a lump on the back of my neck. I did not forget about that. I had it from before. Or was it new? I wondered if Frenkel had injected some poison, or hallucinogen, or truth serum – but then I thought I could feel a lump, something hard underneath my skin. This did not distress me. Perhaps I told myself that there were many pieces of shrapnel embedded in my flesh. Finally I fell asleep, and as I slid into unconsciousness I thought, quite distinctly, this thought: *If I have just been dreaming, then how can I be falling asleep? To be asleep, and dream of falling asleep – does that remove you to a deeper, secondary level of sleep? And what if you dream there of falling asleep . . . ?*

This was all very puzzling. But – Dora! At least I had Dora back. Of course I fell asleep, and in sleep I lost her again. My mind had been mashed about.

I woke in the morning with this peculiar encounter, real or dreamed, in my head.

'My concern,' I told the doctor, 'is that my sanity has been dislodged. I dreamt last night that—'

'I have no interest in your dreams. You are well enough to continue your convalescence at home. A taxi is here to take you away.'

'I did not order a taxi,' I said. But as I said this, the memory flushed through me, like water through a pipe, of my journey from Moscow to Kiev in the back of the cab, and Dora. Saltykov, with his absurd *syndrome*, and glorious Dora. She had been with me the whole time. How could I have forgotten Dora?

'Dora,' I said.

'Who?'

'I must find Dora. I must find her.'

'I'm sure you will, too.' A male nurse was helping me to get dressed. My actual clothes, it seemed, had been effectively destroyed by the grenade explosion. The hospital had a supply of garments. 'Donations,' said the nurse, with a cheery expression on his face. 'Dead people, and such. You know?'

'Which dead people?' I replied, and I fumbled at the buttons of an oversized shirt. Its fabric had the texture of dried, salted beef. It was at least clean, however; and it was certainly better than nothing in the raw Kiev weather.

'Dead people,' he chirruped. 'Lots of dead people, in a hospital, I can *tell* you.'

He helped me pull a sweater over my head, and fed my arms into a canvas jacket. This process had worn me out so greatly that I had to sit back and catch my breath. 'Now,' he told me. 'You've a choice: leather shoes that might be a little on the large side; or other shoes that, I'd say, will fit you perfectly.'

'Other shoes?' I panted.

'I'll not lie. I say shoes. Another person might say slippers.'

'I can't believe I forgot about Dora,' I said.

'Pretty is she?' He was rummaging in a capacious fabric bag, and pulling out slippers, one after the other. He held them up and they wobbled in his hands like live fish.

'I would say beautiful, rather than pretty,' I said, the memory of her returning to me. 'Not pretty, no. But beautiful.'

'That's what men say when their girl looks like a horse,' he told me, cheerfully.

'She doesn't look like a horse,' I said.

'I'm sure she doesn't. A man your age, in your condition, *any* girlfriend is an impressive achievement, I'd say. Wait – I've put the right slipper on your left foot.'

'I'm not sure it matters,' I said.

There were other papers to be signed, and Dr Bello gave me a twenty-second primer for my post-hospital care. 'Take it easy for a month,' she said. 'And don't start smoking again. To start smoking again would be very stupid. Very bad for your frail health. Do you hear me?'

'Yes, Doctor.'

'Will you go back to Moscow?'

'Not straight away.'

'Smoking is very bad for your health.'

'I understand.'

'I shall say it three times,' Dr Bello said, 'and it will become a charm. I come from a long line of forest witches, and what I tell you three times will become true. Smoking is very bad for your health. Here is your taxi driver.'

And there was Saltykov, with his sandy hair and his serious, pale face. The taxi driver of the doleful countenance. He came into the room like a comet drawing all the great nimbus of my memories of him with him. I was so pleased to see him I felt the urge, which I barely contained, to burst into tears. 'You were not exploded in Chernobyl!' I said.

'It's more than I can say for you,' he replied, disapprovingly. He did not look particularly glad to see me. 'It is true you are alive. But getting exploded in such a place was – reckless.'

'Mr Skvorecky is still frail,' said Dr Bello. 'You may need to assist him down the stairs and into your taxi.'

'Assist him?' The tone of Saltykov's voice – tart with suspicion – brought back another little flurry of memory. He was exactly like himself. I remembered exactly what he was like. There was a curious joy in that fact.

'Permit him to lean against you,' said Dr Bello, with a straight face. 'Perhaps lend him your shoulder.'

'It is impermissible for me to come into contact with another person,' said Saltykov, primly, 'and *a man* most especially. I suffer from a certain syndrome ...'

Bello spoke across him: 'I thought he was your friend?'

'He *is* my friend,' snapped Saltykov in the least friendly voice imaginable.

'Perhaps, Doctor,' I put in, 'I might have a stick?'

The nurse went off to fetch me a walking stick, and Dr Bello peered intently at Saltykov. He, for his part, ignored her.

'Saltykov,' I asked. 'Dora . . .'

'Indeed. I shall drive you directly to her. She is most anxious to see you again.'

A great happiness bloomed inside me.

The nurse returned with a peanut-brown walking stick. It was for me. It was tipped with half-perished rubber. Very gingerly I levered myself off my bed.

It was a long walk down the corridor to the lift, and it was followed by another long walk through the main hall out to where Saltykov had parked his taxicab. But emerging into the chill of early spring, under a bright blue sky, felt like renewal. I was still alive. I was going to see Dora again. The grey of the buildings had a pewter, precious tint; the noise of traffic, distant in the air, chimed a strange symphony and even that noise was delightful. After weeks of hospital air, I breathed in the tainted chill with pleasure.

Saltykov, in what I believe he regarded as a kind of concession, opened the door of his taxi for me, and then stood aside as I grunted, and struggled, and strained and eventually manoeuvred myself into a sitting position inside unaided.

He got in and drove away. We drove for long minutes in silence before he said, 'You do not think my taxicab is bugged?'

'I don't believe so,' I said.

'It is not likely, I suppose. Still, one cannot be too careful.'

'No.'

'In that case, I may tell you where we are going. Dora is in a small hotel in Kiev.'

'I would have guessed as much.'

'Really?' He sounded disappointed. 'If you can think of that, then perhaps they will think of it too.'

I knew what he meant by they, although without precision. I don't believe Saltykov had any better knowledge. Nevertheless I said, 'I could not guess which Kiev hotel. I daresay there are many.'

He brightened at this. 'True! I tried to persuade her to return to Moscow. I told her: Go to the US embassy in Moscow.

Seek sanctuary, I said. I said: Consider yourself the hunchback of Notre Dame.'

'You told her to consider herself a *hunchback*?'

'Oh yes,' said Saltykov.

'Did this not strike you as, perhaps, an insulting thing to say to a woman?'

He puffed and chewed his lower lip at this, and then said, 'I was not attempting to be insulting. It is a well known story. The hunchback was in danger and he claimed sanctuary inside the cathedral in Paris. That was the point of the analogy. Do you think Dora Norman would be likely to take offence?'

'Take offence at being compared to the hunchback of Notre Dame? Surely no woman could take offence at *that*.'

'Exactly!' But then his face became stern. 'Unless you are being sarcastic? Perhaps you *are* being sarcastic. You must remember, please, that my syndrome makes it difficult for me to understand nuances such as irony and sarcasm. At any rate, she refused to return to Moscow. Specifically she refused to return to Moscow alone. To be more specific still, she refused to return to Moscow without you.'

My old heart sang like it was young again. 'She said so?'

'Indeed. I told her she was foolish. But she didn't listen to me.'

Driving through the streets of the city might, for the buoyancy of my heart, have been flying through the sun-rubbed blue of the sky. I was grinning, my mouth stretched as wide as my pinched and scarred flesh permitted. I do not doubt I looked perfectly idiotic. I may even have looked like a death's head. But I didn't care.

After a while Saltykov spoke. 'I did not mean to compare her *physique* to the physique of the hunchback of Notre Dame.'

'I'm sure she understood that.'

'The comparison was in point of the *principle of sanctuary*. I was not intending to imply she had a hunchy back.'

'Of course not.'

'In point of fact,' he went on. 'She does not *have* a hunchy back.'

'That's right.'

He indicated, slowed, turned right, and pulled away again. 'In point of fact her excess weight is mostly on her *front*.'

'You must stop talking now.'

'One might say hunchstomach,' said Saltykov. 'Or—'

'No,' I stopped him. 'One might not.'

The hotel was a little way from the centre of town: part of a terrace of a 1960s development, a tall narrow building squeezed between an office block and a clothes shop. Tram wires ran like giant clothes' lines suspended along the middle of the road in front of it. The parade overlooked a dingy little park, dotted with bushes and containing a pond, a cadre of doleful ducks, a bandstand that I feel sure had never seen an actual band, and a concrete structure containing public conveniences that possessed somewhat the proportions of a large tool box. Saltykov parked on the road and, pointedly, neither helped me out of the cab nor aided my awkward progress over the pavement and inside the hotel.

At my re-encounter with Dora Norman, I felt, as the English poet said, [as if some new planet swam into my ken]. What I mean is that I felt a sense of renewed possibility. I have, since that day, often pondered those words. A new planet swims into your [ken], an English word for *knowledge*. Does this mean you are an imperialist, set upon dropping interplanetary troopers onto the surface, enslaving the indigenous inhabitants, colonising them? Or is the planet unoccupied, filled with verdancy, enforested, with bejewelled birds flying from bough to bough? Is it crying out for occupancy? Another English poet once called the object of his affections: 'My America, my newfoundland'. How could I not think of that, that had spent so much of my life reading poetry in English, and who found myself – at *my* age! with *my* ruined face and bashed-up brain! – in love with a woman young enough to be my daughter?

Dora put her arms around me when I saw her again. She was weeping, but with happiness. '[At first I thought you were dead – when Mr Saltykov returned . . .]'

'[Certainly not dead, my dear Dora,]' I said.

I sat down on the settee in the main room of the hotel suite, panting with the effort of the journey, and Dora made me some bitter-tasting tea – nectar, I declared it. Saltykov had the grace to leave us together. Syndrome or not, he empathised enough to see that we needed a little privacy.

'[When Mr Saltykov returned, he had such a doleful face . . .]'

'[His syndrome disposes him to dolour, I think.]'

'[I believe he thought you dead. There was an explosion?]'

'[There was.]'

'[It hasn't been in the news.]'

'[It is not surprising that the authorities have . . . is the English expression *shushed it up*?]'

'[Hushed it up, yes. So Mr Saltykov drove away from the reactor, and came back to me. He's been very good. He arranged this hotel room – I couldn't stay where I was, before. There were cockroaches.]'

'[This is to be preferred,]' I agreed.

'[It was, of course, hard to understand what Mr Saltykov was saying,]' she said. ['He found an English-Russian dictionary in an old bookshop in Kiev. Actually he found an English-Portuguese dictionary, and a Spanish-Russian dictionary, and the two of us sat for a long time looking up words and pointing at them. Communication was not very clear.]'

'[Ah,]' I said, trying to picture the scene.

'[There was some confusion. He wanted to tell me that he thought you were dead, but at first I thought he was saying that you were destined for greatness. Then he said I would never see you again, and I thought he was saying that you have proposed marriage in my absence. I understood eventually. It's so good to see you alive again!]'

'[It is good to *be* alive again,]' I said. Then I added, '[Better still to see *you*.]' Had I been standing, or capable of getting to my feet quickly, I would have bowed.

'[He checked the hospitals anyway. And he sat for hours in the lobby of the police station. Eventually they informed him you were still alive. How overjoyed I was! And here you are!]'

We embraced.

We settled into a sort of routine, the three of us occupying that two-room suite. Dora and Saltykov slept in the separate rooms they had been previously occupying; I slept on the settee in the front room. We agreed to make our way back to Moscow as soon as I was fit enough for the journey. And we agreed also on the need to keep Dora out of the way until she could be delivered to the American embassy in Moscow. I impressed upon them both the malignity and implacability of Frenkel. '[He wishes to kill you,]' I told Dora.

'[It makes me shudder to think of it,]' she said. There was something simply delightful in the way a quiver might pass across the amplitude of her flesh. I said as much to her, and she blushed again.

'But *why* does he wish such harm to Ms Norman?' Saltykov pressed.

'He wishes to kill her for the same reason he killed Dr Coyne,' I replied. 'I am sure of it. Although I am not sure, exactly, why he needed to kill Dr Coyne.'

I told them everything that Trofim had told *me* in the reactor room at Chernobyl; but it did nothing, precisely, to clear up the mystery.

Every day, Saltykov accompanied me as I undertook a ponderous, awkward walk in the park opposite the hotel. Every evening we ate together, and I translated between my beautiful Dora and my friend. We were waiting, simply enough, for me to become well enough to withstand the lengthy car journey back to Moscow; that is all. But some of the happiest moments in any life are moments of waiting. It has taken me a long life, and old age, to understand this important truth, and to slough off my youthful impatience.

'A week. No more,' I said. 'Then we can journey back.'

*

Three days passed in this manner. I told Dora of the strange encounter with Frenkel in the hospital, late at night. '[Perhaps I only dreamt it,]' I said. '[But it was a curious and vivid dream in that case.]'

'[Ugh! You scare me.]'

'[It is my intention. I love watching the shiver run through your flesh. It is a very sensual thing.]'

This had become a piece of common banter between us, and usually she laughed at it. But on this occasion she burst, suddenly, into tears. This wrongfooted me rather. '[My dear Ms Norman! Please do not *cry*.]'

'[I'm sorry! So sorry!]'

'[You have nothing to be sorry for, my dear Ms Norman!]'

'[It was when you said *flesh*.]'

'[I apologise! I am a monstrous and cruel man!]'

'[No! No! I know I have too much *flesh* – that's all.]'

'[All the better!]'

'[It cannot be better – I'm ashamed of being so *fat* …]'

'[There's no shame,]' I said severely. '[Since your flesh is beautiful, the amplitude of your flesh magnifies that beauty. Shame? Shame is not welcome here. Shame is how you feel in front of other people, that is the definition of shame. But there are no other people here, only me, and I am a part of you now. You cannot be ashamed of yourself, by yourself.]'

On another occasion she said, '[You were married before. I bet she was thin.]'

'[I was married in the 1940s. Everybody was thin. People starved to death – that's how thin they were. When you have watched that you never again find thinness to be a beautiful thing. This strange modern aberration that praises thinness – it's a function of an anomalous, global glut of food. Now, at this end of this terrible century, we find ourselves with more food than we can eat. But the human condition, taken as a whole, has not been plenty, but dearth. And it will be dearth again. Yours is the default position of beauty, my dear Ms Norman.]' Perhaps I was not quite so eloquent as I have here recalled, but this was the gist of what I said.

'[You are a sweet and lovely man,]' she said.

'[I don't know about that. I am, I would say, a ruined man,]' I noted.

'[You mean money?]'

'[I mean physically.]' I gestured at my scarred face; at the still livid, scorched-looking marks on my temple; at the bristly cropped hair. '[I am old, and disfigured. I know you cannot love me, you, young and lovely as you are. But it is enough for me to have seen you again. It is enough for me that you are alive.]'

She looked at me for a long time. Then she laid a hand – one of her tiny, delicate hands – on my cheek. '[But you have a beautiful soul,]' she said, simply.

Later she and Saltykov examined the back of my neck: she moved the back of my collar down, so that he did not have to touch me, and he peered. 'There is a lump,' Saltykov told me. 'A redness and a lump. Something under the skin.'

'A boil,' I said.

'Perhaps. Or perhaps your dream was not a dream?'

'You think Frenkel crept into my hospital room in the middle of the night, injected me with this, and then crept away again without killing me? It doesn't seem very likely to me.'

The two of them pondered that.

'You could cut it out,' I said, to Saltykov.

'What!'

''Get a knife and cut it open . . . to see if there's anything inside.'

'Not I,' said Saltykov, very emphatically.

I pondered making the same proposal to Dora, but thought better of it.

'Come,' said Saltykov. 'Time for your constitutional.'

'I would prefer to sit here.'

'[Come along,]' said Dora, tipping the perfect sphere of her body forward in the settee just enough to kiss me on the end of my scarred nose. '[You need your exercise.]'

'[Very well],' I replied. '[But I shall expect you to wait upon me like a geisha when I return, as a reward for my efforts.]'

She laughed, and rolled backwards, settling into her seat again.

Saltykov and I went down in the lift and exited the hotel. We waited for an especially shuddery and noisy tram to pass by and, crossing the road, made our way unrapidly into the park. Above us, barely visible flying saucers darted from the cover of one cloud to another. All the onion domes of all the towers of the Kremlin had detached themselves and flown straight up, and now they were flying in V-formation in the *very* high blue sky. Then, with an effort that brought a sweat to my skin, I walked a hundred yards, with Saltykov walking beside me. 'It would be easier for me,' I said, 'if I could lean upon your arm.'

'Perhaps you have forgotten,' he said. 'I suffer from a syndrome, one symptom of which is—'

'Syndrome, syndrome, syndrome. Do you know the English name for your syndrome? [Fuckwittery].'

'Really? I have come across American studies of my syndrome, and have never yet heard it so described.'

'You live and learn,' I said.

'Is [Fuckwitter] perhaps the name of a doctor who . . .'

'I have to sit upon this bench,' I said, lowering myself into the wooden slats.

'I shall sit beside you,' said Saltykov, primly. He sat at the other end of the bench, ensuring of course that there were several feet of wood between us. It would not do for him to come into contact of any kind with another man.

For a while we simply sat, and the sweat cooled on my face. The chill of early spring was in the air. It being a weekday, the park was more or less deserted.

'I do not comprehend love,' said Saltykov, out of the blue. I understood this to be his oblique way of making reference to the situation between Dora and myself.

'No?'

'People talk about it as a wonderful thing. An exciting and

pleasurable thing. Certainly I can see that it is, in terms of the successful transmission of genes, an immensely *useful* thing. But to elevate *love* to transcendental, cosmic and godly proportions, as people do? Is this not a little self-regarding? As if because I enjoy eating beefsteaks, and because beefsteaks serve the useful purpose of keeping me alive, I therefore declared that the universe is beefsteak, God a beefsteak and beefsteak the universal core value of everything?

'Your words produce in me,' I replied, 'an enormous desire to piss.'

'Are you referring to an actual desire, or a metaphorical one?' he replied, blandly.

'An actual one.'

'In that case the public toilets are over there.'

'Shall you come with me, to assist me?'

'The nature of my syndrome, as far as any intimacy at all with another man is concerned,' he began, but I cut him off with the groans I made as I levered myself upright from the bench.

'I appreciate,' I said stiffly, 'your courteous attempt to raise the subject of the state of emotional affairs between Dora Norman and myself.' He blinked at me. 'It is more than beefsteak,' I added, 'to my soul.'

'Good,' he said. Just that.

I walked slowly into the toilets, and stood at a bra-cup-shaped urinal, and relieved myself. Then I walked, slowly, back through the park. As I approached the bench I could see that another man had sat down upon it, next to Saltykov. But it was not until I had actually sat myself down that I saw that this new person was Frenkel.

'Sit down, Konsty,' he said, patting the wooden slats beside him. I would have preferred to remain standing, and would have liked to have been able to say, 'I prefer to stand'; but it so happened that my clapped-out legs would in no way support my weight. I lowered myself onto the seat.

'Jan,' I said, recovering my breath. 'It is surprising to see you again.'

'Surprising?'

'Saltykov?' I said, speaking across Frenkel's lap. 'Allow me to introduce Jan Frenkel, formerly of the KGB.'

Saltykov was looking away to the left, disdainfully.

'I have already introduced myself to Comrade Saltykov,' said Frenkel. 'I'm afraid he has taken a dislike to me. He is sulking.'

'He suffers from a syndrome,' I said.

'But why,' Frenkel went on, 'do you refer to me as *formerly* of the KGB?'

'I met a senior officer in hospital,' I replied, 'who gave me to believe ...'

'Oh, I'm under internal investigation,' said Frenkel, airily. 'They've taken away my gun. But that doesn't stop me being a member of the KGB. The KGB is not a club that people enter and leave at will.'

'I understand that you are now a colonel,' I said. 'Congratulations on your elevation.'

'Thank you!'

Saltykov was glowering with supreme intensity at some sparrows away to the left, as if *they* were somehow responsible for the career-advancement of so wicked a man as Frenkel.

'Did your promotion have anything to do with UFOs?'

'Ah,' said Frenkel.

'UFOs are good,' I said, 'at imparting *elevation* to individuals, after all. Lifting them up. One way or another.'

'UFOs,' said Frenkel. 'Do you know how many departments in the KGB are dedicated to UFOs?'

'I am of course prepared to guess.'

'Or I could just tell you,' he said, crossly. '*Seven* research institutes and *eleven* departments. All of them are attached to a secret wing of the KGB created specifically for this purpose. So. Why do you think the KGB is prepared to expend such resources on UFOs?'

'Is there a word for an acronym that has, specifically, three letters?' I asked, because the thought had just then struck me, and because it made me curious. 'Acronyms such as *UFO* and *KGB*. *Tricronyms*, perhaps?' But that didn't sound very convincing. 'What do you think, Saltykov?' But my friend was still sulking.

Frenkel glowered at me. 'I think,' he said, 'I preferred you before the lobotomy.'

'I was more anxious then, I think,' I said, thoughtfully. 'And more, as they say in America, [stressed-out]. More sarcastic, for that reason. But on the other hand, I had a better sense of future possibilities. I tried playing chess,' I added, 'with the nursing staff in the hospital, after my accident; but I can't plan my moves. I have lost the ability to play chess. And my memory is very erratic.'

'I really could not be less interested in your condition,' said Frenkel. 'You have lost *focus*, my old friend.' He shook his head. 'You were always an ironist – but now? What are you now? A blatherer! I preferred the caustic old Skvorecky, I don't mind telling you.'

'I don't mind hearing it,' I said.

'And how's your memory?'

'It has holes.'

'Do you remember this? Stalin personally commissioned us to write a coherent and plausible story of alien invasion, and then – surely you'll remember this – not long after, Stalin *personally ordered us* to quit the undertaking. Your memory isn't so malfunctional as to forget that, is it?'

'No,' I said. 'Not to forget that.'

'Kiev,' he said looking around. 'It always was a shithole. I was here in the war, you know? It was a shithole then, and it's a shithole now.'

'It was certainly full of holes, in the war,' I said. 'And, to be fair to it, it has far fewer holes now.'

'Shitheap, then,' he said. 'Eh Saltykov?'

And the conversation stalled for a while.

'After the war,' said Frenkel, in an expansive tone of voice, as if beginning a lecture, 'an official Soviet archeological expedition was digging in Kiev. There was a lot of rebuilding, so there was plenty of opportunity. This was a site on Reitarskaya Street – it's been kept completely secret, of course. It was a tomb, a *vault*, twenty feet below the ground. Inside was a massive chest. Inside the chest were five *hundred* books. Books in Russian, but also in Greek, in Arabic, even in fucking *Sanskrit*. The MVD arrived in a matter of hours, bunged everything into three covered trucks, and carried it all away to Moscow.'

'Intriguing,' I said, 'if not wholly plausible.'

'It's real,' he said. 'I've seen these artefacts. I have held the books in my hand.'

'Really?'

'Books filled with drawings, technical plans, instructions. Orbital stations. Docking equipment for spaceships.'

'If the KGB owns the groundplans for spaceships and space-stations, then am I to assume that the Soviet Union has been secretly constructing advanced spacecraft?'

'No. It was not about building our own spaceships. It was about preparing the machinery necessary to receive *their* spaceships.'

'Like getting instructions from Hitler to build garages in Moscow so he can park his tanks?'

'Not like that! Do you know what else was there? A handwritten manuscript. *Slovo o polku Igoreve*, Prince Igor's adventures. The *Prince Igor*! Written by Pyotr Borislavovich – the famous Pyotr Borislavovich. They've been here for thousands of years.'

'And yet they are still to arrive.'

'That's it!' he sounded, excited. 'That's exactly right!'

'Back in Moscow, when I sent you up to that safe apartment with Trofim. You were supposed to call her, Dora Norman, and get her to meet with me, remember?'

'I remember the chute,' I said, darkly. 'And I remember you putting a pistol into my mouth.'

'Oh that was just to, you know. What do the French say? *Pour encourager les – les—,*'

'Aliens?'

'Exactly. We're old friends, you and I. I went to a good deal of effort to bring you onside. To *help* you believe. You could have done some good. You see, I was foolish enough to trust our friendship. We'd been friends before, hadn't we? When we met Stalin? I didn't see why we wouldn't be friends still. You would have helped me *because* of our friendship. But you're not very good at friendship. Too much the ironist.'

'Irony is a jealous mistress,' I said.

'But,' Frenkel went on, adopting an incongruously oleaginous voice, 'I still think of myself as *your* friend, Konsty,'

'Is that why you sent the red-haired fellow to smother me with a pillow in my hospital bed?'

'I wonder if you'll be able to understand why I would do such a thing?' he mused.

'Wonder away.'

'Besides he was unsuccessful – wasn't he? You're still alive – aren't you?'

'Not for want of trying.'

'The important point is,' said Frenkel, locking his fingers together, and pushing his palms out, producing thereby a Geiger-counter crackle of pops and snaps in his joints. 'You don't believe in UFOs?'

This question, calmly posed, seemed to me to distil the entire hectic week into a quiet intensity. It was, it occurred to me, *it*. I did not rush an answer. I opened my mind to my thoughts, as a person flips through a well-read novel. What evidence was there? None. 'Let us say, no,' I said.

'Would you say that you can *prove* there are no UFOs?'

'The burden of proof is not mine,' I noted. 'It is on the people claiming the extraordinary.'

'But who is to say which state of affairs – aliens, no aliens – is extraordinary? At any rate, you accept that you cannot prove that aliens do *not* exist.'

'It's a big cosmos.'

'Exactly! Let us say, then, that I cannot prove to you that

aliens exist. Even though I believe it with a perfect certainty. And you cannot prove to me they do *not* exist.'

'We should, then, go on the balance of probabilities. My belief is more probable than yours.'

'I disagree.'

'We can agree to disagree. I think we both know what is going on.'

'And what is that?' Frenkel asked.

The words came smoothly, and easily, although I am not sure I had arranged all the elements in the picture until that moment. But as I said it, there, it all cohered. It was my brain's new-found ability to understand the picture. It was my new brain.

This is what I said to him. 'The world is changing,' I said. 'Gorbachev is dismantling the Soviet Union. You, and people like you – people with authority, people hidden and secret – do not want it to happen. You are engaged upon an illegal and covert operation to destabilise perestroika, and unseat Gorbachev; to create – no, wait: to *recreate* – the crisis days of the Great Patriotic War. Because the USSR is losing the Cold War, you have decided that America will not function as the enemy. But because you, like all old and stubborn Communists, revere Stalin, you have decided to resurrect the old man's plan. And so you have spent years building the narrative of alien invasion, and adding heft to it by scattering clues, props, assertion and even creative denial to fix the belief in people's minds. It's nonsense, but it is surprising how much nonsense people will believe. Particularly in worrying times.'

'Go on,' said Frenkel.

'Oh I don't know,' I said. 'Maybe the American, Coyne, was part of a secret team assembled to blow up the nuclear reactor at Chernobyl. That is the main event: that's what you're really doing. You blow up Chernobyl – and then go public with the story. Aliens! War! Special measures – roll back glasnost, remilitarise the nation, the Soviet Union steps to the vanguard! It leads the world against the new threat. And of course, you have all the evidence, all the props and trimmings, kept, you say,

270

in a secret warehouse in Moscow since being dug out of the ground in Kiev after the war.'

'You tell a compelling story,' said Frenkel. 'I always admired your storytelling powers.'

'Thank you,' I replied. 'Except that this story is not science fiction. It is a murder story. Trofim said as much, inside the reactor. These people would be laying down their lives, by the million, for the greater good. The survival of Communism.'

Frenkel seemed to be considering this. 'But Trofim believed, literally, in the aliens. Didn't he?'

'That you were able to persuade Trofim of this absurd story,' I said, 'does not surprise me. He was hardly the most nimble-witted individual I have ever met.'

'And Nik?'

'Nik?'

'The gentleman I sent to your hospital to kill you.'

'Ah – Comrade Red-hair.'

'Did it seem to you that *he* believed?' Frenkel asked.

'In the aliens.' I recalled. 'I suppose so. But, Jan, so what? Naturally you need a story capable of being believed by many people. That is necessary. Naturally you have worked to convince your underlings that it is the truth. It is after the manner of a cult,' I said. 'Look at Trofim: he believed the aliens were attacking Chernobyl, even though he was *himself* planting the bomb!'

'Or perhaps he believed that he himself planting the bomb was the method by which the aliens were attacking Chernobyl?'

I thought about this for a while. It was a curiously resonant, and oddly disconcerting, observation. 'Wouldn't aliens be more likely to use laser cannons, or photon torpedoes?'

'And wouldn't Hitler be more likely to fire V2 rockets and atom bombs at Soviet troops? Yet I once fought a Nazi in a farmyard, and he was armed with a shovel.'

'Hardly the same situation.'

'Isn't it?'

'Jan, you were planning to *tell the world* that *aliens* had blown up

Chernobyl. I was a witness that Trofim was the agent of destruction, not space visitors. Thus I had to be eliminated.'

'That wasn't the reason.' He grimaced, with glee, or pain, it was hard to say. 'And besides you are getting things the wrong way around. *You* think we concocted a story of aliens in order to shore up Communism. I have seen what the USSR was capable of under a strong Communist leadership. So have you. And now we need only look to Afghanistan to see what it is capable of under a weak, reformist, crypto-capitalist leadership. I know which system is better geared to protecting humanity. I do not wish to invent space aliens in order to shore up Communism. I wish to shore up Communism because it is the best defence against alien invasion.'

'By shore up Communism you mean things like ... murder Americans.'

'Coyne?' Frenkel seemed actually shocked. 'I didn't murder him.'

'But of course you want to pretend that the aliens murdered him.'

His eyes were wide open in his solid, Slav face. 'Konsty,' he said. 'You were *there* when Coyne was murdered.'

'He was hooked up in a poacher's snare, by somebody leaning out of a window, hoisted twenty feet above ground, and then dropped down to break his back.'

'Ah,' said Frenkel. 'Lifted up, how?'

'By a rope.'

'Ah,' said Frenkel. 'You remember there being a rope?'

'I do.'

'But I have read the police reports. No rope was discovered at the scene.'

'I saw the rope,' I said.

'The Militia officers did not.'

'I was there.'

'And yet there *is* no material evidence.'

'I suppose the rope was removed from the scene by the murderers.'

'And how, exactly, did they do this? It was tied around his ankle, no? So did you see somebody come down and untie it?'

'No,' I conceded.

'And yet you stayed by the body until the Militia arrived?'

'They arrested me immediately.'

'So, there was no rope. And yet you remember seeing a rope. Now: if the physical evidence contradicts witness testimony, wouldn't you be inclined to mistrust the witness? People sometimes see things that aren't there, after all. They may not be lying; they may be genuinely mistaken. Genuinely hallucinating.' He smiled broadly at me.

'I saw the rope,' I repeated.

'Your disbelief is stubborn,' said Frenkel. 'Disbelief can be like belief in that respect.'

'Let's talk about the UFO phenomenon,' he said.

'I am enjoying this talk,' I replied. 'It is diverting and stimulating.'

'But permit me to ask a question,' he said. 'You do *not* believe in the material reality of UFOs, or aliens, or abductions, or any of that?'

'No.'

'And yet you cannot deny that many people *do* believe in those things.'

'Of course.'

'So you deny the reality of UFOs, but you do not deny the reality of UFOs as a cultural or social phenomenon?'

'Exactly.'

'Well then. Let us say three million people in the USSR, and three million in the USA, not only believe in UFOs, but claim to have experienced them directly. To have *seen* them. To have *been abducted* by them – to have had procedures enacted upon their bodies, semen extracted from their genitals, memories wiped from their minds.'

'Is it so many?'

'At a conservative estimate.'

'It is a large number.'

'Some of these people,' said Frenkel, 'are perhaps lying. Perhaps they are malicious, or bored, or perhaps they are seeking attention and fame and the like. So they tell these stories of alien abduction, even though they know them to be false.'

'Eminently plausible.'

'But surely you cannot believe that all six million people who report UFOs are like this? Six million wicked liars? Impossible!'

'Not all of them, by any means.'

'Perhaps only a small proportion of them are *deliberately* lying?'

'The remainder,' I said, 'are simply mistaken.'

'Mistaken? Nearly *six million people* – mistaken?'

'Indeed. Hallucinating perhaps. Or interpreting ordinary occurrences in an extraordinary way.'

'Six million people hallucinating in unison?'

'It sounds a little improbable,' I said. 'But it is the only explanation that fits the facts.'

'May we not apply your earlier test of *probabilities*, in lieu of proof?'

'But that's it,' I said. 'There are only two explanations for this widespread reportage of alien abduction. So let us test the respective probabilities of the two. Somebody claims to have been abducted by a UFO. Let us discard the possibility that he is deliberately lying, since, as you say, not all the six million can be liars. So what has happened? Either he has been literally abducted. Or else he has in some sense imagined the experience. A dream, a hallucination. Perhaps it was not an alien, but only a spectre from the subconscious mind. Which is more likely?'

'There is a third possibility.'

'That he is lying?'

'No, we have agreed to discount that,' said Frenkel. 'So we have on the one hand, perhaps, an actual alien; and on the other perhaps a phantom from the subconscious mind. But there is a third possibility.'

'Go on,' I prompted.

'You must listen carefully,' he said. 'We are approaching the reality of the situation. What I will say may dissolve your unbelief quite away.'

'I doubt that,' I said. 'But I am listening.'

'You think of alien abduction as something that happens to certain individuals.'

'Are you saying it does not?'

He shook his head. 'No, no. It *does* happens to individuals, of course. But also it happens to a mass of people.'

'Millions of them,' I said.

'If an individual imagines something that's not there we say he hallucinates. But what happens when *a whole people* imagines something?'

'Mass hallucination?'

'You are being distressingly literal minded. I shall give you an example. What is Communism, but the dream of a whole people? If an individual dreams utopia, he is just a dreamer. But once an entire people dream it, it becomes reality.'

'Communism seems to be a dream from which people are waking up,' I observed.

This might have made him angry, but instead he seized upon it. 'Exactly! Exactly. We have stopped collectively imagining Communism, and so it is decaying around us. You suggested that UFOs were either material objects in the universe, or else the abductee simply imagined it. I say that what we need is an act of collective imagination, an act as heroic and world-changing as the October Revolution. I say that we are on the cusp of alien invasion – a *real* one, not an imaginary one – and that the only thing that can save us is a world capable of collectively willing those aliens into our observation.'

'Imaginative revolution,' I said. 'Naturally such rhetoric appeals to a creative writer. But what about an ordinary citizen? What do *you* think, Saltykov?'

'He agrees with me,' said Frenkel.

'You've been silent a very long time, Saltykov,' I said, loudly. 'Don't sulk! What is your opinion of all this blather?'

'A little deaf, I think,' whispered Frenkel. 'In his right ear.'

His head was still turned away. I looked at the back of his neck; his lager-coloured hair; his narrow, pale cranium. 'Old friend,' I said, loudly, 'what's the matter?'

'There's nothing the matter with old Saltykov,' boomed Frenkel, putting his arm around the man's back and clapping his shoulder? 'Eh? Eh?' Saltykov's body jiggled with the motion imparted to it by Frenkel's jollity.

'Oh!' I said, as I understood. Saltykov permitting himself to be touched? By a man? Oh, of course.

I took a deep breath. Matters were more serious than I had realised.

The odd thing, as I contemplated the situation I was in, was how little fear I felt. This was odd because I could still remember what it felt like to experience fear, so much so that I was actually conscious of the gap between the former and the present state of mind. I was also aware of a deep penetration of sorrow, as if a heavy stone fell through an inner shaft in my soul, into my depths. It was a sad business. It is sad to lose a friend, and nothing that had happened in the explosion had robbed me of the capacity to experience the weight of that. Nevertheless there was very little acuteness of emotional attack in my cut-about brain.

'I'm not the bad guy,' Frenkel was saying, earnestly. 'You mistake me. I'm the *good* guy. I'm the one trying to save humanity.'

'By committing mass murder?'

'On the contrary: mass redemption. There may be casualties, of course. But casualties are one of the best ways of bringing home to people – that which they do not yet realise, but which is the bald truth – that we are fighting a war.'

'I've had enough of war,' I said.

'Nonsense! You're a hero of the Great Patriotic War, a warrior of Communism. Come on, Konstantin,' Frenkel boomed, getting to his feet and hauling me up. 'You are staying in a hotel, here in Kiev. Take me to it! Show me some hospitality!'

I was unsteady on my feet, and staggered a little like a drunk.

Saltykov, of course, remained sitting on the bench glowering at the sparrows.

Poor old Saltykov.

'I thought you said,' I put in, in as steady a voice as I could manage, 'that your gun has been taken from you?'

'Pending investigation,' he confirmed. 'But my muscles are still there – I have not lost my muscular strength.'

'You always were a big Slav,' I agreed.

'And now, in your enfeebled state, you are frankly no match for me.' I saw the glint of metal tucked into the sleeve of his coat. 'Come! Take me to the hotel.'

'We'll need to get a tram,' I said. 'It's quite a long way from here. Or we could get a taxi.'

'Distance,' said Frenkel, giving me another slap on the back to move me along. 'In a sense it is a subjective quality, is it not? Distortions in the space-time continuum. For what you describe as a long way, reachable only by taxi, *I* would call just across the road.' He pointed at the entrance to our hotel. 'The very building from which I saw you and Saltykov come out not half an hour ago.'

Another push, and I stumbled a few more steps. 'It's really not a very nice hotel,' I said. 'Why don't we find somewhere nice for a drink? We can continue our conversation. I was enjoying our conversation.'

'Come on,' he said, giving me another shove. 'I have something special for you. You can still serve the greater good.'

The road was not busy, which was fortunate since it took me a long time to shuffle across to the far side. I felt enormously decrepit. I felt this because it was true. And there I was, standing in front of the main entrance to the hotel, with Frenkel's wrestler's torso pressed up against my back. I could feel the sharp point of his knife against my kidney. 'Straight through the lobby and into the lift,' he said, into my ear.

'The key.' I said. 'I'll need to collect the key from the concierge.'

'You really think I'm a fucking idiot,' said Frenkel, not unkindly. 'That I should fall for such a thing? You didn't leave the key with the concierge. She's still up there in the room. You can just knock on the door, and she'll let you in.'

The lift door opened as soon as I pressed the button, and closed as soon as we were inside. I could smell Frenkel's body odour, shrimpy and dense. That I could smell it suggested that it was a potent stench indeed. The blade he was holding against my back had poked through the cloth of my coat, and my shirt, and my vest, and was a sharp point of hurt on my skin. The upward motion of the lift in motion made my stomach quail.

At the top the lift door opened, and Frenkel shoved me out, and into the corridor. It was ten yards, at most, along the dingy thread-bare carpet to our door. I was trying to think on my feet, but my bashed old brain was not functioning well. 'This isn't the right floor,' I said.

'Yes it is. Go along and knock on the door,' he told me.

I stepped towards the wrong door and lifted my fist, but Frenkel 'a!-a!' -ed me, and angled my body in the right direction.

I was carried inevitably towards the door.

'I don't understand why you want to kill her,' I said. It was, to a degree, infuriating to me that I felt so little by way of fear. But I had a bone-deep sense of the intellectual and emotional wrongness of any harm coming to Dora.

'What's she to you?' he snapped. 'A foreigner. A stranger. You barely know her.'

'I barely know Ms Norman,' I conceded.

'So you'll be barely upset when I kill her.'

'I know almost nothing about her,' I said, slightly stiffly. 'I have spent only a few days in her company. She is from a different nation, and a different generation, to me. I would have to say that the word that best describes the relationship between herself and myself would be *engaged*.'

'Engaged?'

'Yes.'

'To be married?'

'Certainly not engaged to be stabbed,' I said.

'Konsty!' gasped Frenkel. But I saw at once that he was not gasping, but laughing. 'You never cease to amaze me. You old goat!'

'In the circumstances . . .'

'In the circumstances it's a *great* shame she has to die,' he said. 'Before she's been able to enjoy the conjugal delight of your wheezy old body humping about on top of her!'

I flipped through the pages of my mental notepad, but there was almost nothing there. I had to do something. I couldn't permit this man to murder the woman I loved. 'Ivan,' I said, 'we've been through a lot together. You said you considered me a friend. I am asking you *as* a friend – do not kill her. I'll help you do what you want to do. I'll do anything you tell me. There's no need for her to die.'

'I tell you what,' said Frenkel. 'Do as I say, and I'll not kill her. Engaged! You getting married *again*? And to an *American*! Hey – you could claim US citizenship! Assuming the authorities ever let you go there.'

'That's not why I'm doing it.'

'No? Why, then?'

'I love her.'

And Frenkel laughed like a barking seal. 'Splendid! Splendid! Well, knock on the door, introduce me properly to your wife-to-be.'

'You promise not to kill her?'

'I promise. On the understanding that *you* promise to do everything I tell you.'

'It's understood.'

'Go on then.'

I knocked. Almost at once Dora opened the door. The light was behind her and her face was enshadowed, though I could see enough to see that was smiling. More, I could see that she was looking past me to the man behind expecting to see Saltykov. But there was no mistaking burly Frenkel for scrawny Saltykov. Her expression darkened.

With a hefty push Frenkel threw me into the room, straight past her. There wasn't even time for me to reach out and touch her as I shot in. I tried to balance myself on my rickety legs, staggered several steps and began to fall, striking the back of the settee with my hip and collapsing over. Then I was on the ground, moaning with the pain, and struggling ineffectually to get up. Dora stepped back, her dainty feet moving with characteristic nimbleness to balance her large body. Frenkel came in. The blade flashed in his hand, and went into Dora's side. It came out bloody, and then it went in again.

She did not cry out. She danced back another two steps, with her head cocked to the side and her face crumpled with pain, or surprise, or the combination of the two; and she rolled down onto the floor with a thud. Hungry knifeblade – to take the life first of Saltykov in the park, and yet not to be satiated! Straight away to take the life of gracious, beautiful Dora Norman in that hotel room! How strange it was that an old and feeble man, such as I, could be blown to pieces by a grenade and yet survive; where a young and vigorous woman, such as she, could be killed by a few inches of polished metal.

I cried out, 'Dora!'

Frenkel was shutting the door to the room. 'Get up,' he said to me. 'Get off the floor. This is no time for lounging about.'

It's a mistake to talk about being *full of grief*, as if grief were a tumour, or a full stomach, or some manner of swelling. Grief is an absence. It doesn't push, it sucks. To make a metaphorical cut or slice in the sealed membrane of the grieving self is not to permit matter to gush out. On the contrary, it is to permit the unbearable world to come surging in. I had lain there and watched as Frenkel stuffed a knife blade into the pliant flesh of the woman I loved. 'What have you done?'

He was hauling me to my feet, and shoving me over towards the window. 'Sacrifices have to be made,' he said. He still had the knifeblade in his right hand. There was blood.

'You promised me you wouldn't kill her,' I observed, nearly falling over my own feet.

'A KGB officer not keeping his promises? You amaze me.'

He shoved me.

'I can't believe it!' I cried. '[Dora? My love?]' Shove, and shove, and I was at the window. '[Dora, can you hear me?]' I was calling. 'Dora!' I could see her, over Frenkel's shoulder, a heap of flesh piled motionless on the floor.

'She's dead,' said Frenkel. 'Forget about her. Consider instead your own imminent extinction.'

I was pressed up against the glass now. The prospect of my own death did not bother me in the slightest. 'You could have killed me at the hospital,' I said.

He was holding the knife against my torso with his right hand and fiddling with the latch for the window with his left. 'I rebuked Nik thoroughly for his failure, don't worry.'

'I don't mean the red-haired man,' I said, still trying to see past Frenkel to the body of my fiancée, humped upon the carpet like a small hill of flesh. 'I mean when you visited me personally.'

'*I* never visited you in hospital. What, you think I'm going to bring you a bundle of flowers?'

'When you injected this thing in my neck.' I wasn't really concentrating on what I said. I was straining to look at Dora's ample body, lying on the carpet. Not moving.

Frenkel had stopped fiddling with the latch. He was looking at me.

'What did you say?'

'You stuck me in the neck with this mosquito bite.'

'I never did that,' he said. He was speaking, all of a sudden, curiously slowly.

'I remember it.'

'You don't remember,' he insisted.

'Again with your hypnotism nonsense? That tone of voice? I remember what I remember.'

He looked at me long and hard. Then he looked at the knife in his hand, turning the blade back and forth. 'Believe me, I never came to your hospital. It was under Militia guard, you know. Nik failing in his bid to have you killed meant I'd missed my chance.'

'You came,' I told him, casting my mind back, 'in the middle of the night, and you shone a torch in my face, and then you reached round and jabbed me in the neck.'

'And how did I get past the guards?'

'You told me you were invisible.'

'I told you that!' he said. It looked at though his face was about to crumple into anger, or perhaps even despair, but then, with that odd little knight's move of the emotions that was characteristic of him, he suddenly burst out laughing. 'I *did* tell you that! I told you I was invisible? Fuck, I *was* invisible!'

'If you'd simply killed me there,' I said, trying to access the full range of anguish I knew to be inside me, 'then I wouldn't have been able to lead you back to her now. I wish you'd done it then.'

Frenkel was looking at me in a very strange way. 'It wasn't the hospital, Konsty.'

'But I remember you! You came in the middle of the night!'

'Ah! Now couldn't that have been a *dream*? Don't you have *dreams* in the middle of the night, like everybody else?'

Of course it could have been a dream. 'On the other hand,' I said. 'This lump is definitely in my neck. The mosquito definitely bit me. Even though the weather is much too cold for mosquitoes.' Saying this brought the memory of Trofim's huge bovine face swimming in front of me. I was back, momentarily, in the Moscow restaurant; back in the place where Frenkel had told me his whole peculiar abduction story. I blinked.

I blinked.

I was in a Kiev hotel room, and the woman I loved was lying dead upon the carpet, and the man who killed her was standing right in front of me. 'You know what?' he was saying. 'It's remarkable.'

'What *is* this thing you've put in my neck, anyway?'

'It's very precious, old man. Miniature and powerful and made by no human hands.'

'Still with this? Genuine alien technology? Give it up, Jan! You and I know better than that.'

'I'm very struck that you remembered,' he mused. 'I suppose it's the brain injury. Who knows what effect that would have?'

'Mashed up,' I said. 'But I'm still capable of feeling *grief*.' I wished that were true.

'Konsty, you goat,' he chortled. 'I *did* jab you in the neck. I did it in a seedy little restaurant in Moscow, weeks ago. Weeks and weeks. Then I made you forget that I had done it. I made you forget, and you really had forgotten for good. And now here you are remembering! What I mean to say is: the memory has been jumbled up out of the ooze of your brain. You've relocated the experience in your memory. I *was* invisible to you when I jabbed you. So you've relocated the memory to the night-time, when people generally *are* invisible. And you've attached it to the hospital. It didn't happen in the hospital.'

'I remember that restaurant.'

'Of course you do!'

'Are you saying,' I asked him, 'that you *hypnotised* me? Are you a *hypnotist*?' A thought occurred to me. 'Did you hypnotise Trofim into seeing aliens? Little green men?'

'No, no. Hypnotism is no good for those sorts of special effects. What hypnotism is good for is encouraging you *not* to notice things that *are* there.'

'There's no such thing as hypnotism,' I said.

'There's no such thing as hypnotism,' he agreed. 'No magical trance state in the brain, no. It is nothing. Shall I tell you what it is? It is wholly a question of suggestibility. I'll tell you something else. It works best with people who are conditioned to respect authority and who are used to doing what authority figures tell them. The Soviet Union is full of such people. Most of this century has been an experiment in creating an entire population of such people. Ex-army are best of all. When somebody with a suitably authoritative manner tells you something, you tend to believe it. Even if what they are telling you is: *I am invisible, you cannot see me, you will not remember this.*'

'Nonsense!'

'Isn't it, though? Still, you didn't see me, and didn't remember. Until that explosion knocked your brain about.'

'Mesmerism, though?'

'It's a technical discipline – one mastered by the KGB.'

'KGB mind control?' I scoffed.

'It's not mind control,' he said. 'It's alternate realities. It's tuning the brain into an alternate timeline. It's purely technical – there's a generator, and it superimposes a slightly different quantum reality upon the . . .' He put a finger out and rotated an imaginary telephone dial in the air in front of him. 'Etcetera and etcetera,' he concluded, airily.

'How very plausible,' I observed, craning my neck to see Dora's body.

'It's of especial use for a secret policeman,' he explained. 'I say, "You can't see me," and you can't see me. The important thing is in making sure you can't see *certain things*. Things,' he added, slipping the knife into his pocket, and readying his stance, prior to pushing me, 'like aliens.'

'You want people *not* to see the aliens?'

'People not seeing the aliens is precisely the point!' This seemed to animate him tremendously. 'You need to understand. Getting people to see the aliens is everything we have been working towards! People are distressingly good at not seeing things. Have you never had the experience of looking for a pen, and searching your desk, and looking everywhere, and only at the end realising that the pen was right there in front of your face the whole time?'

'The elephant in the room,' I said.

'Exactly – that's it exactly. We are trying to get people *to see the fucking elephant*.'

'Not pen?'

'The elephant is a better analogy.'

'It is a bigger analogy, I suppose.'

He ignored this. 'If things go to plan – and you have been a fucking pain in the arse about that, by the way – but *if* they go to plan then people will suddenly *see* the elephant that's been in front of them all along. Like now: you're chatting with me, and in doing so you're entirely failing to see the big thing here, your own death. It's right outside the window, there – look – huge, and you can't even see it.' And the strange thing is that there *was* something outside the window: vast, metal, oval or spherical; it occupied the sky; it hung in air. It was so huge you couldn't miss it. You could *not* not see it. But I looked again, and understood that it was too huge to be seen. I couldn't see anything: just sky, and the Kiev skyline. As if it might be: hold a coin-sized circle of glass, with its shine and its scratches, at arm's length and you'll see it. And hold it in front of your eye and you'll see it. But your cornea, shining and scratched and closer than anything else, you cannot see. For a moment I saw the machine in the sky, and then I could only see sky.

'There's nothing out there.' I said, aloud. I didn't say this for Frenkel's benefit. I suppose it was for *my* benefit. I suppose it was to confirm that I had never seen the thing in the sky.

'Out the window you go, old friend. You can take a closer look, as you go down.'

He stepped towards me, and his left hand clamped onto (because I was facing him) my right arm, and his right arm clamped on to my left arm. Behind me the window was unlatched. A quick shove and I would tumble against it, and it would swing open, and I would fall.

'The elephant in the room,' I said again.

'That's it.'

'The elephant is – *in* the room.'

Dora was right behind him.

She was holding a book in her hand: a thousand-page hardback book with a gaudy-coloured cover illustration of tentacled aliens. '[Mr Frenkel,]' she asked, in the politest tones, '[would you sign my copy of your novel?]'

Frenkel's expression twitched at the sound of her voice. He craned round to look back over his shoulder, and tried to twist his torso to face her. His hand went towards the pocket in which he had cached his knife; but I saw what he was doing and *my* two hands went towards *his* hand. He was stronger than me, but I was strong enough, and motivated enough, to grab his wrist and yank his hand down below the level of his jacket. I did this to prevent him grasping his knife. He strained to lift it and get inside his jacket pocket.

'[Oh my mistake!]' said Dora, and now I could hear the strain in her voice. '[This novel is not by you. It is by Konstantin Skvorecky.]'

'Wait,' grunted Frenkel, still straining to pull out his knife. He was reaching with his right arm, being right handed. My right side had been weakened by my injury. But luckily I was facing him, so I was using my left hand to prevent him from bringing out his knife.

Dora swung the book in towards his face, blushing red with the effort. Her prodigious jowls quivered.

She swung the book so that its spine collided with Frenkel's nose. His head snapped back, and a gasp stuttered from his mouth. I danced to the side as quickly as my old legs could manage, and levered him onwards, and Dora pushed forward with her considerable, her beautiful, her life-saving bulk. With me on his right side, and Dora on his left, and blood coming out of his nose, Frenkel found himself propelled forwards and out. His head struck the unlatched window with a boom. The panel swung open, and Frenkel toppled out, and Dora and I released him at exactly the same moment.

Down he went.

He fell straight down the height of four floors. He didn't say anything. He didn't, for instance, call out. He had tipped over onto his back, and we could see him looking up at us, but the expression on his face was not even especially surprised: although a small quantity of blood *had* come out of his nose and covered his upper lip, like a black-red paint-on Hitler moustache. Like Hitler, or like Charlie Chaplin. It was four floors down to what the Americans call the [sidewalk]. He landed with the sound of cowflop hitting the ground. The first portion of his body to connect with the ground was the back of his head, and then his spine, and hips, and then his arms and legs: each segment of his body followed rapidly one after the other. He did not bounce. He did not move after the impact. Not so much as a twitch.

I felt wobbly, and unwell, and exhausted; but I felt better than Dora evidently did. It was not an easy matter for a fellow as elderly and infirm as I was to assist a woman as weighty as she across the floor, but I did my best, and was able to help her stagger over to the couch. She half-sat and half-collapsed, and I knelt down beside her. '[There is some blood,]' I told her, lifting her shirt and examining the mouth-shaped wound.

'[It hurts!]'

'[My poor love – I'm so sorry – my poor girl.]'

'[It hurts, but I don't think there's any serious damage. Thank heavens I'm so fat!]'

'[Thank heavens,]' I agreed, earnestly. '[It has saved your life.]'

'[Oh!]' she said. ['Oh, it hurts! But if I'd been some rake-skinny girl . . .]'

'[Then you would have died],' I said. '[Frenkel knew what he was doing. He was aiming the knife at vital organs.]'

'[Thank heavens,]' she said, in a fainter voice, '[that all my vital organs are wrapped in my protective layer!]'

'[Didn't he stab you twice?]'

'[My arm.]' She was holding her left arm stiffly, awkwardly. I had not noticed this before.

'[Let me look.]'

'[He got me in the side,]' she said. '[I moved my arm to where he'd cut me, and then he cut me again.]'

Her arm was sopping and wet, and her hand bright red. There was blood, I saw, dipping downwards from her fingers' ends onto the carpet. This wound looked much more serious. '[I will get help,]' I said, creakily rising and going to the bed where the room's phone was. In a moment I had called the reception desk, and within a minute two people were in the room with me. A first aid box was brought in. By the look of it, it dated from before the war.

'Have you called an ambulance?' I asked the concierge. 'There's also a man on the pavement outside. He fell from the window. He might need help.'

He looked from the window. 'There's no one there,' he said.

I went with Dora to the hospital. In the ambulance they gave her something for the pain, and then told me to talk with her. Don't let her go to sleep, they told me. So I talked with her. '[Where did you get the book?]'

'[It's yours.]'

'[I know it's mine. It's the omnibus edition of *Three Who Made a Star*. It's all three volumes in one. That's why it is so big; a thousand pages, more or less. But I have not seen a copy for half a century. I don't even have a copy at my flat!]'

'[Saltykov found it in an old bookshop, somewhere near the hotel. He bought it for me, as a present. He knew I would be interested, because it was by you.]'

There seemed to me something wrong with my burn-scarred face. I could feel a strange loosening behind the skin, near the eyes and the bridge of the nose.

'[I got up, quietly, after he stabbed me. I lay there for a moment,]' Dora was saying. '[Until I got my breath back, and then I got myself up. It stung to move. I looked around for something to hit him with. He was a dangerous man. But I couldn't see anything – well, I thought about the lamp.]'

'[The lamp?]'

'[Only it was plugged in, and the plugs you have over here aren't like proper American plugs, and I wasn't sure I could unplug it easily. Then I saw the book. Your *Three Who Made a Star*. So I picked that up.]'

'[Thank heavens I wrote such a fat book,]' I said.

'[A slim volume would hardly have been much of a weapon,]' she agreed, grimacing; in pain, I thought at first; but, no: because she was laughing.

'[We can be grateful,]' I told her, kissing her good hand, '[that science fiction novels are so fat.]'

'[We may be grateful in a general sense for fatness,]' she agreed.

The ambulance brought us to the hospital – a different building, and indeed a different site, to the place in which I had convalesced. Two rows of cherry trees displayed their ridiculous pink and white blossom in enormous profusion. They wheeled her through the main door. They gave her a painkiller. I sat with her in the emergency room. I held her good hand as they cut off her shirt and bandaged up her wounds. 'The wound to the stomach is superficial,' the doctor said. 'The wound to the arm is a little more serious, but not life-threatening. The tip of the blade has scratched the tibia. I'm afraid it will be sore for some time. There will be bruising.'

I translated this for her. '[Black and blue!]' she said in a mournful voice. '[I have always bruised like a peach.]'

'[You *are* a peach,]' I told her, as tears seeped from my ridiculous old-man eyes. '[You are my peach. You are my beautiful luscious American peach.] I love you,' I added, in Russian.

'[What's that?]'

So I told her then how to say *I love you* in Russian. It involves putting together three English words: two colours and a human bone – as it might be, the colour of a fading bruise, and the colour of a fresh bruise, and a bone in the arm: just those three English words. Say them together, rolling from one to the other as you speak, and you will find that you are saying *I love you* in Russian. It was a delight for me to hear her say that Russian phrase, over and over. It was delightful.

Frenkel's body could not be found, although – according to the Militia – there *was* blood on the pavement beneath the hotel window. I do not believe that Frenkel could simply have stood up and walked away after such a fall. I couldn't help the Militia explain who might have moved his body, or why.

Saltykov's body was recovered from the park. The Militia had no suspects; and since we were the only two people in the whole of

Kiev who knew him, we were formally questioned. He had no dependants, it seemed; and no friends or partners. He was buried in a Kiev municipal graveyard.

We were warned by the Militia not to leave the city, since investigation into the death of Saltykov, and the assault upon Dora Norman, was still ongoing. We stayed in the hotel room, both of us slowly recovering our health. My grief for poor old Saltykov was strangely modulated by my joy that Dora was alive, even though I had thought her dead. Every night I laid my hands gently upon her enormous belly, her fluid hips, and gave thanks to her sheer bulk for saving her life.

We made our doddery way about the city; me actually old and she temporarily aged by her wounds, her arm in a sling. She expressed repeated astonishment at the beauty of the Ukrainian springtime. We took the tram along the lengthy, wide streets, where rows and rows of chestnut trees and cherry trees were in blossom. One day, when we were feeling a little more hearty, we went down to the beach, by the river. It was a bright day, and the space was filled with large Kiev women in polka-dotted swimming costumes, and blocky Kiev men in trunks. The men were sunbathing standing up, all of them putting their chests out towards the sun, and slowly turning like human heliotropes.

'[Why are they all standing?]' Dora asked me. '[Why don't they just lie down?]'

'[They are standing,]' I told her, '[to show that even after a full day's work of building Communism they are not tired.]'

We both of us healed from our respective wounds, although slowly.

What happened next was that the nuclear reactor at Chernobyl suffered a catastrophic malfunction. News was at first confused and contradictory. The explosion happened on 26 April. By the 27th there was no official confirmation – although the reactor is less than seventy miles from Kiev, and smoke was evident over the northern horizon. Rumours circulated through the city. Lights in the sky.

Over the night of the 27th and the morning of the 28th trucks and buses containing the inhabitants of Pripyat, the nearby town, began rolling into Kiev. There was no official news for almost a week, but everybody in Kiev knew that something terrible had happened.

You, doubtless, remember that particular disaster.

I sat with Dora in a restaurant in the city one evening, the two of us as subdued and alarmed as any person in the city. '[Do you think Frenkel—]' she asked.

'[Dead,]' I insisted.

'[Or Frenkel's people. His organisation. Do you think that they . . .?]'

'[Trofim exploded a grenade inside the main reactor. Two months later the reactor explodes. Perhaps that is no coincidence. Perhaps there was damage to the pipes, or the structure, or something; and it took two months or so for the damage to lead to the malfunction.]'

'[Or,]' she said. '[Perhaps Frenkel's people came back and finished the job. That driver you talked about – the red-headed one.]'

'[Or perhaps,]' I said, '[the radiation aliens blasted it from orbit,]'

We agreed that we must leave the city, for I feared the effects of radiation poisoning. Besides, we did not belong. I needed to get her back to Moscow. It was not difficult: the Militia, certainly, had more important things to occupy their time than attending to us. We took Saltykov's cab, and drove out of the city together.

I filled the car with fuel and drove east. The main road to Russia went north to Chernilhiv, and then east along the River Desna; but I did not want to take my beautiful Dora closer to the source of radioactive contamination than absolutely necessary. I took small roads, and felt my way, as it were, through eastern Ukraine. The sky was filled with apocalyptic clouds. Even this far south the fir trees were tinted rust and red by the fallout.

Eventually we reached Russia. We were stopped at the border, something, of course, that had not happened to us on the way *in* to the Ukraine – but things were different now. There was considerable panic. I told the soldiers manning the border crossing that Dora was my wife, a naturally shy woman who preferred not to speak. They detained us for four hours, and finally they let us through on the understanding that we would give one of their number a lift to Moscow – a young lad who had to get back to the capital for some reason.

'I was supposed to take the train,' he said, getting into the front seat beside me, after stowing his kitbag in the boot of the car. 'But none of the others wanted to drive me to the station. It's like the whole Ukraine is a plague zone. Are you Ukrainian?'

'I am a Muscovite.'

The young fellow swivelled in his seat and addressed himself to Dora. 'Good day to you, madam.'

'She doesn't speak much,' I told him.

'Don't be shy, madam! I'll not alarm you, I promise! Cat got your tongue, has it?'

Dora looked at me, and then at the young fellow. 'I love you,' she told him.

He blushed, and faced front. 'Why did she say that?' he asked me, in a low voice.

'She's not all there in the head,' I told the young soldier, as I drove off along the country road. 'She takes sudden fancies to people. Especially to good-looking young men. Don't encourage her, I'd advise. Just ignore her and she'll cool down.'

'Whatever you say, chief,' said the soldier, fixing his eye on the passing landscape.

Dora remained perfectly silent for the remainder of the day.

It took us two days to drive to Moscow; too far for me to drive in Saltykov's creaky old car in one journey. When we got to Bryansk we stopped. We ate a frugal supper together in a paint-peely restaurant, and then drove on to discover some lodgings for the night. The soldier had no money, and slept in the car. I certainly did not offer to pay for him to sleep in a room. That night, as Dora and I lay in the bed together, I said to her, '[I saw something strange, the day you were stabbed. When Frenkel was about to push me from the window.]'

'[Strange?]'

'[I saw it through the window. But it can't have been real. And when I looked again, it wasn't there.]'

'[What did you see?]'

'[In the sky, over the roofs opposite. The roofs on the far side of the park. A great metal craft. A great disc of dull silver, five hundred yards wide, with a vast central bulb, also silver, like the dome of a Kremlin minaret. Hanging there, above those roofs. But I looked again and it wasn't there.]'

'[There was nothing there.]'

'[I thought for a moment it was like a building in the sky. Like one of those church domes you get in Russia, only not quite so gold, and separated from any building. Just in the sky. But I looked again and it wasn't there.]'

'[It *wasn't* there,]' she repeated.

She said this without emphasis, in a perfectly matter of fact way. And as soon as she said it I knew that it was true. The hallucination, or whatever it had been, receded – blissfully, blissfully. It was just a bad dream.

'[It wasn't there,]' I agreed. '[It wasn't there.]'

We woke early the next day, and had breakfast when it was still dark. Crunching over frosty grass to where the taxicab was parked. The insides of all the windows were cataracted over with condensation, and it took me five minutes to rub them clean with a rag. The soldier himself shifted position in his seat, but without waking up.

We drove off, Dora silent in the back of the cab; the soldier snoring softly; and made our way along a perfectly straight road between two fields of purple earth. The sun was above the horizon, making the bands of cloud gleam with mysterious illumination. The sky above was not marked with brushstrokes, but had been painted with a perfect gradation of colouration, as if by an artist skilled in the use of spray-guns. The colours were unearthly and very beautiful: pinks and pale amber, Caribbean blues and gunmetal

293

greys, mauves, cyans, and the rectangle of black still fruiting with stars that filled the rear-view mirror.

We were making our way through south-west Russia, driving a lonely road, and the weather was strange. As we crawled over the surface of the earth, a great and tentacled cloud of radioactive material was spreading above our heads. Most of the contamination went north, and north-north-west, on the prevailing breezes, into Belarus, and beyond into non-Communist Europe – Germany, Sweden, England, Scotland. But a great radiative viewless squid-arm of poison reached north-east: massively raised levels of radioactive iodine and cesium and tellurium were measured as far away as Mahlyov and Kryshaw. The endlessly circulating and recirculating ocean of air above us seeped with invisible death, and we scurried away inside our metal beetle-case along vein-like roads making for Moscow. Moscow was hardly far enough away.

We drove and drove. Dora dozed on the back seat.

Very late in the afternoon, the sun came out. Clouds tucked themselves away, into the corners of the sky like a bedsheet, and the blue stretched itself taut. The sun's face blazed upon us as if it were wholly innocent of the meaning of strontium-90.

The sun went behind us and dipped its face down to examine what was happening over the Ukraine. Everything went dark. It had gone into mourning, of course, for what had happened westward.

I drove on into the night, figuring I would keep going until I became too sleepy to drive safely. We were creeping along the road at forty miles an hour, ever closer towards Moscow.

Suddenly, having slept all day long, the soldier grunted, and twitched his head. 'Stop a bit,' he said. 'Pull over. I need a piss.' He swivelled in his seat again. 'Begging your pardon, madam. Don't mean to speak so rudely in the company of a lady.'

'I love you,' Dora told him.

I pulled the car onto the mud at the side of the road, and the soldier got out. He walked no more than three yards from the car and unzipped his fly. I remember thinking how vulgar it was. The sound of his stream hitting the mud was very audible and, in the cold of night, billows and gouts of steam rose from the ground where the urine landed. This smoke, lit by the taxi's headlights, swirled about his legs. It looked like a stage effect. I remember turning to Dora, behind me on the back seat, to say something in English about the vulgarity of this behaviour, but as I—

It was dark. We were at the side of the road, but not the road we had been on before, because there were buildings around us. The sky was black behind us, but paling to the east, with that unique spread of gleam and opacity of the half hour or so before dawn. The soldier had gone. My stomach felt fizzy and uncomfortable.

I turned again to face Dora. 'What happened?'

'[What?]'

'[What happened to us?]' I said, speaking this time in English. How could I forget that she spoke English, and not Russian? '[We were in the countryside.]'

'[We were.]'

'[Where are we now?]' I looked again. A bus thundered past, its lights on like a carnival. It was a Moscow bus. We were on the outskirts of Moscow.

'[What happened to the soldier?]' Dora asked.

He was nowhere to be seen. I got out of the taxicab and went round to the trunk. I opened it and peered inside. Another car swept past me, loud, and close enough to make the stationary taxi rock a little on its suspension. Inside was the kitbag.

I got back into the car. '[Dora,]' I said. '[What happened?]'

'[What do you mean?]' she asked.

I sat at the wheel for a while, as the daylight strengthened and as buses and lorries and the occasional car juggernauted past us, making the shell of our taxi shudder as if sobbing. Rocking it from side to side on its spongy suspension.

Eventually Dora dozed again on the back seat, and I started the car and drove through the outer reaches of Moscow until I found a road I recognised, and followed it, and turned off, and made my way to the unfashionable block in which my own flat was to be found.

I'm almost at the end of this narrative now, and I have little to add. The important thing – the crucial thing – was to get Dora to safety. Once I accomplished that I had no cares for myself. I could hope that Frenkel was gone, and that I would be safe. But I think I had a premonition of my death: of the red-haired man standing and shooting his gun directly at my heart. If I'd though more about it, I might have reasoned that it would happen on the Moscow streets, that I would be tracked down (I would not be hard to find) and that Death would aim his gun and fire straight through my chest. The point is this: if only I could get Dora safe, I did not care. One of the advantages of a lobotomy, perhaps: the dissolution of *timor mortis*.

Dora and I were, first of all, both exhausted from the long journey, both still weak and convalescent from our respective injuries. We agreed to rest for a day, to recover from the journey, before I took her to her embassy. She lay down on the beige settee in my unsalubrious flat. I went round the corner, and queued for an hour to buy bread and a small pot of blood-coloured jam. Back at the flat I made coffee from grains in a tin box in my cupboard that were six months old and stale as dust.

We talked. Our options were: to marry in Russia and then try and get to America as a couple; or for Dora to go home as soon as possible, and then for me to apply for a visa to go visit her so that we could marry in America. After a long discussion we agreed that the latter option was preferable.

We watched the television news on my shoebox-sized black and white television. I translated for her. The news was still, of course, all about Chernobyl.

'[The world is coming to an end,]' I said.

'[It's a terrible business,]' she agreed. '[But maybe some good can come out of it. Perhaps people will now be more safety-conscious where nuclear power is concerned.]'

I didn't reply.

This is what was happening in my head. I was *remembering*. This is what I remembered. I remembered the engine dying as we were driving in the night. I remembered coasting to a halt, with the headlights spontaneously flashing a code to spies in the surroundings forests and then, alarmingly, going out altogether. None of the electrics in the motor worked. Our passenger shifted awkwardly in his seat, and kept repeating, 'What's going on? What's going on?' 'I don't know,' I replied. 'I don't know.' The car rolled more slowly and stopped. On either side forest towered, dark fat trunks going up and shaggy coniferous heads given a metallic sheen by the moonlight. We were quite alone. 'What's going on?'

I twisted and twisted at the key in the ignition, to no effect.

Then the moonlight swelled and climaxed, and every window in the taxi was blindingly bright. The light seemed to swirl, to focus into a great patch of even intenser brightness that swung from the left side of the car to the right. The soldier was gasping, and yelping like a little dog. 'Stay in the car,' I cried, but there was a rushing waterfalling sound all around and my words fell into it. I could see the young man panicking. I could see the hideous leer of fear distorting his face. He clutched at the door release and hauled it open, as I yelled 'No! No!' and tried to seize his arm. But the fool had opened his door, and then he was sucked out with ferocity and vehemence. I had his forearm, but his legs went straight up, and his torso stretched horizontal. His face snapped up towards me terrified, eyes like unshelled boiled eggs, and a weird grunting coming out of his mouth. Then my grip failed and he flew backwards with great speed, as if gravity were abruptly going sideways.

I saw behind the light: a great globe of silver, and great white-bright twisting ropes of light emanating from it. One of them had coiled itself around the soldier's waist and was—'

'[What?]' said Dora.

I blinked at her. '[The journey here,]' I said. '[I can't believe I'd forgotten! Now I remember! I am remembering now. The soldier ...]'

'[We dropped him at his friend's house,]' she said.

The whole bright-lit fantasy sublimed away from my brain. None of the other stuff had happened, it was true. There had been no dead engine, or bright lights: we had simply pulled up at a tall shuttered house and the soldier had hopped out. '[I,]' I said, momently disoriented. '[I don't think . . .]'

'[Oh I know,]' she said. '[It was a house of ill repute.]' She laughed. '[I'm not so innocent as all *that*!]'

It was true. We had pulled up. He had leapt out. He had evidently forgotten all about his kitbag, because he had had other, carnal things on his mind. There was no question of us waiting around for him. 'I can make my own way to Moscow from here,' he'd said. 'Don't you worry about me. I shall see you, comrades. I shall see you.'

And I had driven on. Shortly, feeling the exhaustion of the long drive catching up with my elderly brain, I had pulled over to nap. Everything else had been – something else. It had swarmed up in my brain like a schizophrenia. But it was sucked away and extinguished in the presence of Dora. Everything Frenkel had said in the park, after killing poor old Saltykov: the allure of this mass fantasy of UFOs; this materialisation of the old religious impulse, this relocation of gods and demons into the spaces between the stars – it all fell back into a proper perspective when I was with Dora. She made me sane again. And that was only one reason, and not the least of them, why I was in love with her.

CODA

'We have built a new society, the kind of society mankind had
never known. And, finally, there is Soviet man, the most
important product of the past 60 years.'

Leonid Brezhnev, February 1972

I started with Frenkel, and will end with him. This is the part
where the red-haired man shoots me through the heart; the inevitable coda. Death can be postponed, perhaps, but not evaded.

I took Dora for a ride on the famous Moscow Metro. We got off
and ascended outside the American embassy, and I waited with her
in the antechamber. The embassy officials were very agitated to
meet her – excited, they assured her, and delighted. They'd reported
her as missing; and the death of James Coyne, quite apart from
creating an enormous stir in *certain circles*, had made everybody
fearful for her safety. Her family and friends would be *delighted* to
discover she was all right. Her whole country would.

She was taken away. She said she was happy staying with me in
my flat, but the authorities lodged her in embassy accommodation
and – I believe – flew her out of Moscow the following day. The
exact nature of Coyne's nuclear business, presumably rendered more
acutely sensitive by the events at Chernobyl, facilitated the rapidity
and secrecy of her exit.

The last thing she said to me was a promise that she would be in touch as soon as she could. I did not know whether I would ever see her again.

But I could hope.

Rather than go straight home I took a walk through the centre of the enormous, populous city in which I had been born and in which I had spent most of my life. I wandered like a tourist. Wasn't the city full of beauty, and youth, though, that morning? *Wasn't* it though? The sunlight, perhaps, had scared away the crones and the wrinkled old retainers; the rising sap had driven out the natural Russian reticence of the courting couples. There was a superfluity of youth: infatuated young girls in headscarfs lolling on the arms of solid-limbed, blunt-faced young men; athletic females, witchy, pale-faced males, walking serious-faced together; the glibness of youth, the cleanness of youth, the innocent ferocity of youth. I had been young in the first half of the 1940s, when youth had existed as expensive filler for ditches and shell-holes, as the cement between two nations coming together like bricks squashed in the wall. It was wonderful, and peculiar, to see such unreaped harvests of youth. And always amongst them, moving, as the red-spiny stickleback headbutts the clear flowing waters and worms his way upstream, is death.

The front of my skull throbbed. I was wholly without anxiety, because, after all, I had lost the capacity for anxiety.

'Come along,' said the red-haired man, burlying up against me. He was wearing a jacket, into which his right arm was tucked, Napoleon-style – he had a gun in there, of course.

'You have followed me from the American embassy.'

'I think you mean to say,' the red-haired man hissed, '*you again?* Isn't that what you mean to say?'

'I can say that if you prefer.'

'You didn't think,' he said, coming closer still, to impress upon me that he did indeed have a pistol, 'that you'd seen the last of me? Did you?' He smelt, a little, of soap. Since my sense of smell is very poor, I suppose that means that, in fact, he smelt *strongly* of soap. But *of course* he was clean! Death is the cleanest thing of all.

'You were lucky in Kiev,' he said. 'But your luck runs out here. Here is where it all ends for you, comrade.'

'I've had so much good luck recently,' I told him, 'I was getting sated with it. It's like sugar, good luck. At first its very sweet, but after a while you start to think: any more of this and I shall be sick.'

We were standing on a main thoroughfare, and people were coming and going. But of course none of them stopped to interfere with two men having so intimate a conversation. I wondered if there might be Militia officers somewhere who might want to intervene, but there was nobody. 'At least,' I said, 'Dora is safe. I'm content to die, given that.'

'Come on,' he said, directing me down the street. 'Down here,' he said, down a side road on the left. 'Along there.' This was much less busy, and a much better arena for an assassin to shoot an old man and leave his body on the side. 'Here?' I asked, in a disinterested voice.

'Further on.'

'Trofim tried to kill me, and he didn't manage it,' I said, conversationally. I was walking alongside a huge pane of glass, in which my shuffling reflection seemed to step ghostly through the dust-covered and empty display spaces. 'Then *you* tried to kill me, in that hospital in Kiev, and you didn't manage it. Then Frenkel himself – your boss – tried to kill me in a hotel room, and *he* didn't manage it either.'

'Fourth time lucky,' said the red-haired man.

'But where are you *taking* me, though?' I complained. We were passing, now, a pockmarked stone façade arrayed with closed shutters. 'My legs get tired easily. Why not just do it right here?'

We walked into an open space with a dry fountain in the middle, and there was Frenkel, waiting for me. I understood then that Frenkel wanted to rant at me before I was dispatched. He had always been a choleric individual. I hoped it wouldn't take too long. I really was very tired of all that.

He was sitting in a wheeled chair, with a red blanket tucked over his lap and a pair of sunglasses – for by now the hot Moscow spring had heated itself up, and the sky was bright and the sun bore down with an almost radioactive intensity. The concrete bowl of the fountain, and its central stone spire from which water had long since ceased to flow, looked rather like a satellite dish; except that all it had gathered from being pointed at the sky was a layer of dried and blackened human detritus: old paper and discarded rubbish cartons.

'Hello Jan,' I said.

'Konsty,' he slurred. His mouth was curled round in a left-heavy sneer. The red-headed KGB man looked into the middle distance with an expression of vague disgust.

'How delightful to see you,' I said.

The red-haired man took up position behind me. There was something ostentatious about the way he had his hand on his gun.

'You pushed me out of a fucking window,' Frenkel gobbled, and saliva cried from his mouth. With a claw-like hand he dabbed at his face with a handkerchief.

'You were about to push *me*.'

'I was trying to close off your timelines, you fucker, not *kill* you. But you were trying to kill *me*. Don't you understand anything?'

'Close off my *what*?'

'You think your luck in evading death is down to . . . what? God just really *likes* you?'

My temper rose half a degree or so. 'You stabbed Dora.'

He nodded. 'I thought I'd killed her too,' he said, shortly. 'But she fucking came back to life, didn't she?'

'Dora Norman has left the country,' I said. 'You won't be able to get to her now. But Comrade Red-hair here knows all about that. He has followed me here from the American embassy. Haven't you, comrade?'

'Don't talk to *him*,' slobbered Frenkel, padding at his face again with the cloth. His arm came up and went down like a mechanical spar, pivoting at the elbow. He was clutching a square of cloth in his birdclaw right hand, dabbing at his mouth with it after each little speech. 'Fucking red-headed imbecile.'

'The injury to his head has disinhibited him,' murmured the red-headed man, in a disappointed tone of voice.

'How unfortunate,' I said.

Frenkel wriggled in his chair. 'Can't keep my fucking mouth *shut*, now, can I? It's not just the swearing. It's the secrets. I can't stop babbling them. We *almost had it* in 1977. People – the world – people almost *saw them* in fucking 1977. Petrazavodsk. We were thwarted by – certain persons. And since then, haven't things gone to shit? Haven't they?'

'Hard to think we could get any closer to shit than we were in the 1970s,' I said.

'Scientology,' Frenkel growled. 'Interference pattern. Mass belief systems. Communism is the creation of the people. *Religion* is the creation of the people. It gets in the way. We can't – oh! ah! Fuck! You know what Lenin said-fuck?'

'Said-fuck? What do you mean?'

'*Said*. Fucking *said*. Do you know what Lenin fucking *said*. Fuck.'

'I also suffered an injury to my head, to the frontal lobe,' I observed. 'I assume, from Colonel Frenkel's propensity to profanity, that an injury to the back of the head is associated with a different set of symptoms?'

'He's lucky to be alive,' said red-hair, grimly.

'Lenin said,' slobbered Frenkel, 'that if we succeed in establishing interplanetary communications, all our philosophies, moral and social views, will have to be revised. Lenin said that! That was Lenin! Coyne was fond of quoting that.'

'Coyne?'

'Fucking American bastard.'

'Coyne was yours?'

'Of course! What did you think? Fuck. He was supposed to persuade you of the reality of the attack on Chernobyl. Fuckfuck.'

'He was trying to warn me,' I said, curiously unsettled by this information.

'In a fucking manner of speaking,' slurred Frenkel, dabbing at the corner of his mouth. 'He was trying to warn everybody. That's what we are fucking *doing*.'

'You killed him!'

Frenkel twitched his face about. 'Don't be, don't be,' he snarled, and pressed his handkerchief against his mouth. 'Don't be fucking – stupid,' he said, through the fabric. Why would *we* kill him? He was ours.'

'Nonsense. Don't swear and talk nonsense, Jan. Do one or the other. Coyne and Dora were . . .'

'He'd called me when L-Ron,' Frenkel interrupted. 'When L-Ron. Fuck! He'd *brought* the woman over to *me*,' said Frenkel, flapping his arm away, with its square of white cloth, as if surrendering. 'She's a *special case*. There aren't many like her! That's why he brought her. He usually came on his own. You think I was loitering outside the ministry that evening just by chance? And then! And then! Hubbard's death was the *perfect* opportunity. The moment had come. We figured: a loosening of that whole system. We figured a defocusing. All we needed to do was give the collective blindness of people one fucking *jolt*. It was the perfect fucking opportunity to pull together the . . .' He coughed, and then dropped his head.

'Scientology? What has that to do with anything?'

'Aa. Oo. I don't know why I keep talking,' slurped Frenkel. 'I can't seem to stop babbling.'

'No,' agreed the red-haired man, snide. 'You can't.'

'Fucking brain injury. Mass hypnosis. They're techniques. Brainwashing. Fuck. That's too strong a term for it, brainwashing, but – you know. *Belief* systems. Belief. Oh, *garoo*. You saw them fucking kill him, and then you magicked a fucking rope out of your brainpan to explain it away. Why would you *do* that?'

'I know what I saw,' I told him.

'That's the whole fucking point! Nobody sees anything – *until* they *know what they are seeing!* There's no such fucking thing as pure seeing. It's always being shaped by what we know. Except it's not what we know, it's what we fucking *think* and what we *presuppose* and what we have been told. *She* doesn't even know what she's capable of!'

'You're not making sense, Jan,' I said.

'Excuse *me*, Comrade fucking Ironist. Making *sense*? Don't give me that. You wouldn't know sense if it came up and bit off your balls.'

I looked around. Red-haired man was still behind me, with his hand tucked into his own jacket. A few people were coming and going. I contemplated calling to them, but it would have been fruitless. What would I have yelled? 'Help help!' perhaps? I would have been taken for a drunk, and Muscovites would have averted their eyes and shuffled on.

'If *they* are here, these aliens of yours,' I said, meaning perhaps to postpone the inevitable, 'then *where* are they? What are they doing?'

'They're making war upon us,' said Frenkel. 'Of course.'

'I don't see—'

'They're invading us, of course. They're fucking softening us up. A century or so of attrition. It's the'– dab, dab, dab – 'battleship anchored off the coast, bombarding our fucking entrenchments. Of course they'd prefer it if we didn't see the battleship. If we saw it, we might start firing back.'

'Bombarding us?'

'You don't think the entire twentieth century is fucking evidence of the shells landing amongst us? You don't think it's strange that this century, out of all the previous epochs of human existence, is the one where the world goes up in fucking flames all around us?'

'Flames? *You* were the one who wanted to blow up Chernobyl!'

'The thing that's incredible about UFOs,' Frenkel went on, 'is not that millions of people believe in them, but that millions don't. It takes a continual effort of will *not* to see them.'

I started to reply. But Frenkel was in spate now.

'*I'm* not the bad guy,' he slurred. 'Two roads. One of them leads to glory – a human renaissance. One led *to the stars*, do you understand?' Dab, dab. 'Not a figure of speech. The other leads to the mundane. The mundane. The fucking mundane. The bourgeois mundane.' He seemed to be getting increasingly worked up. 'The shitting mundane. The Yankee mundane. The deadly mundane. The defeating mundane. The appalling, appalling, appalling mundane. Into the realm of that American woman's perceiving consciousness. The interference pattern that ... fucking fuck. That fucking. Fucking.'

'You seem to be distilling your thought down to a single word,' I observed.

'If only we'd taken her out of the picture ...' Dab dab. '*Everything* was in place. She'll go back to America,' dabbing at his twisted mouth. 'And good riddance. Fucking reality *catalyst* and she's not even aware of it *herself*. Coyne was right about her.'

'You're talking about the woman I love,' I said.

A rasp, the sound of somebody clearing his throat.

I looked behind me. Red-hair was still standing there, his hand still menacingly inside his jacket. But directly behind him was now standing a second man: a fellow enormously bearded and dressed in an old-style black coat. There was something vaguely familiar-looking about him, but perhaps it was simply that he looked as many Russians do. Coat, beard, patient manner. 'Good morning, comrade,' I said to this newcomer.

'Good morning,' he replied.

The red-haired man started and looked around. 'Hey? What do *you* want? Go on – fuck off.'

'I'm just waiting, comrade,' said the big-bearded man, mildly. 'I'll wait my turn.'

'This is none of your business,' said Red-hair. 'Go on, fuck off.'

I looked about the little square. Two women, plump and middle-aged, were standing in the corner watching us; deciding, evidently, whether or not to join the queue. Because, of course, two people standing together in a Moscow street is just two people; but three people standing together must be queuing for *something*.

'Whatever it is the wheelchair-bound comrade is selling,' said

Big-beard, 'I'm sure he'll have enough to sell to a third customer, after he's dealt with you two.'

'Selling?' barked Frenkel, from his chair. 'Fuck off!'

The two women were now making their way over towards the dry fountain.

'Look,' said Red-hair, bringing his hand gunless from his jacket the better to gesticulate. 'Go away. Fuck off. This is a private matter.'

The women joined the queue. 'What's he got?' asked the plumper of the two. 'Oranges, is it?'

'It's not oranges!' snapped Frenkel.

'This is not a *queue*,' insisted the red-haired man.

Big-beard looked at him. Then he turned his head to look at the two ladies queuing behind him. He looked back at us. 'It certainly looks like a queue to me, comrade.'

'Empirically,' I put in, 'I'd have to say he's correct.'

'What is he selling?' asked the less plump of the two ladies.

'Death,' I told them, smiling.

'Death? What is that – cigarettes, you mean? Vodka, you mean?'

'I was hoping for oranges,' said the plumper of the two ladies.

'Nik, get rid of them,' snarled Frenkel, slaver pooling in the sickle-curve of his twisted lower lip. 'Just get rid of them! This is KGB business! Tell them!'

'KGB business,' said Nik, bringing out his pistol and flourishing it.

The three newcomers looked at him. 'Since when do the KGB have to queue in the street to buy oranges?' asked the plumper of the two women.

'I don't believe a word of it,' said the less plump. 'Shame on you, young man. You should be in Afghanistan, fighting for the Motherland, like my nephew.'

'He wants all the oranges to himself,' said the first woman.

More people, seeing the queue form, were starting to come across and line up. 'What's he selling? asked one

'Rope,' I said, in a loud voice. 'Unless,' I added, turning back to Frenkel. 'Unless you're saying, really, that there *is* no rope.'

'There is no rope!' barked Frenkel, spittle flying from his mouth in the sunshine like sparks. 'There *was* no rope, there *is* no rope – you know all about that.'

'Rope?' said somebody, joining the queue at the back. 'Or cord? I will buy cord. I need cord to mend the curtains in my apartment.'

'I heard it was oranges,' said the plumper of the two plump women behind me.

'Nik!' cried Frenkel. 'Get rid of them. Shoot if you have to.'

There were now eight people queuing, and more looking on from the edge of the square. Red-haired man stepped a little to one side, so everybody could see him. 'Listen everybody!' he called. 'Do you see? Do you see this gun?'

Everybody was looking at the gun. He held it in the air. Then he brought it down, and aimed it at my head. Its muzzle was no more than an inch from my temples. 'Do you see?' he called. 'Do you understand?'

There was a murmur up and down the line. Three more people had joined the end of the queue.

Shortly the big-bearded man behind me spoke up. 'How much for the gun, then, comrade?'

'What?'

'How much for the gun?'

'The *gun's* not for sale, you moron.'

Big-beard stiffened. 'There's no need to be impolite, comrade,' he said.

'It's for fucking *killing* people,' called Frenkel, from his chair. 'Tell him it's not for sale. Put the gun in his face, Nik!'

Nik did so. The big-bearded man examined it closely. 'Looks to be in good order. What's the price though?'

'I'm not *showing* it to you, moron,' said the red-haired man. 'I'm *threatening* you with it. Can't you tell the difference?'

There were now twelve people in the queue.

'Twelve witnesses,' I pointed out to Frenkel. 'I suppose that makes killing me a more awkward business than it was before?'

'Nothing of the sort. Twelve morons, you mean. Twelve witnesses

I don't think.' A disapproving murmur ran up and down the line. 'Nik will scare them all away. Nik!'

The red-haired man was glowering at Big-beard.

'Shoot in the air! Shoot in the ground!' called Frenkel. '*Then* put one in Skvorecky's head and we can be on our way before the Militia show up.'

Frenkel smiled, to show his death's-head teeth; the bleached white leather of his cheeks crumpled. Nik made a Γ with his right arm, aiming the pistol at the central stock of the desiccated fountain, to his right and my left, and pulled the trigger. I must have heard ten thousand guns firing in my life – more than that number, I daresay. But it's not a noise you ever get used to. It is always louder than you remember. I flinched. The crash of the gun going off and the clatter of various shards of concrete being blasted from the point of impact were almost simultaneous. The next sound was from further back in the queue, as a small chunk of spattering stone struck somebody – a woman I think – somewhere – on the cheek, I think. '*Fuck off* the *lot* of you,' yelled Red-hair, over the brief echo of this report. Then he rotated his body like the turret of a tank to bring his arm, still sticking straight out at a right angle, to bear on me.

I was aware of the queue dispersing rapidly. The two women nearest me flinched away and scurried, head down, towards the edge of the square, squeaking. Some other people were helping the person hit by ricocheting masonry away. Others were simply slinking off. As quickly as it had assembled, the queue was disappearing.

All except for the large-bearded man, who had been the first to join. He stood his ground, seemingly unfazed. Soon everybody had gone except for Frenkel, Red-hair, myself and this stranger. Although what was strangest about him was how familiar he looked.

But whatever it was, and whatever he was saying, red-haired Nik wasn't about to wait for it. His job now was to shoot me, and to wheel his boss away before the authorities turned up.

He was an experienced KGB assassin, aiming his gun at the heart of his victim.

He pulled the trigger.

The trigger released a firing-hammer, a component inside the body of the weapon, which in turn impacted upon the base-pan of the bullet. The bullet was ready in the chamber. It had been slotted into position by a spring that was pushing up with its coil, and continued its upward push.

Gunpowder ignited, and gases expanded very rapidly, forcing the projectile portion of the bullet along the inwardly-grooved barrel.

'Konstantin Andreiovich Skvorecky!' boomed the bearded man, his mouth barely visible beneath the black carpeting of his beard. The thing that seemed familiar to me about this man clicked in my brain (*click*, as the Pistol Makarova *clicked* and detonated).

'Why,' I said, 'you could be the *son* of Nikolai Nikolaivitch Asterinov! You *must* be Nikolai Nikolaivitch's son! The resemblance is . . . uncanny.'

'It's not the *resemblance* which is uncanny,' he said, smiling broadly, and shaking his head so that his heavy beard wobbled like a bough of black blossom in a spring breeze.

'What do you mean?'

'I mean what I say! *That's* not the uncanny thing.'

I turned my head back to watch the bullet coming out of the gun. Its point emerged first, as if the pouting mouth of the barrel were sticking its tongue out at me. Then the whole thing slipped free and began moving through the air towards me,

'I don't understand.'

'You don't understand.'

'I don't understand why it's coming so slowly.'

'It's easy enough to explain.'

'Asterinov?' I said, looking back at him. 'Are you really Asterinov?'

'The very same! Don't you remember, Konstantin Andreiovich, working together in that dacha? Do you remember you and I walking in the meadows outside. I confessed to you that I had stolen most of what I wrote from other writers. I remember that conversation very well, my friend. It was very heartening to me, that conversation.'

'You've aged well,' I observed. I meant: *You haven't aged at all.*

The bullet was in the air, now, between the gun and myself. It was moving through the air, as a torpedo through water: which is to say, it cleaved the air, or punched a hole in it, sweating DNA-strands of curling turbulence behind it. The strange thing, oddly enough, was not that it was moving so slowly. The strange thing was that it was swelling, like a plump-black kernel of popcorn in the fire. As it expanded it lost its density. In moments it was the size of a grape, and had become semi-transparent. I drew a breath into my lungs. I breathed out again.

'I don't, so, I don't understand,' I said.

The red-haired man was a ghost now, as transparent as tracing paper. As transparent as mist. As transparent as an image projected upon glass, and he had one arm out firing his gun, or he had both arms out throttlingly, or he had his arms by his side, it wasn't clear.

Frenkel was scowling. His face was perfectly opaque. I could not see through his face, and I could see the movement *of* his face. But everybody else in that square was growing wispy, glasslike. The air had assumed a certain quality; the sort of impression you get in a heavy downpour: not that water and air are superimposed, because, clearly, in a rainstorm it is a question of *either* water *or* air. Either water or air or some third thing. The interleaving of water and air is temporal, not spatial, although the effect for the viewer is almost like superposition. I'm afraid this isn't a very good way of putting it.

Frenkel was unaffected; but everybody else in the square was fading. The buildings themselves were flickering on a frequency as rapid as a television image on its cathode screen, too rapidly for my eye to distinguish the *what* and *what* they were flickering between. The sky had a cloudy feel, even though there were no clouds. Or there were clouds.

'Why have things slowed?' I asked.

'I suppose,' said Nikolai Nikolaivitch Asterinov, twining a finger into his beard. 'I think it has something to do with processing density. Something like: if you force water through a narrow pipe it moves quickly, and if you put the same volume of water through a much wider pipe it moves slowly.'

'The water?'

'Time. And the pipe – well you can see.' He looked around. 'But I'm not really expert in that sort of thing.'

The bullet was a foot from my chest, and the size of a tennis ball: dark grey now. I could not see it spinning, as perhaps I expected to do; but that was because I could not see its edges at all. It was fuzzed, weirdly unfocused. 'Should I move out of the way?'

'I don't think you can.'

'No?'

'I don't think you have time. Between, I mean, the bullet leaving the gun and reaching you?'

'But it's taking a *long* time.'

'Ah! Well it seems that way.'

'It's not really taking a long time?'

'How long does a bullet take to travel a few feet? In one realityline, I mean if we isolate just one – the one you were in a moment ago – it would take less than a second. A single realityline is a very narrow pipe you see: time gushes rapidly along it.'

'But, then, I am going to die?'

'You're still *talking* to me,' said Asterinov. 'So, I doubt it. It'll pass through your heart, yes. But it will slip between heartbeats, I'd say.'

'Fuck!' contributed Frenkel. He was wriggling with fury in his chair, although sluggishly.

I looked around once more. 'It's everybody except you, and me, and Frenkel.' I observed. The bullet, now a ball of soot the size of a football, had intersected my chest. I could almost feel it. It was almost wholly spectral. It was both palpable and impalpable at the same time. It with either palpable, or impalpable, or else some third thing.

'It is everybody save for us three,' Nikolai Nikolaivitch Asterinov agreed.

'Why us three.'

'Use your fucking *noddle*,' barked Frenkel. 'Use you fucking *head*.'

'Asterinov – I must say I'm surprised to see you. Delighted, obviously, but surprised. I'd heard you were dead.'

'Reports of my death,' he beamed. 'I forget how that one ends.'

'But you haven't *aged*. Perhaps you're a ghost?'

'No such thing. No *such* thing.'

'I'm trying to get my head around this,' I informed them.

The air around me was less atmosphere and more immersion, or preparation was of a multiple spectral shift, a shift of spectres, or spectra, an uncanny gloom. It was somewhat like the quality light takes on during an eclipse. The ghosts were now pale, and only some were loitering. Others were on the move, making their way towards the streets that led off the square. Or they weren't moving. Either they were moving, or they weren't moving, or it was some third thing.

'You're unaged because of *them*,' I said to Nikolai Nikolaivitch Asterinov. By them I meant – well, *you* know whom I meant.

'I *am* them, Konstantin Andreiovich.'

'When you say the pipe is wider . . .'

'One reality is a narrow pipe: but a bundle of forty thousand, give or take . . . that's a broader pipe. Accumulate them altogether and the flow is . . . Ah, but, look! The bullet went through you, and no ill effects.'

I looked round. The bullet was now a beachball of smoke, or the ghost of one of those knots of tumbleweed that rolls along the street in a Western movie. Or, as I watched, a mere sphere of mist, expanding and disappearing.

'I wasn't shot?'

'You *were* shot, in that realityline. But when you consolidate all forty thousand, given that you weren't shot in the vast majority, then the average is . . .' He seemed to lose interest in his explanation. His finger was in his beard.

'You're saying I was shot in the particular, but that *on average* I wasn't shot?'

'That's a good way of putting it.'

'I'm immune?'

'The probability of you being killed, in this lamination, is very low.'

'Lamination?'

He winced. 'Not a very good way of putting it, I know. Do you know what quantum physics is?' Nikolai Nikolaivitch Asterinov asked me.

'He knows *shit*,' splurged Frenkel, from his wheelchair.

'I know a little,' I corrected.

'Copenhagen fuck!' Frenkel slurmed. 'I wish we'd written that the aliens *blew up* Copenhagen, all those years ago. Fucking Copenhagen.'

'A blameless town,' I objected.

'Blameless? *Fucking quantum* physics.'

'Destroying Copenhagen would hardly alter the facts of the quantum universe,' said Nikolai Nikolaivitch Asterinov.

There was something disorienting happening in my inner ear. There was a faint dazzle, like solar glare over a camera's convex glass eye, in my sense of the city. It was all happening at once. It wasn't happening at all. It wasn't happening at all, or it was all happening at once, or there was some other, third thing.

'Every event that can happen more than one way,' Nikolai Nikolaivitch Asterinov was saying, 'happens more than one way. You might think that would lead to a multiverse of near infinite complexity.'

'*I* wouldn't think anything of the sort, comrade,' I said, mildly.

'The reason it *doesn't*,' he went on, 'is that many of these branching alternatives cancel one another out. Over the broader fan of possibilities, spreading into a complex delta-basin of alternate realities, probability creates reality gradients. Realities below a certain threshold are liable to evaporate altogether. Realities above a certain threshold can solidify in an absolute sense. It's chance, you see, but also observation. That's the Copenhagen part.'

'*Fucking* Copenhagen,' growled Frenkel.

'And some consciousnesses are more gifted with that solidifying effectiveness than others.'

'Dora *fucking* Norman,' snapped Frenkel. 'Fuck! *Fucking* fuck!'

'But there is still a broad range of alternative realities co-existing. Universes in which you were blown up and died in Chernobyl – lots of them. The universe in which you survived is a tenuous one, in terms of probability. If the Norman woman had not perceived you as strongly as she did – does – then you'd have died there. And his beard danced and waggled as he spoke: all the long black lines extruded from those little hair-pits on his chin and cheeks and upper lip, all grown out and matted and packed together.

'You're very well informed,' I said. 'About my life.'

'We have a good perspective upon it.' He twirled fingers in his beard again. 'You can see, our technology gives us access to this realm of – superposition.'

'That's the ground on which they're fucking invading us!' screeched Frenkel, slobber scattering. 'This one! This ground! *That's* why it's so hard to, fucking, pin them down.'

I looked over at Frenkel. 'You ought to calm yourself, Jan.'

'That's what I was trying to fucking tell you in that park in Kiev! Look up!'

I looked up. The sky was full of flying saucers, from horizon to horizon. There were alien spacecraft everywhere, and descending directly above our heads was a craft bigger than all the rest: the pupil of a colossal eye, the radial iris spokes of grey and dark green against a dark blue background, a shield-boss kilometres in diameter framing it. The air was shuddered by the thrum of its impossible engines. It might descend inexorably and crush central Moscow – I didn't know. It was possible I could see clouds through the main body of the thing. I wasn't sure.

'[Good gracious,]' I said, lapsing, for some reason, into English.

'Fuck!' yelled Frenkel, spit coming from his mouth in pearls. 'Fuck! This is the ground they're invading us over!'

'This.' I looked around. 'It's more than one reality, it's the whole sheaf of possible realities?'

'A good spread of them. As many as we can coalesce. And the bullet that passed through your chest – that's a very weak reality, when diluted by all the rest. Very weak.'

'Weak because?'

'Isn't it obvious ! Because in most of the rest you died in Chernobyl ! And in the realities in which you died in Chernobyl, there's no need for Nik here—' but Nik was *barely* here: he was vaguer than the dream to the waker – 'to follow you across Moscow and put a bullet in your chest.'

'So – he didn't shoot me?'

'Of course he fucking shot you!' slurred Frenkel.

'He shot you in one thread. In forty thousand other threads he didn't shoot you. So if you're worrying whether you've been shot and killed by Nik . . . you need to know which thread you're in.'

'Fucking fuck,' Frenkel interjected, with no very obvious pertinence.

'I'm still alive,' I said, running my hand across my chest. 'So I suppose I wasn't in that thread.'

'You were in that thread,' said Nikolai Nikolaivitch Asterinov. 'But you were in forty thousand other threads as well, at the same time, and in those forty thousand you weren't shot. The ones in which you live diluted the one in which you die to the point where . . . Well, look I don't want to strain the point. You see what I'm saying.'

I looked at my feet. They looked weirdly solid against the fluctuating, pulsing, darkly luminous pavement. Good Moscow stone. The ground interested me less as metaphysics, and more as – I don't know. The grave, I supposed. The space opened by pressing the hidden latch-switch, visible only by moonlight, and lifting one of the great pavement slabs up and out, a horizontal door. Those steps lead down . . . where do they lead, exactly? 'I don't see,' I said.

'I see,' I said.

'I don't see,' I said, 'how I'm suddenly living forty thousand

and one realitylines simultaneously. Is it that – what? Is that *normal?*'

'Fuck!' gargled Frenkel. He sounded like he was choking on something. His own rage.

'That's not normal. It's normal to live one realityline, of course. Our consciousnesses work that way; they slide effortlessly left, right, whichever, down all the frictionless cleavages and reunions of possibilities. We never even notice them.'

'I don't see,' I said. Then I said, 'No, I don't see.'

'You're wondering,' said Nikolai Nikolaivitch Asterinov, his beard shuddering like a live thing, like a beard of black bees, 'given that your natural habitat is a single realityline, how you can be presently living in the full spread of forty thousand?'

'I'm wondering that,' I agreed.

'Fucking! Fuh-fuh-fuh!' interjected Frenkel, and then he sneezed. It made his body writhe like an eel in its chair. He almost fell out.

'You want to know how we are doing it?' Nikolai Nikolaivitch Asterinov asked. 'So look up.'

I looked up again. Directly above us, now no more than a thousand yards up, was the main, vast alien spacecraft. It looked like a huge inverted cymbal made of pig-iron: so broad it stretched wider than the eye could take in. A mind accustomed to seeing large things in the sky thinks, automatically, *cloud:* and a shape this big put me in mind of rain clouds first of all – a perfectly circular rain cloud with a vast eye in its centre. But there was no doubting its prodigious solidity. There was all manner of intricate griddle and porthole detail in the underside. It was not rotating, but around its bulging black-blister middle – that central dome alone was more than a hundred metres across, I think – strips of radial illumination, not sharp-edged but not exactly fuzzy either, moved clockwise very slowly: yellow and red ones, blue and white ones. The exact middle of the central dome, like an inverted nipple, was a ridged cavity.

My feelings were of awe.

I tried to breathe in, but my lungs felt like polythene bags, and my mouth was dry. The thought kept running through my head: how could I not have noticed!

Frenkel was coughing furiously in his chair. Either that, or he was having a conniption fit.

'It takes, I don't mind telling you, enormous amounts of energy even to maintain the co-presence of a relatively small spread, like the forty thousand we're in now. And even a ship as large as,' he pointed up with his finger, 'as that one can't do it indefinitely. Do you remember being intercepted on the road to Moscow?'

I did remember. Of course I did. 'That happened,' I said, dumbly.

'That craft, that intercepted you,' said Nikolai Nikolaivitch Asterinov. It was even bigger than the one up there. It had even more powerful ... I suppose, *engines* is the best word. That craft put out a spread of about eighty-thousand threads, but even that, with all the power we could muster – even that we could only maintain for a short time. And that was because *she* was in the car. Do you start to understand?'

'I *did* see a UFO on that road,' I said, feeling foolish.

'Yes.'

'And, at the same time – I didn't. At the same time, we dropped the soldier off at that brothel and drove on.'

'Yes.'

I looked up at the staggering, enormous object sitting in mid-air directly above us. It was incredible. It was certainly there, though.

'And now she's not here ...'

'She's being flown, dispatch, back to America. She's in the plane now, waiting for take-off.'

Frenkel pulled himself up in his chair. 'I fucking told you. Look around, Konsty! *This* is where they're invading! Not Russia, or Ukraine, or America – here. This is why they're simultaneously such a genuine threat and why they're so hard to spot! Because their main battle front isn't in one reality, but – here. In this fucking manyspace. This fucking manyspacetime.'

With a slightly sticky movement, as if wading through a resisting medium, Nikolai Nikolaivitch Asterinov took a step towards me, and laid his hand on my arm.

'Oh, garoo, garoo,' cried Frenkel. 'Don't you fucking ... don't you fucking *walk off* with *him* ...'

'Come along Konstantin Andreiovich,' said Asterinov. 'Just a little walk round the corner. I'm not abducting you. We've intervened for a good reason. We've intervened at my insistence, actually.'

'What's round the corner?'

'Round the corner is a better place to be when the spread is collapsed back down to a single realityline again. Because once that happens, and Nik sees that he has not managed to shoot you dead with his first bullet, he'll shoot again. Won't he! So, better not to be directly in front of his gun.'

'Round the corner,' I said, taking an awkward step myself, and then another, with Asterinov's still-young hand tucked into my elbow. 'To stay alive.'

'Yes.'

'You intervened to save my life?'

'Yes.'

'Because we were friends, all those decades ago?'

Nikolai Nikolaivitch Asterinov's beard moved, and I wondered if perhaps he was smiling. 'It would be nice to think that,' he said.

'Don't! Oh, garoo! Garoo!' shrieked Frenkel, his arms flailing. 'Don't fucking *walk off* with him. He's the enemy, Konsty!' But soon we had left him behind and were moving on. 'Fucking *Copenhagen!*' he yelled. '*Fucking* Copenhagen!'

The corner, when we came to it, shimmered and bulged, and we went round it, and walked in silence for a while, until, suddenly, everything snapped abruptly and rather bafflingly into familiarity again. The buildings acquired sharp-edged lucidity. People filled out their own spectral shapes.

I looked up, but the sky was empty. Instead of a huge alien

spacecraft ceilinging the view there was nothing but a quantity of grey-blue sky.

'I wish it were true,' Asterinov was saying, 'that I intervened to save your life, Konstantin Andreiovich, for old times' sake. Indeed I remember that time in the dacha! Good memories. But, no, we intervened not for your sake. But because of Dora Norman. She is remarkable.'

'I know.'

'Her ability is ... important. We need to understand it better. Her line is now tangled up with yours. It's pretty much as simple as that.'

'You're the enemy,' I said.

'We're the good guys, Konstantin Andreiovich,' he replied, his beard splitting with a wide smile. 'You're the enemy.'

'Now that I understand the particular ... territories you are moving over, I comprehend the particular reasons why UFO sightings have been so problematic,' I told him. I told *it*, I should say. 'So widely reported and believed and simultaneously so widely unseen and disbelieved.'

'The invasion is pretty much over, friend,' it said to me. 'It's been four decades since we met in that dacha.'

'You were one of them, even then?'

It laughed. 'You were a *human*, even then?' he retorted.

'But what were we ... what were we *doing*?'

'We were crafting a realityline. We were preparing the ground for my people. We were ... think of it as, clearing the undergrowth. Think of it as laying a path through possibilities. We were creating the spine of a realityline.'

'We were just writers.'

'Writers create.'

'Not *realities*, though. Only fictions. Only science fictions.'

'What you have to do,' said the creature that I knew as Nikolai Nikolaivitch Asterinov, 'is consider the total spread of realitylines. That's what you need to think of *as* reality is the whole spread. Reality is a matter of probabilities. Likelihoods, and possibilities.

That's the idiom of fiction. That's what artists are good at doing. What were we doing? We were laying a line about which *actual* realities, coral-like, could grow. I was there to make sure we came up with the right *sort* of line.'

'Radiation aliens?'

'Radiation aliens.'

'It seems so haphazard. We knew nothing, for instance – for an instance, we knew nothing of radiation! It was all guesswork. The atomic bomb had only just been dropped, and we hadn't even heard of it!'

'I see you think of radiation in *that* sense,' said Nikolai Nikolaivitch. His beard jiggled.

We were still walking, briskly now, turning right onto a main street, and then left again. I pictured, somewhere behind me, a bewildered Nik blinking and waving his pistol. Because the aliens wanted me alive, of course they wanted me dead. It was war, after all.

'It's her, isn't it?' I said to the alien.

'You mean Dora.'

'Yes. You need her, in some sense. Because of her abilities.'

'Yes.'

'You need me alive only because *she* needs me alive.'

'Love,' said the alien, 'has its redemptive possibilities. Don't you think?' And we had arrived at the marble gateway, and the steps down to the Metro.

'Goodbye, now,' he said. 'Down there, get on a train. And stay away from Jan Frenkel.' He turned to go, but I caught his sleeve.

'Wait,' I said. 'Wait. It's hard to believe that you're not real!'

'But I am indeed real,' he retorted.

'Not human, though.'

'Not human, no.' He made a second move, as if to walk off, and several people pushed past me to go down the steps into the station.

'Do you remember,' I said to him, 'when you and I talked in that meadow? We were discussing your book about the man who could breathe under water. You confessed that you had not written that book; you had merely copied it from another language.'

'I do remember.'

'You stole all those stories ... why? Because you lacked the capacity to invent?'

'Exactly that,' he said, his eyes creasing with pleasure. 'Exactly! That is your talent, the ability to invent realities. It is one of the things that makes your otherwise unexceptional world so interesting to us.'

'But,' I said, 'but. I asked if you had plagiarised *Starsearch*. *I* asked if you had simply copied *Starsearch* from somebody else.'

'I remember.'

'And you said you had not!'

He put his head a little to one side, doggishly.

'I'm not expressing myself very well,' I said. 'What I mean is: you plagiarised all your novels, as you confessed, except *Starsearch*. Therefore you composed *Starsearch* as an original fiction, the product of your own creative imagination. So I think to myself: if this is the truth – if you *could* write that fiction – then why did you need five of the Soviet Union's top SF writers to concoct a storyline? Why not ... do it yourself?'

'That's beyond us,' he said. He didn't sound mournful, or regretful. He spoke in a purely explanatory mode.

'Yet you managed it with *Starsearch*,' I said.

'No.'

'Then how did you write *Starsearch*?'

'It is mere documentary verisimilitude, is *Starsearch*. A factual account drawn from my life. A poor substitute for the splendours of fictional invention, I'm afraid. Goodbye, Konstantin Andreiovich.' That was the last I ever saw of him.

Radiation in *that* sense. I see now, of course, in what sense they were radiation aliens: not in the sense I had understood, of (as it might be) nuclear radiation. It was realitylines that radiated; quantum alternatives that radiated; and the aliens' technical advantage over us is a motor to manipulate this radiative spread of possible *nows*. As Frenkel said, this gives them a mighty advantage, but I tend to think – given how long they have been engaged in their assault upon us, and how slow their campaign has advanced – that they must be in some other sense feeble: few, perhaps; weak or uncertain. Or wouldn't they, else, have essayed a sudden rush and a push? What they are doing, instead, is stealth; picking up individuals here and there, moving their heavy cannon into position. But they are almost ready. We shall know the assault is about to commence in earnest when accounts of alien abduction becomes less frequent, or perhaps stop being reported altogether. That is when we should be most afraid.

That they saved my life, I suppose, means that in some way they consider that I shall be of use to them. But before they saved my life Dora did, without even knowing that she had done it: her mind, somehow attuned, aware of the spread of realities branching from that moment in Chernobyl and thinning them automatically down into the few lines in which I was still alive. Love shining from her eyes. Radiation in *that* sense.

KONSTANTIN SKVORECKY

From Wikipedia, the free encyclopedia
(Redirected from Skvorecki)
Jump to: navigation, search

 This article on a writer is a stub. You can help wikipedia by expanding it.

You can improve this article by introducing more precise citations.

Konstantin Andreiovich Skvorecky (1917–) is a Russian-born writer of science fiction. Most of Skvorecky's fiction was produced in the 1930s, including such minor classics as *Tamara* (1935), *Plenilune* (1936), *Sirius na Rusi* (1936) [translated as *Three Who Made a Star*, 1938], *Mortidnik* (1937), *Vsyo eto* (1938) [translated as *And All This*, 2003], *Nadezhda* (1939), *Zoya* (1939) and various others. He served in the Red Army in the Second World War, but disappeared shortly after the war. His reappearance coincided with the Chernobyl disaster. It is believed by some that Skvorecky, having been abducted by aliens, spent the years 1945-1986 on another planet. His memoir *Yellow Blue Tibia* (1999) provides an account of these missing years that explicitly asserts (or attempts to) the existence of aliens, an assertion which has been widely disbelieved. The memoir also asserts that he died inside Chernobyl in 1986. His more recent pamphlet *When I Met the Aliens (And What They Told Me)* (2000) is a satirical reimagining of the events of that novel, warning people of an alien invasion he claims is on-going.

Skvorecky presently lives in New York with his American wife and their young child. He has applied for US citizenship.

Wikiquote has a selection of material relating to the work of Konstantin Andreiovich Skvorecky.

AUTHOR'S NOTE

There is a great deal of evidence of Stalin's interest in UFOs, as indeed there is for his interest in a wide range of cranky and peculiar things. On 19 November 2002, *Pravda* published an article (an English translation is available at a number of online sites) detailing Stalin's abiding interest in extraterrestrials and the possibilities of alien contact, as well as the many military and scientific bodies set up by the Soviets to secretly investigate the phenomenon. The figure Frenkel gives in the novel (*'Seven research institutes and eleven departments. All of them are attached to a secret wing of the KGB created specifically for this purpose by Andropov'*) is taken from *Pravda*, and is evidence of, at the very least, an enduring Soviet interest in the phenomenon. The alleged 1947 retrieval of an alien artefact during archeological digs in Kiev (at a site very near the present day location of the internationally renowned Kiev Tchaikovsky Conservatory) is attested from several sources, and is a hardy perennial of UFO literature. The strange events at Petrazavodsk on 20 September 1977 have likewise been debated widely in the UFO community. Many thousands of eyewitnesses saw radiation aliens (*'radiating pulsating beams of light'*, *'huge jellyfish of light'*) and tens of thousands of military personnel were mobilised.

The kernel of this novel is an attempt to suggest a way of reconciling the two seemingly contradictory facts about UFOs: that, on the one hand, they have touched the lives of many millions of people, often directly; and that, on the other, that they clearly don't exist. I have sought to suggest one possible explanation for this odd paradox of contemporary culture. Those interested in the UFO phenomenon who would like an uncranky and balanced account are advised to read Bryan Appleyard's *Aliens: Why They Are Here* (Scribner 2005). I would like thank Jane Brocket for sharing her reminiscences of youthful visits to both Kiev and Moscow in the mid-1980s. Thanks also to Rachel Roberts for reading the whole MS and making many helpful suggestions, and to my editor Simon Spanton, whose input on this novel has been unusually important.